RENEGADE THIEF

STAR BANDITS: UPRISING BOOK 2

JENNIFER M. EATON

Renegade Thief
Star Bandits: Uprising Book 2
© 2021 Jennifer M. Eaton
R4

Published by Galactic Razor
Cover design: Covers by Julie
www.coversbyjulie.com

ABOUT RENEGADE THIEF

In space, sanity is a luxury when your crew decides they're heroes.

Dania is doing her best to gain the trust and friendship of the crew, but when she finds out that her best friend has been abducted by the slavers Dania failed to eliminate, she resolves to finish what she'd started and save him.

Going after the slaver ring is suicide. The Star Renegade is a little ship, and Cal refuses to put his people in danger. However, the crew votes to take on the impossible: one ship against hundreds to save a guy they don't even know.

Whether Cal likes it or not Dania is part of this crew, and he needs to protect her. When they're cornered, though, the enemy makes him an offer that he can't refuse: give up the enforcers, or watch his ship, and everyone on board, explode.

Two lives in exchange for six. It's a good deal. The crew will hate him for taking it, but he'll hate himself if he doesn't.

For everyone screaming
WRITE FASTER*!*

"I'm trying, I'm trying!"

DANIA'S THROAT CONSTRICTED. Being human wasn't so bad, except for the constant worry about getting killed.

Vulnerability was difficult to get used to. Dying had never been a concern when she'd been an enforcer.

She sat beside an array of supplies as Alanna leaned through a large hole in the wall of the ship's cargo hold caused by the hydraulic lifts dropping their payloads five weeks ago. The woman seemed unharried by the inevitability of an angry prince catching up to the *Star Renegade* and murdering them all.

"Can you hand me some more of that polymer?" Alanna reached back to her.

Dania opened the container, scooped the slippery white goo into a jar, and handed it to her. "Is it wise to keep using this compound when we aren't sure what it is?"

The jar disappeared as Alanna edged farther into the crevice. "It works as good as anything else for this kind of repair, and I'd rather use it on something that doesn't affect life support."

A shiver ran down Dania's spine. So far, the life support had held out, unlike so many other systems that seemed to need constant attention.

Dania considered the makeshift patch on the far wall of the cargo bay, a remnant of their recent encounter with Dania's former sponsor. Over a month ago, the captain had nearly frozen to death in this very chamber. He'd used this mystery polymer to seal a hull breach—saving himself, and probably the ship. He was resourceful, as were all the humans on this crew.

Alanna backed out of the crevice and tucked her pink-tipped hair behind her ear. "All done."

"That was fast." Dania stepped out of her way.

"I'm getting better at this." The woman beamed. "It's nice to have the help, too. Thanks."

"All I did was hand you things. I can't actually do maintenance."

Alanna eased onto the floor and took a drink from a water flask. "I couldn't, either, when I first got here." She wiped her mouth on her sleeve. "You should have seen me. I was a mess."

Dania doubted the woman had ever been 'a mess' in her life. She was naturally toned and rounded in all the places deemed attractive by human standards. Dania, on the other hand, was lean from a lifetime of training, and the shirts Alanna had been kind enough to loan her hung loose on Dania's much smaller frame.

Alanna looked up into the hole. "The ship was in rough shape when I came aboard. I discovered through necessity that I like to fix things, and I'm pretty good at it, most of the time."

Dania glanced at the floor, rubbing a pain that cut into the center of her chest. Her only friend, Alexander, had been good at fixing things, too. He'd loved discovering how machines worked and making them better. On many occasions, he'd performed maintenance on ships without permission. He'd been castigated for his efforts more than once. However, the captains always kept the improvements he'd made.

Dania's warm smile melted from her face. The last time she'd seen Alexander had been through the window of a fighter craft. He'd begged her to come home moments before Prince Geron had opened fire on him.

Dania had thrown a shield up to protect him. But soon after, she'd passed out and been dragged into the black hole that had stranded her and the *Star Renegade* crew here...wherever *here* was.

The ache in her heart deepened. She may never know if Alexander had survived that day. If he hadn't, Dania wasn't sure if she'd be able to live with the guilt.

She grimaced. Guilt was another new emotion she was learning to live with. Being human had so many unexpected complications.

Alanna stood. "I'm sure that we'll find something you're good at too. It makes living on a ship more interesting when you have a job to do."

Dania nodded, but the truth was, the only thing she'd ever been good at was killing people. Those skills weren't quite transferable to shipboard life unless the captain wanted a bodyguard. Unfortunately, the only beings the captain needed protection from were other enforcers, and she'd probably never be able to stand up to her own kind again.

Alanna held up the jar of polymer. "We might as well use this up reinforcing the edges of Cal's seal."

"I thought you and Ty had already reinforced it?"

Alanna walked over to the hull breach and poured the thick material over the existing makeshift repair. "Yeah. Twice." She leaned back as the gray-white material oozed into the pits and grooves. "I just wish there was a way to heat it all up at the same time to make sure there aren't any more micro-leaks." She wiped her brow. "The maintenance torches only melt sections, and I'm never sure they seal together."

Heat? That shouldn't be too hard.

Dania grabbed an angled steel plate and held it up to the seal. "I think I can help with that."

Centering her focus on the plate, she called up energy from her core, then frowned when the heat didn't come to her fingertips.

She stared at her hands. This should have been simple. Child's play.

She gritted her teeth, searching for the few traces of primordial energy still flowing in her veins. A slight tremor erupted in her chest and then flowed out to her fingertips. She reveled in the vibrating particles before pressing the heat into the metal.

Air currents drew toward her, filling the molecular space between her and the steel, insulating her skin as the plate turned molten red, then cooled back to silver.

Dania's vision wavered. The room spun. As she grabbed her head, the plate slipped to the floor, leaving behind a hazy but solid reinforced patch.

Alanna leaned closer to the repair. "Wow! That's a handy trick. I think we've found your calling."

The cargo containers around her whirled and Dania fell back, clutching her temples.

"Oh my gosh!" Alanna's blurry face appeared in front of Dania. "Are you okay?" She disappeared from view. "Peter, I need you in Cargo Bay One. Dania's sick again."

Again. Dania grimaced. How could she live the rest of her life as the weak link? She'd been raised to be a general. A leader. She didn't know how to be anything else.

The room skewed again, and the doctor's dark hair and kind face appeared. He shined a light into her eyes.

"What were you guys doing?"

Alanna explained how Dania had melted the polymer. Their voices sounded like they were underwater.

"I'm okay." Dania tried to sit up but slumped back down. "Maybe I'm a little tired."

The doctor came back into Dania's view. "Does using your abilities usually sap your strength like this?"

Dania closed her eyes, wishing the answer were different. "No. What I did should have been simple."

But it wasn't. And each day, simple tasks seemed harder and harder.

The doctor finally came into focus. "You need to limit the use of your power until I find a way to replenish your pathogens."

Pathogens.

Dania cringed. The doctor insisted that her prince had infected her with tiny microbes that had changed her inner makeup. He claimed that she'd been human before she'd been made into an enforcer, and she now needed those microbes to survive. He thought he could replicate them with the right supplies. Of course, they'd need to find their way back to civilized space before they could procure what he needed.

Dania nodded, but she wasn't really sure what she was

agreeing to. This news was more of the same, and none of this bode well for her when they didn't even know where they were in the universe, or which way to travel to get home.

A loud tone sounded from the overhead comm system.

"Heads up, people!" Ty's voice shouted. "We're about to be scanned. I need everyone out of those cargo bays and into the center of the ship in ten. Nine. Eight..."

"Come on!" Alanna grabbed Dania's arm, and the doctor took the other.

Dania scrambled to keep up, but the humans mostly dragged her into the hall and dropped her on the floor. Alanna hit the controls. The doors shut before she huddled up against Dania, while the doctor put his arms around her from the other side.

The speakers continued with Ty's voice: "Three. Two. One. Here we go..."

The lights winked out. The chill sunk in quickly, faster than it had in the upper levels. They needed to spend less time in the cargo areas until the incessant scans stopped.

Dania knew they wouldn't stop, though, not until Prince Geron found her. These people were protecting her for no better reason than a human code of ethics that told them it was the right thing to do. And it would probably get them all killed.

The doctor drew her in tighter, and Alanna pressed closer from the other side. At first, this kind of contact had repelled her, but she understood the need for body warmth when the cold of space reached through a ship, seeking lives to erase.

Each time they shut down to avoid detection, the captain worried the power might not come back on. He had good reason to be anxious, considering the amount of damage this ship had seen since Dania had come on board.

This was the eleventh time they'd been scanned over the last five weeks, but Ty and Ethan's strategy must be working, because no ships had dropped out of the abyss to kill the crew and drag Dania back to her prince.

Not yet, at least.

Discovery was inevitable. If they didn't get out of there, if they didn't find safe harbor, they would be found. And once her prince restored her to her former self, there would be nothing she could do to save this crew.

TY'S FACE glowed orange with each flash of the confounded light. Cal might have nightmares about that color for the rest of his days. Oranges were supposed to be a blessing, a tasty snack, and a cure for certain diseases out in the dark expanse of space.

Why Ty had programmed such a wonderful color to mean "death is looking for you," Cal would never understand.

They'd been dealing with a short that made the light blink yellow for a long time now. Yellow was a proximity alarm. No big deal, normally. Orange flashing was bad. Very bad. They'd all learned to hate orange.

Now, more than ever.

"Life support?" Cal whispered.

Ty simply held his fingers to his lips as the glow continued to light up his blond hair.

Could a long-range scan hear Cal's whisper? He wasn't so sure about that. However, it wasn't just anyone out there looking for them, but a full-blown, angry, probably vengeful prince. With the Banes, anything was possible.

Ethan shivered, glancing up to the still flashing light. The illumination made his freckles seem even darker.

Orange. Orange. Orange.

It seemed like the flashing lasted longer with every new scan, like the blasted prince was picking something up but wasn't certain it was them, so he swept the area a few more times, just to make sure.

Cal looked out the viewport into the still-unfamiliar stars. *I guess this is what you get when you liberate a prince's prized possession.*

Still, he wouldn't change anything.

Orange. Orange. Orange.

Dania had been a monster when they'd bought her on board. Now she was just like the rest of them: wanted by the government and on the run.

He drew in a deep breath. The room spun, the thinning air not providing enough oxygen.

Across the bridge, Ethan grimaced and folded in on himself, protecting his hands from the encroaching cold. They couldn't keep shutting down life support like this. One of these days, it wouldn't come back on.

Orange. Orange. Yellow.

Ty held up one finger, and they all breathed a sigh of relief. The scan was still close but moving away. That meant air, and blessed heat, would soon be back.

Cal hoped.

The *Star Renegade* was an old ship, and she wasn't meant for this kind of abuse.

Orange. Yellow. Yellow.

Ty's teeth glowed in the ochre light as he held up two fingers.

Alanna had said it could be months before they found

their way back to civilization. And they didn't even know which way to go.

Yellow. Yellow. Yellow.

"Clear!" Ty called.

Ethan jumped to his station and started pressing buttons.

Ty triggered the ship-wide comm. "Heat and oxygen coming your way, people. Hold tight."

The chill started to itch up Cal's back. "Ethan?"

"Working on it!"

The floor started to hum. Cal exhaled as the vents pushed in beautiful, life-giving recycled air.

Each of them slumped into their chairs, drawing in deep breaths.

Cal rubbed his cold hands on the tops of his jeans. "How long can we keep this up? Are we playing Russian Roulette with the air?"

Ethan shook his head. "We're fine." But he glanced at Ty, who looked away, avoiding Cal's gaze.

Sometimes, what these guys didn't say was more important than what they *did* say.

The truth was they were sitting ducks out here.

Cal hit the comm. "I want everyone to warm up and then meet me in the lounge."

He was done with floating out here, waiting to get caught. They needed to take control. *He* needed to take control. Luck wasn't going to get them out of this one.

————

Cal sank into the seat at the head of the large table in the lounge. "We need to do our best to stop shutting the systems down."

"Tell us something we don't know." Ty leaned back in his own chair.

"We can't keep hiding forever. We need to get out of here." Cal turned to Ethan. "When can you get the engines working to full capacity?"

The engineer smoothed back his curly, copper hair. "Tomorrow."

Everyone stared at him.

"Why are you guys always surprised when I work miracles?" Ethan held out his hands. "Hey, it's me, remember?"

Ty folded his arms. "So you did something by accident, got incredibly lucky, and fixed it?"

Ethan laced his fingers behind his head. "Hey, a miracle is a miracle. The *how* should never be questioned."

"Fine," Cal said. "Are you sure we'll have engines back online tomorrow?"

He placed his hands back on the table. "You can have them tonight if I don't sleep."

The last thing they wanted was a tired engineer when they might need him the most. "Statistically, we have a few more days until that scan hits us again. As long as we're long gone, and don't have to shut off life support anymore, we're fine. So, everyone sleeps tonight." Cal turned to Alanna. "If we're up and running, how long to get home?"

"Still the same as I said earlier. Maybe three months. I don't even know which direction to go."

Dania kneaded her fingers. "I can help with that."

"No more black holes," Cal said.

Dania opened her mouth to speak, but Doc touched her arm. "Honey, you nearly passed out heating something up. As your doctor, I am putting you on permanent light duty until further notice."

"Until further notice? Then that wouldn't be permanent," Ethan said.

"Shut up, Ethan."

Ethan held up his hands again. "Why is everyone always telling me to shut up?"

"What are the other options?" Cal asked.

"I told you I can help." Dania stood and walked to the center of the room. She closed her eyes and then pointed. "Home is that way."

Cal glanced around the room. "Are you sure?"

"Yes." She walked back to her place and slumped into her chair. Her eyes reddened before she closed them and looked down, letting her long, dark blonde hair cover her face.

Alanna put her arm around the former-enforcer's shoulder. "How do you know?"

Dania folded farther into herself. "I'm sick, and every fiber of my being is screaming to run home to my sponsor for healing." She pointed again. "He's that way."

Ethan held up a tentative hand. "Does anyone else think it is a really bad idea to head *toward* the homicidal prince?"

"I'm not saying we should fly directly to him." Dania straightened, looking at each of them as she spoke. "The chance that Geron is sitting right on the border of known space is slim. I suggest going in that direction until one of us, or the computers, recognizes where we are and then quickly go in another direction."

Cal knew better than to trust that it would be that simple. "If we're heading toward him and he scans this junkyard, will the scan intercept us?"

She shook her head. "It's not line of sight. It's projected. The enforcers read the singularity I created before it collapsed, so they know where we went. They just don't know if we survived."

It seemed like only yesterday when the prince had surrounded the *Star Renegade*. They were as good as caught, but Dania had used her enforcer abilities to create a black hole that had sucked them out of civilized space and dumped them here, in the middle of nowhere.

If that scan would skip right over them, though, that would be a big boon. Still, Cal would rather be free and clear. "What will it take to make him stop scanning?"

She stared at her hands. "He won't stop looking for me until he finds my body."

Cal massaged his eyes. He knew that would be the answer. He'd just hoped there would be a simpler solution. Shooting a medical cadaver into space wouldn't save their hides this time. At this point, their best course of action was to get out of this fishbowl before they got hooked.

"All right, as soon as we're operational, let's have Dania point the way and burn the engines steady toward home," Cal said. "Alanna, we'll do some small jumps just so we make sure we don't accidentally appear right in front of Geron's cruiser."

"I can't," Alanna said.

Wait. What? "You can't?"

"Well, I can, but I don't think we should." She looked at Ethan and Ty. "No one seems to know what that polymer Ethan bought is. It might hold, but then again, it might not. Jumping puts a lot of strain on the hull in the best conditions. With a breach..."

Cal rubbed his face. "Yeah, I get it." He looked at Ethan. "You didn't get a metallurgy analysis on that stuff?"

The engineer narrowed his eyes. "I'm not even really sure

what a *metallurgy analysis* is, and for the price I paid, I don't think they really had a whole lot of information."

Which also meant they were trusting their hull integrity on some sort of glue that for all they knew might be rigged to explode.

"I should probably put an additional containment field around that deck," Doc said.

"Good call," Cal said. "Take anything you need from storage." He turned to Ethan. "Let us know when the engines are running." He stood. "Everyone else, prep for immediate departure as soon as Ethan gets those engines online."

One way or the other, he'd get them home. Cal didn't care how long it took, but sooner would be a heck of a lot nicer than later.

CAL STORMED FROM THE ROOM. He didn't seem so much angry as determined. The doctor slipped through the door with him just before the exit closed.

Alanna stood. "Well, we can't jump, but I can at least start plotting a course." She turned to Dania. "Are you ready to point the way?"

Dania flinched. Yes, she'd offered to help, but the ache pulled, drawing her in like a tether.

Come to me, Geron's voice beckoned in the distance.

It was only an echo, but she still hugged herself, wishing it away. Even though she knew he'd erase who she'd become, returning her to an unquestioning automaton—part of her still yearned for that release, that comfort, the bliss of being in his presence, of relishing in his power.

Dania closed her eyes, clearing her thoughts.

She wouldn't give in.

The doctor would help her. She was free.

She didn't need her sponsor anymore.

Alanna frowned. "Are you okay?"

Yes and no. How could she explain this to someone who'd been free all her life?

Dania pointed again. "Can't you just go that way?" She blinked away the burning in her eyes. "I don't really want to think about him anymore. It's already so hard. I've been trying to block it out."

"Sure. I can do that." Alanna bit her lip, as if thinking that over. "When we start moving tomorrow, can you let me know if I veer off course?"

Dania nodded. That should be easy enough.

Ethan stood and scratched his head. "Alanna, can help me in Engineering before you plot the course? I need to reframe the manifold before we go online."

She folded her arms. "Is this another excuse to get me into tight quarters?"

"I'm hurt." His face lit up. "But I have to admit, that is a fringe benefit." He pointed a thumb over his shoulder. "But seriously, I need an extra set of hands."

"I can help," Dania said.

Ethan turned to her. "Are you good with fixing things?"

"No," she said, at the same time Alanna said, "Yes."

"Don't let her fool you," Alanna said. "She helped me a lot downstairs today."

Dania quirked a brow. "I held a jar of polymer and handed it to you when you asked."

"Which was incredibly helpful."

"What I need isn't hard," Ethan said. "I can place the relay on the base, but I can't hold it steady while I solder it."

Alanna smiled. "And if he touches your rear end, you have my permission to fry his face off."

Ethan placed his hand on his chest. "Again, I'm hurt. I would never cheat on you, baby."

Alanna rolled her eyes. "I'm going to catch a shower before I plot the course."

"Procrastinating?" Ethan asked.

"There's no rush until you fix the engines, hot-shot." She turned to Dania. "Seriously, no one will fault you for melting his face off."

Dania grinned. A few months ago, she may have thought Alanna was serious, but the crew bickered and joked like this frequently. There were no airs there, no competition. Just kinship. It was refreshing.

Alanna walked through the door.

"You better be careful," Ethan called after her, "or Dania may try to win me away from you."

"One can only dream," Alanna called from the hallway.

Ty laughed, following her. He stopped at the threshold and pointed at Dania. "Face melting might be extreme, but some broken bones would be totally understandable."

"Hey!" Ethan said, but the door closed, leaving them alone.

Dania smirked. "You do realize that Alanna has no interest in you."

Ethan waved his hand at her. "I'll wear her down sooner or later, because seriously." He pointed to his chest. "I'm irresistible, aren't I?"

Irresistible wasn't quite the word she would use. But each member of this crew had their charms and Dania was starting to feel more like part of the team than a troublesome passenger. With any luck, one day, she would be able to repay their kindness. For now, she would help in any way she could to earn her keep, while hoping that her past didn't arrive to execute them all.

CHAPTER 4

CAL

CAL LET the door to the lounge close behind him. Without Alanna jumping them, their chances of getting out of this in one piece decreased far more than he wanted to admit. He couldn't dwell on what couldn't be, though. He needed to figure out what they could do to get out of this mess alive.

"Boss?" Doc pushed through the door and entered the hall.

"What's up?"

"I'm worried about Dania."

"Of course you are. You're the doctor. It goes with the territory."

"Well, in this case, I'm worried about how tired she got when she was helping Alanna today. I told her not to use any of her powers, but it seems to be instinctual." He sighed. "It would be like asking Ethan not to be annoying. He couldn't do it. It's just part of who he is."

Cal held back a snicker. *Poor Ethan.* "What's your point, Doc?"

"Dania told me that what she did shouldn't have tired her out so much."

"Well, we expected this, didn't we? She's been getting weaker all along."

"Yes and no. Not like this." He scrolled through a hand-held tablet. "You know how I hate to be wrong, but I think I underestimated when the problems would start." He looked up. "I'm afraid it might be her lungs, or worse."

Cal bit back a curse. This was bad, but Doc wouldn't be telling him this without a reason. "What do you need?"

"Once we get to regular space, our first stop needs to be sector Z8 so I can get the supplies I need to try to help her." He stopped scrolling and put the device into his pocket. "I was serious when I said she's like a junkie. She knows that the pathogen load inside her is bad, but her body still craves it. In her case, she actually *will die* if she doesn't get it."

"I hear you loud and clear." Cal continued down the hall. "I promise you, we're not giving up on her. As soon as we reach charted space, we'll do our best to get everything you need."

And he meant it. Dania hadn't been here long, but she was here by unanimous vote. The enforcer was no longer their prisoner, but a member of their crew for as long as she liked.

His chest clenched as he realized he wanted her to stay. Another mouth to feed would be a problem, but at this point, the ship would feel empty without her.

Doc headed back down the hall, hopefully to work on that containment field. Maybe his big brain could find a way to solidify that seal enough that they could use Alanna's jump ability. That would be a huge asset right now.

Cal pursed his lips as he entered the bridge and slumped into his chair. Part of him still couldn't believe he was helping an enforcer. She'd admitted to being every horror he'd had nightmares about. She was the reason they were trapped here.

He rubbed his eyes. Even if she had given that blasted prince their location and put them all in danger, she'd still saved them in the end. Helping her didn't mean that he trusted her, though. He'd never be stupid enough to trust her again. Although deep down, he really wanted to. He just wasn't quite sure why.

The doorway behind him opened and Ty entered the bridge. "Hey, boss. Everything going good up here?"

"Sure, but you're late to the party. I've got the whole ship running like clockwork."

Ty snorted. "Yeah, a broken clock, maybe." He tapped a few keys on his panel. "Do you really think it's going to take us a few more months to get out of here?"

"I don't have the luxury of thinking that. I'm pretty sure you're the one who pointed out we don't have enough food to last that long."

The light on Ty's panel flashed orange once.

Ice coursed through Cal's veins. It was too soon. They'd just been scanned that morning.

Silence hung thick in the room. Cal didn't breathe until he heard Ty let out his breath when the light didn't flash again.

"Must've been a glitch," Ty said.

"We can't have that kind of a glitch," Cal said. "The yellow flashing was bad enough."

"I agree. Do you want me to get on that first?"

With so many other things wrong with the ship? "Not unless it happens again. Our focus needs to be getting out of here."

Ty opened up the panel on his console and started

pulling out the burned and melted wiring. Cal worked on some of the easier repairs. He was getting better at fixing things, but he'd never know the *Star Renegade* as well as Ty. The guy had been renovating the ship since he was a kid, hoping that his employer at the time—Stanley, back on planet Kirato—would give the ship to him once the rebuild was done.

Unfortunately for the kid, Cal had come along. Stanley and his wife had hid Cal for what seemed like an eternity while the enforcers chased him down for a murder he hadn't committed. And when it was time to leave, Stanley had given the ship to Cal.

Luckily enough, Ty had been more than happy to take the position of first mate, and neither of them ever looked back. Except for returning from time to time, repaying the colony's kindness with food and supplies.

Kirato was on the edge of Cartek space, and when the Banes and Carteks started fighting over Earth's territories, traders cut the colony off rather than risk flying so close to the enemy. The war between the Banes and the Carteks was also, in a way, how they'd ended up here. If Earth hadn't bowed to the Banes for protection against the Carteks, Dania never would've been on board, and they never would have been running from that blasted prince.

Cal still had nightmares—when he was able to sleep— about the prince's cold stare on the main viewing screen when he'd demanded Dania's return. Usually, Cal would laugh at that kind of ultimatum, but dealing with pirates and smugglers was far less complicated than dealing with Kever nobility. Normal criminals couldn't blindside you with magical powers you had no defense against.

Still, Cal did his best to hide his fears. Although the

growing circles under Ty's eyes made him wonder how many of them were keeping their worries to themselves.

The *Star Renegade* had always been a place for open discussion. Cal genuinely wanted to know what was on everyone's minds. But lately, they'd been as silent as Cal about what had happened to them.

Maybe, after Cal's migraine episodes, they were too worried about causing more stress. He hoped that wasn't the case. He'd rather be plugged in than kept in the dark.

Ty, of course, had a way of knowing everything happening on the ship, with the personnel as well as the wiring. A fact that Cal needed to take advantage of more often.

"How is the crew holding up?" Cal asked.

Ty leaned underneath his panel with a screwdriver. "They've been through worse."

"Worse than being lost in the middle of nowhere with no way to get home?"

"At the moment, no one is in the immediate vicinity trying to kill us." Ty looked up. "I say this sounds like a vacation."

An alarm boomed through the deck, the sound echoing off the ceiling and walls.

"I was kidding!" Ty punched his chair. "Come on!"

Cal covered his ears, his entire body tensing, the horror of his recent headaches making him want to crawl in a corner and hide. Luckily enough, the pain didn't come.

He lowered his hands. "What's going on?"

Ty cursed. "There's some kind of a leak in the engine room." Ty called up the comm. "Ethan, what's going on?"

"Kind of busy right now."

Ty leaned closer to his monitor. "Radiation levels are rising. Ethan, get out of there. Now."

"And sacrifice the ship? No way. I can hold it."

Cal slammed his fist on the comm button. "No heroics. We'll figure it out. Get out of there. That's an order."

Static filled the line.

"Ethan?"

Ty gulped. His eyes flashed at Cal.

"Ethan!" Cal jumped to his feet and ran to the door, barely waiting for the panels to open.

He sprinted through the halls, red lights flashing and sirens echoing. The sound of Ty's boots slamming on the floor tiles behind him was barely audible over the blaring sirens.

Cal skidded to a stop at the end of the hall a few paces from the engine room.

Alanna stood outside the door, pounding her fists on the glass and screaming Ethan's name.

Still holding his screwdriver, Ty pried the panel beside the door off and fiddled with the wires. "I can't get it open," he said. "The emergency locks have engaged."

"Then how do we get him out of there?" Alanna wiped tears from her eyes.

Ty grimaced, but he didn't say what they already knew. There was no way to open that door. Not with a radiation leak.

"I'm here!" Doc ran up and dropped a shoulder bag on the floor at his feet. He held up some sort of scanner with red lights flashing on a panel in front of the window.

Cal's head started to swim. "Ty, shut off those alarms."

"On it." He moved to a different panel farther down.

"Where's Dania?" Cal asked.

"Oh, no," Alanna whispered, looking back toward the engine room door. "Dania!"

Cal froze. His stomach twisted. This couldn't be happening.

Alanna continued to slam her fist on the thick glass panel window on the door to Engineering. "Ethan! Dania!" she cried, even though they wouldn't have been able to hear her through a reinforced panel even if the alarms weren't so loud.

Doc put his hand on her shoulder. "Alanna, stop."

"No." She slammed her fist on the door again. "Ethan!"

The alarms stopped blaring.

Doc pulled her away. "Alanna, you're going to hurt yourself."

She tried to twist out of his grip. "Let me go." She leaned toward the door. "Ethan! Dania!"

He shook her. "It's too late," he told her.

She froze, her eyes blank and stunned, and a little piece of Cal died inside.

Ty slowly edged back to them. "Too late for what?"

Doc glanced back to the window. A dull, red hue fogged the glass from the other side. "It's about a thousand degrees in that room. It's as good as a kiln in there."

Alanna turned back to the window, placing her hand on the glass. "No." She eased to the floor, shaking. "No!"

Cal punched the wall. "Dammit!" Why hadn't they evacuated while they still could?

Ty tapped on the panel beside the door. "We lost the tertiary reactor. With that much leakage, the outer hull should have melted." He turned to them all. "I don't know what they did to insulate the ship, but if they'd bailed, we'd..." He looked down and closed his eyes. "We'd all be dead."

Alanna doubled over, holding her stomach. Doc held her

as her wail echoed through the hall, before she started to cough.

She sobbed onto Doc's shoulder. "Dania... All she wanted was a new life." She wiped her eyes but tears still streamed from them. "And Ethan... He hit on me less than an hour ago, and I blew him off." She lifted her face, her cheeks damp and shiny. "I was always so mean to him."

"You weren't mean, Alanna." Cal flinched, remembering the yellow bruises on Ethan's face from when Cal had punched him.

Granted the guy had deserved it after he'd shot Cal for no good reason.

Still... He choked down the pain building in his throat. Maybe they'd all been a little harsh.

But they needed to face reality. "We argue. We tease. That's what makes us a family. No one ever could have known that..." The one member of the crew who they'd stepped on the most would die saving all of their lives. And Dania, so strong only a month ago... Why now, when she had so much to live for?

Alanna lowered her face into her hands. Her shoulders quaked as she sobbed.

Cal gritted his teeth. He needed to be the captain, now more than ever. He needed to be strong.

"The hull isn't going to last at those temperatures," Ty said. "I don't know what Ethan did, but..." He held up his hand to the window, where red smoke billowed in raspy plumes.

Cal hated himself for this, but he needed to be the one to make the harsh decisions. "Vent the room. Shoot the particles into space. It's the only way to bring the temperatures down."

Alanna raised her face. Her red, puffy cheeks made Cal want to punch something again.

"Wait." She sniffed. "Won't that shoot their bodies into space, too?"

Ty grimaced. "Yeah, we'll lose anything that's not tied down."

"But we'll survive." Cal kept his shoulders back, doing his best to look more confident than he felt.

Alanna's face contorted into a loose semblance of her serene, happy beauty. "Don't do this, Cal."

Doc crouched next to her. "Sweetie, at those temperatures, there probably isn't much of them left in there."

Alanna lowered her face again. "I think I'm going to puke."

Cal's ears started to ring, and a deep ache started over his right eye. This was too much. But he needed to think about the people on this ship who he *could* save.

He turned to Ty. "What do we need to do to vent the room?"

Ty drew in a deep breath. "I can do it from here." He moved a few feet down the hall, opened a panel, and pulled out an emergency juncture box. He tapped in a series of codes and stepped back. "I need your release codes, too."

Cal nodded. Ty knew Cal's codes, just as he knew Ty's... just in case. Ty didn't want to be the one to vent the room and everything...every*one* in it, and Cal got that.

This was Cal's decision. It should be on his back.

He typed in the codes, and Ty unlocked the clear protection box. He stared at the red lever looming inside.

"Two thousand one hundred degrees," Doc said.

Too hot. Knowing that venting the room would save the ship didn't make it any easier.

Cal flipped the lever.

The walls hummed. The sound of a tornado vacuum boomed through the soundproof walls.

Alanna threw back her head and wailed.

Cal wanted to join her. He fought to not hold his head, he fought to not scream. He wanted to wake up from this stinking nightmare once and for all.

But this wasn't the kind of thing you could wake up from. Ethan and Dania were gone, and they all needed to learn to live with that.

"Clear." Ty flipped the lever and slammed the panel shut. "Returning life support to the chamber." His face was red and blotchy before he turned away.

"When will it be safe to go in for repairs?" Cal asked Doc.

He took in a shaky breath. "It should be good right away. Space would have chilled everything back to normal levels." He held up his scanner. "Internal readings are within habitable levels."

Cal cocked his head to the right. Swirls of reddish plumes still billowed in front of the window. "Are you sure?"

Doc leaned closer to the glass. "What the…"

Cal approached the door. The room should have been clear. "Could that be a trick, or a burn in the glass?"

Doc shook his head. "The vapor is moving." He held up his device again. "The readings look fine. I mean, it's a little cold in there, but oxygen levels are returning to normal."

"Look sharp, people." Cal placed his palm on the square to the side of the entrance, and the door slid open.

They all stepped back, but no red smoke engulfed them. A soft crimson glow emanated from the center of the room.

Cal moved inside. Centered in the widest area of the room, a perfect smoky red orb pulsed like a beating heart.

"Radiation?" Cal asked.

Doc's device beeped when he held it up. "No. Nothing."

Cal stepped closer to the light. The smoke dissipated, revealing a dark shape inside.

Dania stood within the orb, her arms outstretched.

Cal gaped. How was it possible? She… She was alive!

Her wide eyes met his before she lowered her hands.

The orb winked out. She stared at him, motionless, before her head lolled back.

"Whoa!" Cal reached for her, but she slipped through his hands and banged her head on the floor.

Ethan fell to his knees, holding his temples. "Am I alive?"

Alanna tripped, sprawling across the floor as she screamed Ethan's name. She threw her arms around him, pulling him into a hug, repeating his name over and over.

Ethan's arms closed around her. "It's okay, baby. I missed you, too."

She pushed him away and slapped his chest three times. "Don't scare me like that ever again!"

Cal crouched beside Dania as Doc pulled a piece of shiny tape out of his bag and attached it to her forehead.

She looked so weak for someone with ridiculous cosmic power.

Doc frowned. That was never a good sign.

"This is going to be bad news about pathogens, time, and not having any of either, isn't it?" Cal asked.

Doc closed his eyes. The man saw possibilities in everything. Life was simply a puzzle that he hadn't figured out yet. Cal had never seen him look so defeated.

"We really need to get home." Doc stood. "Preferably yesterday."

Ethan crawled a few yards to where Dania lay. "S-She saved me."

"Yeah," Cal said. And now they needed to figure out how to save her.

CHAPTER 5
DANIA

A BRIGHT LIGHT flashed in Dania's eyes before the blurry form of the doctor appeared.

He looked down at her. "We have to stop meeting like this."

She leaned up and blinked as the rest of the med bay came into focus. Dania sighed, letting her head fall back.

A deep pain pressed into her scalp, despite the soft pillow. "Ouch."

He pointed a stylus at her. "You bet your pretty little head *ouch*. You had quite a hit to your noggin when you fell."

The memory of the heat flooding the room rushed back… The sound of the engineer screaming as his skin started to pock and bubble. Yet he'd refused to leave.

"The engineer. Is he…?"

"Alive and well, thanks to you. Actually, he had a few blisters on his hands, but I've already cleared him. That was some quick thinking on your part, whatever you did."

It had all happened so quickly, Dania wasn't sure what she'd even done. Had she saved the engineer on purpose, or had he been inside the radius of her shield when she'd tried to save the ship?

She rubbed her eyes. "I can't really remember."

He pointed the stylus at her again. "It might be that blow to the head. You have a concussion."

"Ridiculous." She tried to get up, but the room spun.

The doctor helped her back down. "You need to take it easy. You get the wonderful privilege of spending a few days with me again."

"A prisoner?"

He tilted his head. "A patient."

But this was also one of the places they'd imprisoned her. Was the captain worried after she'd used her powers again? Was this another ploy to keep her contained?

She flinched as a dull throb beat inside her head. "Enforcers don't get concussions."

"Maybe not, but humans do." He moved the stylus over her forehead. "I experimented with electrical stimulus, and it seems to have elevated the activity on your remaining pathogens, so you'll be okay for the immediate future, but you need to stop using your magic like an extra sense." He poked her shoulder with the stylus. It seemed more like he was making a point than using it for a medical reason. "The magic is a direct drain on the pathogens, and it's increasing the rate of cellular decay. I can't imagine how hard this will be for you, but you have to stop using it."

"Was I supposed to let the engineer die?"

He held out his hands. "Not at all, and we all really appreciate you going above and beyond on that one. Especially Ethan. But you need to understand the risks. You're not part of the enforcers anymore. You don't have that magical healer-guy around to fix things like this. I really need you to limit any unnecessary use of these powers."

A small burn mark marred the ceiling tiles, as if something had exploded in the room at one time. Alexander would never have allowed such outright signs of his failure in his medical treatment area. Of course, she couldn't recall a time Alexander had failed at anything.

"I need you to stay in the med bay for a few days to make sure these little shocks I gave you worked."

"And if they didn't work?"

He raised a single brow and turned away, walking to a station on the far side of the room.

His silence told her everything she needed to know.

This man was not Alexander. She couldn't expect perfection from him. Dania needed to learn to live in a world where her health wasn't a certainty.

She just wasn't sure how to do that.

The glass door protecting the medical instruments hung ajar. Not long ago, she would have seen this as an opportunity to secure a weapon. That was no longer needed, but the lapse in security was interesting. Could it be that they actually had learned to trust her?

Maybe that trust was warranted if she could no longer use her power.

She stroked her stomach, searching for the familiar hum of the borrowed strength of her sponsor. The tingling flows were there, but barely noticeable. The doctor had given her fair warning, yet she'd still expended considerable energy saving the ship and shielding the engineer from a quick, yet horrendous death.

She shivered, imagining being normal, being *human*. She'd tried her best to find a place on the crew, but without her strength, she had nothing to offer. All Dania knew how to do was enforce the king's law. Her power defined her, and asking her not to use it was akin to asking her not to breathe. She simply wasn't sure it was possible.

She wiped away the sheen of fresh tears as the doctor closed the glass doors. The man had innumerable skills, but could he really restore her to health without Geron's help?

Or was this all just a fantasy that would lead to an untimely end, for both herself and the crew?

Days later, Dania woke to the smell of…well, she wasn't sure what. Steam rose from a plate sitting beside her bed. She eased up to find a yellow sphere centered within a flat white substance, and a fork perched on the edge of the dish.

"It's an egg." Alanna sat beside her. "Cal made them this morning. I grabbed you one before Ty gobbled them all up."

"Gobbled?"

"Ate them all." She handed Dania the plate.

Dania sat up and accepted. "You're here early today."

Thankfully, the woman had become a fixture in the med bay during Dania's treatment. Alanna had been teaching her ancient human games, which, while pointless overall, did provide some distraction.

"Ethan got the engines online yesterday." Alanna sat beside her. "I want to get down there early to help with the final repairs."

"Then you certainly don't need to be sitting here with me." It was a ridiculous waste of time but appreciated. The days seemed longer when the woman wasn't there.

She handed Dania a white cloth napkin. "Don't worry about it. The guys are sleeping late today. Doctor's orders."

Doc pointed at them. "And I am not beyond slipping them narcotics to make them sleep if they don't listen, and they know it."

"Besides..." Alanna pointed at the plate. "If I didn't bring you food, you'd get meat sticks and vegetable pills. We want you to get better, not sicker."

"There's nothing wrong with nutritional supplements," the doctor called from across the room. "The entire galaxy lives on them." He leaned closer and whispered. "I have to say that as your doctor. But real food is *soooo* much better."

Dania scooped some of the eggs into her mouth. The odd texture begged to be spit out, but she chewed them anyway. The flavor was palatable once she got over the consistency.

She set the plate to the side. "What game do you have for me today?"

Alanna held up a set of playing cards. "Poker."

Poke her? These games certainly had interesting names.

"If you're going to be part of the crew, you need to learn our pastimes. We play a lot of cards. Poker is a mainstay."

Alanna pulled the tray over Dania's lap and dealt cards, explaining the rules as they went along. It wasn't hard, for the most part, except Dania had no 'poker face,' whatever that meant.

These visits were about more than playing games, though. The doctor, while personable, wasn't too forthcoming with what went on outside the med bay walls. Where Alanna was more amiable about relaying information.

"So, the repairs are going well?" Dania asked.

Alanna adjusted the cards in her hand. "Ethan and Ty keep bickering about the best way to optimize the engines.

You should see them. They're like a couple of old biddies trying to prove who knows more about the ship."

Biddies? Dania didn't know what that meant, but she had seen the two men posturing.

Alanna arranged her deck. Her sweet smile seemed to have nothing to do with the cards in her hand.

"Are you involved with either of them?" Dania asked.

Alanna's lips parted before she answered. "Definitely not." She laughed, placing her cards down. "The guys are more like my family. They're all like brothers to me. Right, Peter?" she called over her shoulder.

"You know it, girl." The doctor bumped fists with her.

"That's interesting," Dania said. "Because your engineer does seem overly fond of you."

Alanna waved her hand. "Ethan is just Ethan. He understands that it will never happen. He's just messing around."

The engineer seemed to be putting far too much effort into the pursuit to be simply *fooling around*. Then again, Dania didn't have much experience with courting. Most men she came in contact with ran in the opposite direction.

The doctor returned to her bed and took Dania's pulse. "I love that you two are playing games every day, but you'll be needing to find alternate arrangements."

"Why?" Alanna asked.

"Good news, I assure you." He turned to Dania. "I'd like to give you one more complete exam to make sure you're strong enough, but then I'm going to release you. I think the best thing for you now is to get out and move around." He held up a finger. "But not too much. If you get tired, you need to rest until you get used to the new you."

The new *human* part of her, he meant. The weak side of her.

Dania closed her eyes. In her world, weakness meant death.

"This is great!" Alanna clapped her hands once. "That means next time we can play in the lounge with the crew."

That *would* be nice, but first she needed to find a way to deserve to be there. She needed to find her place—but she wasn't sure what that place could be.

DANIA PAUSED outside the entrance to the captain's quarters. For some reason, the door seemed larger than the last time she'd been here.

Alanna leaned past her to tap the entry panel. "It's not going to bite you."

Dania glared at her. She knew the door wouldn't bite her. She wasn't a fool. The people inside, however…

The panels slid open, and Ethan jumped up from his place at the large dining table across the room. "Hello, ladies!"

He beamed, his coppery hair shining in the overhead lights as he moved to the opposite side of the table and pulled out a chair. "Here you go, Dania."

She narrowed her eyes at him. Was he purposely calling attention to her lack of strength? Was this a joke to him? "I'm not an invalid. I am perfectly capable of pulling out my own chair."

His mouth fell open. "I-I was…"

Alanna moved around him and took the next seat. "He's trying to be an old-fashioned gentleman." She smacked his arm. "You never pulled out a chair for me."

"You know I love you, babe, but you never almost died saving my life."

Saving his life… Was that what Dania had done?

She drew in a deep breath. The chair assistance seemed to be another strange human custom. There were just so many things to get used to.

Dania took the offered seat. She needed to remember that these people were her friends. Maybe the engineer was just showing his appreciation.

Ethan took his own seat across from her. There were small signs of scarring where the doctor had healed the burns on his skin. His injuries would have been much worse had Dania not been there. But had she saved him intentionally? She massaged the sore patch on her head, wishing she could remember.

The captain came out, serving his crew, just as he'd done the last time she'd been invited to his table. This time, however, the plates seemed barely filled. The crew glanced at each other with questioning looks on their faces. Apparently, they'd noticed the same thing.

Cal came out with a plate for himself, holding a small amount of potatoes and vegetables, and no meat. He placed the dish in his place before sitting. *"Bon appétit."*

They all stared at him.

"Everything okay?" Alanna asked.

The captain picked up his fork. "Just eat and enjoy."

Across from Dania, the doctor reached out and touched the captain's arm. "Cal?" He pointed to Cal's significantly smaller portion.

The captain's fork clanged when he dropped it to his plate. "I wanted you all to enjoy the meal before telling you."

"Telling us what?" Ty asked.

The captain grimaced. "This is the last of the real food. From here on out, it's meat sticks and freeze-dried vegetables."

Dania scooped some vegetables in her mouth. A medley of spices exploded across her tongue. The food was nice, but other than during Alanna's visits, she'd been eating mostly food supplements while living in the med bay. The rations weren't that bad. In fact, they were better than what she'd been accustomed to back home.

She stabbed another forkful of her vegetables but paused when she realized she was the only one eating. Had she committed another *faux paus*?

Alanna broke her frozen state, cut her meat in half, and reached past Dania to place the morsel on the captain's dish. Then Ethan did the same, followed by the doctor, and Ty.

Was this another strange human ritual she was unfamiliar with? Cutting another piece of meat, she reached over and placed half of her own portion on his plate as well.

Cal sat, rubbing his face. "You all don't need to do that."

"Yeah, we do." Ty pointed at the captain's plate with his fork from the other end of the table. "Now eat."

The captain looked at his plate. "You do realize that I now have more than anyone else."

Alanna held up her water glass. "For all the times you've sacrificed for us."

"Hear, hear." Ty held up his glass, and the others followed suit.

Another odd custom, no doubt. Dania held up her glass, and when everyone drank, she took a sip as well.

Ethan stood with his cup. "I'd like to toast our newest crew member, and the woman who saved my life."

"Hear, hear," the others said, raising their glasses in her direction.

Again, they drank, smiling.

Her cheeks flushed, but she wasn't sure why. She looked down, grasping her hands beneath the table. Was she supposed to do something? Should she drink? Had the captain drunk when they'd raised glasses to him?

Cal tapped Dania's shoulder. "Welcome to the crew."

There was a slight edge to his voice, a tone that she would normally take as a lie. He had seemed welcoming, though. He'd even joined the others in voting for her to stay comfortably in a room, albeit under restrictions that she certainly couldn't blame him for. Could he still not trust her, even after she'd saved the engineer?

"You aren't the newbie anymore, Alanna," Doc said.

The navigator leaned across the table toward him. "Oh, come on! I'm barely the newbie now. You were only onboard a few days before I got here."

He held up his pointer finger. "Weeks, my friend. Weeks. You are definitely the newbie."

"Newbie?" Dania asked.

"The latest member of the crew," Ethan said. "So that's you now."

An interesting thought. Dania had taken for granted this solidified unit of a crew had always been together.

"What were you doing before you got here?" Dania asked Alanna.

"Oh, this and that." She pushed her vegetables around. "Cal took a chance on me, and I'm eternally grateful."

"Our girl was a reluctant pirate," the doctor said. "Our own little renegade thief."

A pirate? Alanna?

She sat back. "I'm not very proud of that."

Alanna had always seemed like the least guilty among them. "I can't see you as a pirate," Dania said.

"Because I wasn't. I was a prisoner."

A prisoner? "Please elucidate."

Ty leaned his elbows on the table. "I saw them do a little snatch and grab at the armory near Kemper Station. One minute they were standing there, the next minute they were gone. Poof." He made fists and opened his palms at the same time, then motioned to Alanna. "I noticed our girl here didn't look so happy with her company."

Alanna folded her arms. "They were jerks."

Doc touched his hand to his chest. "Such language."

Ethan snorted. "I'd have used a stronger word."

"Anyway," Ty said. "I told Cal I thought the current crime spree in the area might be the result of a jumper. Apparently, I was right."

Alanna shifted in her seat. "They were blackmailing me. Holding my mom. Threatening her if I didn't help."

"What happened?" Dania asked.

"Her mom is now safe and sound on Europa." Cal took a sip of his drink and placed the cup back on the table.

"And I'll never be able to thank you all enough," Alanna said. "The guys have taught me how to focus better. When I was helping the pirates, I was only jumping them a few meters, just enough to evade authorities. But now..." She held out her hands. "The galaxy's the limit."

The doctor pointed his fork at her. "Within reason, girl-friend. You know I don't like how you pass out at long distances."

Alanna shrugged. "I have to admit it's a bit of a thrill. It was just a game I used to play as a kid. It was fun, and then it became a curse when those jerks caught me." She shivered. "I really thought my life was over, that I'd be a slave to them forever."

"I guess you could say I saved your life." Ty popped a piece of potato in his mouth.

Dania sat back. In retrospect, Ty had saved Dania as well, although that wasn't his original intention when he'd kidnapped her from Midway Station.

A hum filled the room, and Ty looked at the small computer band attached to his wrist and frowned.

"What's up?" Cal asked.

Ty stood. "We got a double orange."

Cal jumped to his feet. "Already?" He headed for the door.

Ethan shoved the rest of his meat in his mouth. "We need to tell that prince it's rude to interrupt our last meal."

Ty grabbed his jacket from the back of his seat and ran for the exit. "Shut up and get to your station before this actually does become your last meal."

CHAPTER 7
CAL

CAL BURST onto the bridge and dropped into his command chair. The unfamiliar stars twinkled back at him, looking unassuming, despite the odd flashing.

Yellow. Yellow. Yellow.

That was normal. The broken proximity alarm.

Yellow. Yellow. Yellow. Orange. Orange. Yellow. Yellow. Yellow.

What in the name of Jupiter's moons did that mean?

Ty blasted through the door and sat. "What we got?"

Cal pointed at the new sequence of lights.

Ty frowned. "That's not good."

"Care to elaborate?"

"I would if I could. I set the systems up separately but wired them to report at the same place."

"Does that mean there's a proximity alarm *and* a scan happening at the same time?"

"I sure as heck hope not."

Because that meant they'd been found.

Yellow. Yellow. Yellow. Orange. Orange. Yellow. Yellow. Yellow.

Alanna dashed through the door and sat. "Taking readings." Her eyes widened. "Oh, no!" She turned to Cal. "Several metal objects incoming."

"Missiles?"

She shook her head. "Larger, with reactive propulsion."

That meant ships. Big ones. *Dammit!*

Ty hit several buttons on his panel. "It has to be that prince. This is dead space. There shouldn't be anything out here."

But if Dania could feel this guy from a million miles away, why hadn't she told them he'd gotten closer?

Yellow. Yellow. Yellow. Orange. Orange. Yellow. Yellow. Yellow.

"Options?"

Ty's Adam's apple bobbled. He looked slightly in Alanna's direction but shook his head and turned back to his console.

Cal gripped the arms of his chair. They'd already discussed the dangers of using Alanna's abilities. But that was when they hadn't been in immediate danger.

"We need to jump the ship." Cal looked out at the stars. If they made it out of this, they needed to find shelter. He wished he could tell where they were so they could aim for a safe port. Or at least a port not friendly to the Banes.

A bead of sweat dripped down Ty's temple. He looked at Alanna, then back to Cal. "Boss, remember the hull breach? The ship might come apart."

"That's not the kind of information you forget." Cal closed his eyes and took a deep breath. "If that prince catches up to us, we're all dead. If we jump, we maybe have a chance."

"You don't understand," Alanna said. "When I jump, I can feel the ship. The hull is like a skin and jumping is like dropping the ship into a pot of boiling water. It hurts, and then when it gets a chance to cool off, it's fine again." She shivered. "I'm afraid that the hot will expand the hull and break the seal."

Cal stared at her. That sounded really, really bad.

Ty hit the comm. "Ethan, are we running engines at full?"

The engineer's voice came over the speaker. "Of freaking course! Can't you feel the shimmy?"

Yellow. Yellow. Yellow. Orange. Orange. Yellow. Yellow. Yellow.

Cal leaned closer to the glass. "Does anyone have visual? Can we confirm what's out there?"

"Negative," Ty said.

Alanna's screen lit up her face. "I see it on the radar. Whatever it is, it's coming in hot."

And there was only one person who'd throw that much metal at them.

"Okay." Alanna lowered her eyes. "I'll do it." She stood. "You're right. We won't survive the prince, but we might survive the jump."

Cal dragged his nails through his hair. This was insane. "Can you pull us out of the jump if the ship starts to...to *hurt?*"

"I'll do my best." She stood beside her station. "Where do you want me to go?"

Cal spun back toward his console. "Stay on course. Our best bet is to get to civilized space as soon as possible." He took a deep breath and released it. "And if the hull looks good, make one more jump right away to send us in another direction."

Hopefully, with a second jump, the *Star Renegade* would be gone before anyone popped out behind them. If they were lucky, the prince's navigator wouldn't be able to triangulate the second location in the three minutes it took before their trail went cold.

That was all if the *Renegade*'s 'skin' was able to handle the hot water.

Alanna held up her hand and the blue gear circle appeared hovering at shoulder height. She turned the dials in the air.

She called up the comm with her other hand. "Okay, everybody. Prepare for jump." She sniffed, wiping away the tears. "I love you guys, you know that?"

Cal clutched the edges of his chair. He'd seen a ship breach after a jump once. If this didn't go well, at least it would be over quickly.

Doc's voice came over the comm. "I thought we were too damaged to jump?"

"No choice," Cal said.

Alanna sniffed again. "I love you, Doc."

Doc cursed and shut down the comm.

Space stretched. The purple hue flashed to pink, then blue before black space and twinkling stars blasted back into view.

Cal's knuckles whitened on his armrests. "Hull integrity?"

"Right as rain," Ethan said. "I can't believe it held. This ship can handle anything."

"Three minutes!" Ty called.

Three minutes? They weren't wasting three minutes waiting to get caught!

Cal turned to Alanna. "How'd the *Renegade* feel? Can she handle another jump?"

She grimaced. "I'm not sure, but I don't think we have a choice. That was a lot of ships back there."

Cal stood. "It's on my ass, not yours. Jump us." At this point, they could either die quick, or die begging for mercy, or maybe, just maybe, they'd squeeze out of this one more time.

Alanna wiped her face. "Okay." She spun the dial. "Here we go."

Cal fell back into his chair just before the world turned purple and pink. The color deepened to a deep blue, flashed orange, and then space returned outside the window.

"Three minutes!" Ty called.

"Report!" Cal said.

"Hull integrity…" Ethan cursed on the other side of the comm. "I'm sealing off the breached hangar. We're still okay, but I don't think she can take much more."

"Where are our friends?" Cal asked.

"No sign of pursuit." Alanna covered her mouth. "Oh my gosh! I think we're clear!"

Ty jumped up and hugged Alanna, swinging her in a circle. "You are amazing!"

Yellow. Yellow. Yellow.

Ty hit the button three times to stop the blinking.

The doors opened and Ethan stormed onto the bridge and gave Alanna a hug. Dania inched in behind her, looking like a wounded animal, her eyes darting around like she was looking for an escape route.

Was she actually more afraid of that prince than they were?

Alanna stumbled back from Ethan's embrace, grabbing her console.

"Whoa there, beautiful." Ethan helped ease her back into her chair.

The color drained from Alanna's cheeks.

Cal cringed. Doc was going to give him an earful for

letting her jump twice like that, but with any luck, it was nothing a few hours of sleep wouldn't cure.

Alanna held her forehead. "I'm okay. I just need a few seconds."

Ethan and Ty high-fived each other. Those two probably didn't have any doubt that they'd make it out of that bind alive.

A dull ache formed behind Cal's eyes again. He needed to try and tap into some of their positivity before he gave himself a heart attack. If he started vomiting from another headache, they'd never let him hear the end of it.

Yellow. Yellow. Yellow.

Cal gripped his armrests again. "Ty, didn't you just hit that thing?"

Ty returned to his seat. "Yeah." He cursed under his breath. "We're still under three minutes. They may have tracked us."

Ethan's grin faded as he walked over to the engineering panel on the wall. "Ready to shut down on your order."

Cal held up his hand. The last thing he wanted was to bring down life support if the ship was already hurting.

Yellow. Yellow. Yellow.

Cal gritted his teeth. "Ty? Is it a glitch?"

His first mate tapped the button three times.

Yellow. Yellow. Yellow.

Ty cursed. "It's not the glitch."

Cal rubbed his face. "Ethan, go ahead and shut everything down."

"Wait!" Alanna pulled her earpiece from her console and placed it in her ear.

She held up a finger, and they all stared at her, but Cal

was sure he was breathing too loud for anyone to hear anything else.

Her face turned red, and she turned to them, tears in her eyes. "I hear background chatter, and direct linking ping static." She wiped her eyes. "I think it's the lower band trade routes. Shadows from the freight skippers could be setting off the alarms."

Could they get that lucky?

"Are you sure?"

She closed her eyes, holding her hand over her ear. A smile burst across her face. "Yes, it's definitely trade chatter!"

Finally, something went right! Now they needed to get away from the guy chasing them.

"Dania?"

She startled at the sound of her name.

"Which way is your stinking prince?"

She shuddered, and then pointed to the right.

"Perfect," Alanna said. "The static bands are coming from the other way."

"Then plot a course and get us out of here.

Yellow. Yellow. Yellow.

"And shut that stupid thing off."

CHAPTER 8
CAL

A BEAUTIFUL BLUE planet filled the viewscreen. Cal had heard that below the dusting of clouds were rolling hills, snowcapped mountains, huge masses of blue and green water, and lush fields with practically no pollution.

Themyscira. Cal hated this place.

Most men agreed because few men ever made it to the surface to see what many people dubbed *New Earth*.

"Engines are humming within local guidelines." Ethan held one finger on the engineering panel on the wall. "We should be good for their scans."

"This should be interesting," Doc whispered, tapping the screens beside Ethan.

Alanna looked up at the screen. "Have faith, guys. Are you all afraid of a little girl power or something?"

"More like girls on steroids." Ty tapped on his panel. "I'm sending out our arrival hellos now."

Cal steadied himself. On Themyscira, they never knew how they'd be received until someone answered the communication. If you weren't a woman, you could get blown out of the sky for the crime of existing if the person on the other side of the comm was having a bad day.

"Is Dania still asleep?" Cal asked.

"Yup." Doc looked over his shoulder. "Do you want me to wake her up?"

Did he want to have another woman handy, just in case? Heck, yes, but Dania tired out too quickly lately. "Let her sleep for now. We're going to need her if we're able to land."

Cal had traded here several times, always with the same complications. Still, the aging satellite trading platform circling their main moon, the only place they allowed men to dock, was the most beautiful thing he'd ever seen after being lost in unknown space for more than a month.

A tone sounded, and a woman's voice filled the air. "Hello, *Star Renegade*. What brings you out this far?"

Cal checked local time and flipped on the comm. "Good afternoon, Themyscira. We are in need of supplies and rations. We're looking for a few good trades." And a place to land and hide for a day or so, but she didn't need to know that.

The one big positive about Themyscira was the size of their military, and they had no love for the king. The local government had printed out and publicly burned every treaty sent to them. They probably wouldn't be too happy to know the *Star Renegade* was stuck in a game of cat and mouse with a prince, though.

The screen flickered, and a woman with warm skin and long, curly black hair filled the screen. She looked off to the side before meeting Cal's gaze. "It looks like you are pretty banged up, *Star Renegade*. Would you like to dock for repairs?"

Repairs would be fantastic, if they weren't worried about

having to leave at a second's notice. "We really don't have a lot of time, nor cash at the moment, Themyscira. Thank you, though."

She raised one perfectly plucked eyebrow. "Veronica."

Cal cocked his head. "Excuse me?"

"My name. Veronica, rather than Themyscira?"

Ty cleared his throat and whispered, "Here we go."

Cal tensed. On a planet inhabited by ninety-five percent women, they were never sure what to expect. Sometimes they looked at you and wanted you dead. Sometimes they wanted you in *other* ways.

Veronica looked at something outside the camera's view. "Tell you what, Captain. I can scoot you to the front of the line and cut you a really sweet deal on the repairs, if you agree to have dinner with me."

And there was his answer on how things would go this time around.

Cal switched off the audio. It wasn't the worst request, but it certainly wasn't the best, either.

This could be an easy way out of a shipload of problems.

His stomach churned. She didn't just want dinner, and he knew it. On a planet without men, the contents of a man's testicles were traded like gold, or maybe even citrus.

"It's a good deal," Ty said. "And she isn't all that hard on the eyes." He held up his hands. "One dinner for cheap repairs?"

Veronica leaned closer to the screen. "It looks like you have a nasty hull breach. And what in goodness' name did you plug it with?"

There was no reason to lie. Cal switched on the audio. "I'm not really sure what the polymer is, but it was all we had on short notice."

Veronica laughed. "Is it the mystery glue the redhead picked up on Triton? Ethan is his name, right?"

Cal switched off the audio again. "How did she know about that?"

Ty shrugged. "That's Themyscira for you."

"I can tell by the look on your face that the answer is *yes*." Veronica shook her head. "You guys are lucky to be alive. Land in Hangar 145 and we'll have that panel switched out for you."

A whole panel? He flipped on his mic. "It might be a few weeks before we can afford a repair like that, Themyscira."

"Veronica." Her brow quirked up again. "I think you missed the part about dinner, Captain Espinoza."

Cal shut off the comm again. The screen went blank as he pinched the bridge of his nose. This colony had been created by women wanting freedom from men. But a small number, usually the ones who'd been born there, still sought male company. And the ones who didn't want anything to do with men still on occasion needed to procreate.

Bile rose in his throat. He spun from the camera and faced the back wall. What could he say to this woman that wouldn't offend her?

To the right of the door, the hook Ty had attached Dania to when they'd taken her from Midway Station caught the light. That seemed like a lifetime ago.

He turned back to the screen. Cal had lived most of his life without a father after the enforcers had murdered his dad for being at the wrong place at the wrong time. Cal had promised himself he'd be there for his kid—if he ever had one. Being a father, not knowing if it was a boy or a girl, never knowing their name...never seeing them...he just *couldn't*.

Alanna swiveled in the nav chair. "We are *not* pimping out our hot captain for cheap repairs."

Cal sighed, doing his best to ignore the *hot* comment.

"What's the big deal?" Ty asked.

Doc leaned on the wall beside his station. "I'd like to point out that if there was a guy on the other side of that call, and he was asking for Alanna, we'd all be rolling up our sleeves, ready to do battle for her."

Ty held up his hands again. "But it's not Alanna. It's just Cal."

A tone sounded, and Cal nodded to Alanna to allow the comm to open back up.

Veronica reappeared on the screen. "Never mind, Captain Espinoza. I've never seen a man look so pale when offered some warm company." She looked to the side again, as if perusing the contents of a data screen. Or maybe, and even more likely, the contents of the ship she seemed to know so much about. "Do you still have that morally ambiguous first mate with the delicious smile?"

Ty stood and walked into view. "Would that be me?"

"You *do* have a nice smile." Her eyes brightened. "How about you? Are you also too uppity for some warm company?"

Ty put his hands in his hip pockets. "No, ma'am. I don't believe I have ever been accused of being uppity."

"Good. I'm looking for a donor, and you're pretty enough. You game?"

Cal hated being right.

Ty glanced at Cal, then back to the screen. "Always happy to help out."

Veronica cocked her head to the left. "Just so we're clear, I want this donation administered the old-fashioned way."

Ty snorted. "Yeah, I figured. One donation, and the ship gets fixed today?"

"It will probably be spit shined and ready to go by the time we're done."

Cal cringed. Repairs usually took days to schedule and complete. Did they have fast-paced repair crews on hand just for occasions such as this?

"Deal," Ty said.

Her grin lit up the screen. "Okay, land in Hangar 145, and consider the repairs paid for."

The screen went blank.

"*Paid for?*" Doc said. "His smile isn't *that* delicious."

Alanna stood. "Ty, you don't need to do this."

Ty returned to his station. "An afternoon with a beautiful woman is really not a chore."

"Why don't beautiful women ever ask for me to have clothing-optional dinners?" Ethan asked.

Ty started maneuvering them to the port. "No one wants to see your hairy butt."

"Hey, once they go ginger, they never go back."

"You wish."

Ty brought them in through the narrow, jagged opening to the satellite station. All along the walls, gun turrets came to life.

Cal lost count after the eighteenth weapon angled toward them. This was the kind of welcome he was accustomed to here. These ladies really didn't trust men. "Doc, I think we're going to need Dania."

He finished tapping a text into his panel. "I already asked her to meet us downstairs."

Good call. They needed a show of women on board. Not many other things mattered to the inhabitants.

Ty set the ship down like they were landing on a cloud, and they headed to the lower decks.

Outside, scores of dock workers… *female* dock workers… circled the ship.

Cal's stomach sank, and he grabbed Ty's arm before he stepped off the ship. "Alanna is right. You don't need to do this."

"The way I look at it, two consenting adults just made a date for a nice afternoon together." Ty brushed some lint from his shoulder. "If we get some free repairs, I'm totally good with it."

"Like Alanna said, I'm not okay with the idea of pimping out my crew."

Ty's gaze centered on the approaching guards. "Would it have bothered you if I'd met her in a bar and we'd hooked up?"

"No."

"Well, for me, this is no different. I mean, really, I'm on a planet filled with women and almost no men. Did you think I wouldn't take advantage and try to score while I was here?"

Cal hadn't considered that.

"Listen. Veronica is a good contact, and I was serious about her being gorgeous. This is not a problem for me, boss."

Cal sighed. He just wished the whole idea didn't make him want to pummel something.

The second Ty's boots hit the steel decking, three of the guards approached and ran scanners over his head, torso, and legs.

"What's this?" Ty asked.

"Standard check for sexually transmitted disease." She crinkled her nose. "You are, after all, a *man.*"

Cal tensed at the way she spat *man,* like it was a curse word.

When the light on her scanner flashed blue, they led Ty away, one on each side, holding his arms like he was a prisoner.

In a way, he was. He was payment for services about to be rendered.

It didn't really matter that Ty said he was okay with it. Cal still wanted to puke.

Nearly a dozen more guards surrounded the *Star Renegade* "for the ship's protection." That was a little more protection than Cal felt comfortable with. It wasn't like they had a choice, though.

Cal slipped back into the ship as Dania and Ethan came down the ladder onto the deck.

Doc and Alanna both stood near the exit with bags over their shoulders, ready to go out and make their trades. Cal and Doc would team up to find medical supplies while trying to avoid getting shot for the crime of having a Y chromosome, while Alanna would do a ration and pantry run.

"Are you okay going out there by yourself?" Cal asked Alanna.

"I'll be fine. My last employer used me as a courier here, so I know where to go."

Cal didn't want to know what her pirate overlords had needed a courier for on a planet run by women.

Alanna gripped her bag tighter. "I'm mostly worried about the cost of food rations. We don't have a lot of money."

That was the problem of the hour. Doc had most of their available funds on his trading card to pay for the supplies they needed to save Dania.

"As soon as we're done, I'll air you the rest of the funds.

For now, just do the best you can." Cal turned to Doc. "You all set to go? We're probably going to be watched every minute."

"My contact says there is a scientist here who regularly kicks ass at galactic competitions. She's already agreed to see us. So, as long as we get there in one piece, we should be fine."

Getting there might be the problem. "Just keep your head down." Because men had no rights here, and if a woman said you looked at her the wrong way, it could mean a week in a cold, dark jail cell.

Ethan looked out onto the landing platform. "What if they try to board the ship while you're all gone?"

Cal pointed to Dania. "They'll have to get through her."

The enforcer smirked, folding her arms. She'd donned her silver uniform for the occasion, which looked no less menacing with the sleeves cut off after they'd been burned escaping from the pirates on Port Walker.

Ethan looked satisfied with that, even though Dania wasn't supposed to use her power.

They started off the ship, and Alanna walked right by the guards. She held her head high and kept moving. Her days as a courier did her justice. Cal and Doc, however, met a wall of beautiful but angry faces.

A guard with tightly cropped black curls stepped forward, one hand on the weapon at her hip. "I am Master Armer Empi. What's your business?"

Cal held his hands where she could see them. "We've been cleared by Veronica to trade."

"Veronica cleared a seed carrier. Nothing more."

Doc flinched beside him when she called Ty a *seed carrier*.

Cal held himself steady. "I also told her we need

supplies." Cal lifted his chin in the direction they'd taken Ty. "He's pretty, isn't he? If you ladies play nice, I could be persuaded to dock here more often."

Empi's eyes slid over Cal's body with a look of disgust, until she reached his groin area.

His little soldier pulled in tight and hid before her eyes met his again. "You'll need guards. Men are not safe here. Nor are they trusted."

"I understand," Cal said. "We just need some food and medical supplies. If you can point us in the right direction, we'll stop stinking up your hangar and leave as soon as our ship is repaired."

She sneered at his remark and waved him forward. As he and Doc started walking, she signaled to another guard, and they followed less than a step behind.

Cal hoped everything Doc needed was legal on this station.

Doc told the guards the name of who he wanted to see, and Empi moved ahead, leading them through the corridors.

When they passed into the more populated areas, Cal was actually glad to have the guards, as some women spat at them and called them words that he was sure weren't pleasant in their culture.

As they approached a non-descript, silver building with no windows, the door opened, and a woman with short light brown hair poked her head out.

"I have it from here," she told the guards, as she pushed up the sleeves of her white lab coat.

"But...the men..." Empi said.

"Do you seriously think I need protection from a couple of little boys?"

Empi backed off, and she and the other guard poised themselves outside the door.

Their host waved Cal and Doc in. "My name is Yonid." Once they were inside, she closed the door and clapped her hands. "So, I'm hearing all sorts of interesting stories about why you're here."

"Care to relay what they said?" Cal asked.

"Not really." She moved behind one of four metal tables and took a steaming beaker off a flame. "I'd love to hear the real reason you're here, though. There are far safer places for a ship with men onboard to get food rations and medical supplies."

Doc moved closer to the table. "They tell me you're the best there is with biocellular renumeration."

She snickered, then coughed into her hand. "I'm sorry. I've never met a man who could even pronounce *biocellular renumeration.*"

Doc held it together, not even flinching at the jab at his male-ness. They started talking in really big words. Yonid's voice got higher, and she spoke faster the more they threw around crazy technical terms. In any other sphere, Cal would have thought they were making things up to make him feel like a simpleton, which he supposed he was, standing in a room with two scientists, even if one of them was self-taught.

To the left, a red laser scanned a thick, bubbling clear liquid. Equations that looked like hieroglyphics scrolled on a screen behind the table. Books and gadgets were stacked neatly across the room in perfectly uniform rows.

Doc stood in the center of all of this, not missing a beat with this woman. It was times like this when he realized that Doc just might be the genius everyone said he was.

Yonid pulled out a microscope. "Can I see what you're trying to replicate?"

Doc drew a vial of reddish liquid from his jacket pocket and placed a drop beneath the scope. A screen about five feet across and three feet high lit up on the wall beside them.

Her jaw dropped. "That's organic?"

"From what I can tell, yeah," Doc said.

"Why in all the stars would you want to replicate something like that?"

"I just do." Doc stared her down. It was probably a good call to keep the details to himself, since this lady was smart enough to sniff out things they'd rather keep hidden. By now, everyone on this station probably knew that Dania was on board the *Renegade*.

Yonid leaned closer to the screen. "These cells look enhanced. I'd think the result would be quite phenomenal, to be honest." She tapped her lower lip. "If they're degrading to the point of needing renumeration, maybe the answer is as simple as re-infection." She looked at Doc. "Have you tried re-exposure?"

"That would not be ideal. I really need to create a synthetic alternative."

She sucked her teeth, grabbed a container from a shelf, and put a drop on the slide. All the little red squiggly things stopped moving and then turned black.

Doc gaped. "What did you do?"

She handed the container to him. "Take this. It's a gift."

Doc stared at the jar like it might bite him.

"It's harmless to you. Don't worry." Yonid pointed at the screen. "But it will kill any organism with that inside them."

Cal's jaw started to ache, and he loosened it. "Why would we want that?"

"Because that." She pointed at the screen. "Could be turned into a weapon."

This was a smart lady, and she had no idea how right she was.

Doc kept a perfect scientific poker face. "Can you help me replicate it?"

Yonid started rattling off all the things she had in the lab that were on Doc's list, and the names of scientists on other planets who could provide the rest.

"Is this all doable?" Cal asked.

Doc bit his upper lip. "I know some of these people already. Some good, some bad. We'll probably have to go to Ebuda to get the polo-silica gels and micro plasma filaments, but then I think I can get to work while we're en route to the other stations."

They'd just have to find something else to trade once they got there because after today, they'd be out of cash.

"You're really going to travel that far to get those supplies?" Yonid asked. "You really are serious about this."

"I do love a challenge," Doc said.

She folded her arms. "And you are also not being completely truthful." She turned and looked at the screen. "Those cells are enhanced in ways that shouldn't be possible. Weaponization is a real threat, but the alternative..."

She glanced at Doc, and he shifted his weight. What would they do if she figured it out?

"The alternative..." She removed the slide of dead cells and replaced it with a new sample. The red cells jittered across the screen.

"So interesting," she said.

She took a speck of the dead cells and added it to the new sample.

Doc mopped his brow with his sleeve. "We really need to get going."

Yonid seemed to ignore him. The red cells fluttered, engulfing the black until the dead cells disappeared.

She starred at the twitching cells that remained. "Yes, the alternative could also be quite interesting." She tapped her lips with her finger, pacing in front of the screen, just like Doc always did. "Polo-silica gels and plasma filaments, huh?" She spun toward them, her eyes wide. "In large numbers, those cells have healing properties. Are you trying to cure a disease? Castian Flu, maybe?"

Doc seemed to think it over. His mouth opened several times, but it looked like he kept rethinking his answer.

She tapped her lips with her pointer finger again. "That kind of medical advancement would be amazing." She started rooting through her shelves. "I have most of what you need here, but only small amounts of everything."

"I thought you didn't have all the stuff we needed," Cal said.

She glanced over her shoulder at him. "I lied." She continued to root through her drawers.

"Why would you lie?"

Yonid picked up a black cylinder, considered the contents, then put it back. "Do you know how expensive polo-silica gels and micro plasma filaments are?" She started loading vials and metal instruments into a box as Doc watched.

"That's a lot of tech," Doc said.

"Yeah, but to cure the flu?" She looked over the box. "I guess I can part with all of this for fifty thousand ducets."

Cal felt like he'd been punched in the gut. That was exactly how much he'd loaded onto Doc's card, which she'd probably known before they'd even stepped foot through the door.

This would drain them dry. It would also mean they had nothing extra to send to Alanna for food.

Doc lowered his eyes. "This is all worth way more than fifty thousand ducets."

Was he crazy? They didn't have any more!

She looked over the box. "I know, but it would be worth it if you found the cure for the Castian flu."

Cal put his hand on Doc's shoulder. "Alanna." He hoped that was enough to remind him that they were going to start getting hungry very soon.

Yonid smiled. "The pretty little thing shopping in the market?" She tapped a few keys on her screen. "She doesn't have enough on her card for all the supplies she's bartering for."

Cal cringed. This planet was a smuggler and pirate's nightmare. There was no privacy anywhere. It was probably why they had no crime, though.

"There is another way." Yonid looked up from her screen, taking on a professional, emotionless tone. "I've been thinking of having a baby, but the men available don't meet my standards."

Doc stepped between her and Cal. "Honey, I know the captain is hot and believe me, I'd love to have a baby with eyes that blue, too, but this isn't his thing." He looked back to Cal, then to Yonid. "Can we possibly come up with another way to..."

Yonid coughed out a laugh. "I'm not interested in the clueless one." She took a step toward Doc. "I've never met a man that even knows what polo-silica is, let alone how to use it with micro plasma filaments."

The color drained from Doc's face. "Oh, sweetie, I'm not even sure I could."

That was the understatement of the century. Cal grabbed Doc's shoulder and pulled him back. Ty was bad enough. Doc was absolutely out of the question.

Yonid held up a finger to wait and then rooted though a drawer. "No worries, I'm interested in the DNA that created your brain, not your body." She held up a small, clear container. "I have no desire for physical contact with a man."

Doc trembled beneath Cal's hand, staring at the container, but he didn't move.

Had Doc ever even considered the possibility of children?

Cal felt Doc exhale. "A jar donation is worth a hell of a lot more than fifty thousand ducets."

"Agreed." She looked at the box. "All the supplies are free, and I'll send enough money to the pretty pink-haired girl to buy everything she has in her bartering square."

Doc gulped. "Are you sure?"

Yonid laughed again. "I'll freeze a sample for my own use and sell the rest. Don't worry about me. This will take care of the bill and then some."

"This is…" Cal shook his head. "No. I can't let this happen."

Doc pushed Cal's hand off his shoulder. His eyes looked scared when he turned. "This could cure the *Castian Flu*." He emphasized Castian Flu, pointing out that this could save Dania, before he turned and grabbed the jar from her hand. "Is there somewhere private I can go?"

Cal remembered a little boy, limping home to his mother, fatherless.

Stars! This was wrong. But on a planet with no men, was it more wrong to deny this woman a child if she wanted one?

Yonid opened a door and Doc slipped inside. She whispered to him, glancing back at Cal.

Doc flushed before the door closed.

Yonid's grin dazzled when she returned. "If you give me Alanna's card number, I'll send her the ducets."

"Before your package is delivered?" Cal asked.

She glanced toward the closed door. "As a sign of good faith."

Cal gave her the number.

A minute later, Alanna sent a text. *"What the bejesus did you do?"*

Cal typed back. *"Just get the food."*

"This is enough for several months."

Months?

He looked up. "How much did you send her?"

"Do you have any idea how many million sperm cells that magnificent-brained-man is about to give me? It's worth a fortune here. This is not a problem whatsoever." She looked at the door Doc had disappeared into. "He's about to make me a very rich woman."

Another wave of nausea swept over him, and Yonid handed him a glass of water. "I've heard about transactions like this bothering people, but it shouldn't."

Maybe not, but his stomach still twisted.

"Think about it," she said. "I have no other way to conceive. It's not like there are any unwanted children here I could adopt. I want to be a mother. That means I need to buy my seed." She looked over to the door again. "And I seriously can't overlook an opportunity to get an IQ even remotely close to my own."

Cal sighed. She made it all sound so clinical. So cold. But he nodded.

He understood, but it still made him feel like sludge. It wasn't any different than sperm banks at the turn of the enlightened age, and he needed to remember that.

He shot off a final text to Alanna. *"Use the extra funds to get anything we can store for the long haul. We'll explain later. Don't worry."*

"I worry."

Cal smirked and put the tablet in his back pocket. "Can I help pack any of this up?"

"That would be great." She pulled out another box.

"Thank you very much for your generosity."

She shrugged. "Hey, you seem like nice people, and I'm sure if you come up with a viable antidote, you'll share it with the galaxy. To me, that's a great investment."

Cal flinched. Themyscira wasn't loyal to the Banes, or anyone for that matter. Out here so close to the pirate sector and on the border of known space, they'd never seen the devastation of the Carteks and had shown a militant response when asked to join in the Bane alliance. Would she be as willing to help them if she'd known who, or *what*, they were really trying to treat?

Yonid leveled her gaze on him. "You're not really trying to cure the flu, are you?"

Cal glanced toward the door. He knew he was out of his league even speaking to this woman. "I'm pretty sure you're the one who said we were doing that."

She sniffed. "I was hoping you'd tell me what you really are trying to do." She stared at the screen again. "If you can replicate whatever those cells are, the healing properties really could be formidable. Castian flu could only be the beginning." She turned back to Cal. "If you're successful and need help modifying your discovery for another purpose, I'd be willing to be a part of that."

Maybe not, once she figured out what they were really doing.

She placed her hand on his shoulder. "Be careful, though. I worry you're playing with something bigger than both of you."

She had no idea how right she was.

The door opened, and Doc stepped out, keeping his eyes down as he handed the container to Yonid.

She held it up to the light. "If I have a successful conception, do you want me to let you know?"

"No," Doc said. Then he frowned. "Wait. Yes. Would you mind?"

"Are you kidding? Most women want to hide their donors. The men who stop here are rarely high-grade." She pulled the jar closer to her, cradling the glass like it was already a warm, healthy baby. "I'd be proud to let my child know who you are."

In one short sentence, and the light in Doc's eyes, the weight on Cal's heart lifted. Why did that make it all okay?

Gathering their boxes on an automated, floating metal cart, they met their guards outside. After a short walk to the trading centers, Empi directed them to the pay station in the transportable food market.

Alanna waved at them. "Hey, guys. You're just in time. I'm finalizing things now."

She had her own cart loaded with standard rations and a container of fruits, fresh vegetables, and...

Cal ran his palm over a freezer wrapping. "Is that fish?"

"I know!" She beamed. "Can you believe it?"

They loaded their supplies on her carts and sent the automated transport back to Yonid.

"Neither of you did anything you didn't want to do, did you?" she asked.

Cal glanced at Doc as they headed back to the ship.

"No," Doc said. "I'm actually feeling pretty good about this, to be honest. This was a good day."

Cal's chest tingled. He really couldn't ask for anything better than that.

"Well, that's a relief," Alanna said. "That had to be the easiest supply run ever."

Red and yellow lights blared to life as sirens filled the corridors. Heavily armed guards pushed past, forcing them against the wall and nearly knocking over their carts.

Doc slapped Alanna's shoulder. "You *had* to say something, didn't you?"

"What's going on?" Cal asked Empi.

Both their personal guards listened to someone talking into their earpieces.

"There is a disturbance in Bay 145," Empi said.

The hangar where the *Star Renegade* was docked.

Ethan had a penchant for getting in trouble, and Dania was a former enforcer to a king these women hated. Maybe leaving Dania and Ethan alone with the *Renegade* hadn't been the best idea.

CHAPTER 9
CAL

THEY SPRINTED DOWN THE HALL, the guards at their sides and their automated cart floating behind them. Each of them skidded to a stop as they entered the hangar.

The guards who had been around the *Star Renegade* had moved to surround a small short-range skipper craft hosting multi-phased weapons turrets on all visible sides. The nose of the ship was nestled right up against the *Renegade*'s engine ports, maybe even touching them.

The guards swarmed the other craft, leaving the *Renegade*, for the moment, alone.

"Get the cargo on the ship," Cal said.

"What about you?" Alanna asked.

"Don't worry. I'll be right behind you guys." After he figured out how to get out of there safely.

Doc and Alanna made their way to the ramp, the supply container following.

Empi motioned for the other guard to join those surrounding the new ship, but she stayed at Cal's side as he tapped his portable comm, calling Ethan.

"Is Ty on board?" Cal asked.

"No. What's going on out there?"

"I have no idea." But it wasn't good.

If whoever was flying that thing wanted to start trouble with the locals, Cal needed to get his ship out of there ASAP.

He tapped Ty's frequency on the comm. "Sorry to cut your party short, but we need to leave."

Ty answered, "The package has been delivered. I'm just pulling things back together."

That was fast. Veronica certainly hadn't injected any romance into the transaction.

In this case, that was a good thing. "Zip it up quick. We have a situation."

"Nothing new. I'm on my way."

There was only one exit from this landing bay for a ship the *Renegade's* size, and although the other craft was smaller, it was firmly seated in their way. If the proverbial shit hit the fan, they were trapped.

"They landed without clearance," Empi said. "Whoever that is just asked for a very big problem."

The cargo ramp on the other ship opened. The Themysciran guards raised their weapons and pointed at the doorway. They shouted phrases in different languages. The English version said: *Stand down and prepare to be boarded.*

Cal edged closer to the *Renegade*. This was going to go bad—and fast.

A tall figure appeared in the opening of the rogue ship. Silvery white boots caught the light before the guards surrounding the craft lifted off the ground like the station's gravity had failed.

Cal flinched and looked down, but his own feet, and his escort's stayed on the deck.

Empi's jaw dropped before a man stepped the rest of the

way into the light. His short, silvery-white hair whisked about his face as if he stood in front of an omnidirectional fan. His glassy, light blue eyes looked up at the helpless guards before a bemused smile crossed his lips.

Cal froze, his mind whirling back to the dirt streets of his home planet, and a man in a shimmering white uniform looming above his father.

This wasn't the same man. Cal would never forget the emotionless, unforgiving face that still haunted his nightmares. It didn't matter, though. Enforcers were all the same.

Cal sprinted toward the *Renegade*. There was a weapons compartment just outside the base of the ramp. If he could just make it there while the enforcer was still busy with the guards, maybe he could…

His fingers grazed the edge of the locking mechanism before his feet left the ground.

Ethan and Alanna gaped at him through the *Renegade*'s bridge window as Cal rose above the ship.

Cal's stomach turned as the air around him clamped down like a giant hand. He could breathe, but that was about all he could do as he lowered a few feet above the ground and hovered toward the approaching enforcer.

The cold ice in his captor's eyes seemed to deepen. "Calvin Espinoza, so you *are* still alive."

Cal struggled against huge fingers made of air. The *Renegade* was beside him, the ship still wide open. His crew was in there, and he couldn't get to them. Even if he could, they couldn't take off. There was nowhere to go, and death was knocking on their door.

Cal did his best to keep his voice steady. "You knew I was alive, or you wouldn't be here."

"True. You have something I need." The enforcer looked

at his fingernails, ignoring the curses of the women hanging in the air above.

Cal lowered to a few inches above the ground, leaving him at eye level with the taller enforcer.

Ty sprinted into the landing bay and skidded to a stop behind Cal. He took a step back. "Whoa. I'm going to take it that's not a friend of yours."

"Not exactly."

Boots slammed down the *Renegade*'s ramp. Dania leapt off the edge of the plank and injected herself between Cal, Ty, and the enforcer.

She raised her palms like she was ready to kick ass. "Don't kill anyone!"

Yeah, like that would work.

The enforcer lowered his head slightly. "As you wish."

Wait. What?

Dania relaxed her stance. She looked back at Cal. Her lips parted before she turned back to Cal's captor.

The enforcer seemed to peruse her. "Geron was correct. You look like you are near death."

Empi raised her weapon. "I need you to stand down. You have landed illegally, and you are holding our people hostage. That breaks at least ten of our laws."

The enforcer smirked. "Your laws do not concern me. However, I can be gracious if you stop pointing your toys at me."

She lowered her weapon, and all the guards hanging in the air dropped to the floor. Their guns moved of their own accord, whisking down the hallway.

Empi lifted her chin, her face full of defiance, but there was a slight shake in her fingers. "Get off our planet. We do not bow to your king, and you are not welcome here."

"Fine."

The enforcer looked back to his ship. The door he'd exited from closed, and the ship hovered, flashed its lights, and flew out of the hangar. That meant there were more than one of them. And that was a short-range ship. There could be an armada waiting for them outside.

Cal's feet met the floor, and the enforcer held out his hand toward the *Star Renegade*. "Shall we?"

Ty shifted uneasily beside Cal. He knew as good as anyone how screwed they were.

"You actually expect me to let you on my ship?" Cal asked.

The enforcer snickered. "Mr. Espinoza, you don't have a choice."

CHAPTER 10

DANIA

DANIA KEPT HER BREATH STEADY, but Kile was more than capable of reading her mood. Her temperature would be elevated, maybe as much as zero point eight degrees. Her breaths were shallow. Any one of these symptoms or more showed her frailty, and she hated herself for it.

Still, how dare her commander say she looked close to death? Her skin was a warm, pleasing tone, like the other people on this ship, and not the blanched white of the enforcers.

She glanced at Kile's nearly white, opalescent hair. He still wore it short on the sides, with longer strands on the top, floating in flux with his primordial energy.

Dania fingered her own honey-brown, lifeless hair. Lack of movement in the strands was the hardest part of her change to get used to when she looked in the mirror, followed by the darkening of her eye color.

Cal slowed his pace. "Ty, get up on the deck and prep us for departure."

Ty glanced at Kile. "But..."

"Just do it."

Kile turned to Ty. "Place the ship in a low orbit and await my instructions."

Cal's cheeks reddened. Dania hoped he wouldn't do anything foolish. So far, Kile was being uncharacteristically congenial. The last thing she wanted was for any member of the crew to become a liability.

Kile stepped toward her. "Is there somewhere comfortable we can speak?"

"Comfortable?"

Kile motioned to the walls. "As in, not a cargo bay."

Dania narrowed her eyes. This was not like him at all. Why would he care where they talked? Still, the best thing to do was to play along and find out what his orders were. He was here for Dania, of course, but he could have easily overcome her in her weakened state, which meant he needed something else... something he probably could not obtain with his normal brute force.

Dania leveled her eyes at him. "We can go to the lounge."

"We can?" Cal asked.

She glared at him. "Yes, Mr. Espinoza, we can."

His lips thinned at the sound of his last name, and she tried to block out the heaviness building in her chest as they followed her to the lounge. Over the past few weeks, she'd taken her cue from the crew and started calling the captain "Cal." The familiarity seemed natural now. But the less human she seemed at the moment, the better.

The look on Cal's face, though, was far too reminiscent of the distrust, the hate that had been in his eyes when she'd first boarded. They'd come so far in such a short time. Hopefully, Kile didn't ruin her one chance at a new life.

The doors to the lounge opened, and the doctor stood from his place at the table.

"What are you doing here?" Cal asked.

He looked at Kile, then back to Cal. "Well, I don't have anything to do with flying the ship, and I was hungry, so I decided to come down here for a snack."

Yet there was no plate or food residue in the place he'd been sitting. Nor did he show any outright signs of hunger.

He raised his chin, which was probably human code for 'I got your back, boss.'

Cal's blood pressure initially lightened, then spiked. That made sense. He probably appreciated the backup, but from what she'd seen, Cal would probably rather have as few people as possible close to a being with primordial energy coursing through their veins.

"So, what do you want?" Cal spun toward Kile. "It's obviously not me, because I'm still breathing."

"He's here for me," Dania said. "Geron wants me back."

Kile glanced at her. "Yes and no. Yes, Geron is angered and upset, knowing you are out here dying and he can't find you, but you are no longer his chief concern."

A flush of heat ran through her. What could possibly be more important to him than finding his renegade general?

Whatever the problem, it would have to be something huge to gain his attention. Geron didn't really care much about politics or the issues of the galaxy. So, what could be more important to him?

A deep ache formed in her chest, squelching the curiosity.

Geron had said he'd come for her. Had he given up already? Forgotten her?

She closed her eyes and willed the sadness away. She didn't need her sponsor anymore. She just needed time. The doctor was going to help make her strong again.

"Still," Kile continued, "I think your unique circumstances make you the perfect person to help me on our new mission."

Dania raised her eyes. "My unique circumstances?"

"You have access to a very well-known smuggling ship. One that would be granted access to landing sites almost anywhere without question."

Cal pushed away from the wall he'd been leaning against. "You want the *Renegade*? No way. Not in this millennium."

Dania placed her hand on Cal's chest, stopping his advance. "Why would you need a smuggling ship?"

Her commander's eyes seemed to search through her, looking for something that she'd tried hard to push aside these past several weeks.

"Enforcers are not trained in stealth," Kile said. "Our value is in sheer might."

"And intimidation," Cal said.

"True." Kile glanced at him. "There are many places that we have trouble infiltrating because those we are seeking can see us coming."

Dania had experienced these issues as well, but pure might always won out in the end.

"So what do you need stealth for?" Dania asked.

Her second-in-command's stare bore through her, his eyes both accusing and empathetic. He took a deep breath and looked toward the rectangular window of stars. "This concerns Alexander."

Alexander? He was still alive! The galaxy suddenly seemed eons lighter.

Until Kile's stoic visage turned grim. "Our healer is missing."

Dania dropped her hand from Cal's chest. "What? When? How?"

Kile started to pace. "Alexander was en route to Morak when he received a distress call from the Opanus colony."

"That's the outer rims," Cal said. "Right on the border of Cartek space."

Kile folded his hands behind his back. "From what we can tell, over a dozen Cartek ships attacked the planet."

"A dozen?" Cal gaped. "Those colonies are defenseless."

Kile quirked a brow. "There were no survivors."

Doc looked at the floor. "All those colonists—dead?"

"No. The human fatalities were actually fairly low." Kile turned to Dania. "Alexander must have been having a bad day. He slaughtered the Carteks. Every single one. It was a bloodbath. You would have been proud of him."

Dania flinched. Alexander was certainly capable of eliminating twelve targets with ease. However, he'd always looked for a peaceful solution. Then again, maybe they hadn't given him one.

"But you said he was missing?" She eased down into a chair at the end of the table.

"Apparently, after the uncharacteristic bloodshed, Alexander's normal programming kicked in. He landed his ship and started healing the colonists. According to the eyewitnesses, he treated people for days until he collapsed." Kile grimaced. "One of the families took him in and did their best to keep him comfortable." He turned away and looked at the blast pattern on the wall. "That's when the trappers came."

Dania sprang from her chair. "What?"

"The father of the family who'd sheltered him, the man's son, and three other colonists were killed trying to protect Alexander, but they were overrun."

"No!" Dania gritted her teeth. This wasn't possible. First Matara, and now Alexander?

"He's been missing for just over three weeks."

Dania stared at him. "Three weeks?" And he'd already been weakened—so weak, he wouldn't have been able to defend himself.

Cal almost reached for Dania but drew back after glancing at Kile.

Instead, Cal looked at her, his gaze somehow comforting, before he turned back to Dania's subordinate. "The slavers are getting more aggressive. Attacking a fully seasoned enforcer is suicide."

"Maybe not," Doc said. "It sounds like they're opportunists. They sat and waited, probably had someone watching your friend. When he collapsed, they knew he couldn't fight back."

Dania rubbed her arms, fighting off a chill deep under her skin. With the growing problems in the outlier colonies, the ones that the king had not given up on, more enforcers with the proper intentions of protecting the innocent would head to the outer rims.

The distance from the Bane home world would leave them away from their sponsors for longer periods of time, putting them at even more of a risk.

The trappers must have figured out the correlation between time away from their sponsor and amount of power expelled and had started using this to their advantage. And now, one of the most giving, understanding people she'd ever known was gone.

Dania paced the room. "He's out there, all alone, and he won't be able to regain his strength without Geron."

Kile turned on her, narrowing his eyes. The nature of enforcer strength was a close-kept secret. Dania had never considered why until now.

"It's all right." She waved her hand at him. "They've been doing testing on me, trying to keep me alive. The doctor already figured out how our power manifests."

Doc leaned on the edge of the table. "Well, I mostly get how it works. One thing I can tell you, though, is that if your friend was so broken that he collapsed, it would mean he was in worse shape than you were when we met. Then add three weeks on top of it?"

Kile spun on him. "What are you saying?"

Doc blanched and glanced at Dania before he evened out his expression. "I'm saying that if he's alive, then he's dying. He needs medical care—and fast."

"That's ridiculous," Kile said. "We've found younglings who have been taken. We've liberated them with no consequences."

Doc shrugged. "How many years does it take to get addicted to the pathogens? Maybe they don't need their prince as badly as you older enforcers do."

Kile gawked at him. "What?"

Dania moved a little closer to Doc in case Kile lashed out when she explained. "You know how we need to go back to our sponsors, how our bodies cry for our power to be replenished?"

He stared at her before nodding.

"Whatever he did to you," Doc said, "you can't live without it. It's possible the younger ones might not have the same tissue degradation, but the older ones..." He looked at Dania. "I hate to say it, but Dania is pretty messed-up inside. Her body is dependent on whatever he does to you, and it's not something easily cured."

Kile looked like he wanted to object, but instead lowered his eyes.

Deep down, maybe he had already considered their dependency was a possibility.

Convincing Kile wasn't their problem, though. If Alexander had been out there for weeks, all alone… "Can you save him?" Dania asked Doc.

He shook his head. "Sweetie, I'm not even a hundred percent positive I can save you, let alone two of you."

The doors slid open, and Ty and Alanna entered.

"Who's flying the ship?" Cal asked.

Ty pointed to the miniature computer on his wrist. "We are in our enforcer-prescribed low orbit. But the Themyscirans are not-so-nicely requesting that we take our new friend here…" He pointed at Kile. "And leave their space yesterday if not sooner."

The door opened again, and Ethan entered. "What's going on? Are we in trouble?"

"We're always in trouble," Ty said. "The question is: How much?"

Doc eased into his chair. "The abridged version: The long-haired enforcer who pulled the bullet out of my chest on Midway Station is missing. They think he was taken by slavers."

Alanna gasped, covering her mouth. "He was so sweet. So nice." She looked at Kile, no sign of fear in her eyes. "You're going to save him, right?"

Kile folded his arms. "That is my intent, yes. Prince Geron is livid. All of his assets have been redirected to saving his healer. In Geron's exact words: *Nothing else matters* to him."

Dania rubbed her shoulders. "Which is why you haven't executed this crew and dragged me home."

"Correct. At this moment, you and this ship are a valuable asset. A means to an end to our sponsor's primary mission."

"And when all this is over?" Cal asked.

"Then you will no longer be a valuable asset."

Cal tilted his head. "So, you want me to help you, and as soon as this is all done, you're going to have to kill all of us?"

Kile looked to the side, as if considering. "I may be inclined to look the other way for ten minutes while your ship tries to escape."

He would? Dania tried to read him for a lie, but enforcers couldn't lie. It wasn't in their programming. But neither was *looking the other way*.

"And after ten minutes?" Cal asked.

Kile met Cal's gaze. "You are, after all, a criminal."

Dania grabbed Cal's arm. "It is the best he's able to offer. With Alanna, ten minutes is all you'd need."

Kile glanced at her, and Dania's veins chilled. She could tell he was cataloging that small bit of information. Alanna's ability wasn't illegal, but Dania didn't want to call unnecessary attention to her friend.

But Alanna wasn't the only one who needed her protection.

"Please, Cal. Alexander doesn't deserve this." She tightened her grip on his arm. "He saved your doctor."

Doc nodded. "When Alanna and I got back to the ship after I was shot, we both told Cal that we thought your guy was different. He actually gave a hoot whether I lived or died, and it wasn't even part of any bigger agenda."

"Can we vote?" Alanna asked.

Cal's hands clenched into fists. "No, we can't vote. Are you all insane?"

Ty slipped his hands into his pockets. "He did save Doc."

"Not you, too."

Cal's face had reddened, and a slight hint of heat radiated from his skin. Was he seriously not going to help her friend?

Dania released his arm. "How many times have I seen you risk your lives for others, for people you don't even know?"

"They weren't enforcers."

She pointed to herself. "You saved *me*."

"By accident."

She stepped back. An odd pain formed in her chest, but she pushed it aside. "You could have dropped me off any time, but you stuck with me. You saw something in me that I didn't even know was there." She advanced on him. "Alexander is far more worth saving than I am."

"All in favor of saving Dania's friend?" Ty asked.

Cal pointed at him. "Do *not* put this up for a vote. This is *my* ship." He turned to Dania. "Look, I understand that your friend was a great guy, but I can't risk this entire crew to save one person who might not even be alive anymore. I'm sorry. The answer is *no*."

Kile pushed away from the wall. The air about him pulsed with the power of their sponsor.

Everyone stepped back, and with good reason. Kile wasn't used to *asking*. He was used to taking what he wanted, when he wanted it. And right now, his patience had worn thin.

She left Cal's side and moved between her commander and the crew she'd learned to think of as family—but she knew, she and Kile both knew, that without her primordial energy, she couldn't stop him from taking anything he wanted, and at the moment, this crew was nothing more than an annoyance to him.

And that meant they were all about to die.

CHAPTER 11
CAL

CAL PREPPED for the worst as the enforcer took a deep breath and let it out slowly. It almost looked like he was trying to keep his calm, which was ridiculous because enforcers had only one switch, and that switch read *homicidal maniac*. Cal would know. He'd seen it up close and personal.

The air about Cal solidified and his feet left the ground. Ethan and Alanna both cried out as they flew up beside him. Across the room, Ty clutched the ceiling and Doc hung pawing at the air over the window. It was like the gravity had failed, but all the cards and dominos remained on the tables.

The enforcer, feet still firmly on the floor, walked toward Cal. "I could always execute you all, and my general and I can confiscate the ship. That would be far easier."

Dania pulled the enforcer back. "You will not. Let them go."

The invisible fingers released. Everyone's voices cried out at the same time. Cal flipped over and his head smashed against the tiles. The room spun.

Cal wasn't surprised by the lack of cordiality. The man was, after all, an enforcer.

Doc helped Alanna off the floor, while Ethan wiped blood from his nose.

Ty grimaced. He pushed onto one knee, his right hand forming a fist.

The enforcer smirked.

Dania stared at him. "You…*listened to me.*"

He folded his arms. "Of course. You are my general."

She stared at him, her lips slightly parted. "Still?"

He sighed like she were a naïve child. "You are Geron's only general. It's not like he can simply appoint another in your stead."

He couldn't? Cal frowned. *Why not?*

Dania glanced around the room but didn't seem to focus on anything. "Who is in command?"

Cal wasn't sure why that mattered when they were so obviously under this one's thumb.

The enforcer's lips thinned. "We're all currently separated, but I was the one to relay responsibilities after Geron gave the order to save Alexander."

Cal stood, shaking off the ache in his shoulder. "I don't care who's in charge. You can't have my ship."

The air about the enforcer started to pulse again.

Dania held the guy back, looking at Cal over her shoulder. "Cal, please. Be reasonable."

Reasonable? Reasonable would be running and putting as much distance between them and this maniac as possible. But that was pretty much out of the question the moment the enforcer had stepped onto the ship.

Cal straightened, ignoring the headache brewing behind his right eye. "Let's say I agree to help. What do you want with the *Renegade?*"

"I want you to do what you normally do. Trade. Pirate. Steal. Murder. At the moment, I don't care."

"I highly doubt that."

"My goal is clear. Save Alexander. Nothing else matters."

Dania had made one thing about enforcers very plain to them. Everything in their world was black and white.

This Alexander guy was the priority, the *only* priority, so maybe the enforcer was telling the truth. Maybe he did want them to act like business as usual.

But the enforcer had also said that he'd probably kill them all once he got what he wanted. Getting out of the tail end of this escapade alive was going to be the problem.

"I'm getting agitated." The enforcer pushed Dania aside. "This human will do as we ask if I start executing his crew." He pointed at Ethan. "How about that one? He looks useless enough."

"Hey!" Ethan jumped behind Alanna. "Why is it always me?"

"No one is getting killed," Dania said.

Thank goodness they had one half-charged enforcer to be the voice of reason. With any luck, that would be enough to keep the bigger one in check.

Still, this was all strange. "You could have just taken the ship if you'd wanted. Why do you need cooperation?"

The enforcer folded his hands and tilted his head like a teacher about to give a lesson the student should already know. "The face and voice of Calvin Espinoza are as valuable as this ship. If this vessel arrives with a different captain, it will not be received with as much…enthusiasm."

Great. Just great.

"Where are we going?"

The enforcer smiled. "Pirating, Mr. Espinoza. We are about to make some very illegal trades."

Of course they were. And then he'd probably kill them all for it.

CHAPTER 12
DANIA

ALONE IN THE HALLWAY, Dania leaned against the wall, taking slow, deep breaths. It seemed even short walks now left her needing to sit and rest. Was this what it was like being human?

It couldn't possibly be. The crew walked, ran, and played games. They only appeared tired in the evenings. Dania wanted to brush off the doctor's claims that Geron had done something unspeakable to her. Every ounce of her being knew her sponsor would never hurt her, yet the evidence against him grew harder to counter with each passing day.

She placed her hand on the entry pad to the medical bay, and the doors slid open.

"Hey, girl." The doctor—*Peter*, Alanna always called him— wiped his hands on a white cloth. "How's my favorite enforcer?"

"I'm not feeling much like an enforcer anymore."

"Good!"

She shook her head. "Not good. How is the new treatment coming?"

"Oh, sweetie, it's only been five days. These things take time."

She knew that. She'd just...*hoped.*

He scanned her forehead with a thermal laser. "What's going on?"

"I was helping Alanna again, and..." She hated admitting this. She'd been trained to never appear weak, but... "I almost fell. She had to help me."

He looked at his device. "Well, sometimes humans get up too fast and their heads spin a little. It's nothing to be too worried about."

His temperature raised slightly. She wished her senses were dulled so she couldn't tell when he lied to her.

"I might have a little something to play with in the next few days." He tapped a glass container. "I have some pathogens incubating right now, but this is the first batch. Experiments don't always work."

The small container seemed so miniscule, yet it might hold the key to her salvation. She wanted her cure now, but she needed to trust in his scientific methods. "I understand."

"Get some rest. That's another basic human need." He held up his pointer finger. "And don't tell me you're getting plenty of sleep. I get the crew's heart rates sent to me. It looks like you're doing calisthenics half the night."

Dania shrugged. "Old habits. We're taught to keep ourselves strong."

"Sleep. That's an order." He pressed a button on the device. "It's actually one of the few orders a doctor is authorized to give the crew."

That, among many other things, were new concepts she'd have to get used to.

Heading down the hall, she stopped in the lounge.

Kile sat alone at a table, scratching an old-fashioned writing instrument on a piece of…was that *paper?*

He glanced up at her, then continued his work. "Are you here in an official capacity, General?"

"No. I was just wondering how you were."

"Other than being concerned for you and for Alexander, I am fully functional." He wrote something on the paper. "I have to admit, I am missing my calling to enforce the law. Being on this ship is…" He grimaced. "Stifling."

Being on a vessel wanted for smuggling, even though they were on a mission, had to be hard on him. "Thank you for not executing the crew."

"I still must follow your orders, as long as they don't contradict our sponsor."

That was good to know. If all went well, she'd be able to stay in control by keeping within the parameters of Geron's orders.

"It might make it easier on you if you knew that Calvin Espinoza did not kill Filluck Palogivan."

He didn't look up. "I don't care."

"But you should."

"But I do not."

Dania sighed. She should have expected no less. "It sounds like you were in charge while I was gone."

He seemed to press harder with the writing instrument. "To the best of my abilities. I'm not you."

"But you led them for years before I was named general."

"Correction. I led them while Geron worked on your programming. My command was always temporary, and I never took it as anything but that."

This was true, but Kile had done a good job. He'd tested

her authority once after she'd taken her place as Geron's general.

But only once. She'd put him down in front of the team, that day. No one questioned her authority again.

The question was: Did he question her authority now?

"No." He scribbled more on the sheet.

Dania startled. Kile wasn't capable of the mental link she had with Alexander. But he'd always been able to read her in other ways.

"You are my general, Dania, and up until recently, you've given none of us reason to question your strength."

But now they did because she'd done the unthinkable. She'd turned away from their sponsor, their prince.

There wasn't much she could do to change that now. She was free, for however much longer she lived, and she refused to go back to what she had been.

She moved closer to the table. "I didn't know you liked to draw."

He nodded, scratching more on the paper.

She picked up a finished drawing, a perfect likeness of a young woman, maybe twenty years old. Pretty.

"A friend of yours?"

Kile lifted his head. The pencil stopped scratching as he considered the image Dania held. "No. She was a colonist on Neptune Nine."

"Was?"

He grimaced. "She gathered a crowd around her and tried to incite a protest against the rule of our king."

Dania's stomach clenched. The girl's eyes seemed so strong. So sure of herself. But that wouldn't have mattered if she'd spoken out against the king. "So she's dead?"

He returned his attention to the paper. "Of course." His

pencil scratched across the sheet. "I create likenesses of those who I've passed judgement on."

He did? "Why?"

"It helps me remember what's important."

Dania frowned, not sure what he meant by that.

Moving closer, she looked over his shoulder as he completed a render of a woman with her arms outstretched, hanging in space, hair floating and eyes glowing.

"Is that me?"

He held up the image. "I wanted to remember you as you were: a beautiful horror. Unstoppable. Infallible." He looked back to her. "What happened, Dania?"

She closed her eyes. How could she put it all into words? Would Kile believe that they were being controlled? Was he even capable of fathoming such a thing?

He stood. "Your sponsor came to you, offered you your life back, but you pushed him away. To save smugglers. To save criminals."

"It's not that simple."

"Then make it simple. Help me to understand. Why are these people not dead? Why is Calvin Espinoza still breathing?"

She turned away, because Kile would have that look on his face...that fatherly concern for her anytime she'd been reckless.

Dania sighed, remembering the blank bliss of being fully charged with Geron's power.

In Kile's mind, she was being irresponsible. He was incapable of understanding that there might be more to life than his mission. More to life than being an enforcer. There was no way to make him see the galaxy as she saw it. Not while he was under Geron's control.

He walked toward the window. "You don't need to answer. Right now, you just need to follow our sponsor's orders and help me save Alexander. I trust you will do that."

"Of course."

"And when that is done, the three of us will return to Keveron." He looked her over and grimaced. "Hopefully, that won't be too late for you."

Ignoring his gaze, she glanced back to the picture and took one last look at who she had been before leaving the room.

She wanted to save Alexander.

She *would* save Alexander.

Somehow, she had to find a way to find him without losing herself.

TY WALKED on deck and Cal jumped, banging his arm on the chair.

"Sorry, boss. Didn't mean to scare you."

"Not your fault." Cal stared out at the stars in the distance. Six days, and it hadn't gotten any easier. He waited, wondering when—not if—that enforcer decided that he only needed the ship, and not the crew.

Dania had stood in Kile's way once, but would that continue?

"He doesn't really seem that bad," Ty said. "I mean, for an enforcer and all."

All enforcers were bad. Cal wasn't sure there were degrees.

Dania was an anomaly that would probably never happen again. She'd gotten lucky. Or maybe they were the lucky ones because without her, they'd be completely at the commander's mercy.

Ty tapped a few keys on his panel. "Hey, I couldn't help but notice that today is Saturday."

"Yeah, and?"

"Well, the crew was wondering if you were going to cook tonight." He pointed out the window. "We're back in normal space, and Alanna loaded us up with supplies at Themyscira. So, we don't need to worry about conserving food."

Was he crazy? "I am not cooking an elaborate meal. Some of that stuff we picked up is considered illegal, and as you pointed out, there is an enforcer on board."

"The same enforcer sending us to known pirate settlements?"

"That's part of his master plan, and when this is all over, he'll probably add all of these stops we make for him to our list of crimes before he executes us all."

"Maybe."

How could he sound so casual about all this? That enforcer was a serious threat. He had to know that.

Ty leaned from his own station to Cal's. "Boss, I know you're nervous. Heck, I'm nervous too. We all are. But hey, we've been in worse spots."

"Like when?"

"Like when we were actually being shot at. And think of it. If anything happens that's bad, we have a fully loaded enforcer on board with a vested interest in making sure we survive. To be honest, I've never felt so secure in all my life."

"You do realize that if we're able to save Dania's friend, all of this will change, right?"

"Yeah, but Dania will still be here, and this new guy is still listening to her, and after we save Tall, Blond, and Beautiful, he should be pretty appreciative of our efforts as well."

"Tall, Blond, and Beautiful?"

"That's what Alanna and Doc are calling him."

Cal shook his head. The last thing he needed was his

doctor and his navigator entranced by a man who'd left no survivors during his last encounter with lawbreakers. "I just have a really bad feeling about this."

Ty shrugged. "All crimes are punishable by death. Eating some good food is not going to make the punishment any worse."

Cal glared at him. "Believe me, there are different degrees of death." Cal had seen quick deaths and long, drawn-out punishment where the accused had begged to die at the end. They all needed to understand the seriousness of this situation.

Ty sat back in his chair. "You need to learn to live in the moment, boss."

The doors slid open. "Knock, knock," Doc said. "Everybody decent?"

"On the bridge?" Cal asked.

Doc winked at him. "One can dream." He walked in. "Anyway, I hope I have good news."

Cal rubbed his face. "I can use some of that right now."

"I just ran some tests, and the pathogens I've created look viable."

Ty stood. "Really? That's awesome. Our girl isn't looking so good."

"Is she getting worse?" Cal asked.

"She's mostly weak," Doc explained. "Stumbling and stuff like that. She's noticed it, though. I think she's ready to give treatment a try."

A week ago, Cal would have been all for treatment as long as Doc thought it was safe.

However, the arrival of their new passenger changed things. Dania was weak, but the enforcer was at full strength.

Doc was talking about replacing the part of her that her

prince had created. How would the other enforcer react if he knew they were thinking of doing something to free her even more from the prince's thrall?

"We should probably do all treatment under the radar. I'm not sure our new guest will find experimental treatment on a sentient being very legal." There certainly was no need to rush anyone's inevitable punishment.

Doc checked something on his panel in the wall. "I think Dania will be willing to keep it low key. She's come to me three times already, checking to see how things are going."

"And you're sure it's safe?"

Doc's brows shot up. "Safe? Hell no. I have no idea if it's safe. The new pathogens are just reacting within set parameters in a Petri dish. I have no clue what will happen when I put them into a human host."

Wonderful. "Make sure Dania understands all the risks. Don't sugarcoat this."

"I'm the one who had to tell her she's dying the first time. I'm getting good at scaring enforcers." He pointed back to the door. "So do I have your okay to proceed?"

Cal's chest ached, knowing this might make Dania even worse. She was coming out of her shell, becoming one of them. Every day she seemed brighter. Happier. But her body was degrading, rebelling against her newfound freedom. It wasn't fair. She deserved better.

They didn't have a choice, though. She needed this treatment. It might make her worse, but it could also make her better. They had to trust and believe in the latter.

However, they all needed to realize that if anything happened to Dania, there was someone down in the lounge who'd probably pass a quick sentence—not only on Doc, but on all of them.

Nonetheless, Cal didn't need to put it to vote. He knew what their answer would be.

"Go ahead." If there was ever a time for Doc to prove himself, now was it.

CHAPTER 14
DANIA

DANIA PUSHED her way through the med bay doors. "I'm here!"

"And you certainly know how to make an entrance." The doctor pulled a protective glove from his hand and tossed it into the recycler. As usual, a folded glove popped out the other side. "I guess you're ready to kick this pathogen problem all the way to Saturn?"

She jumped onto a gurney. "Definitely." She'd spent too many days worrying, too many days with people looking like they felt sorry for her. She was ready to be strong again.

Peter folded his hands. "Okay, sweetie, listen. I'm your doctor, and I need to tell you that there are risks."

"I don't care." And it was the truth. Nothing could be worse than being weak—than being ordinary.

"You need to care. I don't know if what I created will work. Even more, I'm not certain that this won't backfire and kill you."

Kill her? "But you've done research and tests?"

"Yes, and they all look positive. I just can't tell you I'm sure."

But he *was* sure. This much, she'd learned about him in the past month. He wouldn't have offered to get started if there was much doubt of success.

She understood, though, that he needed to be certain that his patient knew the risks.

And Peter needed to understand how ready she was to take this risk, no matter the possible consequences. "Peter, I'm dying. If I die today or three days from now, nothing will change that. You're giving me a chance at life."

"What about your scary friend?"

Ah, so that was the problem. She'd heard mention that Peter had done something in the past. No one would tell her what, but she could ascertain that something had gone wrong with someone's treatment and that had led to him fleeing the planet with the *Star Renegade* crew. Dania hadn't looked into it further. She didn't want to know. For now, she had to hope that he'd learned from his mistakes.

He was right to be concerned, though. If anything happened to her, Kile would be an unstoppable force.

Luckily, she'd already considered this possibility. "There is a recording in my room. It gives Kile instructions to complete his mission and then to let you all go free."

Peter looked to the side and Dania could tell he was working through all the possible outcomes. He probably wasn't so worried about himself, but the rest of the crew. "Do you think he'll listen?"

She hoped so. The only way to be sure was to not test his anger. "It's the best I can do."

He slapped his palms on his thighs. "Okay, I guess we are a go." He picked up a syringe. "There is one crazy *Frankenstein* thing I'd like to do, first."

"*Frankenstein?*"

"You know, Mary Shelley?"

She started at him. Was this a famous Earth scientist?

"O-kay…" he said. "Anyway, what I'd like to do is take an imprint of several parts of your brain."

An imprint? "Why?"

"Call it security. There was a big fad on Earth a few years back where wealthy people would download their brains onto computer chips in hopes that if anything happened, they could upload themselves into a new body."

"That was deemed an illegal abomination of nature by the king."

"Well, people still paid for the imprints, just in case." He waved the syringe. "This would be the same thing. A contingency plan, of sorts."

"You think this procedure will make me lose my memory?"

He sighed. "Let's just say we'd rather keep you remembering that you like us, rather than having you suddenly forget all the lovely time we've spent together."

The idea was ludicrous, but everyone on the crew held Peter in high esteem, even giving him the title of 'doctor,' despite not having achieved a doctorate in any subject. If this above-average mind thought it was a good idea, she should probably comply. "Just don't re-upload me into anyone but myself." The last thing she needed was to wake up one day in the body of the gangly engineer.

"You have my word."

Her heart fluttered as he stepped behind her and pulled her hair up. "Is this going to hurt?"

"No more than those bullets that sliced through your arms."

She cringed. That *had* hurt, but she'd pretended to not

feel anything. A general never wanted to look weak, no matter how much pain they were in. With the training she'd endured, she could keep fighting beside her squadron after losing an arm, if necessary.

She wasn't that general anymore, though. She was now something *less*.

But not for long. "I'm ready."

She grabbed the edge of the gurney when Peter pinched the skin at the base of her skull. The back of her head burned, and then heat shot out around her jaw, up through her nose, and exploded behind her eyes. She took in a deep breath.

"You okay?"

She wanted to answer but just gripped the bed harder.

"Grunt if you're still with me."

She managed that much. The door opened, but she didn't dare turn to see who'd entered.

"One second more."

A lie, of course, but probably not an intentional one. One minute, five point three seconds later, the burning stopped, and he stepped away. Murmured voices echoed in her head.

"Breathe, Dania," Peter said.

Wait—not Peter. The voice was lower. Deeper. More concerned.

She opened her eyes.

Cal smiled. "You okay?"

She took in a deep breath. "It is over?"

Peter moved beside her. "Just the imprint." He frowned. "You look pale. How about you lie down for the pathogen replacement?"

She eased back. Her hands trembled on the top of the soft

mattress. If the easy part had been that bad, how hard would the actual procedure be?

Cal moved to the side of the bed and held her hand. "Hey." He leaned over her. "I'm here, okay?"

She nodded, squeezing his hand back. A short time ago, she'd threatened to kill this man. Now, she clung to him. Why did his presence give such comfort?

Peter rolled a bag of fluids attached to a long pole to the other side of the table. "Ready?"

She drew in a deep breath and let it out slowly. Cal gave her hand another squeeze and she turned to him. His eyes were kind, concerned—the look on his face similar to when Alanna had been shot after trading on Port Walker, and he'd run out amid a rainstorm of bullets, trying to save her.

"Here we go." Peter inserted a needle in her arm.

She winced and wanted to close her eyes, but instead, she focused on the light blue irises of her captain. Of Cal.

Dania squeezed his hand. She could get through this.

CHAPTER 15
CAL

CAL DIDN'T NEED to be here, but the look in Dania's eyes… He couldn't leave her.

She winced. Her eyes widened, but she focused on him, her gaze intent as her grip tightened.

"Okay," Doc said. "Here come the pathogens."

Her eyes widened even farther. The fear there… This wasn't the same woman he'd dragged onto his ship in energy-draining handcuffs. Part of him missed that spirit, that strength. But he knew the fire was still there, hidden under the surface.

Hell, he'd be scared, too, if a self-taught doctor were shooting him up with experimental replicated microbes, or whatever the hell these things were.

"So far, so good." Doc touched his hand to her forehead. "You okay, sweetie?"

Her gaze stayed locked on Cal. "Yes."

"Good. I'm going to increase the flow a little." He adjusted the lever.

A tiny high-pitched sound slipped from her lips. Her grip

loosened, then tightened with even more force. The determination in her gaze turned to panic.

Cal mustered up his best grin. "Tell me about this friend of yours we're going to save."

"Alexander?" She flinched, her grip tightening again. "He's sure of himself. Arrogant at times. I think you'd like him."

Cal puffed out a laugh. "Is that your way of telling me I'm arrogant?"

"Arrogance isn't always a bad thing. It's important to be sure of yourself." There was an air of affection in her tone Cal hadn't heard from her before.

"You like him a lot, huh?"

"He's very important to me." Her eyes saddened. "If anything happens to him…"

Cal placed his other hand over hers. "Nothing is going to happen to him. We're going to get to him in time." Of course, they had to find the poor guy first.

For the first time in his life, Cal hoped Doc wasn't right, and that Alexander wouldn't be in as bad a shape—or worse —than Dania. If these treatments worked, and she still lost her friend, it might send her in a spiral they wouldn't be able to bring her back from.

A tear dripped from the corner of her eye and into her hair.

Cal tapped her hand. "Hey, I'm serious. He's going to be fine. Right now, let's worry about you."

And the odd thing was, Cal really *was* worried about her. This, a woman who'd wanted him dead less than two months ago, and who had almost gotten them all killed several times over. The only certainty in the galaxy, it seemed, was uncertainty.

"Cal?" Her grip tightened, her eyes glassy.

"What's wrong?"

Her fingernails dug into his palms. She wasn't fixed on him anymore, but something distant, like she was no longer in the room with them.

"Doc!" he called. "Something's wrong."

Sweat beaded Cal's brow and drenched his palms, but he didn't let go.

Doc appeared on the other side of the bed, flicking the white switch controlling the contents of the bag attached to her arm. He took a reading on the machine.

His eyes widened and he cursed under his breath. "She's not fluxing."

"Not fluxing? What the hell does that mean?"

Doc pulled apart her shirt and cut the band of her bra with scissors he'd grabbed from the side table. "Let go of her hand."

Her eyes were still fixed on the ceiling, her grip calcite solid. "I can't."

"I need to read her blood. If you're holding her hand, it might pick up your vibrations." Doc positioned a heavy-looking black mat with wires attached onto her chest. "You need to let go of her, now!"

Dammit! Cal yanked away, nearly pulling her off the gurney. She reached for him before a long, sharp tone sounded from the machine beside the bed.

Her hands went lax, one arm falling off the mattress.

"What happened?"

"I don't know yet." Doc flipped on a monitor and looked at a zoomed-in view of large, dark red particles running through a lighter-red fluid. He dragged his fingers through his hair. "It's not working. It's not working."

He looked at Dania's prone form. Her parted lips.

"It's not working." Doc blanched. His eyes reddened as he pulled at his hair.

Was this what had happened with that kid? Had doc frozen when the treatment had gone bad? Was that why the kid had died?

Cal grabbed Doc's shoulders. "Hey!"

Doc shook his head. "It's not working."

Cal tightened his grip. "Then make it work!"

"I-I don't know how."

"Yes, you do. You've thought this all out. You've dreamed every possible scenario, or you wouldn't have tried. Think. You know what to do."

Doc looked at her, then the screen.

"That's it," Cal soothed. "Think it through."

The sharp tone continued. In fictionals, that sound always meant a patient was close to death, that they weren't breathing, or their heart had stopped. Fictional doctors always hooked them up to machines.

"Should we do electric shock or something?"

Doc shook his head. "The pathogens are partly metallic. It might kill her."

"Then what's the next option?"

"I-I…"

If she wasn't breathing, how long did she have?

"Come on!" Cal jumped to the table and started chest compressions. Something inside her cracked, and Cal's stomach turned, but he kept going.

Doc held up a hand. "Wait. Stop."

Cal shook his head. "We have to do something!"

"I think you were on to something with the shock." Doc pulled the weighted mat off Dania's chest and replaced it with adhesive pads, working around Cal as he continued the compressions. He placed a small suitcase beside her, the word *defibrillator* scrolled on the side in red letters.

"I thought a shock would kill her?"

"The pathogens I injected her with died in her bloodstream." He pointed at the screen. "They aren't moving."

Cal compressed her chest ten times. "And?"

"They have metal elements. A shock might ignite them."

Cal stopped, leaning away. It was as good a plan as any. "Go for it."

Doc took a deep breath. "Clear!" He flipped a switch, and Dania's body twitched.

But the tone still sounded.

Cal did another round of compressions. His arms ached. He wasn't even sure if this was doing anything, but he couldn't just stand there and watch her die.

"Let's try it again. Clear!"

Cal stepped back. Doc threw the switch and her body jolted. The tone continued to sound.

And then it beeped.

Cal reached for her to start compressions again, but Doc stopped him.

"Wait." Doc stared at her as the machine beeped, then beeped again. "We have a heartbeat."

Doc pulled off the pads and replaced them with the weighted mat again.

He spun to the screen, where the dark red circles one by one turned oblong and started to move in different directions.

"Is that what I think it is?" Cal asked.

Doc ran to the other side of the table and hugged him. "We did it! We did it!"

Cal gently pushed him back. "All right, great. Now, how do we keep her okay?"

Doc took another deep breath and fiddled with the bag. "Let's just start with the pathogens she already has inside her and see what happens." He ran a full-length scanner over her. "So far, so good."

"She's going to make it?"

"For now, yes."

That didn't sound as promising as Cal had hoped. "Just for now?"

He sighed. "We weren't able to give her enough pathogens to save her long term. But they're alive. In time, they'll cycle through to her organs and get to work. Now we just need to wait and see what happens before we give her another dose."

"She'll definitely need another one?"

Doc looked at his data pad and grimaced. "We're going to need to do this at least two more times."

Two more times, and the first time had nearly killed her.

They needed to figure out a way to keep her heart beating before they tried this again.

Seeing her like that…it had been too much. They couldn't risk losing her.

Cal frowned, bit his lip, and left the room.

CHAPTER 16
CAL

THIS HAD BEEN ENTIRELY TOO LONG a day, and it wasn't even lunchtime yet. Cal rubbed his forehead as he placed his other hand on the pad to open the door to the bridge. What he needed were a few quiet hours sitting in his chair and staring at the stars.

"Calvin Espinoza." The enforcer stood in the center of the bridge, taking up most of the small room.

Ty leaned around the shimmering opal behemoth. "Oh, um, boss, the enforcer is looking for you."

Kile turned toward Ty. "You communicated that you had already informed him."

"I did. And sometimes transmissions don't get through. This is an old ship, after all."

The *Star Renegade* certainly was an old ship, but the communications were one of the few things that worked like a charm.

Big, Tall, and Scary didn't need to know that, though.

"Where is Dania?" the enforcer asked. "She is not answering my calls."

Cal sidled past him to his chair. "Well, like Ty said,

communications sometimes don't work. And maybe she's resting and has them turned off."

He'd better not push the issue, because that was partially the truth. Dania was resting in the med bay, working hard to become human again. Which big, bad enforcer-guy probably wouldn't be too happy about.

For now, it was probably better to keep the focus on Cal.

"So, you were looking for me?" Cal ran a scan across their forward trajectory. Ty had most likely done one recently, but it would be best to make the enforcer feel like he was bothering them. Then again, the guy probably wouldn't care.

The enforcer loomed over their chairs. "Yes. Your first mate has been hesitant to follow my orders."

Ty pretended to turn a nob on his panel that didn't actually turn. "That's because you're not my captain."

And he was probably buying Cal some time. Ty had pinged in to the med bay over an hour ago, and Doc had filled him in on Dania's status.

At the time, there'd been pretty much nothing to tell him. All they could do was wait. Still, Cal wished he could have stayed down there with her.

She'd look so scared. What if she woke up and...

He blinked, shaking his head. If she woke up and needed something, she'd call for her doctor, not the useless captain.

Kile took a step toward Cal's chair. "You are to change course and head toward Teson Minor."

"What's on Teson Minor?"

"I have reason to believe that the transmission relay has been compromised."

"Are you a comm tech now?" Ty asked.

"Hardly. I intend to tap into their system, extract data,

and then comb through the communications for pirate transmissions."

"Isn't that illegal?"

"Not if you do so under the direction of the royal family."

"So, the Banes can do anything they want?" Ty asked.

"The Banes have always done whatever they want," Cal pointed out.

Ty looked over his shoulder. "I may have some training that would be helpful in such a situation."

Kile scoffed. "Training? You are a known systems infiltrator wanted in two systems for illegal data bartering."

Ty shrugged. "And there's that, too."

"I do intend to utilize your skills." He crouched and looked through the window as Cal changed course.

"Do you think they have information on this Alexander guy?" Cal asked.

The enforcer seemed to peruse the stars. "I do."

"Okay, let's see what we can find." And with any luck, this would keep him busy enough so he didn't start asking about Dania again.

Or poking any further into his crew's pasts.

Teson Minor wasn't the largest of planets, but it was big enough that anyone could be hiding in the ancient mountain caves, or in the deep forests that would put Earth's Rainforests to shame.

Alanna touched her control pad. "They're sending a welcome ping."

"Let them know we'd like to trade. Send them our available stock."

The enforcer leaned against the wall where Doc's station was, out of sight in case the visual came on. "We do not need to trade. I just want to see their data files."

Spoken like a man who'd never done any smuggling.

"Yes, we do." If anyone on the *Star Renegade* acted suspicious, they'd call too much attention to themselves. "Business as usual, and while Ethan and I are trading, you and Ty can do the data extraction, just as we agreed."

Alanna fiddled with her earpiece. "Cal, they want to know if we have spices."

He turned to her. "Spices? Half their planet is jungle. Can't they grow their own?"

"Apparently not basil, oregano, or turmeric."

Basil and oregano were easy. Doc wasn't going to be happy to give up his turmeric. The stuff was a commodity out here, and not on Cal's list of available supplies. Maybe they'd heard Cal had a kitchen on board.

"Try to get by with basil, oregano, and rosemary." Cal had never used the rosemary, anyway.

Alanna's board pinged. "They agreed. I'm plotting a course to land."

"Is it a populated landing site?" Kile asked.

"Yes. The main canopy compound."

"That makes my job easier," Ty said. "I can accidentally access the system from the bathroom if I needed to."

"Accidentally?" Kile asked.

"Well, I would never do anything illegal, of course."

But everything they were about to do was illegal, except for trading spices. They needed to do all they could to make sure the local authorities didn't put a black mark on the *Star Renegade* after they left. They were starting to run out of friendly ports to hide in the next time they needed safe harbor.

They flew through the opening of the metal webbed dome the locals insisted was to protect the compound from the large, flying reptilian indigenous species on the planet. The webbing was secure but still left the compound open to the air, giving those living inside the benefits of the sunlight and a planetary environment that was similar to Earth.

The dome was an engineering marvel, but Cal still shivered as the massive, webbed door closed behind them. Like it or not, they'd just flown into a giant cage.

A cool breeze swept over the landing platform as they stepped off the ship. Cage or no cage, you had to appreciate the open-air design.

Cal drew in a deep breath. Too bad they couldn't bottle fresh, real air for long voyages. Recyclers did their job, but after a few weeks in space, the air started to smell like dust and lubricants. They needed to make stops like this more often to let some natural oxygen inside.

Ty headed out toward the main buildings, probably planning to feign dysentery, while Cal and Ethan went to the generic supply tables lining the landing platforms.

A petite woman with curly brown hair stood taller as they approached. "You are the guys with spices? Do you really have rosemary?"

Cal quirked a brow. "Yeah." He leaned toward her. "I picked it up months ago on a whim. The flavor is just so strong. What do you cook with it?"

"To be honest, I use it to soothe muscle aches. It's supposed to help with immunity, too, but the forests here absorb most disease, so we really don't need anything like that."

Interesting. Maybe he should have checked with Doc first, but it was too late now.

He looked over his shoulder to where Ty had disappeared. He wasn't sure how long the data snatch would take. Hopefully, Ty could stay on target and not get distracted by the local sites. Or women.

Ethan perused the table and came back with a metal box about a foot high.

"What's that?" Cal asked.

"It's a broken water recycling relay." He fingered a crack along the side. "I think I can fix this."

"I guess it would be a good thing to have a backup for."

"I was thinking more of the trade-up value." Ethan held the box higher. "These are worth a lot. Maybe not this close to Earth, but the outer rims beg for supplies like this."

Cal had to agree, but native-grown oregano was worth more than a broken piece of equipment.

He turned to the woman tending the table. "What else you got?"

She looked around. "We have some older supplies, stuff from junkers."

Cal would never consider the *Star Renegade* junk, but he had seen a few of her model in salvage yards. "Let's see what you have."

He kept his eyes on the door to the main compound while Ethan sorted through the box, sometimes laughing at what he found, until the engineer froze and cursed under his breath. He held something up. "How much for this?"

The woman narrowed her eyes. "The rosemary and the oregano."

Ethan quirked a brow. "For that? Forget it." He threw it

back in the box and picked up something else. "How about this?"

She blinked. "The basil and the rosemary?" Her tone seemed less sure.

Ethan shook his head and dropped the small piece of metal. "She's ripping us off." He pointed to another table. "They might have something over there."

"Wait!" She grabbed his arm, eyeing the rosemary. "Those are vintage parts. I thought... I-I thought..."

Cal tried to keep his expression neutral. Did they really have that much trouble finding herbs out here?

Ethan's face turned uncharacteristically stony. "Last chance." He picked up a thin metal rectangle, a little longer than his hand, and maybe an inch wide. "How much for this?"

"Take the water relay, and that, for the rosemary and half the basil."

Ethan smiled. "Now, that's more like it." He plucked the rosemary from Cal's hand and gave it to her. "Good trade."

Cal measured out the basil. He wasn't sure what they were getting in this trade, but he was more than happy not to have to part with the oregano.

They handed off the spices and shook hands.

"What did you trade for?" Cal asked as they left the table.

Ethan tapped the bag slung over his shoulder. "A sync navigator. It looks like it's in nearly mint condition, too."

Cal's eyes widened. They'd lost their sync navigator weeks ago when the enforcers had been battling each other in space outside prince Geron's ship.

Ethan beamed. "Maybe I'll give it to Alanna for her birthday."

"After paying with my spices? I don't think so."

They ended up making another trade using a quarter of the oregano to get a small power unit to help increase the voracity of their shield matrix.

The power unit was an easy yes for Cal. The way their luck was running lately, they'd probably need it.

Cal's comm band pinged. He lifted his wrist. "Talk to me."

Ty's voice. "Hey, Captain, I got a little sick as soon as I got here. I've been in the bathroom the entire time."

As they'd planned. "Are you feeling better?"

"Yeah, a lot, but I think I'll head back to the ship. I'm not sure all this fresh air is agreeing with me."

Which meant he'd gotten what the enforcer had asked for, and now they needed to get out before local law enforcement discovered the breach. "Roger that. We just finished up here. We'll meet you at the ship."

If all had gone according to their plan, all eyes had been on Cal and Ethan, and far, far away from the pilot with digestion issues.

He turned off the comm and grabbed the package with the power unit, while Ethan doled out the oregano.

"You ready?" Cal asked.

"Yup." Ethan handed the spice to the trades woman and started walking back with Cal. "It's a little strange. We've never landed for such a small trade."

"Yeah, but grabbing the power unit and the sync navigator was a good call. It probably looks like we need a lot of repairs and don't want anyone to know about it." Of course, if anyone looked at their ship, it would be more than obvious they needed a lot of repairs.

Shots fired in the distance, coming from the building Ty had disappeared into earlier.

"Please tell me that's not what I think it is," Ethan said.

Unfortunately, it was. It seemed their secret data extraction wasn't so secret anymore.

Cal handed him the power unit. "Get back to the ship."

Ty sprinted toward them, holding a hand over his head—like that would stop a bullet. Two more shots rang out and Ty stumbled but quickly righted himself and continued the sprint.

Cal called up the comm. "Alanna, get us ready to take off."

"Yeah, I see Ty racing in, as usual. Get him on board and we'll be in the air before you guys get to the bridge."

Cal headed for the landing ramp, but the enforcer stood on the tarmac, blocking the ship entrance in all his shimmering white uniform and floating-haired glory. So much for keeping his presence a secret.

When Ty reached the ship, Kile grabbed him by the back of the neck and hoisted him into the air. "Did you get the download?"

"Yeah, I got it."

The enforcer released him, and Ty dropped to the ground with a thump.

"Ouch!" He got up on one knee, holding his neck. "You're welcome." He whispered something under his breath that sounded like *bass-pole*.

Cal doubted that was what he'd said.

The enforcer walked farther from the ship.

Cal helped Ty get to his feet and they raced up the ramp and into the cargo bay.

"Get to the bridge and get us out of here," Cal said.

"Roger that." Ty sprinted for the stairs.

The enforcer stood on the tarmac below and held up his palm. The guards running toward them lifted off their feet, floated, and whisked back toward the buildings in a flurry of hoots and screams. Their weapons clanked to the floor and bounced as if dropped from the dome above. More people came from the building. He raised his palms again, and the machines lining the edge of the platform shifted, blocking the doorways.

A few guards squeezed past, and the enforcer threw them back like a one-man army. He barely seemed tired as he focused on the next group.

Lights winked on in the gun turrets surrounding the platform. Those suckers shot artillery a lot larger than bullets.

"Commander, come on!"

The enforcer turned and started up the ramp. Once he'd made it inside, Cal hit the button to close the door, and the ship left the ground.

Now they just needed to get past planetary defenses, which on Teson Minor, weren't all that minor.

CAL SPRINTED TOWARD THE BRIDGE. The commander's boots pounded on the floor behind him. They pushed through the door and Cal dropped into his seat. They were already hovering, heading toward where the opening of the dome had been when they'd first entered.

Alanna called up the comm. "Teson Minor, we are leaving whether you like it or not. Open the door or you will be sorry." She made a pained expression and leaned closer to the comm. "Umm, please?"

Ty and Cal glanced at her. She meant well, but with that sweet voice, she might as well have been inviting them to tea.

"Turn the communicator on again." The enforcer leaned over her shoulder. "Teson Minor. Open the dome, or I will open it for you. You've seen what I can do. You have been warned."

Yeah, that voice was just a little more menacing. The grid didn't budge, though.

"Head for the exit at high speed," Kile said.

Ty glanced at Cal. They had to hope the enforcer didn't have a death wish.

Cal nodded, and the ship hummed beneath them as they shot toward the thick metal grid.

Kile held up his hands and the air about him seemed to solidify. A cool, almost solid, vapor shot out through the hull of the *Renegade* and blasted into the webbed dome. A flash of light filled the screen, followed by the roar of a hundred explosions.

Ty growled as they passed through what was left of the grid and soared into the clouds.

"Let's get out of here," Cal said.

"*So* with you there, boss." Ty tilted them straight up.

As the *Renegade* left the atmosphere, several ships lifted off the satellite stations around the planet and headed for them.

Kile returned to Alanna. "Is the communicator still on?"

She flipped a switch. "It is now."

The commander leaned over her again. "Teson Minor, I have no problem destroying your ships as easily as I destroyed your protective dome. Disengage now. You have been warned."

One ship turned tail and ran. The others continued to pace them.

Kile's nose flared. "Fools."

He rubbed his hands together and held up his palms again.

"Wait!" Alanna stood. "You'll kill them."

"That's basically the idea."

"But they're just doing their jobs. I mean, we stole from them, right? They're the good guys here."

The enforcer stared at her for a moment. "I have been

gracious up to this point. They are not accepting my warnings."

"But we don't have to kill them. You're like this big, great enforcer guy. You can overpower any of them. You don't need to prove anything. You can also show mercy."

He glared at her before placing his palms down on her navigation panel. "Fine."

His palms lit up, and the ship jolted. The stars blinked, and Kile lifted his hands.

"Where are the other ships?" Ty asked.

"Behind us." Alanna spun toward the enforcer. "Did you just jump us?"

Kile straightened. "I do not have the ability of skip space. I simply jolted power to your engines."

"They're breaking off," Ty said.

Cal leaned back in his chair and puffed out a breath.

Kile moved away from the controls. "Depending on the veracity of the information we procured, they may still give chase."

Ty tapped on his data pad. "I'll get on that now. I should be able to decrypt the files pretty fast."

Alanna touched her earpiece again. She frowned.

A text from Ty pinged to Cal's station.

> It's Doc on Alanna's comm.
> She looks worried.
> Could it be about Dania?

Cal wished he knew.

Alanna stood. "I'm feeling a bit tired. I think I'll go down to the med bay and get my vitamin levels checked." As she passed behind Kile's back, she mouthed the words, *'It's okay'* to Cal before slipping out the door.

Cal sighed. Any good news was appreciated at this point.

He still didn't like taking directives from Dania's subordinate without her here to steer things in the right direction, though. Heck, they didn't even know what Ty had taken from that station.

Cal turned his seat toward the enforcer. "I hope whatever we just stole was worth almost dying for."

Disjointed characters started scrolling across Ty's screen as he began working on the file. "Give me a few hours and we'll find out."

SECONDS AFTER CAL had placed his head on his pillow and closed his eyes, a tone sounded through the overhead speakers in his room.

This wasn't fair.

He grabbed his pillow and pressed it over his ear. Why didn't he get to sleep like everyone else?

His pulse quickened and he sat up in his bed, squinting in the darkness.

What was he thinking? He shouldn't be sleeping at all! There was an enforcer on their ship who'd just thrown a battalion of security forces with a whisk of his hand, which wasn't all that much of a surprise after Dania had burned those slavers alive on Port Walker.

But watching as that enforcer had lifted his hand and exploded a *Renegade*-sized hole in a solid carbon-enhanced dome grid wall had been sobering.

No, not sobering—it had been as frightening as the center of Jupiter's eye.

There were stories floating about the galaxy of crazy

things enforcers could do. Cal had witnessed their brutality firsthand, but that show of force yesterday…

There were thousands of these turbo-charged beings out there, not to mention the Banes themselves, who were supposed to be even stronger. Now that Earth had formed an alliance with these ridiculously powerful beings, could they ever free themselves if the Banes decided to change their deal?

Cal massaged his burning eyes. Doc was going to be pissed about Cal's sleep cycles. Cal needed to be sharp, but he needed to get them all out of this mess even more. He needed to get back up to the bridge.

The tone sounded again.

"Lights!"

The room illuminated halfway. Cal reached for the panel over his bed and tapped the blue button. "What's wrong?"

Alanna's voice. "Ty wants us all in the lounge."

Lovely. Cal was awake, but that didn't mean everyone else was. "It couldn't wait until morning?"

The line hummed for a moment. "Cal, it's almost ten o'clock."

"What?" The hovering time stamp beside his bed glowed 9:49 in green numerals. He blinked the sting from his eyes. He'd been out for over ten hours. How was that possible?

He pulled on his pants and a clean shirt and headed down the hall, stopping Doc before he entered the lounge. "Did you drug me?"

"What?"

"Did you knock me out last night?"

A smile broke across his lips. "No, but I'm happy you got so much sleep. You look worlds better."

"I don't believe you."

"You don't think you look better? Then you haven't looked in a mirror." He snorted. "Listen, you don't have to believe me. Science is science. Exhaustion will make you sleep, even if you don't want to." He reached for the lounge entrance pad. "Why do you think I watch everyone's sleep patterns? I don't want you face-planting into your consoles and driving us right into a planet."

Fair enough.

Cal *did* feel better. Passing out like that wasn't like him, though. He needed to keep it together.

Inside the lounge, Ty and Ethan sat at the table. The enforcer stood with his arms folded, staring Cal and Doc down like they were late for a meeting with the principal.

Doc grabbed the back of his chair and glared right back at him. "I'm going to take a wild guess and say you didn't sleep at all last night."

Kile's nose flared. "I don't need sleep." His eyes darted to the side. "At the moment, at least."

"You need sleep just as much as anyone." Dania walked in with Alanna behind her.

Dania strode toward Kile, her back erect and her chin high.

Kile lowered his hands and took a partial step back.

Cal couldn't blame him. There was a tinge of pink to her lips, Alanna's shade, and her hair hung in soft waves. She walked with intent, ready to kick ass—and she'd never looked more beautiful.

Alanna fist-bumped Doc as she took a seat.

Last night when Cal had checked on Dania, she'd been awake, but Alanna had stopped him at the med bay door, saying their patient needed as little distraction as possible.

Maybe this was why. Hopefully, Dania really felt as good

as she looked, and this was not a short-lived ruse to keep the commander off her back.

Dania pointed at her subordinate. "The doctor is right. You look like you haven't rested in days. I need you alert and in good form."

His jaw dropped again. "I am always in good form."

She paused, probably taking in the odd darkening under his eyes marring that enforcer perfection. "Time will tell."

Ty waved them forward. "Come on, guys. I need to tell you what I found before I drop. I'm the one who actually *was* up all night."

His hair stood out on the sides like he'd been pulling at the sandy strands, and his eyes were even darker than Kile's.

Cal sat at the other end of the table. "What did you find?"

"This is going to sound crazy, but hear me out." He pinched the bridge of his nose. "I got the first half of the messages decrypted, and no one is going to like this." He looked at the enforcer. "It looks like the Carteks are the money men behind the slavers who took your friend."

Kile somehow managed to stand even taller. "Impossible."

"I wish it were. It also looks like they're helping smuggle alien technology into Earth's territories."

Dania folded her arms on the table. "That would be an odd move from them. Are you sure?"

Ty tapped on his data pad. "I've seen more than one directive, giving them locations of younger enforcers. They're trying to weed them out before they get too strong."

"For what purpose?" Kile asked.

After what Cal saw yesterday, he really needed to ask that question? The enforcers were already a menace when they were supposed to be keeping the peace. If they actually turned on humanity, it would be unthinkable. If the Carteks wanted any real chance in their war with Keveron, they needed to even the odds.

"They want to cull your numbers," Cal said. "You guys are hard to kill when you're strong."

What they were doing was against nearly all modern peace accords. It was like genocide, going after the young before they become what they feared. It was actually a good war plan. Not good for those enforcer kids, though.

Ty rubbed his eyes. He looked like he might fall over at any moment. "They were supposed to kill the enforcers they caught, but as we all know, they found out that selling them on the black market as exotic slaves was even more lucrative." He glanced around the room. "The Carteks didn't care because they still got what they wanted."

"Fewer enforcers," Cal said.

Ty sent the contents of his data pad to a screen on the wall and pointed to depictions of sound waves. "What's strange, though, is it seems like they're talking to each other over long distances with no delays. They should have to wait for the messages to travel through space, but these time stamps are almost immediate."

That probably wasn't good. "Could the Carteks be closer than they appear?"

Ty shook his head. "No. These messages are definitely coming out of Cartek space."

Kile held his chin, walking over to the window. Did he know something about this, or was this new information?

If the Carteks had a way to send instantaneous transmissions through the universe, that could be a huge win for their empire. They could coordinate attacks before the Banes even knew what hit them. Whether that was good or bad for Earth, time would tell.

Doc stared at the enforcer's shoulders before easing out of his seat and plucking something off of Kile's back.

The enforcer spun on him, and Doc lowered his hand and waved his other. "Hi. Nice view, huh?"

Kile's eyes bored through him before he turned to Ty. "You will continue to analyze. I want plans. I want locations. And I want them *now*. You will start on this immediately."

Cal stood. "He will not." He walked to the other side of that table and put his hand on Ty's shoulder. "You need sleep."

Ty shook his head. "The big, annoying wall-with-legs is right. This is an asteroid field of information. I need..."

"You need sleep." Cal squeezed his first mate's shoulder. "You'll go quietly, or I'll have Doc *make sure* you sleep."

"I really didn't drug you, Cal." Doc turned to Ty. "But I have no problem with knocking you out because, boy, you look like hell."

Ty held up his hands. "All right, all right. Maybe a few minutes."

Doc smacked his shoulder. "Try six hours or more."

Ty nodded and left the room.

Cal pointed at Doc. "Make sure he really sleeps."

"On it." Doc pulled out a data pad and tapped on the screen.

The enforcer folded his arms. "This is highly inconvenient."

"Yeah, well, you're going to have to get over it. And you could use some sleep, too. Why don't you rest now that we're all awake? That way, you'll be bright and chipper when Ty can make his next report."

Dania leaned back in her chair. "I agree. The captain has afforded you perfectly suitable quarters. I suggest you use them."

Kile lanced her with more of that glare. Did the guy have any other expressions?

Dania stood. "I am now turning this into an order, Commander. Get some sleep. I can handle things for a few hours."

He muttered something before heading out of the room. *He better not be planning on catching up with Ty to drag him back to a computer console.*

When the door shut behind him, Cal turned on Doc. "Are you crazy? What did you do to him?"

"Nothing." He slipped the data pad into his jacket pocket and held up something nearly invisible in his fingertips. "There was a piece of hair on his shoulder. I was intrigued."

"By hair?"

"Do you know how much DNA is in a piece of hair?" He pointed at Dania. "I might be able to find something to help our girl."

"You're crazy."

"If I can find out anything about his living pathogens from this piece of hair, I might be able to figure out how to strengthen the synthetic ones."

Always the scientist, even to a fault.

"Can we please try to not get killed for science?"

Doc held up his fingers again. "It's just a little piece of hair. How much harm can it cause?"

CHAPTER 19

DANIA

DANIA STARED at an indent in the door to the captain's quarters. It appeared to have been hit several times with a blunt object, and then had the dents pushed back into place from behind. This ship certainly had an interesting history.

The door suddenly opened, and Cal leaned on the frame. "Are you going to keep staring at my door, or are you going to knock?"

She did her best not to gape. How did he know she was out here?

Cal stepped back. "Would you like to come in?"

She nodded. Why had she suddenly lost her ability to speak?

His receiving room looked very much like the last time she'd been here…a couch nestled in the corner, and a large table centered in the room where she and the crew had eaten dinner a few times.

She flinched. That first dinner had been a few hours before she had accidentally brought the power of the Banes down on top of them. She closed her eyes and looked at the floor. How could she have been such a fool?

"Hey." Cal placed his hand on her arm. "You okay?" He looked her over. "How's your chest?"

"My chest?"

He paled, looking down. "Yeah, I think I broke one of your ribs when…"

When he and Doc were trying to save her life.

Dania rubbed the tender spot. "It's a little sore. Peter did some work on it and gave me something for the pain." She leaned back and took a deep breath of the air. A million wonderful scents touched her senses. "What is that wonderful smell?"

He pointed his thumb over his shoulder. "I'm making lunch."

"For the crew?"

He made an exaggerated grimace. "Not this time. Once in a while, I cook for myself."

"I think Ethan might have an issue with that."

Cal tilted his head back and laughed, a pleasant sound that made her smile.

"I think they'd all have issue with that." He waved her toward the kitchen door. "I usually try recipes out on myself first. If they taste like moon crab droppings, I usually scrap it. Better to waste a small batch of food on myself than ruin a whole meal."

Heat and humidity wrapped around her as she stepped into the next room. Stainless steel cabinets and an old-fashioned stove and oven lined one wall, while a long counter and a double sink lined the other wall.

"This is what a kitchen looks like?" She spun, taking in the shiny walls.

"Yup. This is my little piece of heaven."

A pot of water boiled on the stove. A thick, white block

lay on the counter next to it, with three red fruits perched atop.

"What are you cooking?"

"Right now, I'm skinning tomatoes."

This was all so different, so new. "Can I help?"

His eyes sparkled. "Sure." He picked up a knife and made a star pattern over the top of the fruit. "You cut them like this and then do the same on the bottom."

He handed her the knife. It felt strange in her hand. Knives were ancient weapons, and enforcers never had the need for weapons. His arms moved around her, helping her to hold the fruit.

"You only cut a little bit of the skin, not into the fruit." He helped guide her hands. He smelled of spices and a hint of a woodsy scent, which was impossible, since they were in space.

Cal let her go, and she released her breath. His presence was soothing, like it had been in the med bay.

She turned toward him. "Thank you for staying with me during the procedure. That was kind of you."

"You are most welcome, my lady." He bowed low at the hip. "I'm just glad you're feeling better."

But she wasn't better—not in the true sense of the word. "Peter says I'll need another treatment. Maybe more than one."

"At least we know how to kickstart the pathogens now. I'm sure that Doc can find a way that doesn't involve accidentally stopping your heart."

Cal reached across her and plucked the tomatoes off the block.

He placed one on a spoon. "Now, we gently place these into the boiling water."

"We want to cook them?"

"Nope. This is a magic trick my mom taught me." He pointed to the fruit, bobbing just below the surface. "Watch."

The fruit shifted in the water before the edges of the star pattern she'd cut in the top started to peel back. "Oh! Look!"

"Easy as that." He scooped the fruit into a separate bowl of water beside the pot, and the rest of the peel slipped free.

Dania giggled like a little girl. "Can we do the other one?"

"Sure." He handed her the spoon.

She lowered the second fruit into the boiling water. When the peel began to curl, she scooped the fruit out and lowered it into the second bowl of cooler water. Again, the peel slipped free. "That was fun!"

Cal's grin lit up the already bright room. "It is, isn't it?"

She looked around the room. Everything suddenly looked like a playground. "Now what do we do with them?"

"Whatever we want. Tomatoes are really versatile. We can..." A tone sounded from the speakers above. He tapped a button on the wall. "Talk to me."

"Hey, boss," Doc said. "Have you seen Dania? It's time for her next treatment."

His smile turned to a frown, and the room became a little less bright.

Dania wished she could bring back that shine. "Does it have to be now?" she asked. "We're cooking."

Silence lingered on the other side. "Cooking, are you? Interesting. Umm..."

Cal tapped the button, turning off the comm. "We don't want to miss your treatments."

The smell of the tomatoes swept up around her. "But I was having fun." And oddly enough, it was the truth. This was creation, when her entire life had been devoted to destruction. It was odd, how something so simple could give her such joy.

Cal's hand appeared on her cheek. The touch was warm, comforting, as it had been during the treatment.

"It's okay to be scared," he said.

She blinked. Was she scared?

"For the treatment, I mean. I'll stay with you again. Let's get you fixed, and then we can peel all the tomatoes you want."

Tendrils of steam rose from the fruits, disappearing into the air. Her stomach tightened, like she was about to lose something, and there was nothing she could do to stop it.

"Hey." His hands moved to her shoulders. "I mean that." He looked behind him. "Hold on."

He released her, placed the tomatoes in a jar, and then stowed them in a refrigerated case. "These will keep until we're done. Let me think of something great to make, and then after your treatment, you can help me make it. Deal?"

Deal? Were they bartering? Maybe, but that was a barter she could be agreeable with.

She shook his hand. "Deal."

———

Lying on the mattress in the med bay, Dania closed her eyes as the doctor removed the syringe from her arm.

Cal squeezed her hand. "Hey, you're almost done."

"Correction." Peter pressed a ball of white material on the spot where the needle had been. "You *are* done. Hold that tight and press on it for me." He looked up at the screen with flowing water and dark dots inside. "It looks good. It looks *really* good." He put a small bandage on her arm and sat her up.

"That was a lot easier this time," Cal said.

"I had a little help from enforcer DNA."

"That actually worked?" Cal asked.

Dania held her bandage. "What did you find?"

"It's hard to explain in laymen's terms." Peter moved the stand holding the empty bag away from Dania. "Imagine you are a puzzle, and there were missing pieces in you that I couldn't find. Your big, scary friend sort-of provided the last pieces of the puzzle."

She supposed that made sense. "It's going to be hard to keep hiding these treatments from him, though. How many more will I need?"

He shrugged. "I'd like to do one more in a few days. After that, maybe we can see if what you've already received can keep you afloat." He looked down. "You need to understand that you might need small treatments for the rest of your life. At this point, you are patient zero, so I really don't know."

He looked at the screen, then turned away.

"What is it?" Cal asked.

Peter scratched his chin. "I did a genealogy on your friend. I was hoping to maybe find some family like we did for Dania."

Dania cringed. Her own parents had sold her to the Banes at a considerable profit. She wanted to hate them, but she found herself more curious. If she ever found them, she would ask why they had given her up and decide how she felt after she knew all the facts.

Her commander, though, came from a completely different background. "Kile is royal. His family comes from old blood."

Peter's brow quirked. "I wouldn't say that. Well, his father's bloodlines are what Kever culture considers old, but it's not Bane."

She gaped. "What?"

"I traced it back in the archives and linked the DNA to an illegal forced union."

"Illegal forced union?" Cal asked.

Doc grimaced. "On Earth, it's called rape."

What?

Dania shook her head. "That's not possible. He was reared in the highest houses before the Banes offered him a position as an enforcer."

But had they *offered* him a position, or had he been taken, as Dania was?

Peter shook his head. "Someone may have shown him mercy, but his father was a guard in the Bane household, and the mother was a human servant from House Lessuer."

A servant and a guard? A criminal guard, at that. If the genealogy was known, that guard would have been punished for the crime, which would have left Kile fatherless to a servant girl with no means to care for him.

However, if they'd tested Kile and found him to be worthy of carrying the Bane power, they may have taken him in, as Peter had suggested.

Dania looked at the floor. Kile's complexion was pale, like all enforcers, but his skin wasn't scaled like the Banes'. How had she not noticed that before?

She grimaced. She may have been programmed not to notice. Geron could, and did, make her believe anything he wanted her to believe.

Kile had always held himself in such high esteem. No one

ever questioned his upbringing and no one, even the Banes, corrected any mention of where he'd come from.

Of course, this made Kile a valuable leader. Kile believed he was a Bane, the highest-grade enforcer. This made his loyalty absolute, unlike Dania, who'd failed them.

If her commander's heritage was all a fallacy, this news would crush him. No enforcer ever wanted to appear to be *less* of anything.

"Don't tell him," Dania said. "Promise me."

"You don't think he'd want to know?"

"Definitely not." His ties to the Banes were strong… strong enough to be important to him. "He might lash out and destroy the evidence." Which would mean also destroying the doctor who'd made the discovery.

"Okay," Doc said. "I just found it interesting. I mean, you enforcers come from all over the galaxy."

That, they did. But there were hierarchies that had nothing to do with rank. Kile was not a general. His past was his only claim to aloofness. And he might do anything to protect what little stature he had.

CAL LEANED his head into Engineering. The enforcer stood next to Ethan, both of them staring up at a piece of machinery.

Ethan pointed at a silver plate. "Right there. Can you give me about eight-hundred degrees in a two-second burst?"

Kile raised his hand and the plate turned red before cooling to a shiny, mirror-like material.

"Perfect!" Ethan said.

Cal stepped into the room. "It looks like you kids are getting along."

The enforcer frowned. "My general tells me I need to *earn my keep*." He looked at Ethan. "Apparently, everyone on this ship needs to *do their time* in Engineering."

Cal choked back a laugh. He had made Engineering rounds required for everyone on the crew when people had started avoiding Ethan. It had actually worked to the crew's advantage, helping them to look past Ethan's shortcomings and see him as a person, rather than a nuisance.

"Dare I ask what you're working on?" The creases in Cal's face shone back at him in the newly-heated metal plate. It looked freshly machined next to the more worn-out plates beside it.

Ethan reached up nearly six inches to put his arm around Kile's shoulder. "Me and Big Bad are putting the finishing touches on our new tertiary reactor."

The enforcer glared down at him, and Ethan slowly withdrew his arm.

"We had the parts for that?" Cal asked.

Ethan turned toward the new panel. "Well, the circuitry fried, but most of the parts were intact. The problem was getting the metals super-heated to reconstitute the elements. But Big Bad here is like a human blowtorch."

Kile folded his arms. "I am neither human, nor a blowtorch."

Ethan gave him a light punch on the shoulder. "Aww, don't sell yourself short, ya big balooka."

The enforcer glared at him again. "Balooka?"

Cal stepped closer, although he wasn't sure what he would be able to do if the enforcer decided he'd had enough Ethan-ness. "Dania has given an order not to execute anyone in the crew, right?"

Kile closed his eyes and turned away. "Unfortunately, yes."

Cal released a breath. "In that case, as you were. It looks like you two are working well together."

The enforcer spun back toward Cal. "Are you sure you don't need assistance on the bridge?"

Cal held back his smile.

Well, he *almost* held back his smile. "And ruin all your fun down here? Never."

He slipped out of the door before the enforcer could object.

Ethan was definitely an acquired taste. It was probably better that Kile got used to him on days when Dania remembered to reinforce the no-kill order.

Cal headed down the hall. Getting the tertiary reactor up and running without having to dock for repairs was a huge bonus. With Alanna working on the new sync navigator they'd just picked up, the only other big repair was the secondary comm juncture. They were doing fine without it, but if they lost their main comm, not having a backup would be a big issue. Maybe they'd have some luck finding one at their next stop.

"I take it Ethan is still breathing?" Dania barred his way, smiling.

"For the moment." Cal looked back toward Engineering. "I think they're actually getting along."

Her eyes were still changing color, now a lovely hazel tone —a drastic transformation compared to Kile's freakish icy-clear irises.

"Kile isn't so bad. There are far worse enforcers we could have been dealing with." From the look on her face, that didn't mean the commander wouldn't melt anyone's face off at the first chance.

"Ethan is safe with him, right?" Cal asked.

She tucked some of her brownish-blonde hair behind her ear, as if considering her answer. The rest fell in perfect waves across her shoulders. "If Kile wants to kill him, he'll come and ask me first."

"Good to know."

She slipped her fingers into the pockets of her borrowed pants. "So, I was wondering, how do my tomatoes look?"

Tomatoes? Cal's eyes widened. His gaze dropped twelve

inches before he could stop himself. His cheeks heated, and he looked away. *Idiot!*

"Did I say something wrong?"

"No!" He turned back to her.

Her brows furrowed. Her beautiful eyes looked...*hurt*.

"It's-It's me." He pointed to his temple. "My brain. It's just stupid sometimes." What in Neptune's moons was wrong with him?

Her expression hardened. "You're too hard on yourself. This crew respects you more than you know."

Cal scoffed. This is the same crew that had mutinied when they hadn't agreed with him. The same crew who'd accidentally shot him.

She touched his arm. "Enforcers are trained to see people's weaknesses."

Cal cringed. It probably made them better killers.

She drew her hand back. "Your biggest weakness is this crew. You care for them, but that's not a bad thing."

Cal glanced back toward Engineering. "Will your guy use the crew against me?"

"If he has to. But I'll be there to stop that from happening."

He grimaced. That should have made him feel better, but it didn't.

Dania stared at him, maybe trying to figure him out. Maybe if she did, she could give him a heads up...tell him why a kid who'd had his whole life taken away from him had managed to find a new family, and how they'd managed to adopt not only one, but two enforcers...the very twisted beings who'd ruined Cal's life.

She straightened. "All things happen for a reason."

He startled. "What?"

"That's what Alanna keeps telling me. Whatever it is that's bothering you, even if you think it's bad, it's really good."

"That sounds like Alanna, but it also makes absolutely no sense."

She laughed. "I'm glad to hear you say that, because the way she explained it seemed to make so much sense, but at the same time it just…"

"Didn't?"

"Right." She pointed her thumb in the direction of the forward crew quarters. "So, how about those tomatoes we peeled? Have you decided what to do with them?"

Tomatoes. Of course. "Actually, I've had some pasta in storage for quite a while now. I thought we'd make a slow-cooked sauce."

Her eyes darted to the right, as if searching her memory. "I don't know what pasta is."

Cal gritted his teeth. The more he learned about the Kevers, the more barbaric they seemed. *No pasta? Ever?* Now *that* was something to make a law about.

He slipped his arm around her shoulder and drew her toward the crew quarters. "There is a whole galaxy of culinary delights waiting for you, my lady." And, oddly enough, Cal couldn't wait to show her.

A tone sounded overhead. "Boss?" Ty's voice. "Call in, please."

Dania stopped walking. "So much for culinary delights."

Cal pointed at her. "There is a home-cooked tomato sauce in your future, and a bowl full of rigatoni. I just can't guarantee when." He pressed the comm. "Talk to me."

"I got the rest of the files decrypted."

"And?"

"I think I know what happened to Dania's friend."

Dania blanched, grabbing Cal's shoulder. The fire returned to her eyes, the grim determination he'd seen the first day they'd dragged her onto this ship.

Cal hit the comm again. "Meet me in the lounge."

"Already there."

They doubled back over their steps and up the stairs.

Heat seemed to radiate off Dania, and her hair shifted slightly—not quite alive like it had been, but definitely an unnatural movement. Maybe those pathogen treatments were finally working. Hopefully not *too* well.

When they entered the lounge, Ty sat with his face in his palms, leaning on the table.

"You okay?" Cal asked.

Ty lifted his chin. Dark circles under his eyes betrayed his lack of sleep.

"Didn't I order you to rest?"

"I did, for a few hours, until the big bad enforcer called and threatened me."

Dania folded her arms. "He won't kill you."

Ty scoffed. "He didn't threaten me directly. He didn't have to."

Dania had said enforcers learned people's weaknesses. That meant that Kile had threatened to hurt something, or some*one*, that Ty cared about...maybe someone not on this crew.

Cal turned to Dania. "I think we need to expand on his no-kill directives."

"Agreed." She leaned on the table, looming toward Ty, looking no less the enforcer without the pearly uniform. "What did you learn about Alexander?"

Ty rubbed his face and sighed. "You're not going to like it."

Her knuckles whitened on the tabletop.

"Ty, let's get to it," Cal said.

He held up his hands. "Okay, okay. Geeze." He rubbed his face again. "So, as we know, everybody's favorite intergalactic terrorists, the Carteks, have turned up the heat on all the outlier colonies."

Dania straightened. "Yes, it's been getting progressively worse."

This was what had happened to Kirato. Being far from Earth had been a blessing at first, an adventure to the colonists…until the people of Kirato had found out they had some unfriendly neighbors just a few hundred million miles away from their new home.

Ty leaned back. "The Carteks are attacking on purpose, just to destroy. They aren't even taking anything or trying to occupy the planets."

"Useless bloodshed. Nothing new for them," Dania said.

"Yeah, well, it's not so useless to them. What happens when colonies that the king hasn't written off get attacked?"

Dania tilted her head. "He would send the military to protect them, of course."

"What kind of military?"

Dania's eyes narrowed. "Enforcers."

Ty pointed at her. "Bingo." He leaned back again. "They're causing all that ruckus on purpose to draw you guys away from Keveron. They figured out that if they can keep the enforcers from their sponsors long enough, that they get weaker and easier to kill." He glanced at each of them. "And, since there are fewer baby enforcers because of the pirates…"

Dania took a step back. "There aren't enough to replace the enforcers lost in battle."

Ty pointed at her again. "Double bingo. Give the pretty lady a prize." He took a deep breath. "But that's not the worst of it." He blinked several times. "The slavers figured out what the Carteks were doing and decided to swoop in and snatch themselves an even more exotic catch—an older, fully charged enforcer."

Dania gasped.

"Alexander," Cal whispered.

"Yeah. We knew he'd been taken, but it looks like it was planned and executed with precision. They were supposed to kill any enforcers who came to help, but they waited it out, hunted the poor bastard, and the rest we already knew."

Dania closed her eyes, biting her lower lip. "Were you able to find any more details on his capture?"

"Not a lot, but there was a ton of galactic high-fiving going on. I mean, they bagged an adult enforcer. Lots of jabber about how pretty he was and how much money they'd get for him."

Dania's eyes flared.

Ty held up his hands. "Sorry. I'm just the messenger."

She took a deep breath. "I know. Continue."

Ty sighed. "I want to sift through the static, but I think there was enough chatter going on to trace their flight path for a few days after they grabbed him."

"Just a few days?" Dania asked.

"Yeah, but that might be enough to triangulate which way they were headed. It's at least part of a clue."

"That's more than we have now." Cal tapped the table. "Get some sleep."

"But..."

Cal pointed at him. "Sleep." He turned to Dania. "And make sure your boy isn't threatening anyone else in the crew. If Ty's exhausted, he might miss something that would make us lose a chance to find your friend."

She lowered her eyes. "I'll talk to him."

Cal turned from the room.

She better take care of this problem because Cal still had a tiny pistol tucked into his boot that Doc had given him to take her out. Not that he'd use it on Dania anymore, but he'd protect his crew from her commander if he needed to, even if it brought that wrath of the Banes back to his doorstep.

CAL SANK into his seat on the bridge beside Ty. "You look better this morning."

His first mate gave a curt nod. "Doc gave me melo-*something-or-other* to help me sleep. I barely remember lying down."

"That's good. You needed it."

Ty tapped a few keys on his panel. "Alanna ran some numbers off of the coordinates I gave her, and she's tracing possible trajectories from all that pirate chatter. I re-charted our course to head in that general direction until she finishes doing her magic."

Cal glanced over at her empty chair.

"Relax, boss. A girl's gotta eat. The algorithms are running."

"I had no doubt." But Cal might be a tad overanxious to get this mission over with so they could get rid of the extra enforcer.

The doors opened, and Ethan stepped onto the bridge. "Morning, gents!"

"How's the reactor?" Cal asked.

"Fantastic. Actually, I think it's in even better condition. The super-heated wiring—thanks to my new favorite assistant—has really increased the power flow. I think losing that reactor was a blessing in disguise."

A blessing? Ethan and Dania had nearly died. But he couldn't fault the guy for looking for the positives.

"So, things are going well with Kile?"

"Totally. Me and Big Bad are tight." He crossed his fingers before walking to the engineering panel.

Cal looked over their new trajectories. "If you ask me, he's just as bad, if not worse, than Dania when she first got here."

"Maybe," Ty said. "But you have to admit that he's pretty bad ass. I mean, did you see how he threw all those soldiers around? And those machines he moved must have weighed a few tons."

"Your point?"

Ty turned his chair toward Cal, resting his elbows on his knees. "I think if we could convince him to stay, he'd be a pretty valuable addition to the crew."

"What? Have you forgotten about him flying us all in the air and then unceremoniously slamming us to the deck?" Cal pointed at Ethan. "Doc had to cauterize Ethan's nose."

The engineer shrugged. "I don't know, boss. He doesn't seem all that bad. I mean, yeah, he's all rough and tough and *'I'm gonna kill you'* and all, but I think he has a mind of his own. He seems to think things through."

"That enforcer is on a mission. He's made it perfectly clear what will happen to all of us once that mission is over. We are a means to an end, and nothing else."

Ty leaned closer in that annoying way he did when he

expected to win an argument. "I'm not denying that, but we did change Dania."

Yeah, but Dania wasn't fully charged when they picked her up, and they'd melted the only Palian steel they had off her wrists on Port Walker.

Ty held up his hands. "We just have to find a way to break his resolve like we broke Dania."

Cal wiped his face with his hand. "Showing this guy a declining outlier colony isn't going to help."

"We could always get him laid," Ethan said.

Ty and Cal turned and stared at him.

"Hey, why not? It's a good idea."

"It's a ridiculous idea," Cal said, although he had seen Kile's eyes drape over Alanna a few times. If had been anyone else, Cal would have punched him in the face to prove a point.

Ethan leaned against the wall. "Think of it this way. He was probably human before he became an enforcer, right?"

Well, maybe half-human, if what Doc had said was true.

Ethan continued. "If the prince's effect is waning even a little, maybe certain physical needs might be taking over again."

Cal stood. "We are not asking Dania or Alanna to…"

Ethan's eyes widened, and he held up his palms. "Oh, heck no. No one is touching my baby girl."

Ty leaned back in his chair. "We are dangerously close to Hedonaii. We could make a pit stop, see if we can rally a little feminine company."

Cal clenched his jaw. Hedonaii specialized in all things considered disreputable on other worlds.

A smile burst across Ethan's face. "What happens in Hedonaii stays in Hedonaii."

Cal pointed at him. "You are not gambling."

"No fair!"

Cal shook his head. Where did they come up with these ridiculous ideas? "A pretty woman is not going to convince him to stop being an enforcer."

Ty smirked. "Maybe it depends on how talented the woman is."

They were both crazy, but Cal had to admit, Kile had proven himself a valuable asset in a fight. One woman wouldn't change the enforcer's mind, but maybe one woman could make him consider freedom.

Based on their progress with Dania, they'd need to take small steps and hope no one got their faces fried off in the process.

Cal walked to the window and gazed into the distance. A million stars twinkled back at him. One day, he'd look out again and see their beauty and not wonder what might be hiding behind them.

"Go ahead and set a course for Hedonaii."

Behind him, Ethan and Ty high-fived each other.

Changing course was the easy part. Now they just needed to come up with a good reason to give the enforcer for stopping in the debauchery capital of the galaxy.

———

Kile's eyes narrowed on Cal. "You have plotted a course for where?"

"Hedonaii is a perfectly respectable trading port."

"I do not believe that *respectable* and *Hedonaii* have ever been used in the same sentence. And it is of no consequence. There is nothing there that will lead us to Alexander."

"This is true," Cal said. "However, we are on our way to Hitus, as you asked. You also directed us to 'act normal.' I always stop at Hedonaii to give the crew a little R and R. If I don't, it will look odd. People who know me, who know this ship, will start to ask questions."

Kile folded his arms. "That would be inconvenient."

"Correct. We only need to stop for a few hours. We set down, do a little shopping, have a few drinks, and we leave."

"Just a few hours?"

"Yes, and then we're off to Hitus. With any luck, we'll have a good lead on your friend by then."

And you, my enormous friend, will be one step closer to humanity.

They hoped.

CHAPTER 22
DANIA

DANIA ADJUSTED the carry-bag on her shoulder as she walked toward the exit. Her mission today would be to join the captain in procuring a *communication juncture*.

Dania assumed a *communication juncture* had something to do with long-range messaging, but she wasn't sure and was embarrassed to ask. However, she was looking forward to getting off the ship, and Cal seemed excited about her "riding shotgun," whatever that meant.

On the far side of the gathering space, Alanna leaned against the opening to the gangway plank, scanning the hangar outside with her arms folded. It seemed a shame that on a recreational outing such as this, anyone had to stay behind with the ship.

The captain leaned around Alanna, looking outside. "Hey, are you sure that you don't want to take some R and R?"

The navigator shook her head. "No. I volunteered to stay onboard. This place gives me the creeps, to be honest." Her cheeks reddened. "I mean, I'm all for a free lifestyle, live how you want and all, but this place has always been a little much for me."

Peter placed his arm around her shoulder. "Besides, I'm going to teach my girl how to play Parcheesi."

She furrowed her brow. "Parcheesi? Do you know how to play Parcheesi?"

"No. But that's okay. I'll look it up."

"Why Parcheesi?"

He held up his palms. "Because it sounds cool, and it's a pre-colonization game, and we are all into pre-colonization games, if you hadn't noticed. And…"

They started to discuss whether or not they needed a special board for that game, when Kile stepped into Dania's view. "I don't understand why you want me to go out there. There is nothing on this planet that will help in the quest to find Alexander."

Dania had actually wondered the same thing. She flicked a glance to Cal.

"That was Dania's request," Cal said. "She was a little worried about Ty and Ethan making it to where they needed to go, and you make the perfect bodyguard."

Kile glared at him, then Dania. "Why would I need to protect them?"

This, Dania didn't know, either.

She flicked another glance at Cal, who lifted his brow in a way that sent a tingle of warmth spreading through her chest. Alarming and odd, but…*nice*.

Sensing no ill intent, she leveled her gaze on Kile again. "It will just make me feel better."

It wasn't exactly a lie. She would feel better with Kile protecting anyone. He was a strong sentry, and his powers were formidable, even for an enforcer.

Kile grimaced. "What exactly are your orders, General?"

She wished she knew.

Cal took a step forward. "She'd like you to walk Ty and Ethan to where they need to go. From there, you can just enjoy yourself until they are ready to leave."

Kile narrowed his eyes. "Enjoy myself?"

"Yes. This is the entertainment capital of the galaxy."

Ethan arrived and slapped Kile on the back. "Hey, Big Bad. Are you ready to have some fun?"

"No."

Ethan turned, smiling. "Okay, then. Let's get to it."

Ty snickered, following Ethan and Kile down the gangplank.

Cal grimaced, his brow furrowing.

"You look worried," Dania said.

"With Ty and Ethan, I'm always worried."

Dania adjusted her bag. "Is that why you wanted Kile to be with them? Do you think he'll keep them from getting into trouble?"

Cal laughed as they headed down the ramp. "I'm not sure even our mighty enforcer is powerful enough to keep Ty and Ethan from getting into trouble."

Alanna leaned her head out of the ship. "If they have choices, I'd love a pink one."

Cal looked over his shoulder. "You want a pink comm juncture?"

She nodded. "To match my hair."

"You do realize this gets mounted on the outside of the ship, right? You're never even going to see it."

She folded her arms. "Maybe, but *I'll know* it's pink."

Cal opened up his mouth twice to reply, but nothing came out.

"We'll see what we can do." Dania pulled his arm.

"We will?" Cal followed her down the plank.

"How hard can it be to find pink paint? And imagine the look on her face if you actually came back with pink hardware." Dania snickered. "She's most likely kidding, but she'd probably love it."

Cal shook his head. "Women are strange."

"Alanna has told me the same thing about men on more than one occasion."

And it was little conversations like this that had made Dania realize how connected this crew had become over the years. 'Strange' was not a bad thing. They embraced each other's quirks, even growing to look forward to them.

As an enforcer, she'd known her squadron's strengths and weaknesses and had blended them to keep teams fine-tuned for specific missions. Personalities were never considered. Maybe they should have been.

The crowd ebbed and flowed in parallel lines. People on the right moved deeper into the facility, while those on the left seemed to flow back out toward the hangars. The farther they got from the ship, the more the crowds began to thin, but people still bumped into them until they passed beneath a sign that read: *Bartering*.

A woman with long, blonde hair approached. She tugged on the hem of a skirt that barely covered her hind region as her eyes swept over Cal. "Can I help you with anything?"

Cal kept walking. "No thanks."

"Are you sure?" she asked.

Cal bit back a grin, grabbed Dania's arm, and gave her a tug. "Yeah, I'm pretty sure."

What was so amusing? And what was the rush? "Maybe she knew where the traders were?" Dania said.

Cal's smile broke free. "Somehow, I doubt it."

A man with short, dark hair and a tight T-shirt that

showed off his muscle definition started walking with them as they passed. "Are you two looking for the traders? Which ones?"

Cal stopped. "I was told there is a remanufactured parts dealer around here who specializes in older ships?"

"Paradise Supply over in Section Three." The man pointed his thumb to the right. "Me and my dad used to go to Paradise Supply all the time when we fixed up old ships together. I can show you."

He started walking backward.

"My name is Charles, by the way. I saw you kind of blew past my friend back there." His eyes perused Cal just as the other woman had. "Any chance you're looking for a different kind of company?"

Cal nearly stumbled before he shook his head. "Just the parts dealer, thanks."

Charles turned to Dania. "How about the lady?"

Cal drew her closer to him. "Definitely not."

Dania glared at him. Definitely not *what*?

Charles laughed. "Hey, it's okay, I get it. How about the three of us…"

"No." Cal stopped, his grip tightening on her arm.

Was he, for some reason, threatened by this human? Dania checked Charles's temperature readings, posture, changes in expression, but nothing prodded her instinct to strike. He seemed genuine, amused, friendly.

Cal held up a hand. "Charles, trust me, she doesn't even know what you're talking about."

Dania exhaled. He was right, but she hated that he was right.

"First timer? A beauty like that?" Charles's eyes raked over her. "Are you from New Lancaster or something?"

Cal pulled her in so tightly she almost stumbled. "Something like that."

"Well, you've come to the right planet. Let me…"

Cal held up a hand. "Would you please just point us to Paradise Supply?"

Charles's eyes shot back to Dania. "You sure, beautiful? Because the things I can show you…"

Cal pulled out his jacket, showing a small sidearm. "I'm getting a little annoyed. Seriously, that's not why we're here, and the lady has no idea what you're talking about."

Charles held up his hands. "I got you, my friend. No harm intended. Just thought I'd offer. Hedonaii's hospitality is legendary. I just didn't want you to miss out on any fun while you were here."

Cal's temperature had spiked but lessened by zero point zero six degrees as they walked. His grip on her arm abated, but only slightly.

"Was he offering illegal substances?" Dania asked. "Were you trying to protect him?"

Cal shook his head. "No, there is very little illegal here outside of robbery and murder. He's just a guy looking for a good time."

Walking in front of them, Charles called over his shoulder. "And still looking, if you two crazy kids change your minds."

Dania frowned. Why would Cal be so opposed to a good time? She'd never realized how little she knew about humanity until she'd had to live as one of them.

Charles stopped and held out his hand. "Here we are."

The sign above pulsed in a soft pink glow. *Paradise Supply.*

"Thank you, my friend," Cal said. "May I pay you for your time?"

Charles scoffed. "Not necessary. It was a pleasure to be in your company." He bowed slightly. "Enjoy your stay on Hedonaii." He righted himself, winked at Dania, and headed back the way they'd come.

"Why do I feel so lost?" She'd never been so confused by an encounter. Then again, most humans ran from her on sight. No one had ever simply walked up to her and started talking. They were usually dragged to her feet, kicking, crying, and begging for mercy.

"Like I said, he was looking for a good time. That's what this planet is all about."

"I understand the concept of a good time. Why did you say I didn't know what he was talking about?"

He looked at the ground and sighed. "At the end there, I'm pretty sure he was offering a threesome."

"A threesome of what?"

Cal laughed. "Like I said, you have no idea what he was talking about."

Heat flooded Dania's veins. She was not a child. How dare he...

Cal looked up. His eyes were soft, warm, and there was something there that...

She blinked and looked away.

"Hey." He touched her shoulder. "It's actually a good thing that you didn't know what he was talking about. To me, at least."

His temperature stayed steady, and his voice soothed with no sense of malice. He wasn't making fun of her. He was telling the truth. And for some reason, he didn't want her to know what the man had been offering. Was he being protective, or was it something else?

Dania looked up at the flashing sign. She didn't like not

knowing something. Knowledge was important, but the sincerity in Cal's voice, in his demeanor, were as comforting as ever. She wouldn't push the point. Maybe she could look it up on the interweb, or she could probably get someone else on the crew to explain what a *threesome* was.

Maybe Ethan. He never seemed to have a problem with relaying information that no one else wanted him to say.

Cal walked toward the door. "Shall we?"

They entered the store and a man with a tousled gray beard and thinning white hair slammed an old-fashioned book down on the counter.

He glared at them. "For the last time, this is not Paradise *Pleasure* Supply. This is Paradise Supply. You are in Section Three here. You want Section Eight!"

Cal stared at him, gaping. "Umm, we *are* looking for Paradise Supply. Old ship parts, right?"

The man adjusted his stance and folded his hands. His temperature lowered a full quarter degree. "My apologies. It's just that the two of you..." He motioned to them. "You looked like a couple, and, as you could probably tell, this happens a lot." He moved to the center of the counter. "So, what may I help you with today?"

"Do you have pink paint that can withstand space travel?" Dania asked.

Cal's wide gaze turned to her.

"What? I didn't want to forget."

The man behind the counter frowned. "I have a base that I can tint, but that's only an add-on service. I don't just sell paint."

"That's fine," Cal said. "I'm looking for a late model light-mounted comm juncture."

The man ran his tongue over his teeth. "Interesting. They're not used much anymore. Too many got lost from ships landing on planets. The hardware ripped off in takeoff and reentry."

From what Alanna had explained, they'd lost theirs when the ship had gotten pulled too close to the black hole that Dania had conjured to save them from Prince Geron. Of course, that same black hole had nearly killed them after Dania had passed out and lost control of the singularity.

"I'm told that's what our ship needs. My crew is pretty good at modifying tech to make it work."

"Yet you lost one." The man quirked a brow.

If she'd been standing here with Kile, he would have pulled the man out from behind the counter by now.

Cal's temperature spiked slightly again, his only sign of annoyance. "Do you have one or not?"

"I actually do. And your lady friend might be on to something. For an extra fifty ducets, I can dip it in an extra layer of heat-sealing polymer before the paint. It will make it much stronger."

"Sounds like a plan."

Cal paid a down payment for the service, and they headed out to the food market.

A smoky scent flowed through the air, followed by something citrusy sweet. Smiling people walked in groups, many laughing as they congregated at wooden tables and booths piled with different types of unfamiliar foods.

Cal took a deep breath of the delectable air. "You can usually find things here that you can't find anywhere else."

"Like what?"

He walked to a vendor and purchased a brown substance molded in perfect spheres.

He handed Dania a piece. "Try this. Just let it sit on your tongue."

Dania sniffed the orb. The scent was odd—spicy with a hint of sweet.

Cal pointed to the confection. "Trust me."

She put the material into her mouth. There was no flavor at first. Then the substance melted into a rich paste. An explosion of sweetness and spice taste rolled over her tongue.

She placed her fingers over his lips, savoring until she had to swallow. "What was that?"

"It's called chocolate. It's made from a bean that will only grow on Earth." He asked the vendor for some more. "This is one of the few places that always seems to have it, and since they're more worried about people being happy than turning a profit, they don't skewer you on the cost."

They strolled through the market, picking up mostly spices and a few more confections.

"Shouldn't we be purchasing more practical supplies?"

"On Hedonaii, very few things are practical. We're better off looking for food the next time we stop."

They collected the comm juncture, which ended up a few shades darker pink that Alanna's hair, before loading the tech onto a hovering cargo cart and heading back to the ship.

All around them, people laughed, some danced, a few even formed small groups and sang. Those who looked at Dania grinned, some even waving. Not a single person looked afraid or ran.

"A penny for your thoughts?" Cal said.

"Pennies were eradicated centuries ago."

Cal laughed. "It's an expression. It means, *what are you thinking about?*"

The streets became more crowded as they neared the ship. "I don't know. It's just so nice here. I feel so..." So what? Alive? Free? Human?

But it really came down to one thing.

"No one is afraid of me."

"And how do you feel about that?"

She should be angry. She should call up what little strength she had and demand the respect of her station.

But she wasn't a general anymore. She was something less.

Or was she something more?

Cal stopped and spun her to him. "This is another step toward freedom. You don't need them to be afraid of you." His grip lightened. "I can see it in your eyes. That's not what you want anymore."

He was right, but that didn't change the gnawing in her gut.

"It's just hard. I'm not used to it." Even that man earlier, who'd wanted to spend time with them... No one outside of her enforcers or her prince had ever wanted to spend time with her. It was startling, upsetting, and...*nice*.

Cal touched the side of her face. Again...*nice*.

"Are you okay?" he asked.

Another couple passed, arm in arm. They smiled at Cal and Dania, and a warmth spread over her.

"Yeah," she decided. "I think I am."

CHAPTER 23

CAL

THE LARGE CROWDS dissipated after funneling to the individual landing ports. Cal and Dania strolled toward the hangars. She didn't seem to be in any more of a rush than he did, looking up at the blinking lights overhead and grinning at the smiling people. Cal wished they could spend a little more time here so he could take her to a show or maybe a gaming center. The possibilities on Hedonaii were endless.

Dania slowed when the Star Renegade came into sight.

The enforcer paced in front of the ship, alone. That probably wasn't good. He should have been with Ethan and Ty—and spending a little extra time with the welcoming committee, if Ty and Ethan's plan had gone well.

Dania stopped walking.

"You okay?" Cal asked her.

It seemed he'd said that a lot today, but this was her first real outing since the visible signs of her former life had disappeared. It must have been strange for her to not have people run like she was the Angel of Death.

The cargo cart caught up to them, hovering just behind her.

"Yeah," Dania said, still watching her commander pace.

If she still had that strange ability to judge people by temperature and stuff like that, she might be reading something on her enforcer friend that she didn't like. Which probably wouldn't bode well for any of them.

Kile stopped when he saw her, straightening his back and lifting his chin, standing perfectly still.

Dania took a deep breath before approaching.

The enforcer barely moved until she was a few inches away. "I've failed you, General. And I am prepared to face your wrath."

Dania closed her eyes, took another slow breath, and opened them. "What happened?"

"I followed the humans like you asked. I led them to a gathering hall and eatery, and they said that was as far as I needed to take them. They said I could remain outside or do whatever I wanted until they called me."

Dania flicked a glance at Cal. "And?"

"I allowed..." He looked down. Oddly enough, that pearly white skin got even paler. "I allowed myself to become distracted."

Cal bit his lips to keep from smiling. Could Ty and Ethan's plan have worked? Had the high-and-mighty enforcer spent his afternoon with someone in the Hedonaii welcoming committee?

Kile swallowed like a kid about to be scolded by a parent, or worse. "When I returned to collect the pilot and the engineer, they were gone. I checked heat signatures, tracked them, I even interrogated some of the patrons, but I was unable to..."

Wait. What? Cal held up his hand. "They're missing?"

"I wouldn't say that." Dania looked toward the far end of

the landing platforms, where Ty and Ethan sprinted toward them. Both their faces were red. Ethan's eyes seemed wild and fixed on the *Renegade*.

By the time they reached the ship, Ty was laughing. "Time to go!"

"Where have you been?" Kile growled through clenched teeth.

"Later, Big Bad!" Ethan tried to tug the enforcer toward the ship, but the larger man barely budged. Ethan shrugged and sprinted up the ramp.

Ty suppressed a chuckle. "I really do think it would be a good time to leave."

"What did you do?" Cal asked.

He placed a hand on his chest. "Me? Nothing." Ty checked the hall they'd come from. "Can I explain later, like…when we're no longer on the ground?"

Dania had already led Kile and the cargo cart up the ramp. Cal shook his head. "Get on board."

Pressing the button to retract the access ramp, Cal headed into the ship after Ty as several large men in black ran into the hangar. One of them glared, pointing at the *Star Renegade*.

Great. Once, just once, Cal would like to leave a spaceport without running for their lives.

CHAPTER 24
CAL

CAL FOLLOWED Ty onto the bridge. Alanna was placing a comm node in her ear, while Ethan tapped buttons on the engineering panel.

"This was supposed to be an easy stop, gentlemen." Cal paused in front of his chair. An old-fashioned board painted in bright colors and intricate designs lay across the controls. "What's this?"

Alanna's eyes widened. "Oh! Sorry." She jumped up and grabbed the board, sliding it under her own station. "Parcheesi. We were playing up here in case anything happened and I needed to start preflight."

Cal didn't even want to know where they'd gotten the board. "Can we lift off?"

She slipped back into her chair. "I had clearance but let me confirm."

The men in black stood outside the window on the deck below, waving their hands in the air and arguing with the workers, pointing at the ship.

"Sooner is better than later. Ty, let's suppose we're going

to get that clearance and get us off the ground and ready to fly out of here."

Hopefully, the hangar stayed open, because they definitely didn't want a black mark from one of the few totally open ports in the galaxy.

"Comm to the captain coming to the main screen," Alanna said.

The window showing the hangar outside shimmered into the face of a woman with short, angled blonde hair and a bright smile. "*Star Renegade*, there appears to be a misunderstanding between someone in your crew and another visitor."

Cal glared at Ty and Ethan. "Really, Hedonaii? I wasn't aware."

Her grin didn't waver. "Our police confirm that you are in the clear. You are free to leave." Her eyes flicked to the side. "Buuuttttt… I'd like to warn you that three ships owned by the other party are firing up their engines and asking for clearance to leave immediately."

Of course they were. "May I ask, since you have confirmed no laws were broken, that you detain those other ships?"

"Everyone is a guest in high regard here on Hedonaii, *Star Renegade*. And we do our best to make sure all of our guests are happy." Her voice was syrupy sweet. "However, we do prefer to stagger ships on exit for everyone's safety."

That sounded promising. "What's a standard stagger?"

"Ten minutes?"

"And today, that standard stagger could maybe be…?"

"Fifteen minutes. That's the best I can do." Her happy expression seemed almost plastic. "But do try to ask your crew to be more courteous to other guests the next time you honor us with your company."

"Yes, ma'am."

Cal wasn't even sure he wanted to know what they'd done. Fifteen minutes was close, but more than enough time to avoid anything unpleasant with Alanna onboard. Cal was just glad that Ty and Ethan hadn't done something so bad that they weren't invited back.

"Ty, take us out."

"With pleasure."

The men in black sunk out of sight as the *Star Renegade* rose off the platform, spun, and headed for the exit. They breezed over the trees before banking up into a greenish-blue sky dusted with light clouds.

Cal sat back as the sky faded into a blanket of black dotted with twinkling stars. He closed his eyes and took a deep breath. *That could have gone far worse.*

"Hold up." Alanna adjusted her earpiece. "I've got chatter. Ty, do you see anything?"

"No, I…wait. We have incoming."

Couldn't be. They still had at least seven minutes. "Are you sure?"

Ty cursed under his breath. "Ethan, it looks like your new best friend had a scout ship out here waiting. Just our luck."

The engineer *tisked.* "Aww come on! Doesn't anyone have a sense of humor anymore?"

"Apparently not." Ty banked them up.

"Is a scout ship a problem?" Cal asked. "Those little skipper ships barely have any firepower."

"Nah, those things are meant for surveillance, not…"

A flash of light lit up the bridge. The ship rumbled.

"Whoa!" Ethan called. "Would you believe they targeted the exact spot the lovely ladies of Themyscira fixed? They were going for the only spot they knew was vulnerable. Someone has really good intel."

And probably didn't know that they'd received a first-class repair. "Let's get out of here."

Ethan cursed. "Hold on. They hit us with some sort of freeze something-or-other. The hull in that section is icing over."

"Icing?"

"The temperature in the cargo hold is plummeting and the rear right hull is a sheet of ice."

"Will it melt?" Cal asked.

Ethan pursed his lips. "In space? I don't know. I don't even know what they did to us. This is a new one on me."

"Ice on the hull?" Cal looked at Alanna. "Does this affect you?"

"I'm with Ethan. I have no idea. I'd be super scared to try jumping."

So they'd just lost their ace in the hole.

Cal's throat dried up. "We are not getting taken out by a tiny scout ship."

The doors slid open, and Kile entered. "May I be of service?"

Alanna stood and pointed at him. "Don't kill anyone."

He narrowed his eyes. "It appears you are rubbing off on my general because she keeps commanding the same thing."

She lifted her chin. "Well, it's a good thing. You should make that a personal motto."

Yeah, like that would ever happen with an enforcer.

The scout ship shot across the view pane. "Can I trust this ship is the cause of your annoyance?"

"Basically," Cal said.

Kile raised his hand and the lights on the ship flying

toward them went out. They kept moving, but more so from momentum than propulsion.

"Do they still have life support?" Cal asked.

"Of course."

Cal turned his chair toward him. "If you can do that, why didn't you do that to the *Star Renegade* when you were chasing us?"

The enforcer quirked a brow. "This is not a scout ship." He pointed out the window. "That vessel is expendable and non-reinforced." He looked at the ceiling, the walls. "And you've made some very illegal modifications to this ship that could cause a good deal of annoyance to anyone trying to catch you. Including me."

Cal couldn't argue with that. He turned back to his console. "Are we okay to move with regular engines?"

"Looks like it," Ethan said. "Just nothing that would supercool us any more than we already are."

Cal stood. "All right. Give me a complete ship scan and let me know if there is anything to worry about." He turned to Ty. "Reset the course to Hitus."

Kile's reflection shone in the window as the enforcer inclined his head slightly. "Thank you."

Thank you? For what—resetting our course? "You're, umm, welcome."

A tone sounded and the speakers flicked on.

Doc's voice. "Boss?"

Cal flipped on the comm. "Talk to me."

Doc sighed on the line. "I think we have a problem."

"No more problems allowed. I'm making a motion that the next twenty-four hours are problem-free."

"Well, that's fine and good and all, but I need a rollcall."

A what? "Come again?"

"Who's on the bridge?"

Cal looked around. "Me, Ty, Alanna, Ethan, and…" He glanced at the enforcer. "And the commander." Which was far too many in the tiny room.

"Okay. Dania is with me."

So what was his point? "Good. Everyone is present and accounted for."

"Not really so good." He made some tapping sounds. "There are seven of us, but I'm scanning eight heartbeats on the ship."

Cal glanced at the others, but they all looked just as dumbfounded. "Come again?"

"I'm picking up an extra heartbeat in the primary cargo hold."

"That's impossible."

"I checked it five times. It's erratic, but it's there."

Ethan pressed some buttons on the panel to his right, where Doc normally worked. "He's right." He spun toward them. "Boss, I think we've got a stowaway."

"A what?"

"You heard me." Ethan paled, looking back at the engineering screen. "Boss, it's below freezing down there. If they're still alive, they won't be for long."

CHAPTER 25

DANIA

IN THE MED BAY, Dania stared at the comm box as Cal cursed on the other side of the line. "Doc, get Dania to the cargo hold ASAP."

Peter flicked a glance at her before hitting the comm. "What's going on?"

Ty answered. "The enforcer just took off, and Cal ran after him. We might have a stowaway." The line clicked, like he'd switched to a portable device. "Dania? Is stealing a ride on a starship a capital offense?"

Dania flinched. Under the law of the king, everything was a capital offense.

Peter flipped the comm. "We're coming." He grabbed her arm and they sprinted down the hall.

Just a few days ago, Kile had confided in Dania that while he knew he was on a mission, he'd missed enforcing the law. If he'd raced for the cargo hold, he might inflict punishment before she'd be able to stop him. If this stowaway had broken the law, the person needed to be dealt with, but they needed to give the person a chance to explain and maybe give them a punishment that wasn't quite so...*final.*

They made it down the ladder to the lower level just as Cal and Ty disappeared behind the first row of cargo, heading toward the same area Dania and Alanna had repaired before they'd found their way back to charted space. A chill swept over Dania, as if snow were falling on the other side of those containers.

She rubbed her shoulders as she stepped onto the deck and followed. "What happened?"

Ty held up a device with flashing lights on the end. "A skipper ship hit us with some kind of coolant beam."

Dania shivered. A very effective coolant beam.

Kile stalked toward some containers, his eyes wide and predatory.

She moved toward him. "Do not kill anyone."

He glared over his shoulder. His breath puffed out in a white cloud. "A law has been broken."

"But not a big one. This crime does not necessitate death."

He opened his mouth to speak when Peter called out. "I got him!" He started shifting boxes, Ty helping.

Dania approached with Kile as they stopped moving the boxes.

"Whoa," Ty whispered.

A woman with dark coppery, almost-brown hair lay curled up in a ball with her eyes closed, creasing a dirty brown flight suit. She was probably a little older than Ethan.

Kile's hair flailed up and the air about him wavered. Dania grabbed his arm.

Cal jumped between the commander and the stowaway. "It's okay, this is no big deal."

Kile's eyes were wide. "This is a very big deal."

Cal held up his palms. "No, it's not. We can just drop her off at the next way station. It'll be no inconvenience at all."

Kile spoke through clenched teeth. "You do not understand."

"She's breathing!" Peter announced. "We've gotta get her out of here and warmed up, though."

Ty leaned down to help pick her up.

Kile's hands trembled, his gaze locked on the unresponsive girl as Ty cradled her in his arms.

Dania's heart tightened. Crimes needed to be punished, and all punishments led to death. This wasn't a choice; it was part of who an enforcer was. There wasn't an option for them. It was just the horrific truth.

Kile needed to execute this lawbreaker with every cell of his body, and since the girl didn't have any part in the mission to save Alexander, even Dania's orders might not be able to stop him.

She tugged him away from the stowaway. Thankfully, the much larger man complied.

"Come on. You're not needed here."

"T-The girl." He nearly choked on the words—the stutter was so odd from him. A year ago, she may have thought he needed to be fed.

Could that be the case? Was he wavering?

From the angry look in his eyes, it was unlikely.

"This is a matter for the crew," she said. "Let the captain take care of it." Hopefully, he would comply, because if their places had been changed, and Dania had been the fully charged enforcer, that girl would already be dead.

CAL STOMPED toward the med bay. He'd helped Dania calm the enforcer down, but the commander had kept trying to find ways to check on their unwanted guest.

Everyone on the ship was on the same page: the enforcer got nowhere near the stowaway. Period.

Cal shook his head. That girl had chosen the wrong ship. If the commander had dropped the emergency airlock doors in the cargo bay when he'd gotten there, he may have been alone when he'd found her, and she'd be dead.

Cal had hidden in a fair share of cargo containers in his youth. He knew what it was like to need to get off a planet but not have a means to pay. He understood it was wrong, but he also understood what it was to be desperate.

That didn't mean he wanted anyone else they didn't know on the ship, though. The girl better be happy with Hitus because that was where she'd be getting off.

He stepped into the med bay. Ty stood beside one of the beds, his arms folded, while Doc ran a scanner over the shivering girl. She sat on the edge of the gurney, a blanket partially covering a brown casual work suit with one of those short useless over-jackets like Alanna always wore. Fashion was something Cal would never understand.

Ethan handed Doc something out of a cabinet on the wall while Alanna placed another blanket around the girl's shoulders.

The stowaway looked up at him through long, straight strands of red hair—not the harsh bright red like Ethan's but a dark chestnut-red.

Doc handed her a steaming mug. "Drink this. Let's see if we can get you warmed up on the inside."

"How's she doing?" Cal asked.

"Mild hypothermia." Doc leaned closer to her. "Is your sight getting better?"

She nodded and sipped the drink.

"Ethan says the compartment should be back to normal temperatures within a few hours. The ship seems fine otherwise," Ty said.

"Good to know."

The girl perked up. "He's giving you a report. Does that mean you're the captain?"

Cal didn't have a chance to respond.

She jumped from the mattress, spilling the drink. "I want to see the big guy."

Cal cocked his head. "Big guy?"

Ty made an exaggerated grimace. "The commander?"

Had she lost a few brain cells when she'd nearly frozen to death?

Doc eased her back to the gurney. "That's not going to happen. And believe me, it's for your own good."

The door opened, and the girl's eyes widened.

The enforcer stepped through, with Dania beside him. Had she lost her mind?

"There you are!" The girl threw her blanket back and ran to Kile, throwing her arms around him.

The enforcer stood stiff, his arms at his sides, barely budging when it seemed like the small woman hit him with all her strength.

"I knew I'd find you," she said, her voice muffled in his chest.

The enforcer looked straight ahead, still not moving. "You've broken a law."

The girl leaned back. "Just a little one. Everyone hitches a ride sometimes."

Kile closed his eyes, took a deep breath, and continued to stare at the far wall, seeming oblivious to the small female body attached to his torso. "You did not hitch a ride. You snuck onto a vessel and purloined transportation off planet." He swallowed deeply pulling her from his chest. "And for this, you must be punished."

"Whoa!" Cal held up his hands. "She had a ticket. Everything is fine."

Kile glared at him. "She did not have a ticket."

"Yes, she did. I'd just forgotten."

The stowaway rose from the floor. Her eyes widened as she kicked her feet.

"Kile! Stop!" Dania called.

Cal moved closer. "I swear, I only forgot that I'd sold her a ticket."

Dania pushed between them. "Put her down, Kile."

The woman's feet touched the floor, but he didn't release her.

The enforcer glared at Cal. "You are lying. No money changed hands, or you would have said something."

Cal took a step farther. "She just hasn't paid *yet*."

The woman's eyes widened, maybe only just realizing what a precarious position she was in. She shoved her hand in her pocket and handed Cal a silver ducet. "Here you go, Captain. Is this enough?"

Cal put the coin in his own pocket. "Yup, that will do fine. You are paid in full."

Kile's breathing started to even out. The stowaway let out a breath and took a step back.

"Wow." She mopped her brow with the sleeve of her jacket. "That was interesting." A smile burst across her face. "And fun!" She threw her arms around the commander again, plastering his arms to his sides. "We need to do that again sometime."

Ethan took a hesitant step forward. "Do you two, umm, know each other?"

Kile said *no* at the same time the girl said *yes*.

What in the name of Jupiter's storm was going on?

Kile's nose flared. "Technically, I suppose we are acquainted. This is..." He grimaced. "I do not know your name."

She leaned away to look up into his eyes "That's okay. I don't know yours, either." She stepped back and held out her right hand. "My name is Quirky. Rachel Quirky."

The former stowaway waited while the enforcer frowned at her.

"You're supposed to grab my hand." Rachel placed his right hand in hers. "And then you shake." She held their hands together, moving their arms up and down. "And now is where you say: *Pleased to meet you* and tell me your name."

He continued to stare down at her, his expression blank.

She released his hand. "That's okay. I can just keep calling you 'Big Guy.' That kind of fits." Rachel spun, taking in the crew. "So, I guess this is everybody?"

She turned to Cal. "You must be the egotistical captain who has no business giving orders to the Big Guy's general."

Cal glared at the enforcer, but the commander continued to look forward.

The woman looked at Alanna. "Pink hair. You are the pretty one with the crew wrapped around her moderately adept fingers. You sound like my kind of girl."

Alanna blinked, looking at Doc and Ethan. Doc shrugged like he might agree.

Rachel pointed at Ty. "Are you the pilot with the completely unjustified superiority complex?"

Ty gaped.

"I'll take that as a *yes*." She spun to Ethan. "Red hair. That makes you the capable, yet infuriating engineer."

Ethan straightened, beaming. "Did you hear that? I'm capable."

She looked in Doc's direction. "I guess that makes you the utterly incompetent illegally practicing doctor."

Doc scowled, mouth open.

Then to Dania. "And you would be the most gifted person he's ever met, who's throwing her life away for some foolish reason he can't even begin to comprehend."

Dania closed her eyes and lowered her head.

Rachel clapped her hands. "That was fun! Did I get it all right? Did I miss anyone?"

Ethan raised his hand. "I just want to reiterate that I'm the capable one."

"Shut up, Ethan," Ty and Doc said in unison.

"See?" Ethan looked at the newcomer. "I get no respect."

"Enough of this ludicrousness!" Kile turned to the girl. "What are you doing on this ship?"

Rachel caressed his cheek. "I missed you."

He narrowed his eyes. "I've only been gone a few hours."

"That was too long."

Kile cocked his head. "We don't know each other."

"Yes, we do. I just introduced myself. But that's okay. We have plenty of time to get to know each other better." She turned to Cal. "I paid for my passage. I'm a real passenger, and now I want you to make me a member of the crew."

Cal balked. "What?"

"The crew." She tilted her head. "Are you really daft and clueless? Because I figured the Big Guy was just exaggerating."

Cal sighed, glaring at the enforcer before returning his gaze to Rachel. The last thing he needed was another mouth to feed. "Sorry, we don't have any openings."

"Sure you do. The Big Guy says you're a sorry lot that barely knows how to ignite their engines." She rubbed her chin. "I honestly don't know how to ignite an engine, but I do know some other stuff."

"Like what?" Ethan asked.

Cal pointed at him. "Stay out of this." And to Rachel. "I don't have enough room for anyone else on this crew."

"You don't need room." She hugged the enforcer again. "I'll just stay with the Big Guy. No room needed."

"I am not sharing my room," Kile said.

She looked up at him. "Why not? You said sleeping with me was *a most agreeable experience that you wouldn't mind repeating.*" She tapped his chest. "If we share a room, we can repeat yesterday every night."

The enforcer lowered his eyes. A slight grin touched his lips before the stoic blankness returned to his face.

Of all the moons in the galaxy...was this the person that Ty and Ethan had set him up with? Had this petite woman been on the Hedonaii welcoming committee?

Cal turned to them. Ty raised his hands, while Ethan shifted his weight.

"I can earn my keep," Rachel said. "I don't want a free ride. My mama raised me better than that." She glanced at Doc. "I was a med tech on Hedonaii. If you are as incompetent as the Big Guy says, you could use my skills."

Cal gritted his teeth. "Doc is not incompetent." He turned to Kile. "I am not happy with you bad-mouthing my crew behind their backs."

Kile folded his arms. "I am an enforcer. I am incapable of not telling the truth."

Cal shook his head. "You are such a charmer. Stop trying to cozy up and get on our good sides."

Dania held up her hands. "Stop this." But she looked like she was at a loss as to what else to say, as was Cal.

"I think it's a great idea," Ty said. "I mean, why not let Big Bad have a friend to pal around with?" He leaned closer to Cal. "Keep him busy."

That wasn't exactly the kind of distraction that Cal had in mind.

They had hoped to find a way for Kile to find his human side. Rachel Quirky might be just the right kick in his libido to jumpstart his return to humanity. But Cal had never intended on this little experiment leaving Hedonaii.

This was the longest of long shots, and probably one of Ty and Ethan's dumber ideas. There were a million ways that this could go wrong, and only a few ways it might go right.

Ty raised his hand. "All those in favor of letting Miss Quirky stay, say *aye*."

Ayes rang out through the room. Kile muttered no.

Rachel elbowed him in the gut, and he barely moved. "You big kidder. He wants me to stay!"

Kile looked at Cal, an odd hint of defeat in his eyes, but also a look of hope, like the *egotistical captain who has no business giving orders* might swoop in and save him.

Maybe Cal did have an ego problem because he found this incredibly amusing, and he wanted to see how it played out. Maybe this petite redhead was just what they needed to bring the enforcer to his knees.

Cal raised his hand. "Aye."

CHAPTER 27

DANIA

WARMTH GRAZED Dania's fingertips as she placed the lid on what Cal had called a *crock-pot*, although she was still sure he was making that name up. The essence of the tomatoes and spices already eddied up from the green ceramic pottery.

"What was that green leafy substance you stirred into it?" she asked.

"Oregano. It's the magic ingredient. It's what brings it all together for that old world taste."

She closed her eyes and drank in the aroma. "It smells so good."

Cal reached over and changed the setting from high to low. "You haven't smelled anything yet. In about eight hours, this will be like walking around in Heaven." He licked his lips. "The longer it cooks, the better it tastes."

"Is that true? Why is that?"

"I really don't know, to be honest, but it does. And even better…" He wiped his hand on a white towel. "If we let it cool and then refrigerate it overnight, the flavors will just explode the next time we heat it up."

"That makes no sense."

He held up his hands. "I surrender, General. And I agree it shouldn't be possible, but wait until you taste it. Facts are facts."

The green ceramic sat on the counter, looking so unassuming for what sounded like the catalyst of some sort of witchcraft. She still didn't believe that cooking anything longer, let alone reheating it, would make it taste better, but she couldn't wait for him to prove her wrong.

"Are we going to talk about the elephant in the room?" Cal asked.

Dania took in the shiny cabinets and freshly-wiped countertops. "I don't believe there is an elephant in this room."

Cal laughed. "It's a saying. It means, 'the big thing we're not talking about that we should be talking about.'"

She turned and washed her hands in the sink. "You mean Kile and that woman."

"That woman's name is Rachel, and while she doesn't seem to be worried about the commander blowing a fuse around her, I need to know if she's in any danger with him."

Dania shook off her hands and grabbed a towel. "I don't think so." The whole situation was just so...strange. "I just can't imagine what they could have talked about while they were on the planet that would make her want to stowaway on a ship to see him again."

Cal pressed his lips together as a pink flush tainted his cheeks.

"What?"

"Nothing." He shook his head. "I just needed to make sure he's not going to lash out irrationally, because she seems a little more...*open* than he's used to."

Open was an interesting way to put it.

The comm dinged.

Ty's voice. "Boss?"

Cal hit the switch. "Talk to me."

"My surrogate mother on Kirato, a.k.a. Mel, made me promise I'd never drive this ship tired. I gotta admit I'm seeing double up here."

Not surprising. The pilot's temperature fluctuations made it obvious his body had not caught up to his long days scanning Kile's pilfered data.

"We also just got a new course from Dania's bestie," Ty said.

Cal frowned. "We're not going to Hitus anymore?"

"Nope."

Cal groaned. "I'm coming." He tapped the comm to turn it off before turning to Dania. "Sorry to cut your cooking lesson short."

"It's okay." She looked at the crockpot. "But I want to taste that in eight hours."

His smile dazzled. "It's a date."

———

Kile stood on the far side of the lounge, hands folded behind his back as he stared out into the vast space beyond the window. Rachel Quirky leaned against the wall beside him with her arms folded and a scowl on her face.

She pursed her lips when Dania entered. "He's being broody again." She pushed away from the wall. "I mean, it's sexy and all, but it's getting a little annoying. I hate not getting my way."

Kile continued to look through the glass. "I told you I don't have time for trivialities."

She giggled and rubbed a hand down his back. "That's not what you said last night."

Kile's temperature warmed.

Maybe Cal was right to be worried about her safety. Kile did tend to be hot-tempered. However, the temperature change was not spiky like anger, and not a slow, internal burning like a lie. The heat seemed somehow...*deeper*.

Rachel leaned up on her toes, but she still barely reached his ear as she whispered, "Please come back to the room with me. We can do that floaty thing."

"I told you I was otherwise occupied."

She plopped back on her heels. "Looking out a window? It's just stars. How interesting are stars?"

Kile finally looked at her. "No!"

Dania raised her hands, ready to defend the woman, but Kile didn't lash out further than raising his voice before he returned his gaze to the window.

Rachel waved her hands in the air. "Fine I'll go see if the doctor wants to play with me." She headed for the door.

Kile looked over his shoulder. "The doctor?"

Rachel walked backward toward the exit. "Jealous?"

"Hardly."

The stowaway snorted. "Liar." She turned to Dania. "He's all yours." And to Kile, "You know where to find me."

Kile's lips twitched into a grin as he watched her go before turning back to the window.

Interesting. "She amuses you?" Dania asked.

"Oddly enough, yes."

That was good news. If she amused him, Kile was more apt to put up with her idiosyncrasies.

The ship hummed beneath Dania's feet, and the stars

outside the window shifted as she stepped into the room. "You ordered a change in course?"

He didn't turn around. "I did."

"May I ask where?"

"Yes, you may. You are my general." He turned toward her. "We are heading to Elbus. I'm not sure which of the clustered asteroids we will be visiting, but the co-pilot's trace on the ship that took Alexander ended there."

"Elbus?" It was a long-range communication station in a cluster of three asteroids in orbit around a small sun. A few million years ago, they'd started to spin enough for gravity, and engineers had discovered a way to make them hold an atmosphere, but there was no soil to grow food, so outside the facility, there wasn't much to offer. Other than being a beacon to bounce long-range communications, there was nothing there. "We usually consider Elbus a dead zone."

"Which is why it is the perfect place to trade something as illicit as a sentient being."

Possibly, but Alexander had been missing for quite some time. "You can't expect him to still be there."

"No, but it is our last lead. We need to find something there." His eyes flared. "We have no other choice. We may be able to find record of where they took him, and what condition he was in." He looked back to the window. "At this point we have nothing to help our search. Even the smallest morsel of information would be something."

He tried to keep himself erect, but his posture wasn't as stiff as it normally seemed.

Kile was always in control, always sure. Not knowing where Alexander was probably hurt him just as much as it hurt Dania, though maybe in a different way.

He lowered his eyes. "Before Alexander disappeared, we

found evidence of two other enforcers passing through Elbus. The files were hidden well, but we had been investigating this area for some time."

"Who were the others?"

"Asaina DuRaden."

Dania had heard the name, a young enforcer from a lower house. "And the other?"

He grimaced. "Matara."

Dania winced. Matara had been a strong enforcer not far from ending her training. Dania had molded the girl, worked with her to make her stronger than most of the men…and then she disappeared. Part of the reason Dania had first volunteered to be taken by the trappers was to get Matara back. She never dreamed she'd be looking for Alexander as well.

"Two of our best," Dania whispered.

"Indeed."

"We'll find them," she said. "Failure is not an option." And it wasn't. She'd find them and make their captors pay for their crimes. Dania wouldn't tolerate her people, her friends, being enslaved.

"I'm glad to hear you say that. I was beginning to wonder."

She cocked her head. "Wonder about what?"

He looked back to her reflection in the glass and raised his hand. His fingers glowed slightly before the reflection sharpened, making the glass more like a mirror. "Look at yourself. Certainly, you have to see what I see."

Yes, she could see it. Her hair no longer floated. Her eyes had darkened, and her skin and hair were no longer strikingly pale. She looked warm, inviting, *human*.

"You're smiling," he said through clenched teeth. "This.

You." He pointed at the reflection. "This is not amusing. You cannot tell me anything about this crew is even remotely interesting enough to make you forsake all that you are."

Dania sighed. "It's not just the crew. They've shown me things."

"What could they possibly show you to make it worth a slow death without your sponsor?"

Dania cringed, inwardly reaching for the new pathogens Peter had injected into her blood. They weren't as strong as, and didn't have the warmth of her sponsor's love, but she had to admit, she was starting to feel better, or maybe if not better, more human.

Of course, she couldn't tell Kile about Peter's pathogen experiment. He might execute the doctor in a vain attempt to save her, despite her no-kill order.

But freeing her from Geron wasn't the only thing of interest.

"They showed me that I have a family somewhere."

"The Banes—the enforcers—are your family, as they are mine."

She shook her head. "No, my *birth* family. I'd like to know more about them, and I like that I can make the choice to do so on my own."

"A frivolous need that you would not be encumbered with if you were still under Geron's care."

"You don't understand. I *want* to be encumbered. This feeling of freedom, it's like nothing I've ever experienced."

"Better than being fully charged? Better than having the power of a prince running through your veins, ready to release at your will?"

Dania looked down. She had to admit, she missed the strength, the bond, and never having to worry. Being human was hard, but being able to go where she wanted, do what she wanted, not having to kill people for frivolous or accidental crimes…

Enforcers were cursed, and they didn't even know it.

Kile glared at her reflection. "You are encumbered in ways that you do not even realize, and it sickens me."

She straightened. "I'm not."

"You are. You are so enraptured by these humans that you cannot see it." He pointed out the window, to the star in the distance becoming brighter. "When we get to Elbus, we could very well be going into battle. And you can no longer be trusted to do your duty."

"How dare you! I have every intention of doing my duty. I love Alexander with all my soul. Don't you think I want him back?"

His lips twisted. "You did love him, maybe as much as you loved our sponsor, but not anymore."

"That's not true."

"Really?" He sneered at her, a gesture she would have wiped the floor with him for only a few months ago. "If we find Alexander, and there is a skirmish and you can only save one person, Alexander, or the captain of this star-forsaken junk ship, who would you save?"

Dania's stomach turned, imagining both Cal and Alexander on their knees, guns to their heads.

"Who would you save, Dania? The criminal or your best friend? The smuggler or the man your sponsor ordered us to find?"

Her chest thickened, and she wanted to vomit because there was only one answer.

"Alexander," she whispered. And it was the truth. If it came between the two of them, she'd let Cal die.

Kile shifted his weight, his eyes widening slightly. "Are you sure?"

She took a deep breath, doing her best to squelch the need to puke. She leveled her gaze on him. "Yes. I'd save Alexander."

He stared at her, maybe gauging her temperature before his features softened. "Good. When all of this is done, I hope you come back to your senses and return to Keveron with us. It's time to end this insanity."

She flinched, backing away. Her chest ached as she stumbled from the room. A hint of tomato scent still hung in the air. She backed against the wall as the hallway spun around her.

How could she do that? How could she imagine the unthinkable and so quickly condemn a man who'd taken her in, saved her when she was so far from being saved?

Worse, how could she even consider for a second letting Alexander die instead of Cal?

She shook her head, trying to clear the fuzz.

That was the problem—she hadn't considered letting Alexander die, and she really wasn't now. Even away from Kile, the answer was simple, as it always had been for her. An enforcer follows orders. Nothing else mattered.

She sprinted down the hallway to Area Two, slapped her palm on the med bay door, and stumbled inside.

Peter's eyes widened. "Whoa there. Where's the fire?"

"I need pathogens." She grabbed his shoulders. "I need you to give them to me now."

"Calm down." He guided her toward a bed. "Sit down and take a deep breath."

"I don't want to take a deep breath. I need you to fix me."

He shined a light into her eyes. "What happened?"

Nothing happened. Not yet.

She rubbed her shoulders. "I just need them. Please. Give me the pathogens."

He leaned away, turning off the light. "I can't. The next batch isn't ready."

"What do you mean they aren't ready?" Her voice cracked, and she covered her mouth. She held her breath, but a sob broke free.

Peter sat on the bed beside her. "Sweetie, what happened?"

She shook her head. "Kile gave me a hypothetical ultimatum, and I answered truthfully."

"And you didn't like the answer?"

She shook her head. "I answered like an enforcer. I didn't think. I just answered."

"But you're thinking now, right?"

"Yes, and I hate myself because even when I've had time to think about it, the answer is the same." She rubbed her face. "I don't want to be that person anymore. I want to do the right thing. I want to…"

To what, let Alexander die? No. Of course not.

She hugged herself. "I'm so confused. Being an enforcer was so easy. There was always only one answer to every question."

Peter nodded. "And sometimes questions are difficult, and there is no good choice, no matter how hard you think about something."

She wiped her eyes. "Then what do you do?"

"Well, some people say you find out what you are made of in situations like that."

"What if you have to decide who lives and who dies?"

He took a deep breath. "That's always tough. Everyone

hopes that they will never be in that situation, but I'd like to think I'd be quick enough on my feet to think of an alternate solution."

Dania trembled. "I'm so afraid that I won't be able to."

He rubbed her back. "Sometimes we face no-win situations. That's life. You just have to trust that you'll be strong enough to make the right decision when that time comes."

The whole idea seemed so abstract, so stressful. As an enforcer, if someone broke a law, they were executed without question, without remorse. There was never a choice. Her actions were robotic. Pre-determined.

But if they were innocent… If there were a choice…

She shivered. How could there ever be a right decision if she were forced to decide who lived and who died?

CHAPTER 28

CAL

THE MASSIVE ROCKY surface of Elbus One hung below them as Ty flicked on the comm. "Elbus, this is the *Star Renegade* coming in from your Hitus side. Please confirm we are still cleared for landing."

Static filled the line before a man's voice answered. "Affirmative, *Star Renegade*. We have a crew waiting for you at landing site nine. Please cut your main engines and fly in manually."

Ty glanced at Cal. Had they just said what he thought they'd said?

Cal flipped on his mic. "Elbus, did you just say there was a crew waiting? May I ask what for?"

"Engineers and technicians," the voice said. "You are scheduled for repairs."

"Repairs?" Cal said to Ty.

His first mate shrugged. "You got me."

Cal flicked the comm again. "Elbus, we have not requested any repairs."

"I have three hours of general maintenance bought and paid for by one Christopher Columbus."

Cal sat back, while Ty gaped.

Ty turned off his comm. "Maybe he's paying us back for almost getting us killed?"

Cal grimaced. "Or maybe he's paying it forward for almost getting us killed again." With Chris, they could never be sure.

The huge asteroid loomed closer as Ty adjusted their speed. "What do you want to do?"

Run. But the enforcer would never go for that. They needed to trust that Kile was enough of a badass to scare even Chris, if the pirate had something dirty up his sleeve.

Ty, Ethan, and Cal stepped off the landing platform. Kile, Dania, and Alanna watched from the bridge above. The enforcer hadn't even blinked when Cal had told him about Chris. However, he was annoyed when Dania suggested they should both stay on board, which made sense because the last thing they should do was parade around an enforcer if these asteroids really were friendly to slavers.

Chris held out his arms walking toward them. His brown hair was swept back in the same style he'd always had, but his stubbly beard was a little longer. "Cal, old buddy. Good to see you guys in one piece." He gave Cal a hug. "Ethan!" He shook the engineer's hands. "Did you have any problem installing the frame relay transducer? Damn nice piece of tech, huh?"

Ethan flinched, glancing at Cal.

Soon after they'd picked up Dania, Chris had met them on Cannis Proper, ready to do a fair trade. But like on many pirate worlds, fair trades rarely went as expected. The people pulling the strings planned on screwing them, so Chris had slipped them a frame relay transducer to make up for their losses.

He'd probably meant it to spruce up the *Star Renegade*'s engines, but instead, they'd traded it to Cal's friend Glenn for enough citrus fruits to keep the colonists on Kirato happy for another month or so.

Cal folded his arms. "You're far too well informed to not know we traded it."

"I knew you traded something big on Port Walker, and then all hell broke loose when you tried to leave. But the way you busted out of there and then showed up at the Brim Cluster in record time, I had to wonder." Chris looked back to Ethan. "I figured maybe you were some kind of technical genius to get the tech installed and operational that fast."

Cal tensed. They *had* made good time, but that was only because Dania had conjured a black hole. It was like nothing Cal had ever seen. Of course, she'd used the same trick to escape her boss and had gotten them stranded in the middle of nowhere. After the second time, he knew he never wanted to see anything like that again.

"Past aside," Cal said, "what are you doing here?"

Chris's eyes narrowed. "I was going to ask you the same thing."

Cal stared him down. He should ask about the paid-upfront repairs. He should push the issue. But the itching in his gut told him not to. "What do you want, Chris?"

"I thought maybe we could have a drink, and I wanted to help repair your ship after we got screwed back on Cannis."

Heat flushed through Cal. "*We* got screwed? I believe I'm the one who got screwed."

Chris held out his hands. "That was not what I agreed to.

You know me better. I'd never cut a deal that would put a friend in danger."

That, Cal would have believed maybe a year ago, but now Chris ran in pirate circles, and he'd been cutting closer to the edge of cutthroat every time they saw him.

Cal inched closer to Chris, adjusting the sack on his shoulder. "For old time's sake, should I be ready to blast the ship out of here, or should we expect a nice, relaxing exit?"

Chris pointed his chin at Cal's crew. "Ty and Ethan are standing on the same planet when you ask that question. I can make no guarantees that those two won't get into any trouble, but if they do, it will have nothing to do with me."

Cal wished he had Dania here to tell him if the pirate were lying. He turned to Ty and Ethan. "Why don't you guys go ahead and see if you can trade for food?" Which was code, of course, for 'talk to Kile on the comm and find out whatever information you can.'

"You sure?" Ty asked.

No. But he nodded yes. "I'll meet you back at the ship in two hours." Unless he could speed things up with Chris, without making it look like they'd sped things up.

As Ty and Ethan disappeared into the facility, Chris shielded his eyes, looking at the *Renegade*. "Hey up there, Alanna!"

She waved from atop the ship.

"What's she doing?" Chris tilted his head "Is that a piece of pink hardware?"

Cal grinned. "Actually, it is. Her personal request."

Chris furrowed his brow. "Pink? She knows she won't even see it after she installs it, right?"

"Hey, it made her happy."

Chris lowered his hand. "Do you want the maintenance guys I bought for you to help her up there?"

Alanna moved about the ship, unfazed by being that high off the ground. In general, she didn't like being treated like a girl. They'd all learned to not offer help unless she asked first. "They might be putting their lives at risk by offering, but they can certainly try." He tapped off a text, advising her to make sure no one put any trackers on the hull.

Chris clapped his hands. "So, I thought we'd go get some lunch. Catch up on old times."

This was when the trouble would probably start.

The invitation was actually not unlike Chris. Before the incident on Cannis, Cal wouldn't have even blinked before accepting. Chris was a good contact, even if he couldn't be completely trusted.

If Cal didn't go, Chris would get suspicious. Which might lead to him trying to finagle his way onto the ship. Cal just needed to be smart and keep his eyes open.

They walked through the large metal doors meant for cargo containers.

Cal held his breath, waiting for the massive metal frame to slam down, trapping him inside. When that didn't happen, he breathed a little easier.

The air was still heavy with questions, though. "You never answered when I asked what you were doing here."

Chris shrugged. "Trading, making deals. Keeping my friends alive." He flashed a smile at Cal. "You guys make that hard sometimes."

"It's been a rough couple of months."

"Yeah, you guys drifted off the grid for quite a while. Chatter said the Banes were hot on your trail." Chris pushed through a door that led to a small bar. "I'd have lain low, too."

Chris waved to a guy whose neck was thicker than Cal's legs, and they were escorted to a back room.

The hair rose on the back of Cal's neck. "I didn't know you could afford a private room, buddy."

Chris puffed out a mirthless laugh. "I could always afford one. I just never saw the need."

"Until now?"

"I'm not an ass." Chris looked away. "Well, I am, but I'm not a complete ass."

"Meaning?"

Chris puffed out a breath, dragging his hands through his tightly cropped hair. "I meant it when I said I protected my friends. That's why I came down here in person."

Sweat beaded Cal's brow. He checked for exit points.

Other than the door they'd come from, there were none.

Chris didn't even look at him. "They promised you'd walk out of this room in one piece."

Cal gritted his teeth. Sometimes he hated it when he was right.

He checked over both shoulders, but the room was bare. "Who promised?"

The door opened, and a single man entered. His long, dark coat changed from black to brown, then back to black as the fabric shifted over his legs. His skin tone wavered from dark to light, and his black hair shortened, grew, and shortened three times before he stopped in front of Cal.

The man turned to Chris. "Mr. Columbus, your debt is now paid. You may leave the planet unfettered."

Chris's eyes darted to Cal. "I was made a promise. Cal leaves with me."

"The terms were never that he would leave with you. You will leave immediately, or terms of our agreement are defunct."

Sweat dotted Chris's brow. He pointed to Cal. "He walks out of here alive when this is done. That was our deal."

"Unlike the Bane king, the Cartek Empire always keeps its promises."

The Cartek Empire? *Shit!*

Chris met Cal's gaze with apologetic eyes, and backed out of the room.

Whatever they had on the pirate, it had to be good. At least his friend had the decency to barter for Cal's life before he'd betrayed him again.

The Cartek's eyes changed from black to pink to gray. Cal had never met one before, but even after reading accounts, nothing could have prepared him for how unsettling the cloaking effect was.

He swallowed deeply. "That human-outfit doesn't look like it fits all that well on you."

The Cartek snickered, a sound akin to walking on broken glass. He held out his hands and looked down himself. "We are told that this puts humans more at ease."

More at ease than looking at a walking squid-like creature? Maybe. Maybe not. "What do you want?"

"Right to the point. You certainly do meet expectations, Captain Espinoza."

"You have me at a disadvantage."

The Cartek held out his hands and bowed. "I am known as Rgrythei."

"Great. What do you want, Rgrythei?"

A hint of a tentacle flashed into view as he walked. That kind of cloaking technology could be a game changer, if they figured out a way to make it work without the flashing and changing colors.

Rgrythei held out his hands wide, probably trying to mimic human movement, and failing. "We know you have two enforcers on your ship."

"After blasting out of that pirate colony, everyone knows we have at least one on board."

"We want you to disseminate information to us about their sponsor."

Prince Geron? "Why?"

"The Cartek Empire, as always, hopes to free the people of Earth from the wrath of the Banes."

Cal's chest tightened. The Carteks had decimated several of Earth's colonies before the Banes arrived, offering assistance. Earth had agreed to the Banes' protection without fully understanding all the consequences. However, living under the king's stringent laws was still better than being exterminated by the Carteks.

"I think you have the wrong royal," Cal said. "From what I've been told, the prince is mostly a pretty boy who uses his family money on women and partying. He's not part of the military, or anyone even remotely important."

"This information is inconsequential. The Cartek Empire wants him dead."

Interesting. Why not go after one of the military princes or princesses... someone who actually mattered politically?

The Cartek folded his arms. "I believe this is the time in a human negotiation where you are supposed to say, 'What's in it for me.'"

Okay, I guess I'll bite. "What's in it for me?"

Rgrythei held up his palm, and a holographic image of the *Star Renegade* appeared. "Your ship is small, but formidable."

He looked up. "It would be even more of a nuisance to the Banes with a transient spatial inhibitor."

Cal stared at the spinning hologram. Should he admit he had no idea what a spatial inhibitor was? Let alone a transient one? Maybe not. "We've done pretty well without alien tech."

Rgrythei closed his hand, and the hologram winked out. "Yes, you have. But lately, you have been involved in more skirmishes than you are accustomed to."

Yeah, things like that happened when you added an enforcer to your crew.

The Cartek's cloak changed from black to gray to black again. "My spatial inhibitor is mobile and does not require permanent installation."

"So?"

"So, dear human, you can change placement at will. You can decide with minimal effort which system to add the additional power to."

Add additional power?

"I see the question brewing in your neuropathways. Yes, this device will supercharge any ship system for approximately thirty-five of your minutes."

"Including the engines?" Cal bit his lip, wishing he'd held that question back. It was always better to not look too hungry in a negotiation.

"Of course the engines. A valuable asset for a smuggling ship, and more than enough to spike an engine to escape the law, or to propel a message through space in minutes rather than hours."

Propel a message through space? So that's how they were talking to the pirates. And if he could juice the engines, he wouldn't have to rely on Alanna so much.

That kind of tech could really save their hides. Especially if they were able to save Dania's friend and then found themselves running from Kile, rather than working with him. Heck, for all Cal knew, they might even be running from that Alexander guy when this all played out.

"Your answer, Captain Espinoza?" Rgrythei asked.

The big question in the air, was why did they want Dania's prince...a nobody...dead?

There was a piece of this puzzle missing, and Cal didn't like it. He needed to talk to someone smarter than him. "I need to think about it."

Rgrythei bowed low at the hip. "Understood. You have a standard twenty-four Earth hours."

A jitter itched down Cal's spine.

Twenty-four hours to decide whether or not to put a prince's head on a chopping block, when two people sworn to protect him lived on his ship.

This was going to be a very long day.

CHAPTER 29
DANIA

DANIA EASED into a chair between Alanna and Peter at the head of the table. Ethan sat on Alanna's other side, speaking in hushed tones to Ty on his left.

The newcomer, Rachel Quirky, sat cross-legged on the floor in the corner, her gaze both curious and concerned.

Kile stood to the right, leaning against the wall with eyes narrowed on the captain as Cal paced the floor of the lounge, dragging his fingers along his scalp.

Tension flew through the air, mostly coming from Cal. He did tend to be a worrier, but it seemed the whole crew was on edge.

Peter leaned back in his chair. "I saw something interesting in the net chatter."

Cal continued to pace, but the rest of the room turned to the doctor.

"I'm not sure what happened, but it looks like the colonies of Ephershia have unanimously voted to break ties with the Banes." He glanced at Kile. "There are talks of a few others leaning in the same direction."

The edges of Kile's hair danced erratically. "That's foolish. The king will no longer protect them."

"I don't know." Rachel uncrossed and re-crossed her legs. "I mean, I come from Ephershia. To be honest, all we ever got out of the treaty were a bunch of new laws to follow, and half of them people laugh at." She looked at Kile. "Ephershia has always been in great shape. The Banes never really did anything for us."

The commander folded his arms. "Spoken like someone who has never seen war. No one thinks they need protection until they are threatened or forced to watch their friends and families die."

She bent her knees and hugged them. "I don't know. My whole family is still there, and Ephershia is so far out, we're kind of on our own. I think we feel as safe as we always have."

Kile took a step toward her. "The Carteks are, and always will be, a threat, especially to the outlier colonies. Just because your planet has not yet felt their wrath does not mean that..."

"The Carteks are definitely a threat." Cal dragged his finger through his hair again. "They are farther inside our borders than I think your king knows."

A slight glow shimmered around Kile before he drew it in. He clenched his jaw prior to stepping back and leaning against the wall again.

Odd. Kile was usually more collected, at least on the outside. Of course, something about Cal seemed to get under his skin. Something more personal than Geron's call for Cal's head.

Cal stopped pacing. His gaze lanced each one of them, as if deciding how to continue. "I got blindsided by Chris

Columbus. He took me to a private meeting space, then bailed."

Cal closed his eyes. A slight sheen coated his skin, and his temperature fluctuated up and down by a thousandth of a degree. Shame. Guilt. Fear.

Fear was understandable from their recent dealings with this pirate, but shame? Guilt?

"I ended up in a one-on-one meeting with a Cartek."

"What?" Everyone in the room seemed to bellow at once.

Kile's temperature increased a full one point five degrees, but he didn't move.

"Did it really look like an octopus?" Ethan asked.

Cal darted a glare in the engineer's direction before turning to Dania. "They want information on your sponsor."

Dania clutched the table as Kile pushed away from the wall.

"What kind of information?" Kile asked.

"Anything they can use against him. My guess is they're looking for schedules and places where they can catch him unescorted."

Kile bore down on Cal. "Why?"

"You know why. You're at war. The Banes want the Carteks exterminated just as much as the Carteks want the Banes gone." Cal turned to the crew. "They offered us a transient spatial inhibitor for our efforts."

Ethan leaned over the table with his mouth open. "That's some serious tech—serious covert Cartek kind of tech." He looked at Kile. "They must really hate your boy."

Kile's hair swirled around him. His power pulsed, and Dania wanted to drink it in.

She shivered, clutching her knees.

Peter reached under the table, placed his hand over one of

hers, and squeezed. "I got you, girl," he whispered. "We can beat this together."

Dania needed to believe that was true. She needed to trust that the doctor's treatments would work.

"We will not place our prince in danger," Kile said.

"I kinda doubt Cally is that dumb." Rachel shifted her weight. "I mean, I know you say he's a *useless waste of space on this already crowded ship* and all, but I just don't think he'd do that."

"I agree," Dania said.

Cal narrowed his eyes at her.

Why was he staring at her like that? She'd just agreed that... *Oh...* "I don't agree that you're a useless waste of space—I agree that you wouldn't hurt Geron."

He should have known that. They all should have known that.

Dania turned to Kile. "Cal would never even consider such a thing."

At least, she hoped not. She was free of the prince, but that didn't mean Dania wanted any harm to come to the man who'd taken care of her for so many years.

Kile's hair continued to swirl, his power flexing, and she understood why. Even now, the need to defend and protect her sponsor coursed through her veins.

"We need to contact Geron immediately," Kile said. "We need to make sure he's taken to safety."

Cal walked over to the window and gazed out. "The kind of tech they are offering is a little hard to pass up."

Kile's cheek ticked. "Which is why they offered it. I repeat, we are not putting our prince in danger."

But maybe they didn't have to place him in danger.

Dania stood. "Kile, you told me that Geron said nothing else matters to him but saving Alexander. Is that true?"

"Yes."

"Then that could be construed that his own safety is secondary."

"He knows of no threat against himself." Kile's nostrils flared. "I cannot even fathom that you, his own general, are even considering such betrayal."

He closed his eyes and looked away, no doubt to stop himself from pointing out the obvious, that she'd already committed treason.

His icy eyes pierced hers. "You cannot ignore a threat to your sponsor, no matter how weakened you are."

True, but there were other alternatives. "I'm not ignoring this threat, but maybe we can feed them information that would be incredibly unhelpful, like the location of his personal retreat, the one he abandoned last year because he decided he no longer enjoyed the company of the consorts housed there—old information or random facts that would not compromise him."

"Dania, I think we might be rubbing off on you." Cal cocked his head. "You're starting to think like a smuggler."

Her cheeks heated, and she looked down. A slight tingle fluttered in her chest, and she tried to will it away. Maybe she should discuss this with the doctor.

Cal moved dangerously close to Kile. "If we are lucky enough to find your friend, we're going to need all the firepower we can get to free him. This tech could be a valuable asset. It could mean the difference between success and failure."

Kile folded his arms again. "Spoken like a man who covets what he *does not have*."

Dania frowned. Kile punctuated the last three words as if he were alluding to more than the technology.

Cal's lips thinned. They continued to stare each other down.

Kile was probably right that Cal wanted the tech as much as Ethan seemed to. However, Dania had no doubt that Cal would use the tech to help Alexander. Then again, he'd probably also use it to get away from Kile once the mission was complete.

That's what Dania would do in his position.

Despite Kile's assumptions, Cal was not a fool, and he knew what was going to happen when this crew no longer added value to the mission. The possibility of the final escape when this was all over was probably the true value of this technology.

"All those in favor of cheating the squids with bad information, say *aye*." Ty raised his hand.

"Aye." The human crew all raised their hands.

Kile glared at Dania, but there was still one thing in her favor. She was his general, and he was coded to listen to her.

She raised her hand. "Aye."

CAL STARED at the landing platform below them from his perch on the *Star Renegade* bridge. He really didn't want anyone leaving the ship knowing there was at least one Cartek on the asteroid, and who knew how many more.

"Are you sure you know where to get the data you need?" Cal asked Ty.

His pilot knelt on his own seat, leaning on his console and looking out over the same platform. "Yeah. I'm telling you, there's not many places in those buildings to hide anything. Yesterday Ethan and I found one sealed door. It has to be their data banks."

"And how much trouble are you going to get in by accessing it?"

Ty pursed his lips. "You always assume that I'm going to get caught."

"When have you not gotten caught?"

He thought for a moment. "Neptune Nine."

Cal raised a brow. "That was over a year ago. How many times have you been caught since?"

Ty started counting fingers. Then stopped. "None, come to think of it. We always get away."

Cal shook his head. The *getting away* part of it was always the problem.

Ty squeezed Cal's shoulder. "Hey, we got this. I go in, grab Big Bad's data. You feed the squid phony info, we get the tech, and we're home free."

Cal closed his eyes. He'd love to live in Ty's world for a while, where everything was so easy. No matter how many scrapes they'd gotten into, Ty always figured the next one would be a stroll through a virtual garden program. The problem was things were never that easy.

The enforcer's voice came over the comm. "I grow impatient. I'd like to finish this." Rachel giggled in the background.

"Where are they?" Cal asked.

Ty tapped a few keys. "In the quarters we assigned him." Ty snorted. "I guess they were blowing off a little steam."

The girl was certainly keeping the enforcer occupied. Which was not a bad thing overall, but Cal wasn't all too sure that she'd have the effect that Ty and Ethan had hoped for. He couldn't see the enforcer turning coat on his prince and deciding to stay once they freed their missing friend.

Ty flipped on the comm. "We're ready to go. Get set to receive the data feeds."

Skimming the data feeds was the easy part. Cal was the one who needed to stare down an alien and convince him that they weren't feeding him useless information to get his tech.

Taking a deep breath, Cal pushed up from his console and stepped off the bridge.

Dania stood outside. "I was just coming to look for you."

"Are you going to try to talk me out of it?"

"Maybe." She started walking with him. "It is a Cartek, after all. You can't trust them."

Cal kept his eyes straight ahead. The thing was, he probably could trust the squid. They were known for being straight shooters. Although many times you had to read between the lines of their agreements. "I heard the Cartek promise Chris that I would walk out of this alive. I need to trust in that, or I'll go nuts."

Her face reddened, and she took a deep breath.

He stopped, grabbing her arm. "Hey, you and your guy came up with the bogus information yourself. We aren't actually putting your prince in any danger."

"I know." She pulled out of his grip. "It's you I'm worried about."

Something in his chest tingled. Cal gritted his teeth and pushed the sensation aside. "You're just mad that you haven't gotten to taste the tomato sauce yet."

She laughed, a beautiful sound he wished he'd hear more often. "Well, yes. That, among other things." She shoved his shoulder. "Come back in one piece."

Cal saluted. "Aye, aye, General."

———

Kile leaned against the inner frame of the *Star Renegade*'s exit, Rachel fidgeting at his side.

The enforcer's cheeks reddened. The coloring looked odd against his normally pallid complexion. "She insisted on being here."

Rachel folded her arms and stomped her foot like a child.

"I'm making sure he doesn't play hero and leave the ship on his own. There are bad people out there."

Cal snickered. "You do realize he's the person those bad people are usually screaming and running from?"

She lifted her chin. "That doesn't matter. I want my Big Guy safe where I can see him."

Kile glared at her, but a slight smile hinted on his lips before he covered the expression with his usual stoic calm. He looked at Ty. "You will stay in contact at all times. If there is a problem…"

"I know, I know." Ty waved his hand and pointed at the comm piece in his ear. "We're covered. You can talk to me the whole time." He grabbed the bag of goods he was supposed to be trading and headed down the platform.

Kile sighed, watching him disappear inside the building. "Your pilot is a sufficiently skilled data runner. I have little doubt he will retrieve what I require."

Huh. That was high praise from the enforcer who thought they were all worth less than the dirt under his shoes.

Kile looked out over the docks. "Your task, Mr. Espinoza, will be significantly more trying."

Cal shook his head. "I sure hope not."

Phantom fingers constricted around Cal's throat. He tried to take a breath, but the air didn't reach his lungs. Spinning toward the enforcer, he reached for hands that weren't there.

The commander's glare came into focus. "You will do nothing that would put Prince Geron in jeopardy."

The grip released. Cal took a breath, massaging his throat.

He wanted nothing more than to punch this guy in the face. But he'd promised Dania he'd come back in one piece. Dying on the exit ramp did no one good.

Cal lowered his hand. "You and Dania came up with the information. I don't know anything about your blasted prince, let alone anything that would put him in danger."

"And I intend to keep it that way, *smuggler*."

Rachel slipped her hand around Kile's arm and shrugged. "Good luck, I guess?"

Cal smirked. She was a tiny little spitfire ray of sunshine, clinging to the big, broody deadpan behemoth. There must be some truth to all that *opposites attract* stuff.

Cal double-checked the coordinates fed to their computers and headed off base, out into the rocky area on the edge of the oxygen shield. Dust kicked up around his feet as he sank into silt that didn't appear to have been disturbed in years. The crunch of his boots into the soft ground echoed in his ears, the only sound other than an occasional distant voice from the base behind him.

If he hadn't seen the Cartek promise Chris that Cal would walk out of here alive firsthand, he may have gone right back to his ship. This felt like a setup if there ever was one.

"Mr. Espinoza, I'm so glad you decided to return." The Cartek faded into view from the shadows. He looked at his watch arm, which had no watch on it. "And with barely a few minutes to spare."

"Well, it wasn't exactly easy getting an enforcer to cough up any intel. As you know, they aren't all that helpful to normal people."

Cal shifted his weight. He didn't really expect trouble. Not yet, at least, but the quiet out here, the solitude…it was enough to leave anyone on edge. Especially staring at a man whose clothes changed from black to gray to dark blue.

The Cartek tilted his simulated head. "Really? Not even the female with the long hair? I do believe she's considered fetching, by human standards." He tilted his head in the other direction. "It is our understanding that humans tend to relay mass amounts of confidential data during…" He looked to the side. "It is called *pillow talk*, yes?"

Cal frowned. "Pillow talk?"

"Yes. Idle chatter after copulation? Our research tells that your kind becomes overly truthful after you mate."

Mate? "What makes you think I've been with the enforcer?" He cringed. He didn't really think of her like that anymore. 'The enforcer' was now Kile: the one they had to be wary of. Dania was part of the crew. His friend.

"Oh, come now, Captain Espinoza. Even a mere mention of her has spiked your heart rate, and a slight sheen of sweat has appeared on your brow. We've noted those as signs of human male territoriality."

"I'm territorial about my crew. The enforcer is a different story." Which was the truth, as far as Cal was concerned. Dania was part of that crew, and he'd protect her just like he'd protect any of them.

"I'm actually glad to hear you say that."

Cal flinched. "Why is that?"

The Cartek held out his hand. "First, the data you promised me."

Cal took a step back. "I'm not dumb. How about you show me the tech first?"

The squid held up a hand, and a hovercart floated from the shadows with a metal box about three feet long and a few inches high perched atop.

Finally, this is almost over. Cal reached for the disk on the side of the cart that would re-assign the equipment to him. As his fingers neared the dial, the craft inched back.

"I'd like to see the data you promised first, Captain Espinoza."

That was fair enough. "Here." Cal threw the data node in the air, and a tentacled tail whipped out of the Cartek's shirt-sleeve and plucked it from the air. Cal reached for the cart again, and it still backed away from him.

"I'd like to confirm what's on this node before we make the trade."

"I don't have that kind of time." That wasn't entirely true, but Cal wanted out of there.

The Cartek held up his wrist, which looked more or less human again. The node had sunk into the creature's flesh, and lights blinked on all sides of it.

The creature placed his hand down. "My people confirm that the Bane prince has been at one of these locations in that past three days. This makes your data reliable."

"Great. It's been fun and all, but I'm ready to part ways."

Cal reached for the cart, and a tentacle wrapped around his wrist. Cool, wet goo chilled his skin, and his stomach churned.

"We had a deal," Cal said.

The Cartek nodded. "This technology is considerable, and we've decided that its value warrants more in the way of trade."

Cal gritted his teeth. "I thought you guys didn't go back on your word."

"This is not going back on our word. It is an addition." He held out his hand, and another box hovered and settled beside the first one.

"What's this?" Cal asked.

"The first cart contains the transient spatial inhibitor that we agreed upon."

"And the second box?"

"The second box is directions translated into your language, and a module that will allow for immediate use in your ship, rather than taking up months of your engineer's time and a ridiculous number of failures to get it up and running."

There was always a catch. "And what do you want for the instruction manual?"

Rgrythei swayed slightly. "A trifle. Something you already told me you'd like to be rid of."

Cal gritted his teeth. "I'm trying to be cool about all this, but I'm getting impatient. What do you want?"

Rgrythei sneered. "The enforcers."

Cal flinched. "What?"

"You will use this considerable technology to continue your quest to free the third enforcer. This endeavor should considerably weaken the other two. When it is over, you will hand over all three of them to me."

Cal backed up a step to keep from punching the squid in the face. "No way. This was not part of the bargain."

"Then no instructions."

"Keep your instructions. My people are competent. They'll figure it out."

Rgrythei's eyes narrowed. "They are competent indeed."

The Cartek flicked his wrist, and a bright light flashed over the top of the stones leading to the landing site. The ground rumbled, and the *Star Renegade* hoisted into the air. But there were no signs of the engines. No hum of power.

A white orb appeared around the ship, then started to shrink.

"Do you know what this is, Mr. Espinoza?"

Cal shook his head. His heart rattled in his chest. "No. What are you doing? Let my ship go!"

"This is a rotating shield rampart. It is quite formidable and easily cloaked, especially in a piece of older technology, like a secondary communication juncture."

The comm juncture? The pink tech they'd picked up for Alanna?

They'd installed alien malware on their own ship!

"Shield ramparts are supposed to buffer the hull armor. Why is it shrinking?"

"Because it can also be used as a weapon. That shield can fend off a military-grade missile. And when reversed, it can shrink until the ship it is attached to is no more than a small circle of fused metal."

Killing everyone inside.

Cal fought to control his breathing. "Stop! Please!"

"If I kill the enforcers now or later, it makes no difference to me."

"You will kill my crew. You promised Chris we'd walk out of this alive."

Rgrythei held up a finger. "I promised Mr. Columbus that *you* would walk away. And you will." He looked up at the ship. "If the rest of them die along with the enforcers, they will be logged as acceptable casualties."

Acceptable? Cal's comm pinged.

Alanna's voice. "Cal, something's wrong! I don't know what to do!" Static filled the line, cutting her off.

Cal took a step toward the squid, his hands clenching. "Stop."

"You'll give me the enforcers?"

The white glow ebbed closer to the hull. Within seconds, everyone inside would be dead.

Think, Cal. Think!

But there was nothing to think about. There was no way out of this. Not right now at least. He had no other option but to comply.

Once they were far from here, safe, they'd get rid of the comm juncture and make a run for it. That was their only chance.

He spun to the Cartek. "Okay. I'll do it."

"You will hand over all three enforcers."

"Yes." He'd told worse lies in his lifetime.

Rgrythei looked up, and the circle of light winked out. The Cartek grabbed Cal's wrist and slammed his palm on the controls, transferring the tech and the manual to Cal.

Rgrythei released him, and cool goo dripped from Cal's wrist. "This transaction is complete. You may now collect the young pilot stealing data from this establishment and continue your mission. Your lovely enforcer will be none the wiser."

Or she'd be very wise, and in on the plan to get them all out of this mess.

Cal flicked his wrist and the cart followed him as he walked back to the ship.

"Mr. Espinoza," Rgrythei's voice called from behind.

Cal took a deep breath, doing his best to keep his cool. "What?"

"The Cartek Empire does require that all deals are completed to our satisfaction."

That wasn't much of a surprise. Cal started walking again.

"If anyone, for any reason, tries to remove the secondary communication juncture, the shield rampart will engage and shrink at a rate of six inches per second. I highly suggest no one endeavors to do any maintenance on the device."

Six inches per second would crush the ship in a few minutes. Maybe they could abandon the ship, but how would they afford to buy another one?

"Don't try to get a new ship, Mr. Espinoza. You will regret it."

Cal flinched. He hated it when people were one step ahead of him.

He spun, trying to keep his voice calm. "Keeping my ship hostage was not part of any deal."

"Then allow me to add to the deal to make things more to your liking. Once the enforcers have been delivered, I will personally oversee the recalibration of the device, returning it to a shield rather than a weapon." Rgrythei smiled with his pointed teeth. "You'd be the only non-Cartek ship with a shield that could withstand a blow from the king himself."

And all Cal had to do was give up the enforcers. Give up Dania.

But Dania wasn't an enforcer anymore. She was part of the crew. Part of his family.

He couldn't give her up.

But if he didn't, they'd all die.

He needed to trade three lives to save six. It was a good deal.

These were the kinds of hard decisions captains needed to make. He'd known that when he'd taken on a crew.

His gut twisted. How was he supposed to live with himself for doing the right thing, when it felt so wrong, and when it meant losing so much?

CHAPTER 31
DANIA

KILE PACED in front of the window in the lounge, his feet stomping on the floor. "Nothing seems right. All of my internal receptors are in attack mode."

Dania took a deep breath. She had to admit, she'd felt uneasy since Cal had returned. The ship taking flight on its own was disconcerting in and of itself, but Cal wouldn't even look her in the eyes.

Kile stopped. "Whatever had hold of us, I couldn't stop it. I shot out power into that bright light, but nothing happened."

"And then it stopped, so maybe you *did do* something." Or, more likely, Cal was telling the truth, and the Cartek had shown what would happen if he found out that the information they'd given him was wrong.

Hopefully, the information would seem true enough. Dania didn't want to spend her last few moments alive knowing she'd caused the deaths of the few people who'd given her back her humanity.

Kile folded his arms. "I don't like not being in control of a situation."

"Neither do I."

"But you chose this." He pointed at her. "You want this insanity in your life. I, for one, prefer order."

Meaning the ease of having Geron make choices for you, of him pointing you in a direction, and telling you who to kill, and accepting those orders without question.

When Dania had been on the bridge with Alanna, and the ship had flown on its own, and then the orb had appeared around them, Dania had felt helpless. Maybe if she'd had her powers, she'd have been just as ineffective against the alien technology as Kile had been. Maybe there was really no defense against this new weapon.

Cal stepped into the lounge and looked at each of them. "You two okay?"

Kile marched toward him. Dania took a step forward, stopping his gait.

"What do you know about this weapon they used against us?" Kile asked.

Cal paled, looking at the floor. "They slipped something onto the pink tech we bought Alanna."

"How is that possible?" Dania asked.

Cal shook his head. "You got me. We did leave for quite a while so the shop owner could paint it."

"Inconsequential," Kile said. "We will dock somewhere and remove the threat immediately."

"We can't. There's a failsafe that will destroy the ship if we go anywhere near it."

The commander seemed to consider this. "Then we abandon this ship and procure another."

"He said they'd know. With that kind of tech, it could be reading who is where in the ship, and what we're doing."

"We can't just ignore that there is a self-destruct technology attached to this ship that we have no control over."

"No, we can't. But I know my crew. Ethan probably went into hero mode the second the shield circled us. That means he already has a list of things that didn't work. Alanna told me she tried to jump but read the fluctuations and realized she'd hit the barrier like running into the side of a mountain."

Dania held her breath, hoping with so much information flying through the air that Kile wouldn't notice the comment about Alanna *jumping*. So far, Kile had not found out about the navigator's interesting ability. Cal must have been really distracted to make a mistake like that.

Cal continued his rant. "Ty wasn't on board, but he's hot to figure this out, too. Doc ran readings during the whole thing, and if anyone can figure this out, he can. And Rachel..." He finally took a breath. "I'm not sure where Rachel was, but she might be able to give us some ideas, too."

Kile's nose flared. "I think not. Once I realized there was nothing I could do to save the ship, she climbed into my lap, sobbing."

Dania frowned. "And what did you do?"

"I held her, of course. What would you expect me to do?"

Throw her off? Tell her she wasn't worthy?

Anything but *hold her*. Dania couldn't imagine Kile holding anyone. The man was built for war, not consolation.

"Anyway," Cal said. "Ethan is already geeking out over the new tech. He roped Alanna into helping him figure it all out."

Dania narrowed her eyes. That was an odd change in

subject. The new technology was important to their mission, but not as important as the current risk.

She caught Cal's gaze.

He blanched before giving her weak grin. "It's going to be okay."

His temperature spiked by .02135 degrees, and his heartbeat quickened.

A lie, but one seeded in a deep determination. Kile had already started pacing in front of the window again and hadn't seemed to notice the transgression.

But Dania had. "Cal?"

"It's going to be okay," he repeated, but she didn't need to check his temperature to know that he didn't believe that himself.

She'd thought they were friends. Why didn't he trust her with whatever was wrong?

Her stomach tightened. What could be so bad that he thought he needed to face it alone?

CAL TOOK three steadying breaths standing outside the med bay. He wasn't dumb enough to think Dania hadn't noticed he'd lied to her earlier. He needed to figure this all out before the Carteks came back and demanded their spoils.

Maybe, if he worked it right, he could convince the squids that Dania had died during the mission, and they'd accept the other two enforcers as payment. She'd hate him for giving up her friends, but at least she'd be alive to hate him.

He might need to pull Doc in on a plan like this. He needed a much bigger brain than the one in his own head to pull something like that off.

But what was Doc going to think when he told him? He wasn't sure he wanted to admit to any of them that he'd agreed to betray one of their own. They'd mutinied for less.

He needed to tell someone, though. He was in over his head, and he needed help.

Taking one last soothing breath, he entered.

Dania's face lit up as he walked in. "Cal, you came!"

Rachel placed a tray of instruments on the table beside Dania's bed. "Of course he did. Cally is great like that."

Cal cocked a brow at the stowaway. "You don't know anything about me."

She shrugged. "I hear things. Besides, everyone knows you're hot for Dani here, so…"

"I think that's about enough," Doc said, snapping gloves on his hands. He leaned closer to Cal. "Sorry about that, boss."

"I'm not hot for anyone," Cal whispered.

Rachel snorted. "That's the lie of the century. I'm not empathic and even I picked up on it."

"Picked up on what?" Dania asked.

Rachel tapped her shoulder. "I'll explain a little later."

"No, you won't," Cal said.

If this kept up, this woman might end up being even worse than the enforcer she was supposed to be here to distract.

Cal pulled Doc aside. "Do you really want Quirky here while we do this? She kind of has a problem keeping her mouth shut, if you haven't noticed."

"That's okay, Cally." Rachel smacked his arm. "Doctor Pete already explained that Dani has a rare cancery-kind of thing." She pulled on a pair of gloves. "Anyway, I needed something to do while my Big Guy is looking over all that data the cute pilot stole from the asteroid." Her eyes lit up. "Are you guys really pirates like my sweetie says? Because that's kind of exciting." She looked back to Dania. "And about her being sick… I mean, my Big Guy would definitely have a meltdown if he found out. He's all sorts of protective about Dani, and he might even drag her right home to that prince of theirs." She turned back to Cal. "Is His Royal Highness-ness some kind of super-healer or something? Because that's the way my guy talks about him."

"It's something like that," Cal said, although he wished it were that simple.

She glanced over her shoulder at Dania, then pulled them both close. "I love Dani as much as anyone, but if my guy takes her back there, I'm not sure either one of them will come home."

"We're aware of that," Cal said.

Doc held up a syringe. "Thus, the covert operation."

Rachel saluted. "I am your loyal stealth operative." She twisted her fingers over her mouth. "My lips are sealed."

Cal certainly hoped that was true.

She pointed at him. "Don't look at me like that. I love my Big Guy. I'm not losing him. And I trust Doctor Pete. If he says he can help Dani, then I believe it. She'll get better. Big Guy doesn't need to know, and everyone stays here like one big happy family."

Odd, how after being here for such a short time, she seemed to include herself in *that big happy family*. Also strange that she could be that crazy about a guy she just met, let alone that dry, arrogant enforcer.

Cal pinched the bridge of his nose. Women had always been a bit of a mystery to him, but as long as Rachel wanted to keep this a secret as much as they did, they'd be okay.

Rachel clapped her hands. "Okay, so what do I do?"

Doc motioned to the vials on the warmer. "Watch the little dark spots floating around in the glass. When I ask for a new one, give me the one that is moving the most."

"On it!"

Cal sat next to Dania and took her hand in his.

She looked at Rachel. "She is so odd."

"That, she is."

But she seemed like a good person, deep down. They could have ended up worse, as far as stowaways go.

Cal squeezed Dania's hand again. "Doc told me you were feeling sick, like you were worried the treatments weren't working?"

She pulled her hand away. "He told you that?"

"He's worried about you. We all are."

She closed her eyes and let her head fall back on the pillow. "I just want this to be over. I want to be free."

Her hair flowed over the sheets in neat waves, and her lashes fluttered as she took a deep breath.

"That's all any of us wants for you," Cal said.

And it was the truth. Somehow, he'd make that happen. He just needed to find a way to do that without sacrificing her, the crew, or the ship.

Doc walked over, holding a syringe at shoulder height. "Ready?"

Dania nodded, and Cal placed his hand over hers again. "I have a surprise for you."

Doc injected the pathogens into the bag. The dark liquid swirled before darting down the tube like the particles were alive and searching for a host.

Maybe they were.

He looked away, trying to push that thought out of his mind.

"What's my surprise?" she asked.

He returned his gaze to hers. "You'll just have to get through this to find out."

"I think it has to do with food," Rachel called from the other side of the room. "Because there was this incredible smell coming from Cally's room."

Dania's lashes fluttered open. The light danced across her eyes when she smiled. "Tomatoes?"

There was no use denying it. "They are in for their second slow simmer. It will be ready by the time we're done."

She closed her eyes again. "I think I'm more excited about that than I am about feeling better."

Cal tapped her fingers. "Let's get through this first. We have all day to learn the joys of pasta."

At least until Kile and Ty finished with the data analysis. After that, things would change, and Cal was afraid all hell would break loose.

———

Cal slipped out of the med bay when Dania fell asleep. The good news was that she hadn't seemed to have a reaction like the first time, but Doc said her body needed about an hour to absorb the new cells. That was probably just enough time to check on Kile and Ty to get a gauge on when they'd know if their trek to the asteroids was worth their run-in with the Cartek.

When he pushed through the lounge door, Kile was bearing down on Ethan.

The engineer held up his palms. "It's no big deal!"

"It is a very big deal." Kile's hair floated about him and a slight glow surrounded the enforcer's skin.

That couldn't be good.

"It's me!" Ethan backed up against the wall. "I'm the capable one, remember? I mean, yeah, I'm infuriating, but this isn't my fault!"

Ty jumped between them, and Cal did the same, but he wasn't sure either of them could stop Kile's advance.

Cal held out his hands. Heat actually radiated off the enforcer's chest. "What's going on?"

Ty moved closer, blocking off Ethan. "We came across a sealed file in the med bay documentation while we were searching. I told Big Bad to mind his own business, but he opened it anyway."

If Kile had gone poking around where he shouldn't be, he could have found any number of incriminating things. But if it was the med bay, had he found out they'd been treating Dania?

"Your doctor has been looking into my past." Kile backed up a step. His hands clenched and unclenched.

Cal wasn't sure if he should be relieved or terrified. He'd known looking into the enforcer's DNA had been a mistake.

He held up his hands placatingly. "Dania asked me to seal that information. She didn't think anyone needed to know." Especially Kile, and now Cal knew why.

The enforcer's hair flared up again. "You know, too?"

Ethan looked around them. "See? There's no reason to kill me if everyone already knows."

Kile growled at him.

Ethan pushed past Ty and Cal. The guy never did have much common sense.

"Come on," Ethan said. "So your parents aren't who you thought they were. Who cares? You're still..." Ethan pointed up and down the enforcer's frame. "You're still a big damn scary dude. Nothing's changed."

"He's right," Ty said. "Besides, this gives you a more open door to what you want."

Kile's eyes narrowed. "You have no idea what I want."

"I'm thinking I do." Ty reached for the video comm on the wall and tapped a few keys.

Rachel appeared on the lounge viewscreen. She rested her elbows on a desk in the med bay, apparently reading something.

"That genealogy shows you're half-human. That makes you and Miss Quirky a plausible option."

"How does that make her a plausible option? I am an enforcer. When this mission is over, I am taking Dania and Alexander home to our sponsor."

Rachel laughed at something she was reading. The glow about Kile lessened as he took a step toward the screen and placed his hand on the glass. She looked up, right into his eyes, like she could feel him looking at her, even though the transmission was one-way.

The enforcer flinched and swiped the screen to black. "Enough of this nonsense." He walked to a table with data pads strewn across it. "I am tasked with finding Alexander, and that is what I'm going to do."

But he didn't grab a data pad. He eased into a chair and looked back at the blank screen on the wall.

Cal glanced at Ty, then Ethan, but both of them had the smarts not to move. Cal wasn't sure Ethan was even breathing.

They needed the enforcer to work through this in his head. They could only hope that Rachel Quirky was enough to make the commander decide humanity was a better option than returning to that star-blasted prince.

It was very possible their lives depended on it.

———

Cal guided Dania into his kitchen area. "Keep your eyes closed."

"I don't need my eyes." She took in a deep breath. "I can't believe it smells even better than it did last time!"

Cal took a spoonful of the sauce from the crockpot and blew on it until the steam subsided. He touched the spoon to her lips. "Taste."

She opened her mouth and took a sip from the edge of the spoon.

Cal's pants tightened as she licked her lips. He took a deep breath, warding off his own stupidity. What was wrong with him?

Her eyes shot open. "Wow!"

"You bet your ass *wow*."

She leaned over the crockpot, taking in a deep whiff. "Just cooking them that long makes them taste so good?"

"I did add spices along the way. There is a bit of an art to it."

She took the spoon and licked off the rest of the sauce. Her lips were only a little less red than the fragrant traces left behind.

His cheeks flushed. Cal blinked and turned away.

They were wrong about him. Dania was his friend. A crewmate. He didn't think of her any differently than the others.

Right?

"You said something about pasta?"

"Yes, ma'am." He poured the rigatoni into the already-boiling pot of water. "It will be ready in a few minutes. Pasta has a shelf life of about a thousand years, so I stock up when I can get it. That way, I can still make the crew something, even when the fresh food gets scarce."

She seemed to consider the noodles dancing in the boiling water. "You really care about them, don't you?"

Cal frowned. Odd, that she didn't seem to consider herself in that group.

"I care about *all of you.*"

She nodded, then leaned closer to the pot, taking another deep whiff.

It was refreshing, how much enjoyment she was getting from something as simple as boiling pasta. Maybe they all needed to appreciate some of the simpler joys that were right under their noses.

He leaned down next to her and took a whiff of his own. The scent wasn't quite as appealing as the sauce, but it brought back memories of cooking beside his mom.

Dania turned and looked up at him, their noses inches apart. Cal's breath caught in his chest as the reflection of the water danced in her eyes.

Simple joys were definitely important.

A strand of her hair fell toward the water, and he tucked it back behind her ear. Cal froze as she leaned into his hand, closing her eyes.

When Rachel had joked about him wanting Dania, Dania had acted like she didn't understand. Coming from her background, it was quite possible she didn't.

Had she ever been touched before? Was a small sign of affection like this something new to her?

Her skin was so warm. So soft. She wasn't even a trace of the enforcer she used to be.

There was no way in the stars that Cal could hand her over to the Carteks, even to save the crew. He cringed, knowing he'd even considered the idea. It wasn't in him to sacrifice anyone, and he knew it. He needed to figure this out.

Dania's eyes opened. She looked lost for a moment, until her gaze found Cal's.

She reached up and put her fingers over his. "Cal?" Her touch was so gentle...a million times different from the woman they'd dragged on board in handcuffs.

He leaned down toward her, their lips inches apart. He paused, and when she didn't object, he—

The comm sounded overhead. *Dammit!*

Cal flicked the switch on the wall. "What?!"

"Sorry to bug you, boss, but we found him," Ty said. "We know where they took Dania's friend."

Dania stood, gaping at the speaker. "We're coming."

She turned and sprinted from the room.

Cal growled and threw the spoon across the kitchen. It slammed against a cabinet and splashed sauce on the wall.

What the hell did he almost do? She was a member of his crew, for goodness' sake.

The pasta started to boil over. Cal pulled the pot off the burner and unplugged the crockpot. They were never going to eat this meal...which was a ridiculous thing to worry about.

He wiped his hands on a towel, tossed it on the counter, and headed for the door.

He had an enforcer to save.

CHAPTER 33

DANIA

DANIA'S HEART pounded as Ty and Kile stood to the side of the long table in the lounge and called up information from their data streams.

Ty walked over to the screen on the wall. "Your friend was purchased by a pirate turned government official on Cerberus." He called up a map showing the *Star Renegade*, Earth, and the planet Cerberus, glowing green between them. "Governor Tison fancies himself a collector. Big game, mostly. He keeps a museum of his finds from all over the galaxy, complete with banquet halls and guest quarters so he can show off his collection."

Dania cringed. Caging wild animals, let alone people, was a crime. This governor didn't deserve his rank, or his life.

"Bragging rights," Peter said.

"Exactly." Ty pointed to Cerberus. "Our guy runs in the circles of people who try to one-up each other with the most dangerous and beautiful quarry."

Dania shivered. Alexander was both dangerous and beautiful.

"He doesn't stuff them, right?" Ethan asked.

Ty shook his head. "Nope. If they're dead, they aren't dangerous anymore. There's no thrill in the conquest. There's thrill in control."

Ethan leaned on the table. "So let me get this right. He pays someone else to do the dangerous part of catching these animals, and more recently, people, and then he keeps them —to what? Look at them?"

Cal tapped on the edge of the table. "I've seen the type. He probably gets off on it...controlling what he's probably too much of a coward to go after in the first place. Those animals...your friend...are probably drugged beyond reason."

"That's good, though, right?" Alanna asked. "That means that the nice enforcer is still alive?"

"We think so, yes." Ty called up a representation of the wooded planet, and a red circle appeared on the screen. "We can't find an outside picture, but the mansion is supposed to be a fortress."

"Nothing is impenetrable." Kile slammed his fist on the circle. "We will flatten the building if we have to."

Ethan pointed at the screen. "Whoa there, Big Bad! I'm the one who will have to fix that screen if you break it."

Kile's eyes flared. "I care not about your trivial concerns." He turned to Dania. "We can call in a squadron and annihilate the target."

"And crush Alexander inside? Are you out of your mind?" Dania said.

Kile stared at her, heat radiating from his skin, until he looked down. Alexander was the one who usually coordinated humanitarian efforts, and this was the reason. The rest of them were programmed to destroy.

"Flattening the building is definitely not an option." Ty

scrolled through a list. "The governor is a pretty sick dude. Your friend might not be the only person he's holding in there. There are rumors about his enemies getting too close and never being seen again."

"There is a lot of tourism on Cerberus," Alanna said. "We shouldn't have any trouble landing. Maybe it won't be too hard to get to this mansion?"

"But they don't allow visitors to carry arms," Cal pointed out. "I'm not going in there unless we can defend ourselves."

Dania opened her mouth, ready to remind him that Kile was a walking weapon. But Cal's glance stopped her from speaking, and she knew why. Yes, Kile was formidable, but everyone on this crew was expendable to him, which certainly was not ideal.

She still might have some leftover power to help, but using any of her remaining strength might incapacitate her, as it had when she'd heated the panel for Alanna. She had no idea how much the new pathogens would really help, or if her power would ever return. The best option would be more firepower.

"We could call in reinforcements now that we know where he is," Dania said. "They can break into the building and find where he's being held.

"I doubt it." Ty called up an infrared image showing a star pattern of lines leading away from the central circle. "There are dozens of tunnels under this place. Enforcers aren't exactly sneaky. The bad guys will see them coming before they break the atmosphere and smuggle out anything *and anyone* they don't want found before the enforcers get there."

Kile folded his arms. "Which is, again, why this ship is valuable. We can land and extract Alexander on our own."

"The tricky part is that you can't bring your own weapons

onto the planet," Ethan said. "But that is a free-trade colony. We can buy whatever we want while we're there."

"We don't have that kind of cash," Cal said.

"Ridiculous." Kile tapped a few keys on his data pad, and Cal's pad pinged.

Cal read the screen, then frowned at him. "All this time, we've been scraping together ducets and you had that kind of cash on hand?"

His lip quirked slightly. "I don't believe you ever asked."

Or, more likely, he'd been enjoying watching how a smuggler thought, while collecting data to make himself a better hunter, in case he did end up chasing Cal down after this was all over.

Dania stood, walking toward the screen. "Is there any way to get a schematic of the governor's home so we can look for likely places he may be holding Alexander?"

Ty shook his head. "I had the same thought, but he's managed to keep that under lock and key. There are some articles talking about a banquet hall, and a recent communication about seeing some sort of alien tusked boar in a cage lunging through the bars, but beyond that, we got nothing."

Cal scratched his chin before slowly standing. "So, we're going in blind like any other time. Nothing new for us. But there is one small thing." He took a deep breath, then released it. "We've got a bug on the ship, and I think there is a big possibility that if we all get off at the same time, the ship will explode."

"What?" Ty, Ethan, Doc, and Alanna shouted.

Rachel's jaw dropped. She stood and grabbed Kile's arm.

"When were you going to tell us this?" Ethan asked.

Cal stared him down. "Come on, Ethan. Don't tell me you didn't already suspect."

Ethan scratched his cheek. "Yeah. It's in the secondary comm juncture, I'll guess."

Alanna straightened. "The one I installed? No way. I didn't let those guys anywhere near the ship. I played the PMS card. They all backed away like I had the plague."

Rachel snorted. All the human men just stared at her. Ethan's cheeks grew sallow.

Dania needed to remember to ask her new friends what a *PMS card* was later.

Cal cleared his throat before he continued. "We think it was already in the tech when we got it."

"I'll look at it more closely," Ethan said.

"No!" Cal pointed at him. When everyone stared, Cal said more calmly, "I don't want anyone touching that thing. Scan it, x-ray it, look at it, but no one is to even touch that thing."

Ethan eased back in his chair. "Umm, okaaay."

Cal looked at the others. "It's normal protocol for someone to stay behind anyway. I just know this is a tempting stop to want to get out and take a look around, so I needed everyone to be aware how important it is to actually stay this time."

"Miss Quirky would be a good candidate to remain on board," Kile suggested.

Rachel pounded her fist on the table. "I would *not* be a good candidate."

"On the contrary. You are the newest member of the crew. The rest of them work as a reasonably competent unit. You would be a liability."

She gaped. "Liability, my left butt cheek!"

"Hold on!" Cal lifted his hand. "What I need is someone on board who can have the ship ready to leave because there is a damn good chance we'll either need a pick up, or, if we make it this far on foot, we'll need the engines up and running." He scanned the crew. "That means me, Ty, or Alanna."

Alanna grimaced. "Ty's a better pilot."

Ty rubbed his eyes. "I'm probably going to get kicked for this remark, but the chances are good that people will be shooting at us."

"So?" Alanna leaned across the table. "I'm a way better shot than you."

Ty smiled. "Maybe, but you never duck."

Alanna blinked and looked at the table.

"Am I wrong?" he asked.

Alanna shifted, probably still feeling the wounds in her shoulder and side from the last time she'd been involved in a firefight. "Okay, I'll stay on board. But I'm not the greatest flier if you need a pickup. You know that."

Cal looked relieved. He was probably hoping she'd come to the same conclusion. Alanna was a good shot, though. It would be a shame not to have her with them.

"You're fine flying in gravity. If we need a pickup, Ty or I will be able to take over before we get to zero-G." Cal leaned on the table. "All right, people. Get some rest. We're going to need everyone in top shape when we get to Cerberus."

The crew began to disperse, and Dania looked out at the stars. Somewhere out there, Alexander was in a cage, probably on display for people to laugh and jeer at. Bile built in her throat, and her hands trembled.

Kile appeared beside her. "It's good seeing that look on your face again…like you want to kill something."

She closed her eyes and gulped the sting away. She wanted to deny it, but it was true. Dania wanted to embrace her new life, but she'd still kill for Alexander. And the more she thought about him alone out there, in a cage, the more she *wanted to* kill for him.

Kile stared at the stars. "Fear not, General. I have a feeling we'll both get our chance."

CHAPTER 34
CAL

A FEW OF Cerberus's recreational vehicles flew overhead, lifting the leaves on the surrounding trees.

Cal moved his bag from one shoulder to the other. Getting weapons from local vendors had been just as easy as Ethan had said. Maybe too easy. Either that, or the traders here were far more interested in profiting from their over-priced hardware than they were worried about any of the colonists' safety.

Ty pointed to a dirt trail that led up what the locals called "the hill," but their idea of a hill rose at a slope that would make most stairways envious.

Cal had given Alanna an hour off the ship to get some fresh air, and also to buy a hat and a less-conspicuous shirt and pants for the enforcer to wear before she'd taken up her perch on the bridge and started her takeoff checklists so the *Renegade* would be ready at a moment's notice.

Other than his large size, the enforcer did blend in well in the colony clothing. He walked ahead with Rachel beside him, doing what Rachel did best…talking. Who knew any one woman could know so much about birds, plants, and reptiles living in Cerberus's forests?

They treaded up the dirt pathway, each carrying a backpack of untested munitions. Anyone paying attention would see them coming up the trail. With any luck, they'd just look like a bunch of hikers and sightseers.

Up ahead, the tops of a stonework building jutted out over the treetops.

Ty squinted, shielding his eyes from the sun. "It looks like a medieval castle."

"I have a feeling that castle is going to be guarded a little better than King Arthur's court," Cal said.

"Agreed." Kile turned toward Rachel. "You should return to the ship."

"Why?"

"Because it is not safe. We will have to get past a considerable amount of security, and you don't have any expertise in such matters."

Rachel stopped, spreading her feet like she was preparing for a fight. "I don't have any expertise?" She pointed at the castle. "You're going to have to sneak in there." She poked Kile in the chest. "The only expertise you have is being big and intimidating and blowing stuff up. This is going to take a little more finesse."

"Finesse?" Kile folded his large arms. "What kind of finesse do you have?"

Rachel gave an exaggerated roll of her eyes. "How many people in this group have recently snuck onto a starship, right under the noses of two enforcers, and stowed away undetected until after takeoff?" She raised her hand. "That would be one. You need me, Big Guy. Admit it."

Kile twitched. "You did not sneak onto the ship. You paid for passage."

Rachel opened her mouth to protest, but Dania grabbed her arm. "You paid for passage."

The girl's eyes widened, probably remembering Kile's internal need to enforce the law. "Yeah, umm, I did. I did all the paying stuff. Legal-like."

Kile stared at her before he sighed. "I'd very much prefer it if you were back on the ship. Safe."

"And leave you out here with them?" She thumbed toward the crew. "Like it or not, I am the only one who cares if you come out of this alive. You are *not* getting rid of me." She adjusted her backpack and headed up the trail.

The commander stared at her as she disappeared into the trees.

Ty inched up beside him. "You do realize you're an enforcer, right? You have more than enough power to stop her."

Kile continued to stare at the trees. "You cannot even fathom the power of that diminutive woman."

Ethan snorted. "Us humans call that being pussy-whipped."

Kile glared at him.

Ethan held up his hands. "I'm just sayin'."

Cal grabbed the engineer's arm and pushed him up the trail before he got his face fried off.

Dania moved beside him. "I'm sorry we missed dinner."

Cal stepped over a rock. "Me, too. At this point, we're going to need to start from scratch." Although that wouldn't be such a bad thing, except for the wasted food.

"I thought it would be better the longer it sat?"

"Yes, but not after being reheated and then left out for so

long."

She kept her eyes on the tops of the battlements. It really did look like an old European castle from Earth.

Cal doubted that she was interested in the architecture, though. And she probably wasn't worried about dinner, either. She was going into what would probably turn into a firefight without any powers. This was going to be a totally new experience for her.

To make it worse, she probably saw herself at her weakest when her friend needed her the most. Cal needed to show her that she wasn't defined by who she'd been, but by who she had become.

The high grass shuffled ahead before Rachel stuck her head out. She waved them over to where she'd hidden.

"The front and back are heavily guarded." She pointed through the grass to a nondescript black door. "That's our entrance. It looks like it leads to the kitchens, and it attaches to what seems to be a big dining hall over there." She pointed to a row of large stained-glass windows. "It all looks like one building, so we can probably find a way to the main residences once we're inside."

Ty wrinkled his brow. "You figured all of that out in the last couple of minutes?"

She glared in Kile's direction. "Of course not. I'm just a useless girl with no skills." A guard passed. She held up her hand until he went around the corner. "Let's go."

They sprinted across a small clearing of bright yellow grass cut in a swirling pattern. Rachel felt along the edge of the solid panel.

"Are you sure it's a door?" Ethan asked.

"Of course it's a door. Why wouldn't it be?"

"Because usually doors have handles."

Ty picked up a thin metal tool lying in what looked like an herb garden. "We can try to pry it loose."

The enforcer grabbed his shoulder. "Are you daft?" He looked at Rachel. "How long until the guard returns?"

"If they keep patrolling the way they have been, then about two minutes or so," she said.

Kile turned back to the entrance and pressed his hands to the metal. The door creaked and bent like a thousand strong hands had folded the panel down the middle and pushed it inside.

The enforcer had done that without breaking a sweat... like it was no harder than creasing paper.

Cal felt for the small weapon that Doc had fashioned to use against Dania not long after she'd boarded. But of course, he'd left it on board so it wouldn't be confiscated by customs. It was back on the ship, useless...while they were out here on a planet with an enforcer that could bend steel by just thinking about it.

Dania placed her hand on his arm, and Cal jumped.

"He promised not to kill any of you," she said.

At least until they'd freed Alexander. Cal had a sinking suspicion that once that happened, all agreements would be forfeit.

Dania had been weakened when she'd first boarded. She'd already started down her path to humanity. Kile had just proven he was very much the same enforcer who'd boarded their ship back on Themyscira.

They all moved inside.

Rachel gaped at the crumpled door, then looked back to the enforcer. "Okay, two things." She held up her pointer finger. "Number one, you are lucky that I'm still mad at you because that was incredibly hot, and you definitely need to do that again for me later." She held up her next digit. "Number two, what did you just do? The door is, like, gone. And I just said the guard was coming back!"

She had a good point. Enforcers were more the crash-and-burn types. As Kile had pointed out, stealth was not their thing.

The commander stared at the broken door. The metal creaked, wobbled, and flattened itself. It floated to the opening, where he set it down, leaning against the frame. Ty and Ethan shoved it into place. The entire panel was still creased and pitted from the ordeal.

Ethan shrugged. "Maybe if they don't look too hard, they'll miss it?"

"We should probably find a different exit, just in case." Ty looked across the chamber. "Let me check the next room. I don't want to walk into a cleaning crew."

Kile started heading toward the door. "If we do, we will just neutralize the problem."

Rachel yanked him back. "You're going to kill the janitors? I don't think so."

The enforcer sighed as they moved between long counters and past large humming doors that had to be freezers and refrigerators.

"Where is the staff?" Ethan asked.

"No party, no need for kitchen staff," Rachel said. "There's probably a smaller kitchen in the main residence."

"Why would you know that?" Ethan asked.

"It just makes sense. All you big-brained people think too much. Sometimes you just have to open your eyes and pay attention." She put out her arm, stopping Kile's gait again.

A small reptile scurried across the linoleum, right where his foot would have fallen.

"Like I said, you all need to pay more attention." She pointed up at Kile. "And don't squish things."

"I have bigger issues to worry about than small animals," he said.

"You should care about everything. All life. That's what the king says: that all life is precious to him."

"He didn't mean animals."

Rachel placed her hands on her hips. "Did you ever ask him?"

Kile opened his mouth to answer, then looked away. "We need to find Alexander."

Ty leaned back through the door. "It's clear. This place is deserted."

Which was odd. Even if there wasn't a party going on, shouldn't there be people around?

"I don't like this," Cal whispered.

"Don't look at a horse with a gift in his mouth," Ethan said, following Ty.

"That's not the saying." Cal followed him into a room with a long table in the center surrounded by chairs. A massive electric candelabra hung above, attached to a ceiling filled with skylights.

Ty crouched near a blackened square in the floor and pointed at the outer edge. "Look at these holes. Something was bolted here." He fingered the scoring. "And recently."

Doc pointed at the darkened marks on the ground. "Whatever was in here was burned." He brushed his fingers over five deep ridges in the stone flooring. "This looks like someone was clawing at the floor."

Cal took in the deep grooves. His stomach turned. "Could those marks have been made by a human being?"

Doc looked up. "Unfortunately, I think they were."

CHAPTER 35

DANIA

DANIA KNELT ON THE GROUND, placing her own hands on the marks. "Someone was trying to get out. Someone strong enough to claw through stone."

Her eyes filled with tears. The only humanoid capable of clawing through stone would be an enforcer.

She choked back the ball lodged in her throat. Hopefully, they weren't too late.

Rachel covered her mouth. "This sicko didn't burn anyone alive, did he?"

Dania's heart clenched. *No.* It wasn't possible.

Peter crouched beside her, waving an instrument over the burn marks. "There is significant pathogen discharge."

"Pathogen discharge?" Kile asked.

Peter's eyes saddened. "I think your friend was here, and he wasn't happy."

Dania grabbed her neck. "They really set him on fire?"

Peter shook his head. "I don't think so. I think he was trying to set *them* on fire. It looks like he was fighting to get out." He ran his fingers along the edge of the blast area.

"This must have been one hell of a cage. The amount of energy spent is off the charts."

A deep ache seated in Dania's chest. "He didn't get out?"

Peter shook his head. "It doesn't look like it."

Dania stood, shaking. If he didn't get out, then what had happened to him?

Ethan stared at the table and then back to the burns on the floor. "Dinner and a show." He mumbled what sounded like an explicative under his breath that wasn't strong enough.

These people...they were monsters. Had they just sat there, eating and socializing while Alexander was fighting for his life?

Alexander didn't deserve this. He wasn't even a military-grade enforcer. He was a healer. His mission was to save people. He wasn't a threat to anyone.

"Is this blood?" Ty pointed to the floor. "And drag marks?"

Dania's pulse pounded in her temples. Kile moved first, following Ty and then overtaking him. A large, paneled door made to look like wood stood in their way. Kile blasted it off the hinges. The metal frame slammed against the other side of a hall and clanged to the floor, the sound echoing down the stone corridors.

"So much for stealth!" Ethan cried, pulling out a gun and racing after them.

"Big Guy," Rachel called. "Wait for me!"

They moved out into the hallway. A camera on the wall turned toward them. Cal and Ethan both raised their weapons and shot the lens.

"It's pretty safe to say they know we're here," Cal said.

Kile stood halfway down the hallway in front of an

opening in the stonework. He placed one hand on either side of the framed arch that had probably been a door before he'd ripped it open and thrown the panel to the side.

Rachel stopped beside him. "Big Guy?"

His lips were parted, and his lower lip trembled. He backed up, looking over Rachel's head and meeting Dania's gaze.

A chill raced over Dania. The loss on Kile's face—the blank essence of dread.

"What?" She sprinted for the door. "What is it?"

Her commander grabbed her by the waist, holding her back. "Dania, don't."

"Let me go!" And like a good soldier, he did, following orders without question.

Cal looked inside and grimaced.

Dania's chest ached. Whatever was in there, she needed to deal with it. She owed Alexander that much.

"General," Kile said. "I truly think we should…"

She held up a hand, quieting him, and stepped past Cal.

A tall cage webbed in glass sat centered in a small room that must have at one time been a large closet. The blood smear traced along the floor and under the open cage door.

But why would they leave it open?

Crumpled in the back of the cage lay a body arched at an odd angle. Long, blonde hair with hints of faded silver streaks draped across the floor.

This was not a man's body, though, but a woman's. Dania took in a relieved breath before reaching down and brushing the lifeless pearlescent hair from her face.

Open eyes looked back at her.

No. They didn't look at her. They stared at nothing. Void.

Dania's breath caught in her throat.

She knew she had to breathe, but she couldn't.

Hundreds of training sessions flooded back to her. A young girl, getting stronger and stronger. The men scowling when she bested them in combat, and the proud applause of the girl's sponsor.

Matara was being groomed to be a general. She had been the strongest female enforcer since Dania had risen in the ranks. And now she lay on the floor, a lifeless shell. Gone.

The breath finally came, and Dania tilted her head back, screaming at the ceiling.

Strong arms encircled her. She tried to push them away, but Cal only held her tighter.

Ty's voice sliced through her sobs. "If we have any chance of finding the other one, we need to go now."

The other one?

Dania held her breath, keeping in another sob. Alexander.

They were here to find Alexander.

Dania opened her eyes and met that cold stare again. What if they found Alexander like this? What if he'd been killed as some sort of spectacle? As entertainment.

Cal grabbed her face and forced her to look at him. "I don't know who this girl was, but we can't save her. If we stay here, we're going to get caught. We need to go. Now."

Dania allowed him to pull her to shaky knees.

Kile blocked their exit. His stare penetrated Dania, sinking clear through to her bones. "When we find the people who did this, the kill is yours," he told her.

Dania nodded, but the usual excitement at the thought of punishment didn't come. Even the most gruesome deaths she could come up with didn't seem like enough.

Rachel ran down the hall toward them.

"Where were you?" Ty asked.

"Doing recon." She pointed her chin to the closet. "Was it our guy?"

"No." Dania squeezed Cal's arm.

How wrong was it to be relieved it wasn't Alexander?

Matara was dead, and she hadn't died a hero's death. She hadn't died enforcing the king's law or protecting her sponsor. It was all so senseless.

Footfalls and voices came toward them.

"Why did it take them so long to get here?" Ty asked.

Rachel pulled his arm, directing them back in the direction they'd come from. "Because the governor isn't in the building, but I found something."

Around the corner, she pushed on the wall, and the stones shifted, opening a secret entrance. "Inside. Quick."

They huddled within, and Rachel closed the doors. The guards outside ran right past them.

"What are you, like a super spy or something?" Ethan asked.

"No. I..." She looked at Kile. "I'm a thief."

Kile tensed, his eyes wide.

Ty squeezed between them in the tight hallway. "I'm sure she means that rich people hire her to break into houses to find faults in their security, which would make everything she did in the past perfectly legal. Right, Quirky?"

Rachel rolled her eyes. "Yeah, whatever."

Kile relaxed, but only slightly. "I thought you were a medical technician."

She moved her gun from one hand to the other. "There was that, too. I was also on the Hedonaii welcoming committee. A girl needs to have options." She pointed behind them. "Go that way."

They squeezed down the hall until it opened wider. Something dripped in the distance, and a dank, murky smell filled the air.

"How did you find this hall?" Dania asked.

"The floor was scuffed from the door shifting. I just pushed all over the place until I found the trigger to open it."

"That was resourceful," Kile said.

Rachel lifted her chin. "I was thinking *ingenious*, but I'll still take that as a compliment, Big Guy."

"Why is this hall even here?" Dania asked.

Rachel motioned them through the partially lit hall. "I found a data node. Apparently, the governor had this castle moved stone by stone to this planet and had it rebuilt here. He's crazy. Rich, but crazy. This is some sort of old family ancestral home or something. This passage was in the original architecture."

"Why is this important?" Kile asked. "We need to find Alexander."

She placed her hands on her hips. "Well, we also need to not get caught, and you needed a way to move around without being seen. So you're welcome." She shook her head and turned to Dania. "The node I looked at said there's a zoo on the other side of the property. But there are two special exhibits that are the governor's current favorites. Those are up in his private residences. I'm hoping that's where we'll find his latest purchase."

His latest purchase, meaning Alexander. "Do you know how to get there?"

She pointed farther down the hall. "I think we can go that way and get past the security, but once we're out of here, we'll be in the living space. If the data node was current, then the family doesn't seem to be home, but security knows we're here, thanks to my overzealous boyfriend."

"I'm not…" Kile growled under his breath before he turned away.

But was he going to deny being overzealous, or deny the romantic entanglement?

The relationship had to be one-sided, though. Kile wouldn't be interested in a human. At least, Dania didn't *think* he would. However, he did seem to let this woman get away with far more than he normally would.

Still, Rachel was right. Kile had been reckless, and now that security knew they were here, they'd probably have to fight their way out once they found Alexander. And who knew what kind of shape her friend would be in.

Dania straightened. This was what she'd been trained for. Maybe even made for, if what Peter had said was true. She needed to brush off Matara's death. There would be time to mourn later. Now, she needed to be a leader. A general.

She quickened her pace until they reached the end of the stonework. A rim of white molding material marked the last of the ancient stones and the start of a metal-lined arch leading to a modern door, similar to the sliding doors on the *Star Renegade*.

Dania glanced back to Kile. "Ready?"

"Hold on," Cal said. "Stealth, remember."

Dania steeled herself, looking back to the door. Cal was a good man. They all were. But this might be the time for the enforcers to step up. Kile may have been right before. It was easier to force your way through situations, rather than hiding around corners. Matara was dead, and she wouldn't let the same thing happen to Alexander if she could stop it.

She gritted her teeth. "Commander?"

Kile stepped beside her. "May I assume anyone breathing who is not in a cage is guilty?"

Part of her, the human part, considered the possibility of servants. But any servant who did not report crimes were just as guilty as their employers.

"Do what you need to do, Commander."

"Dania?" Cal's voice nearly ripped through her soul. But she pushed the feeling aside and strode through the door. This wasn't about Cal, or anyone else standing behind her, but Alexander.

Kile's hair swirled beneath the hat Alanna had purchased to hide his pearlescent tresses. He reached up like it itched before tossing the hat to the floor.

He moved into the empty hall beside her. His loose, beige-toned colonist clothing shifted from the power coursing over his skin. He looked no less menacing without the uniform.

Dania no longer had her power, but she had her training. She would save Alexander, no matter who stood in her way.

Kile glanced at her, a smug grin on his lips. "It is good to have you back, General."

CAL LOOKED left and right as he stepped out of the hallway. The enforcer looked way too excited, and Cal didn't like Dania's rigid stance.

"Dani is acting a little weird," Rachel whispered.

Weird wasn't the right word. She was acting like an enforcer.

Doc held up the device he'd been using to take readings. "I have a heartbeat in this direction. It's pretty strong."

He started walking, but Dania and her commander pushed past him, moving ahead around a corner. Halfway down the hall, a similar cage to the one they'd found the dead girl in stood pushed against the wall with a low light shining above.

Dania sprinted ahead and grabbed on to the bars. "Alexander!"

Her hair came alive, swirling in the air about her.

Cal skidded to a stop beside her. "Dania!"

A huge black mass inside lunged for her. Cal grabbed her, pulling her from the cage before five-inch claws sliced through the space where Dania's face had been.

"Whoa!" Ethan skidded to a stop a few feet from the cage. He gaped at the snapping teeth and the long tusks poking through the bars. "Is that a Trellan jungle boar?"

"It can't be," Rachel said. "They're extinct."

"Which would make that thing rare and dangerous," Ty said. "I'm not so sure it's beautiful."

Dania twitched beneath Cal's grip, like a live wire waiting to explode. "That isn't Alexander!" Her hair swirled like she was underwater.

Doc approached, holding up his hands. "Sweetie, you need to calm down."

She pulled out of Cal's grip. "I will *not* calm down!"

"Sweetie, you need to." Doc's gaze rolled over her twisting hair. "It looks like you're expending energy, and it might be the last of your original pathogens. If you burn them all out, I'm not sure what will happen."

"I don't care."

"But you should. If you collapse, you won't be any help to your friend when we find him."

She looked down at her hands, then at the creature snarling in the cage. Her hair lowered a few strands at a time until she looked like herself again.

The creature lunged at the bars.

"That is one scary fuzzball," Ethan said.

"But he's worth a fortune if everyone thinks he's extinct," Cal said. So of course, they stuck him in a cage.

Doc took more readings. "He's worth a lot more than you can imagine." He lowered the device. "He is a she. And she's pregnant. That's probably why she's up here. They're trying to keep her safe."

"That means there's probably a daddy boar somewhere, too, right?" Rachel said.

A blast of heat rolled over them. They all spun to see a soft glow about the enforcer. "This is inconsequential," Kile said. "We are here to find Alexander. As my general pointed out, this is not Alexander."

Rachel pointed to the cage. "But she's extinct. Or, like, going extinct."

Kile's nose flared, looking at the cage. "This is not my problem. Come." He started walking.

"No."

He spun on her. "No?"

"You heard me." Rachel pulled on the bars. The creature lashed at her.

Kile pulled her back. "That beast will hurt you."

"I don't care. I'm not leaving her here."

Ethan raised his hand. "Umm, I'd like to point out that jungle boars are nearly extinct because they were hunting down and eating the Trellan settlers. The colonists started killing them to keep their families safe."

Meaning that thing would kill us, too. Cal sighed. "He's got a point, Rachel." Not only that. Security could drop on them at any moment.

She reached for the bars again. "I'm not leaving her. She's scared, and she's going to have a baby. That little guy will get sold to the highest bidder, and you all know it. Someone will probably eat him just to say they got to taste the last living jungle boar."

"Stop!" Kile pushed her back. "This is ridiculous."

"You can keep saying that all you want, but I'm not leaving her here."

He closed his eyes and growled. This woman definitely had him under her thumb, but this wasn't quite what Cal had in mind when they'd wanted a distraction.

Kile surveyed the cage and looked at Doc. "This does not seem to be the same grade enclosure that housed Matara."

Doc scanned the bars. "No. I guess they weren't worried about our fuzzy mama throwing merciless magical power at them."

Kile touched three of the five hinges, and the lock. The three hinges dripped to the floor, and the lock started to droop.

Snarling, the creature slammed against the inside of the cage. The remaining hinges buckled. The boar seemed to notice the change and crashed even harder against the failing metal.

Kile stepped back. "If my calculations are correct, the last of the fasteners will fall free within twenty minutes. I highly suggest we finish our assignment and exit the building before that happens."

They had twenty minutes before a very angry animal known for ripping settlers to pieces and skewering grown men on their tusks got free. Perfect.

Rachel smiled, lifted up on her toes, and kissed the enforcer's cheek. "You are a big softie, after all!"

Dania started walking. "Let's go. We now have an actual ticking clock, and who knows when the guards will find out we made our way through their defenses."

As they moved deeper into the building, the décor seemed more ornate. Lots of gold and tapestries woven with tight, uneven threads...not the precise perfect stitching of modern machinery. Could these tapestries be the originals? Could old fabric last this long outside of a museum?

They turned a corner and a yellow light started to flash. Yellow...Cal's least favorite color. No. Strike that. The light could have been orange.

"We're going to get company," Ty said.

Dania pointed at the corner they'd just come from. "We need a defensive stance right here. Two guns, while the rest of us advance."

Cal took a deep breath. "Well, in case your friend is in one of those high-tech cages, I think I'll need Ethan. And we'll need our doctor in case he needs medical help." Which was more than likely, after the condition they'd found the girl in.

"I'll stay," Rachel said. "I can scream pretty darn loud if I see anyone coming."

Ty pulled out his weapon. "And I'll take her six. We got this." He pointed down the hall. "Go get your boy."

Dania took off down the hall, Ethan and Doc chasing after her.

Kile took a step toward Ty. "If you touch her, I will disembowel you."

Ty's eyes widened. "Dude, touching your girl never crossed my mind. I *do like* breathing."

Kile grabbed him by the back of the neck. "Likewise, if she dies, you will die. Slowly and painfully." He released him, and the pilot thumped to the floor.

Ty rubbed the back of his neck. "Have you ever thought of being a motivational speaker? Because you have such a way with words."

Cal tapped the enforcer's arm. "Come on. Ticking clock and guards coming, remember?"

Dania, Doc, and Ethan stopped at each juncture ahead, with Doc pointing which way to go.

"Heartbeat, this way." Doc pointed left and they followed.

The hall opened into what must have been a throne room in the original castle. A corridor on the far right led out of the large, circular room. Centered on the far wall stood a raised dais with a large stone chair on top decorated with lions resting on the armrests.

To the left of the chair hung a glass chamber, eight-foot tall and filled with a swirling semi-clear gas, or maybe it was liquid. A bare-chested man floated inside, his long, opal-white hair swaying about him like he were underwater.

"Alexander!" Dania ran to the cylinder, placing her hands on the glass.

Yellow lights on the wall flickered, reminding them that things were about to get a lot harder.

Ethan moved beside Cal. *"That's* Alexander?"

Dania turned to Doc, tears in her eyes. "We have to find a way to get him out."

Kile marched forward. "Just break the glass."

Doc held up a hand. "Whoa there, partner. For all we know, that liquidic gas in there is keeping him alive." He pointed through the frame. "I see a lot of bruising. Let me take a look at the controls before we do anything hasty." He moved over to a panel on the wall.

Ethan tugged Cal's arm. "Umm, boss, I think we might have a problem."

"No more problems." But of course, whatever it was, he needed to know. "What?"

The engineer pointed his chin toward the glass. "I know Dania said that guy is her friend, but he's probably just as bad as the commander. Maybe even worse."

"What makes you say that?"

"Because Ty and I saw Dania with him back on Midway Station." He moved closer, looking over his shoulder at Dania. "Boss, the guy in that container raped Dania right in front of us."

Heat flashed through Cal's veins. "What?"

"I'm telling you. We saw it. She fell to her knees, crying, and he told her to shut up and not tell anyone before he walked out and left her there." He looked back at Dania again. "That's why we were able to catch her. She was a wreck about it."

Cal's hands formed fists. He resisted the urge to pull out his gun and shoot right through the glass.

Dania pressed her hands against the cylinder, whispering things like, "We're here," and "We're coming."

Why would she be so worried about someone who'd hurt her—violated her in the worst way? "You've got to be wrong."

Ethan shook his head. "I'm not. Maybe it's like Stockholm syndrome or something, but that guy is an even worse problem than our own Big Bad."

And they were about to set him free. And then there would be two of them ready to execute them all.

"Does anyone have any good news?"

Doc returned. "Well, I'm going to be able to open the container, but it's going to take time. He's breathing in the gas, and it's keeping him alive but drugged. It looks like he's given them one hell of a fight on more than one occasion." Doc looked at some figures on his data pad. "His vitals look decent, but he's been through a lot. He's probably going to be screwed up in the head in more ways than one."

So the criminal enforcer might be psychotic, too? Great. Why couldn't anything go easy for them, just for once?

CHAPTER 37

DANIA

ALEXANDER'S EYES WERE CLOSED, and he floated in some sort of liquid gas. He looked at peace, but Dania knew better.

The lights on the wall still flickered yellow. How long did they have before they were found? They needed to stop playing games and do what needed to be done.

She spun and walked to Cal, Ethan and the doctor. "How do we get him out of there?"

"I'm thinking maybe we should leave him in there," Ethan said.

She stared at him, wondering if possibly she'd misheard. "What are you talking about?"

The engineer held up his hands, like he was preparing to ward off an attack. "I saw what he did to you."

What in the name of the stars was he talking about?

Dania looked at the flashing lights. "We have no time for games."

The engineer pointed behind her, to where Alexander floated inside the glass cylinder. "I saw that piece of drifting fuselage hurt you. I'm sorry, but you're my friend and…"

Had he gone insane? "Alexander never hurt me."

"Oh, come on! Ty and I saw him piledrive you under the tree in the aviary on Midway Station."

In the aviary? Midway Station?

Under the tree…

Her eyes widened. The imbecile actually thought Alexander had *used* her.

"He pretended to hurt me. He was making me look weak so I would appear to be an easy target." She folded her arms. "And apparently, it worked." She shook her head. "Do you really think I would let a man use me? And that he would walk away with his skin intact if he had?"

Ethan gaped. Apparently, he'd never considered that he'd been played and had walked right into a trap set for someone else.

"Either way, we need to be really cautious," Doc said. "There's some video in that feed…" He shook his head. "Dania, I'm not sure he's going to be all right after what he's been through."

After finding Matara, Dania knew that Alexander wouldn't be the shining pinnacle of perfection that she'd known. But they didn't know him like she did. "Alexander is strong."

"Maybe he was, once, but…" He sighed. "I'm thinking that we need to find a way to get him out of there while he's still unconscious. Then maybe give him a sedative so we can wake him up under controlled circumstances."

"Controlled circumstances?" What did he think Alexander would do? And did he expect them to carry a full-grown man out of here?

"This is ridiculous." Kile walked to the monitor. "I will judge if there is a potential threat."

"I'm not sure he can be a neutral party in this, either," Peter said.

This made no sense. The doctor had always been the voice of reason and facts on this crew.

"What aren't you telling me?" Dania asked.

Peter's eyes saddened. "I've learned stuff about the brain over the years, and there are certain things that the brain can and can't handle. Some traumas can change a person, and, sweetie, I'm sorry, but I don't think he's going to come out of this the same person."

His temperature spiked, then receded, like a man conflicted. He did want to save Alexander, but he was…afraid.

Dania tensed. If Alexander was compromised, he would be a very serious threat to them all.

She looked back to where her friend floated in the cylindrical tank. Dark bruises covered his normally immaculate chest. Could it be true? Could he be…*different*?

Cal's wrist pinged.

He hit the comm. "Talk to me."

"We're hearing movement through the walls," Ty said. "No sign of them, but they might be on their way."

"Roger that." Cal turned to Peter. "How can we get him out of that tank safely?"

Kile roared. Behind him, the monitor displayed a video of Alexander, his mouth twisted in a scream.

The room filled with white light, and a comet-sized firestorm spewed from Kile's palms. The light slammed against Alexander's cylinder, exploding the glass. Shards impaled themselves in the walls, some hitting stones and shattering to dust.

Dania's blood iced. The doctor had insinuated that they needed to take care with how they released him!

Gas and water filled the air and spilled across the floor as Alexander's limp body fell onto the dais.

"I guess we don't have to worry about how we're going to get him out anymore," Ethan said.

Dania broke out of her fog, slipping on the slick, watery goo dripping town the dais as she sprinted to Alexander.

Peter splashed through the water beside her, instruments at the ready.

Dania got there a second before him, touching her friend's face and repeating his name over and over.

Kile stormed toward them, his eyes even whiter than normal. If he'd hurt Alexander, she'd take retribution out of his hide.

"Alexander," she whispered.

His skin chilled her fingers. She resisted the need to grab him and warm him up, giving Peter room to do whatever he was doing as he ran the instruments over Alexander's body.

Cal jumped in front of Kile, stopping his advance. "He needs a doctor. Let Doc do his thing."

Kile pointed at Peter. "He is not a real doctor."

"Neither are you," Cal told him. "You're trained to kill things. Right now, Doc is your friend's best chance at survival."

Kile growled, showing his teeth before he stepped back. "I am going to eviscerate the people who did this to him. I will paint this blasted place with blood. I will…"

"I get it, I get it." Cal turned to the dais.

Dania swept back Alexander's hair. "What did they do to you?"

Whatever was on those security streams must have been

just as bad, or worse, than Peter had said for Kile to react that way. She took a steadying breath. Alexander couldn't really be permanently changed, could he?

Dania smoothed more of her friend's wet hair from his face. "Alexander, please be okay."

"His heartbeat is erratic," Doc said. "I'm not sure he…"

Alexander's eyes sprang open. His hand shot out and gripped Peter's throat.

The air flashed. A blast of wind punched Dania in the chest, throwing her back. Ethan, Cal, and Kile landed on either side of her.

"Stop!" Dania sprang to her feet and ran back as Doc gasped for air. "Alexander!" Dania clawed at her friend's hand, but her fingers slipped from his wet flesh. "Alexander, stop!"

Peter choked, his face turning red.

"Stop!" Kile returned to her side and placed his hands over Dania's, but he slipped just as much.

Peter's eyes grew heavy.

Cal grabbed Ethan's arm. "Find something to hit him with!"

Dania cringed. It wasn't a bad idea, but in Alexander's weakened state, they might kill him by accident. She wanted to beg them not to hurt her friend, but how could she do that, when Alexander was choking their doctor!

"Alexander, please!" Dania begged.

Kile grunted and pulled Alexander's fingers from Peter's neck.

The doctor fell to the floor, free, holding his throat and gasping. Color returned to his face.

Alexander snarled, screaming in gibberish, like his tongue had forgotten how to form words.

Kile shook him. "You will stop. You are strong. Show it!"

A blast of light shot over Dania's head and a laser blast scorched the wall behind her.

Cal raised a gun and fired, and someone out of Dania's line of sight hit the ground.

"We're out of time!" Cal turned to Ethan and pointed where he'd just shot from. "Cover that hall. There will be more where he came from."

"On it."

Cal pointed his own weapon in the direction they'd left Ty and Rachel.

Alexander twitched. His back arched at an odd angle before his body started convulsing.

"Alexander!" Dania placed her hands on him. Could she heal him?

Even if she knew how, she didn't have the power anymore!

Rachel screamed from the hallway. Guns and laser fire echoed down the corridor.

Peter stopped rubbing his throat, took a long breath, and picked up his medical device, running it over the spasming man. "He's bottoming out."

Dania wiped tears from her eyes. "Help him!"

Peter coughed, sitting back, holding his neck. "I don't know how."

And that was it? She was supposed to accept that?

Ethan shouted something and shot his gun. Someone cried out in the distance, and another blast of light exploded over their heads.

Alexander took one last breath and stopped moving.

Kile shoved Peter, sprawling him back on the tiles. "Imbecile. Your job is to save him. Nothing else!"

Peter shook his head. "I have no idea what that stuff was that he's been breathing. *You're* the imbecile for breaking the glass before I'd had time to…"

Dania closed her eyes, blocking the men out. She pulled Alexander into her arms. His dripping, wet hair chilled her neck as she rocked him against her shoulder.

Some of her earliest memories were of Alexander. They'd run through the halls of the king's estates, setting things on fire by accident. Alexander had always had ingenious plans to not get caught when they'd done something they shouldn't have, which had been often. He was maybe her only friend, and the only person she knew who, without a shred of doubt, she could trust.

"I wanted to save you," she whispered into his hair.

And she'd never spoken words that were more true.

She'd failed her prince. She'd failed Kile. And now she'd failed Alexander.

Maybe Kile was right. Maybe she was no one if she wasn't an enforcer. She was supposed to enforce the law and protect the innocent. What good had she done for Matara, for Alexander?

She stroked his hair, and a tiny *thump* met her fingertips at his temple. His chest didn't rise and fall, but she could sense shallow, barely discernible breaths. When they'd been young, he'd taught her rudimentary healing. She'd enjoyed it at first, until she'd been admonished and turned toward the more valuable tutelage—like methods of execution.

Alexander had become skilled over the years. Then again, so had Dania, but in such different arts.

There was one skill she had that no other enforcer under her command was capable of, though, even Alexander. As a general, Geron had granted her the ability to give her enforcers strength when he wasn't available. They called it feeding, but it was really so much more than that. It was a sharing of power, will, and energy.

Alexander twitched.

If he was still alive, maybe strength was all he needed?

Peter stood and backed away from Kile. Her commander had never been good at accepting defeat, always looking for who to blame. Today, apparently, he placed blame on the doctor.

Peter had given her so much, but the strength he'd given her—these pathogens—were artificial, and nothing like the strength of her prince.

However, her hair had started to float when she'd thought the boar was Alexander. If she did have strength in her, maybe she could still share it?

Peter seemed unsure if she could survive without her original pathogens. This might be the perfect time to find out. She'd always believed that Alexander was better than her in so many ways. More worthy of his gifts. This might be her last chance to prove that. She pulled him tighter, pressed her cheek against his, and called up the last few swirling particles inside her—the last of her prince's gifts.

Taking a steadying breath, she focused her energy and pushed the particles out through her skin until Alexander began to warm. If Peter was right, and this killed her, at least she'd die a noble death. She took a deep breath and smiled.

Alexander was worth it.

CAL LOOKED down the target tracer of the unfamiliar weapon. He hoped these things weren't cheap knockoffs the locals sold only to tourists. He reached for the comm on his wrist to call Ty.

"Dania! No!" The commander's voice boomed through the room.

Cal spun.

Dania lay on the floor, holding her friend. A soft haze filled the air about her. Her hair stood out, not floating as it had when they'd first met, but like she'd been hit with a static charge.

Kile ran toward her as she slumped over Alexander.

More shots echoed down the hall, followed by another angry cry from Rachel.

"Dammit!" Why now?

"What do I do, boss?" Ethan's gaze shifted between the hall they'd been attacked from, and Dania.

"Shoot anyone you don't know coming down that hallway." They needed cover, and then they needed to give Ty reinforcements.

Cal slid to a stop as Doc peeled Dania off her friend. "What happened?"

"I think she fed him," Kile said. "She's too weak. She shouldn't have."

Doc took readings on both of them and cursed under his breath. "This isn't good." He looked at Kile. "Can you explain what feeding is?"

The commander looked confused, like maybe even he wasn't sure as he crouched beside them. "It's like an exchange of energy. It makes us stronger. More alert."

Doc dragged his fingers through his hair. "Can you do the same thing for her? Can you give her some energy?"

Kile looked down. "No. Only the sponsor or a general can feed their soldiers."

Doc cursed. "I suppose there's no way to give you a promotion?"

The enforcer tilted his head. "The process takes years of programming."

Doc gaped at him. "I'd say that a pretty big design flaw."

Kile grimaced. "Under the circumstances, I would have to agree."

Cal's comm pinged. "Ty, you okay?"

"Taking heavy fire. I have to admit, Rachel is a bit scary with a gun, but there're too many of them."

Kile stood. His hands shook as he looked past Cal to the door they'd entered from.

The last thing they needed was for the enforcer to lose it over Rachel getting hurt. With two people down, Cal needed his help.

"We're on our way." Cal turned off the comm and looked at Doc. "We can't stay here."

Doc blew air from his lips. "Well, our boy here..." He

pointed at Alexander. "He looks pretty good, all things considered."

"And Dania?"

Doc shrugged. "I think we need to get her a *treatment*, and fast."

A treatment…meaning pathogens. That wasn't good. "I guess there's no chance of waking either of them up?"

"Not within the next several hours."

Of course not.

Cal slapped Kile's leg. "I need your help. Can you carry Alexander?"

"Of course, but I'll be encumbered."

Yeah, Cal had the same concern. "Can you hold him on your shoulder to keep your hands somewhat free and just put him down if you need to?"

Kile nodded, reached down, and placed Alexander's limp, half-naked form over his shoulder, and then stood, as if he weren't carrying any additional weight. Damn, the guy was strong.

Cal looked over his shoulder to Ethan. He was probably the shortest member of the crew, and slight, which helped him get around the tight areas in Engineering. He wasn't the greatest build for carrying someone. Doc was a better candidate, but the truth was, Doc had been shot with a bullet recently, and Ethan, even if he were strong enough, was still nursing the wound from the particle beam.

Even though Cal was a better shot, he was the only one who could carry Dania without aggravating an existing injury.

He pulled her into his arms. Her eyes were closed, and her lips parted. "She looks like she's sleeping."

Doc grimaced. "I really can't tell you if it's more than that yet. Her physiology is just too complicated for these hand-held instruments."

Cal rested her head on his chest. "Ethan, Doc, you're on point. Let's get back to Ty and take stock."

Blasts flared ahead, lighting up the hall despite the twists and turns.

At the last corner, Ethan held up a hand, stopping everyone's advance. "Ty! What's the deal, man?"

"Kinda busy!" Ty called back. "But I'd love a little help."

Ethan peeked around the corner, then waved them on.

As they came up from their rear, Ty shot once around the corner to his right. "Welcome to the party." He shot again. "Dania, you were right about this defensive position. We're taking them out before they can even level their sights on us."

Rachel took two shots around the corner.

Ty looked over his shoulder. "Dania?" His gaze fell on her in Cal's arms. "Whoa! What the hell?"

"Dani!" Rachel moved toward them.

Three blasts lit up the hall. Doc and Ethan took her place.

"Is she okay?" Rachel asked.

"We're not sure," Cal admitted. He looked past her. "Ty, status."

Rachel waved her hand. "Let him shoot. I can do status." She pointed toward the hallway. "There are guys down there shooting at us. We're shooting back. What more do you need to know?"

Cal didn't think it was possible, but they may have just found someone more infuriating that Ethan.

"Is that the only way out?" Cal asked.

"It looks like it," Ty called. "We're too high up to jump out a window."

"This is ridiculous." Kile eased Alexander's unconscious body to the floor. "Those people are guilty."

"They're just guards," Ty said. "I'm trying my best just to wound them. They're only doing their jobs."

"Only doing their jobs?" Kile stood. "Protecting the people who harmed Alexander? Protecting the people who killed Matara for their enjoyment?"

The enforcer walked into the hall. A blast hit him in the shoulder, jolting him back.

"What are you doing?" Rachel lunged for him. Ethan grabbed her around the waist, drawing her back.

"Stop!" she cried. "Stop him!"

Another hit slammed Kile in the same shoulder. Smoke rose from burn marks in the edges of his loose brown shirt. He started to walk toward the attackers.

"Stop!" Rachel clawed at Ethan. "Let me go!"

Cal placed Dania on the ground beside Alexander and motioned to Doc. "Watch them." He pointed his gun around the corner and fired to either side of Kile's head, but the enforcer was too damn big to fire around.

Leaning his head on the wall, Cal took a deep breath.

Ty sat next to him. "Are you going to do something dumb?"

His pilot knew him all too well. "Yeah. Stay here and cover Doc." Before he could change his own mind, Cal rolled to his feet and ran after Kile, throwing cover fire over the enforcer's shoulder.

"Boss, are you crazy?" Ethan called.

More shots came from farther down the hall, and Ethan and Rachel raced after him. Cal continued to throw cover fire around Kile. Rachel and Ethan did the same.

Kile jolted again, like he'd been hit in the other shoulder.

"Dammit, Big Bad, duck or something!" Ethan screamed.

Heat radiated off the commander. His hair stood on end.

"Please stop!" Rachel called.

Kile finally raised his hands. The air in front of him swirled as he continued to stride forward.

Cal looked around the larger man just as the guards sprinted down the hall in the opposite direction. The ones remaining behind fired three times. Cal ducked as one shot grazed Kile's shoulder. More smoke rose from the enforcer's clothing.

Was he letting himself get shot on purpose?

Flames erupted from the enforcer's palms. Kile roared, his voice booming off the walls as the fire shot from his hands like an extension of his fingers, plucking the fleeing guards from the floor and lifting them off their feet.

The skin on Cal's arms, face, and hands burned. The enforcer had turned the hallway into a damn oven!

Cal slowed, grabbing Rachel as she continued to run toward Kile.

"Let me go!" she cried.

"Get a hold of yourself!" Cal shouted above the booming hum ahead. "Can't you feel that heat?"

"He needs me!"

How in the name of anything sane in the galaxy did she think that death machine needed anyone?

An explosion of heat ricocheted back, blasting from Kile. Cal hit the floor, dragging Rachel down with him. Ethan slammed to the floor beside them, shouting several colorful obscenities.

Rachel started to twist in Cal's grip again. "Something's wrong!"

The ground started to rumble beneath them. Cal had to

agree with her, but that didn't mean he was going to let her run to her death. She was only a stowaway, but she was still his responsibility until he could officially drop her off somewhere, preferably safe and sound.

"Cal?" Ethan pointed to the wall, where the stonework had started to turn red and drip down toward the floor.

Cal tried to take in a breath, but the heat stung his lungs. He pulled Rachel's face to his chest to protect her and buried his own face in her hair, Ethan pressed up against them, probably protecting Cal more than he was protecting himself.

Cal's clothing clung to him, drenched in sweat, but stinging like the fabric boiled on his skin.

They needed to get out of there before they all baked alive.

Rachel twisted and jammed her knee into Cal's groin. He gasped, releasing her. Pain exploded through his body, slicing up his abdomen as she scrambled away.

"R-Rachel," he rasped, getting up to one knee. Heat blasted his face.

"Let her go!" Ethan pulled him back down. "You tried, boss."

But maybe not hard enough. *Dammit!*

Rachel stumbled forward, covering her face with one arm. "Big Guy, stop!"

The flames only rose higher. If he didn't stop, he'd turn the whole place into a kiln!

Rachel fell to one knee, then got back up again. "Stop!" She took another two steps.

Sweat dripped from Cal's hair. He couldn't take the heat from this far away. How was she still standing that close to the source?

The enforcer's hair swirled around his head. The heat wavered the air about him.

Rachel stumbled, falling to her hands and knees and crawling, but still several yards from the enforcer. Smoke rose from the edges of her long, russet hair.

She reached out but drew her hand back, as if it hurt. "Kile?"

Cal startled. He'd never heard her use the commander's name. He thought she hadn't known what it was.

"Kile!" she repeated. "Kile, please. You're hurting me!"

The enforcer looked over his shoulder, his eyes so white, they nearly glowed. Fire dripped from his hands, making him look like some kind of demonic hellhound.

He blinked, shaking his head.

Rachel reached for him, then collapsed to the floor.

The roar stopped. The heated wind died to nothing.

Ethan lifted his head off the ground, squinting down the hall. "I don't believe it."

Neither did Cal. She'd done it. She'd stopped him.

But at what cost? She lay on the floor, still.

Cal sat up, looking back in the direction they'd run from. Ty was pushing himself up to his feet, holding on to the edge of the wall he'd been hiding behind. The others were still hidden around the corner.

"Doc, you still there?" Cal called.

"Here!" Peter looked around the corner. Soft tendrils of smoke drifted up from the edges of the wall. "Did a nuclear bomb just go off?"

Cal looked the opposite way. Metal and stone pooled on the floor, some still red and molten. The once-white marble floors were black with soot and ash.

There was nothing left in the hall. No furniture, no artwork, and worst of all…no people. No guards. Just ash.

The enforcer fell to his knees, his hands shaking and still glowing a heart-chilling red.

Rachel lifted her head and crawled a few more feet toward him, but the commander stared, his eyes still white and unblinking.

That was not the man Rachel thought she knew. Stars, if he touched her with those hands…

"Quirky, stop!" Cal got to his feet and raced toward her.

She pulled herself to her knees in front of the enforcer. "Big Guy?" She reached for him, then drew back.

Cal slid to a stop behind her. "Be careful."

"Shut up." She kept her eyes on the commander. "I'm not afraid of him."

But she should have been. Couldn't she see the destruction?

The enforcer took a labored, staggered breath before the glow in his eyes abated. He covered his face, sobbing.

The enforcer…the rock-solid automaton…was *crying*.

Rachel reached for him. "Big Guy." She grabbed his wrists and pulled his hands from his face. "Big Guy! I'm here!"

He choked out a breath. "You didn't see what they did to him. They needed to die. They all needed to die."

His shoulders shook, drips of fire still fell from his fingers and splashed to the ground on either side of Rachel's legs.

She held his wrists, not flinching from the heat. "It's okay. You got them all. They won't hurt anyone again."

A pile of ash kicked up as if hit with a breeze and blew down the hall, flattening and dispersing to nothing. Cal's stomach clenched as he considered what that pile may have once been.

Kile grimaced. "They deserved worse. I should have killed them slowly and painfully."

The fire stopped dripping from his fingers. His skin was still pale and un-scorched. How was that even possible?

She placed one hand on the enforcer's cheek. "But they're gone. We don't have to worry about them, but I worry about *you*."

He pushed her away. "I don't care about me."

"That's fine. But do you care about *me*?" Rachel asked. "Because I need you to get me out of here. And Dani and Alex too. Can you save me and your friends?"

Kile blinked, shook his head, and looked in the direction where they'd left Dania and Alexander around the corner. He closed his eyes, and the flames on the floor beside them dwindled to nothing. "I will get you out."

"Good. That's my good soldier." Rachel touched his arm. "I'm going to tell Dani all about how you took control and did all the good stuff."

He wiped his eyes. "Tears are not good."

"Tears show you care, and I, for one, thought it was very sexy. But if you want, we can all forget about the tears, and Alex and Dani will never have to know."

He glanced down the hall. "That would be preferable." He stood and faced Cal. "My apologies. I had a minor break in protocol."

"Minor?" Ethan whispered.

Ty came up from behind him and smacked him on the head.

Cal cleared his throat. "It's all right. But we need to get back to the ship. I want off this planet."

Kile scanned the rubble again. "As do I."

THE AIR COOLED with each step they took from Kile's fiery chaos. Cal's skin tingled and itched as the sweat continued to pour from his hair. This enforcer was every bit the menace Cal had thought he was. Now that they had Alexander, Cal would somehow have to save his crew from a man who could melt stone.

Luck wasn't going to get him out of this one.

As they turned the corner, Doc pulled an instrument away from Alexander's pale, bare chest. "What the hell? You guys look like you just had a fight with a sun." He ran the device over Cal. "Your temperature is through the roof."

Yeah, Cal didn't doubt it.

He swatted Doc away and took a step toward Dania. Her skin had paled, now maybe even worse than Alexander. Either that, or Alexander was getting better.

He knelt and placed his hand against her cheek. Her skin iced his palm. He hoped that was his own heat, and not Dania's lack of warmth. "How's she doing?"

"Not good," Doc said. "We need to get out of here."

"Then we will depart." Kile reached down and lifted

Alexander back over his shoulder. "We should find no more resistance." He held the younger enforcer's legs with his right arm as the rest of Alexander's body sprawled across the older man's back.

Doc winced. "I don't think we should be moving him so much. He has broken bones."

Kile glanced over his shoulder as he walked. "He won't care if he's dead. If he lives, he will forgive me."

"He has a point," Rachel said, hurrying after him.

"Is it safe to move Dania?" Cal asked.

"Do we have a choice?" Ethan adjusted his gun on his shoulder.

"There's nothing broken," Doc said. "It's just the damn pathogens."

Or lack of them. As always, time was of the essence.

Cal pulled Dania into his arms. He wanted to pretend she was asleep. He wanted to take her back to the ship and tuck her into her bed and then call her in the morning to ask if she wanted to learn how to cook eggs.

That wasn't going to happen. He knew that, but he couldn't bear to think about her stuck in the med bay again with tubes attached to her.

They moved through the corridors and back into the dining room. Alexander's long, silver-blond hair hung limp and wet, dangling over a foot below his shoulders.

Cal tightened his grip on Dania. Alexander was Kile's goal. He'd made that more than clear. Now that they had him, he'd be returning to the star-blasted prince who wanted Cal dead.

Cal slowed his pace. Doc and Ty slowed their stride on either side of him, with Ethan behind. Maybe they also worried that they were walking toward their deaths.

Kile had just proven he was the very menace that Cal had been running from since he'd been a child…a cold-blooded death machine. The commander would treat the crew of the *Star Renegade* with no more regard than those men back in that hallway now that he had what he wanted.

Cal's walk slowed to a saunter, broadening the distance between his crewmates and the enforcer. Rachel had her hand on Kile's shoulder, talking to him, but the commander's gaze remained forward, either focused or ignoring her. If she were farther away from the enforcer, Cal would have grabbed her and pulled her back. He needed to hope that Kile wouldn't consider her a part of this, and he'd let her go. For the rest of them, the only chance they had was to make a break for it.

Dania's hair—her very human-looking hair—hung in her eyes. Maybe Cal could convince the Carteks that she wasn't an enforcer. Maybe if they were able to get away from Kile, Cal could point the Carteks to this planet, and the squids would be happy to take the two, still letting Cal and his crew go free. Dania would hate him for leaving Alexander behind, but after what Cal had just seen, there was a damn good chance that Kile would take the Carteks out before they got anywhere near him. Then, all Cal needed to do would be to keep a step ahead of the enforcers. Again.

That new tech had better be worth all this trouble.

Doc placed his hand on Cal's shoulder and pointed to Cal's comm band.

Luckily, they were all smart enough not to speak because they'd learned that Dania could hear them whisper from far away. If she had enhanced hearing, it was likely Kile did, too.

Cal twisted his arm slightly, keeping a grip on Dania but giving Doc access to the band. Doc grimaced before pressing the panic button. His hand trembled as he drew his fingers away.

"That's it," Ty whispered.

Ethan shifted nervously. There was no turning back now. Alanna was on her way.

Cal took a deep breath and let it out slowly.

Ty glanced up and down the corridor, probably looking for an alternate exit. Once Alanna got here, Ty would need to get to the bridge in seconds and break the atmosphere so Alanna could jump the ship. Best case scenario, neither the Carteks nor the enforcers would ever find them.

Now, they just needed to keep as much space as possible between them and Kile, so once they left the building, Alanna could drop down and scoop them up before the commander got a chance to put Alexander down and knock them out of the sky.

Ethan gulped. Cal tried to not do the same.

This wasn't going to work. The entire plan was ridiculous, but it was the only chance they had.

Doc waved them forward. "Come on. We need to find a way out."

Something spun through the air, making a whooting sound like an old-fashioned helicopter. Rachel ducked, placing her hands on top of her head as another spinning dial sped toward them.

"Keep down!" Kile shouted.

Rachel stood, shouting something at him while another spinner shot toward them. Kile shoved her and she stumbled back, raising one hand. The spinner wrapped around her wrist like a bola and yanked her to the ground. She screamed as the restraint sizzled and sparked.

"Rachel!" Doc sprinted toward her but slammed into a wall of shimmering light.

Ty moved beside him, slamming his fist into the gleaming surface. "Containment field. Dammit!"

Cal took a step back. *Containment field?*

Kile dropped Alexander to the floor with a thump. Doc cringed as the younger enforcer slammed to the ground. Three more spinners headed in their direction, but Kile raised his hands and they burst into flames, falling to the floor as glowing ash.

Cal took in the shimmering wall before them. "How do we disable this thing?"

Doc looked up and down the glowing partition. "This looks short-range."

"I agree," Ethan said. "But the controls could be in a dozen places."

Kile knelt and tried to get the bindings off Rachel but drew his hand back like it stung.

Cal cringed. If it hurt him, what was it doing to Rachel?

"We need to get around this thing," Cal said.

Ty pointed down the hall. "There were a few hallways back there. It's worth a try."

Rachel screamed as another round of projectiles headed toward her and Kile. If they didn't get her out of there, she was going to be sliced to pieces. "Let's go."

Ethan spun and headed down the hall with Ty. Ethan cried out, hitting another wall of light. Ty slammed into the wall right beside him.

"Parallel triangulation," Doc said.

Cal glanced at him. "Care to translate?"

Another spinner exploded in front of the enforcer as an additional one shot toward him from the right.

"Two for one. It's like getting stuck in an old-fashioned mouse trap. We got lucky."

"How exactly are we lucky?" Ty asked, rubbing a burn mark on his forehead.

Kile spewed fire from his hands, exploding spinner after spinner aimed at him. He started to breath heavily, though.

"For one thing, we got stuck inside it, and not out there with them." Ethan sprinted to the rock wall. "But even better, it means that the controls are between the two beams, at one of the origination points."

"He's right," Doc said. "We must have tripped it walking through. We slowed down, so Big Bad and Rachel got caught out there instead." Doc headed toward the other wall. "I'll check on this side."

So once they got that wall down, they'd be facing fire-power from the front. The only thing they could do was run the other way.

Rachel screamed again, trying to cover her head.

Cal gulped. They couldn't just run. They had to save her.

"Stop thinking stupid." Ty moved closer. "We have to do what we have to do. Big Bad can protect her." He grimaced at Dania in Cal's arms. "We really could use her right about now."

Cal adjusted his grip on her. He'd thought the same thing, but from what Doc had said, she wasn't going to be an option any time soon.

"No!" Rachel cried out as Kile flung backward. A bola wrapped around his neck, pinning him to the floor. "No!" she cried again, trying to crawl to him, but her wrist remained fastened to the ground.

Cal gaped, holding Dania closer to his chest as Rachel screamed Kile's name.

"Doc, Ethan," he whispered. "Get us the hell out of here. Now."

Someone started clapping slowly. Three men walked through the smoke billowing in the room.

"That was exciting." A tall man in a well-tapered suit walked toward the enforcer. He looked scant and thin next to the behemoth. "What a rush!"

Sparks sizzled around Kile's neck as the man looked down on him. The newcomer's gaze was wide. Manic.

"Ty," Cal whispered. "Take Dania."

Ty didn't take his gaze from the crazed man. "Yeah, boss."

Cal kept as still as possible, barely breathing. Ty brought Dania over to the wall and placed her beside Doc as he looked up and down the rocky surface for the controls. Dania slumped against the wall, looking just as frail as Alexander. With any luck, this maniac wouldn't recognize she was an enforcer, too.

The man looked up at Cal. "Thanks so much for bringing him to me. He's quite something." He crouched, looking closer at Kile.

The commander lunged for him but only got a few inches off the floor.

"Lots of fight," the man said. "It was a thrill watching him wear himself down. I lost a lot of good men down there, but this specimen is more than worth it."

He lost men? "I thought the governor wasn't here?" Cal whispered.

Ethan looked over his shoulder. "Wouldn't you come home if you found out someone broke into your house?"

Especially if one of those someones was considered a valuable collector's item.

Had this all been a setup? Had security let them get deep

into the building, hoping to pin them down so Kile would be forced to expel as much energy as possible?

If that was their plan, they had to have known that most of the guards would die. Or maybe the guards working here had no idea what they'd been up against.

"Do all your people know that they're expendable?" Cal asked the governor.

The man stood. "They're paid well. And they know the risks." He continued to stare at Kile.

The enforcer just glared at him. Those sparks must also have acted like some sort of gag.

"Let me go!" Rachel screamed, yanking against the fastener holding her wrist to the floor.

Apparently, the gag part didn't work if the victim was only restrained by the wrist. Now would probably be a really good time for her to learn how to keep her mouth shut until they figured out how to get her out of this in one piece. The chances of that happening, though, were probably slim.

"That was a lucky shot," said a man in gray fatigues. "If he hadn't been so distracted by the girl, we might have run out of ammunition."

Ammunition, as in bolas, probably enhanced with Palian steel, and goodness knew what else.

Ty returned to Cal's side. "This isn't good," he whispered.

"You're not kidding."

"Let him go, you freaks!" Rachel shouted.

The man in the suit laughed. "Sorry, but he was stealing my favorite toy." He leaned down and smoothed the hair from Alexander's face. "This is unacceptable. I take better care of my things."

"Like you took care of the girl we found dead in the cage?" Cal said through the shimmering lights.

The man looked up. "An unfortunate accident. Those responsible were dealt with." He stood and walked over to the barrier wall.

Rachel growled and tried to kick his legs out from under him, but the man simply walked around her.

"What was it like," the man asked, "being so close to an enforcer as he expelled that kind of power?"

Ty glared through the shimmering screen. "Why don't you ask your guards? Oh, wait, you can't—because they're all dead."

The man laughed again. "Quite the wit. From the profiles, that would probably make you the first mate, or are you the engineer?"

Ty didn't answer.

The man leveled his gaze back on Cal. "My understanding is that you came from the ship docked in market slip number five. Call sign SR877 something or other." He looked Cal over. "Would you be Captain Esquire?"

Cal gritted his teeth. "Espinoza. And you are?"

He gave a mock bow. "Governor Tison, at your service."

That wasn't all that much of a surprise, but at least Cal knew for sure now. "If we are at your service, how about you let us all go?"

Rachel yanked against her bindings. "Yeah, let me go, you bastard, so I can kill you!" Blood smeared across her wrist.

She really needed to work on her negotiation skills.

"I have no qualm with you," the governor said. "I'm willing to let you and your people go free."

"Just like that?" Cal glanced at Rachel, and then at Kile, who seemed to stop struggling. Hopefully, the commander was saving his strength for a more opportune time to escape.

"Just like that," Tison said.

Rachel twisted in their direction. "Don't do it, Cally. They're going to kill him."

The governor snorted. "On the contrary. That enforcer is still very well charged, and it took almost all of my defenses to take him down. I will be selling him to the highest bidder as soon as I can get rid of him."

"You can't do that!" Rachael screamed.

The governor walked two steps back to her and pointed at Kile. "Do you think that animal actually cares about you? It doesn't."

"Yes, he does."

"They aren't capable of feelings. If you were dumb enough to let that thing screw you, then it probably kept you around like a toy. But don't think it's anything more than that. Enforcers only care about themselves."

Cal glanced at Dania, slumped on the floor next to Doc. He'd thought the same thing only a few months ago. It had taken a lot to ween her from that prince. Unless they were able to do that for Kile, the governor might be far too accurate in his evaluation of Rachel's relationship.

"You don't know anything." Rachel curled in on herself slightly, looking toward Kile.

Had the commander ever told her that he cared? Was she maybe realizing this now?

The governor crouched near her. "You can probably take solace in knowing you tickled his loins enough for him to keep you alive. I'm sure he has a line of bodies behind him of women who didn't make the grade.

Rachel sneered, spit in his face, and then kicked him.

"You stupid bitch!" He grabbed her by the throat.

Cal flinched. "Doc, Ethan, sooner would be better than later!"

"Working on it!" Ethan pulled a wire out of a panel hidden in a fissure between two rocks.

"You found it?" Doc sprinted past Cal, joining Ethan on the other side of the hall. Dania still lay against the other wall, probably as safe as she could be under the circumstances.

Rachel clawed at the governor's face.

Her cheeks darkened in color.

"Guys!" Cal slammed his fist against the shimmering wall.

"Working on it!"

Kile bucked against the brace holding his neck to the floor. His normally pale face reddened and his teeth gnashed as he growled. His skin took on the slight glow they'd seen before, then winked out.

The Palian steel was doing its job far too well.

Rachel's struggle started to fade. She kicked less. She pushed at the governor's face rather than clawing.

"We're running out of time," Cal said.

"Almost there!"

A roar filled the corridor, echoing off the walls.

A chill itched up Cal's spine. "What was that?"

"Got it!" Ethan called.

The shimmering screen separating them winked out.

A huge black mass rolled into the room. One of the guards screamed, firing his gun. The other guard reached for his own weapon but cried out as a long, dark tusk skewered his chest. The animal threw him to the side, and he slid off the tusk and slammed to the floor in a heap.

"What the hell is that?" Ethan asked.

Another shot rang out.

"Stop!" the governor called, but the beast charged,

flashing long, white teeth and grabbing the second guard by the neck, throwing him against the far wall.

Rachel coughed, clutching her throat with her free hand as the governor jumped over Kile's prone body and opened a panel in the wall.

The creature charged, and Ethan took aim.

Cal grabbed his arm. "Wait."

The governor turned, weapon in hand, but the animal plowed into him, sinking its teeth into the man's neck before he could fire or scream.

Doc cursed under his breath, raising his gun as the creature turned and stalked the still-immobilized commander.

"Can I shoot now?" Ethan said.

"Wait," Rachel rasped.

Doc raised his weapon, too.

"Doctor Pete, no!" Rachel held up her free hand.

"Are you crazy? We're not going to let that thing maul him."

Rachel got up on one knee, her wrist still attached to the floor. "But she's extinct!"

Extinct? Cal gaped. Was that the boar that had been in the cage earlier?

"*Big Bad* is about to be extinct!" Ethan shouted.

Kile's eyes widened as the creature neared. His gaze darted to Rachel.

Inching closer, Rachel held up one hand to the monster. "Hey, girl—listen, remember me?"

The beast snarled. Drool dripped from its teeth.

"Rachel is in the way," Ethan said. "I can't get a shot."

"Me neither," Doc said.

Rachel raised her hand higher. "Yeah, I know. You've had a really bad day. Heck, probably a lot of really bad days, but

Big Guy there." She pointed at Kile. "You remember him, right? He melted the locky-hinge things on your cage. And that's probably why you're here now, free, right?"

The boar growled.

"Where I come from, it is considered really rude to eat someone who saved your life."

Ethan shifted from side to side. "Quirky, that thing cannot understand you. Get out of the way!"

She looked over her shoulder. "Shut up, Ethan!"

He scowled. "I'm getting really tired of people telling me to shut up."

The boar lunged for Kile.

"No!" Cal cried, bolting for Rachel. If he pulled her out of the way, one of the guys could…

"Stop!" Rachel cried as Cal slammed into her. "Stop!" She held up her one free hand.

The boar's jaws were around Kile's neck.

"Shoot it!" Cal cried.

"No! She's extinct!" Rachel shrieked.

Ethan fired. The shot exploded into the beast's shoulder, but she barely flinched.

What the hell?

Ethan cursed as Doc pulled the gun from the engineer's hand.

"Look at the blast marks on her hide." Doc pointed at the creature. "That mama is tough. Your little gun is just going to piss her off."

The boar lifted its mouth and roared in Ethan's direction, gripping the bola that had been around Kile's neck. It shook the weapon before dropping it to the floor.

It fixed on Cal, snarling.

Cal climbed off Rachel, backing up. "Whoa there. Nice, big bear-dog-like thing."

"He didn't mean it." Rachel stretched herself between Cal and the boar. "That thing about shooting you. He didn't mean it." She glanced at Cal. "Well, he did, but he didn't understand. He's just a guy. Guys are dumb. Ask any woman, and she'll tell you."

The boar snarled again, walking toward Rachel.

She cringed, unable to flee. "You do remember that I helped you, too, right?

The boar growled, showing teeth longer than Cal's fingers, before it slipped a claw under her bound wrist. The bindings fell to the floor.

Rachel lifted her hand, massaging her wrist. "Thanks."

Holy hell. Had that thing actually understood her?

The creature snarled, sniffed the air, and walked in the direction the governor and his guards had come from.

Rachel slid across the floor to Kile. "Big Guy?"

The enforcer blinked but didn't move.

She placed her hand on his cheek. "Come on. Please be okay!"

Doc ran some instruments over Kile's forehead and shoulders.

Ethan gaped, watching the boar leave. "No one is worried about that thing walking away?"

"Not as long as it's walking away." Cal crouched beside Kile. "What are we looking at?"

Doc shrugged. "Well, as we know, Palian steel sucks if you're an enforcer."

"Will he be okay?" Rachel asked.

"He'll live." Doc leaned over the commander. "I'm going to give you a jolt of adrenaline. I'm not sure, but I think it will help you move. It might hurt, though, so don't kill me, okay?"

The enforcer glared at him.

Rachel smacked Kile's shoulder. "You will not hurt the nice doctor trying to help you. Be a good patient."

Kile sighed.

"Here goes nothing." Doc pressed a vial to the side of Kile's neck.

The enforcer winced but seemed to breathe easier.

Ty looked around them. "What's the plan, boss?"

Dania still lay propped against the wall. Alexander lay in a heap on the floor. And Rachel helped Kile into a sitting position. The enforcer held his hands over his ears and said something to Doc about ringing.

"We can still make a break for it," Ty said.

The question was: Would they leave Rachel with the enforcer, or drag her kicking and screaming back to the ship?

THEY CROUCHED in the kitchen where they'd first entered the mansion. The late day sun shone through the open doorway.

Cal ducked as a particle beam exploded over his head.

"Aww, come on!" Ethan shouted. "Can't we get a break?"

Somewhere out there, Alanna was probably flying in circles, looking for them. They just needed to get out there without getting their heads shot off.

Kile stood, holding the shoulder he'd been shot through earlier in the day. "I tire of this."

"Yeah, we're all tired of this." Rachel yanked him back down, and oddly enough, he slammed to the floor beside her. That steel must have taken quite a toll on him.

"I am an enforcer," Kile said. "I will not be cornered like an animal."

Rachel shook her head. "Well, I'm not going to let you get shot like one, either." She looked at Cal. "What's the plan?"

The plan? The plan is to leave your boyfriend here and make a run for it.

Cal looked out the window. In Kile's weakened state, he

was probably in worse shape than Dania had been when they'd picked her up. If they left him here, he'd face the same fate of that girl they'd found dead in the cage. But if they took the homicidal enforcer with them…

"Cal?" Ethan frowned. "Is your comm going off?"

"What? No." He turned his wrist. The band flashed with a low glow, like the power was fading.

"My comm is dead," Doc announced. "It must have been that energy shield."

The trap they'd been caught in? "Do those things drain power?"

"Yeah." Ethan shook his own band. "Mine's dead, too."

And Cal's was nearly out of juice.

He frowned, hitting the flashing button on his wrist. "Alanna?"

"Cal?!" Alanna fumbled on the other end of the comm. "I thought you were all dead. No one was answering!" Her voice trembled, like she was on the edge of tears.

"We're all fine."

"Are you sure?" she asked. "Ethan?"

"Here, babe. No worries."

"Peter?"

Doc waved, as if she could see him. "I'm good, sweetie!"

"Ty?"

"Yeah," he answered. "Alanna, we're really okay!"

"Dania?"

Cal rubbed his face. She wouldn't be happy until she heard everyone's voices. "Dania is…" He couldn't lie and say she was okay. "She's alive, but she's unconscious."

"Unconscious? What happened?"

"Can we discuss this back on the ship?"

"Did you find Dania's friend?"

Cal's gaze passed over the other enforcer, propped up against the wall beside Dania.

"Yeah, but he's unconscious, too."

Alanna whispered what might have been a very uncharacteristic curse.

Rachel folded her arms. "I'm okay, too, if anyone cares."

Alanna sighed. "Well, if the rest of you are all okay, why am I flying around in circles up here? It's hard to fly casual when you're passing over the same place a thousand times."

Another blast came through the door. Sparks scattered across the far wall.

"We're trying hard not to get shot here."

"What?" Alanna said. "You have an enforcer. Point him at the bad guys and just walk out."

"Big Bad is hurt," Ethan said.

"*What?*" Alanna's voice raised in pitch. "How bad?"

"I'm fine," Kile said through clenched teeth.

Rachel smacked his arm, and he winced.

"Pretty bad," Cal told Alanna.

"Wait a minute," she said. "Are you telling me that you have a bum enforcer and two unconscious people down there?"

That pretty much summed things up. "Yup."

Alanna paused. "Cal, there's a freaking platoon waiting for you outside."

"Which is why we're still in here." But she was right. They couldn't stay in here much longer. Eventually, the bad guys would stop playing nice and come in here with the big guns. Especially once they found out their boss was dead.

"Umm," Alanna said. A drumming sounded over the comm, like she was tapping her fingers on the console.

Doc grabbed Cal's wrist. "Girl, don't you do anything

stupid."

"Umm," Alanna sounded like she'd leaned away from the comm. "Umm…"

Doc let Cal go. "She's going to do something stupid." He looked over both shoulders and cursed, pulling something out of his bag. "I'm going to regret this."

He lunged for Kile, shoving Rachel out of the way.

The stowaway cried out, landing on top of Dania. Alexander's limp body fell on top of them both.

Doc jabbed a needle in Kile's neck. The enforcer reached for Doc's hand, growling, before his eyes closed and his head lolled back.

"What did you do?" Rachel struggled to get Alexander off her.

"Oh, no!" Ty looked out the door and into the sky.

Above, the *Star Renegade* spun in erratic circles, almost level, but on its way down.

"She's going to crash!" Ty grabbed the edge of the door like he wanted to run out, but what could he have done?

Cal tapped his comm. "Alanna!"

There was a flash of purple light outside.

Ty cursed and pointed his gun out the door. "Cover fire!"

Cover fire?

Ethan dropped to one knee beside Ty, shooting through the door and into the courtyard.

"No, no, no, no, no!" a woman's voice cried from outside.

Was that…

Alanna burst through the door. Her eyes were wide as she spun, taking them all in. A blue dial of light swirled at the end of her fingertip. The gears shifted and flashed.

Cal gaped. "Who is flying the *Renegade*?"

"No one!" she cried, holding her head with her other

hand. "Shoot! Umm..." She turned, dove for Rachel, and a purple glow lit up the room. In a poof of white light, they were gone.

All of them. Alanna, Rachel, Dania, and Alexander.

"What the what?" Ethan shouted.

"There was something wrong," Ty said. "Her spinny-dial thing didn't look right."

Doc stood. "She's still hurt. She shouldn't have even tried that."

No kidding. The ship was about to crash without a pilot. And hopefully she wasn't off ship long enough to alert the Cartek tech.

They raced back to the door. The Renegade wobbled, then headed straight down.

"Come on, baby," Ty whispered.

The guards outside raced into the trees as the ship roared to the ground. Others shouted, running toward the front of the mansion. Cal's stomach sank, his breath caught in his throat.

"Pull up!" Ty slammed his fist into the wall.

"Come on, Alanna," Cal whispered. "You got this."

Cal flinched, turning from the door. "She's not going to make it."

Cal reached for Ty to pull him away from the opening, hoping to save him from the explosion, but the ship banked up at the last minute. Flames spread across the ground from the heat of her engines and the people outside shouted as the *Star Renegade* shot back into the sky.

"That's my girl!" Ethan punched his fist in the air.

Cal grabbed his comm, taking a much-needed breath. "Alanna, are you okay?"

There was shouting on the other end. "Rachel, shut up!

Yes, Cal, I'm fine."

"Who do you have with you?"

"Rachel, obviously, Dania and the cute enforcer. Sorry, I was losing my link back to the ship, and you guys weren't close enough together to grab you all."

Cal closed his eyes.

Not having to fight their way out while carrying two unconscious people would make this a lot better. Not easy, but no longer impossible.

"It's all right. You did good," he told her. "Get ready to pick us up."

"On it," she said, then to the side: "Rachel, have you ever shot guns from a ship?"

The comm went dead. Cal chose to ignore the last thing he'd heard.

Ty slipped to the floor, leaning his head against the wall. "When we get back to the ship, the first thing we need to do is teach Alanna how to use the autopilot."

"Agreed," Cal said. Now, they just had to get back up there.

Ethan grabbed Kile's hair, lifting his head back. He glanced at Doc. "Is there a reason you knocked out Big Bad?"

Doc pulled himself up off the floor. "It will only last about a minute." He looked at Cal. "I know my girl. Alanna is impulsive, and I didn't want the complication of Big Bad seeing her jump."

"Jumping isn't illegal," Ethan said.

Ty scratched his head. "No, but Dania always has a weird look on her face when she sees Alanna jump. Dania's on our side now, but Big Bad isn't. It was a good call."

"Good call, my ass." Ethan turned to Doc. "He's going to kill you."

Kile's eyes shot open.

Dammit, Ethan was probably right!

Cal jumped between Kile and Doc. "It's all right. Take a deep breath. It worked."

Kile snarled. "What worked?"

"Doc knocked you out because he knew you'd be worried about Rachel."

His eyes narrowed. "What about her?"

Cal gulped. "We, umm, gave her cover fire, and she ran out with Dania and Alexander and Alanna picked them up."

He looked at the empty space on the floor. "She couldn't carry them both."

Cal took a deep breath. "Ethan helped, but he slipped and fell and didn't make it into the ship before they had to take off."

Kile flicked a look at Ethan, and then nodded. Apparently, the idea of Ethan falling was an acceptable ruse.

Cal breathed a sigh of relief.

"Why me?" Ethan whispered to Ty.

Ty just snorted.

Kile looked at Doc. "I am unhappy with you but satisfied with the resolution. Next time, I would hope that you'd do me the service of asking me first."

Doc gulped. "You're right, I was a stupid, impulsive human. I'll try to do better."

Kile stood. "You do that." He looked out the door. "Can I assume your pilot is making an additional round to acquire the rest of us?"

Cal looked at the currently ship-less sky. "Yeah, but we're going to have to fight our way out."

The enforcer rolled both shoulders. "Good. I prefer it that way."

KILE STRODE OUT, his head high, but slower than he had been earlier in the day. Three blasts came toward them, and he held up his hand. Two shots bounced off, but the third skidded past. Ethan ducked, feeling his hair to make sure it was still there.

The enforcer frowned. He'd probably never missed before. Which meant he was just as hurt as they'd thought.

"Keep that cover fire coming, boys!" Cal raised his gun and fired to the commander's right.

The *Star Renegade* shot past them, and a spray of artillery rained down on the guards—missing all of them but forcing them back. Knowing Alanna, she'd done that on purpose. Either that, or Rachel had really bad aim.

Alanna spun the *Renegade* above. The landing platform started to unhitch.

Good move. If they played their cards right, she wouldn't even have to land.

"Let's go!" Cal moved out, sprinting for the ship.

Alanna, or maybe Rachel, sent out another spray of fire, keeping their path clear.

A voice cried out behind them. Cal counted heads. Ethan. Doc. Ty.

"Go!" Cal ordered, and Ethan jumped up, grabbing the platform rotating above.

Behind them, the commander lay on the ground. Still.

The platform continued to spin above. It was like trying to jump up and grab a single blade of a ceiling fan as it spun over your head.

"Cal!" Alanna called over the comm. "Maybe I should just land?"

The guards started out toward them again. "No. We might not get off the ground before we get overrun."

Ty cursed, ducking as the platform sliced too close, but too fast to catch. "I will never complain again about how many times Stanley made us run hovering drills."

Cal agreed. The *Star Renegade* wasn't made for this kind of work. Still, Alanna was doing the best she could. It was a miracle a junior pilot could keep the ship off the ground at all.

Ty helped Doc up onto the floating platform. Doc's legs dangled, and Cal helped Ty push him up every time his legs spun in their direction.

When Doc pulled his feet in, Ty glanced at Cal. "You do realize this ship could drop and smash us any second, right?"

"That's why I need you up there." Cal wove his fingers together to make a step.

Another spray of fire from above stopped five guards from advancing on Kile.

Ty wiped back his hair. "What are you going to do about Big Bad?"

Cal wished he knew.

The enforcer rolled over and started crawling toward them using only one arm, the other held tight to his chest.

This was their opportunity to get away. They should take it.

He just never expected the commander to look so helpless.

The *Renegade* choked above, dropping a few inches.

Cal held out his hands. "Get up there and fly the ship before she kills us all."

"On it!" Ty pulled himself up, then held a hand down to Cal. "Come on!"

"No. Go fly the ship."

"You get on board first."

Cal glanced back to the enforcer, then stared at Ty's hand. Did he take it? Did he run, like he always did?

Ethan joined Ty, reaching down. "Boss, come on!"

They were giving him an out. Neither of them would judge him. All he needed to do was grab their hands, and they'd be home free.

So why didn't he reach up and take their hands?

Ty's eyes widened before Kile moved beside Cal.

The commander still held one arm close. "We need to go."

Relief flooded Cal, and he hated himself for it. If anything, he should have felt the opposite.

He grabbed Ty's arm, then Ethan's. His legs swung as if he were on some sort of ridiculous amusement ride until they pulled him onto the ship. Cal shook his head, his vision still spinning. When his eyes cleared, Ethan and Ty had hauled the enforcer on board. Kile inched a few feet from the edge of the platform before collapsing.

Cal pulled himself to a standing position. "Close the

ramp." He staggered to the wall and hit the comm. "Alanna, we're all on board. Head for space."

"I don't know how to fly in space!"

"I'm coming!" Ty shouted, sprinting up the ladder toward the bridge.

Rachel ran down the freight processing ramp, jumping over the edge and slamming to the deck. "Wait!" She ran to the closing door. "Stop it!"

"Stop what?" Ethan asked.

"Stop closing the ramp! We need to land."

A blast hit the side of the hull, raining sparks on the deck.

"Are you crazy?" Cal said.

She hung out the opening, the wind whipping in her hair as she pointed down. "We can't leave her there!"

"Leave who where?"

The ship leveled off. Ty must have made it to the bridge.

Below them, a huge, Trellan jungle boar charged toward the ship, mouth open like it might be roaring, although Cal couldn't hear her over the scream of the engines. Another smaller green creature with a long fluffy tail scampered beside her.

"Did she have her baby?" Rachel asked. "A little green baby?" She looked over her shoulder at Doc. "What do Trellan boar babies look like?"

"How the hell would I know?"

"Whatever. It doesn't matter." She hung her head out farther. "We're coming, Mama!"

"No, we are not!" Cal said. "Did you hear the part about those boars hunting down the settlers?"

"But she's extinct!"

Cal held out his hands. "Will you stop saying that?"

Kile grunted, holding his chest as he moved toward the opening. "Lower the ship."

Had he lost his mind, too? "There are people shooting at us!"

Kile glared at Cal and looked to Ethan. "This is a smuggling vessel. I am sure you have large cargo containers."

Ethan's eyes widened. He looked to Cal. "I-I…maybe?"

Cal folded his arms. "You want to put that animal in a cargo container?"

The comm pinged. "Boss," Ty said. "Alanna is threatening to jump me back to the planet if I don't pick up the giant tusked fuzz ball."

The smaller animal beside the boar got up on its back legs. Cal could have sworn it had been green a minute ago, but now it was more a sandy color, like the ground beneath them.

The bigger one looked right at him and bared her teeth. Lovely.

Kile appeared beside him. "I can create a shield to guide her into the cargo container. Casualties should be minimal."

"Minimal?"

Kile lifted his chin. "Nonexistent. I'm hurt, but I can control a wild animal."

"And then what? How are we supposed to take care of her?" The ship started to lower. Cal punched the wall. "Hey, I never gave the okay."

Behind them, Doc and Ethan maneuvered a large empty container toward the ramp.

Why did this crew insist on making decisions without him?

"I won't allow anyone to die," Kile said.

"Why do you even care?" Cal asked.

The enforcer flicked a glance to Rachel. "She is tenacious and aggravating. I have learned it is easier to do what she wants."

Cal shook his head. Why had the enforcer had to fall for an animal lover?

Another shot blasted toward the ship. Ty flinched as it hit the reinforced hull.

This animal was going to get shot trying to get up the ramp. If they were going to do this, they needed to do it right. "We need to give her cover fire. Ethan, Doc?"

"On it." They grabbed guns, threw one to Cal, and started shooting as they lowered the ramp to the ground. Ty sprayed fire from above, keeping the rest of the guards back.

The smaller creature ran up the ramp first. It stopped at the top, went up on its hind legs, and sniffed the air. It looked a lot like a larger version of a rodent from Earth that he'd seen pictures of, with five-fingered hands ending in sharp claws, and a bushy, arched tail. It wasn't completely sandy-colored. Oddly enough, its feet were almost the same color as the deck plates.

The larger one moved up the deck behind it, slower, and still pretty fat, so this little one probably wasn't her baby.

"We need you to go into the cargo container." Rachel pointed to the massive metal box.

The small one chittered. The larger one roared.

Rachel held up her hands. "Hey, don't shoot the messenger. The captain is afraid you'll eat the crew."

"I've got her," Kile said.

Both creatures jumped toward the box like they were being pushed—probably because they were. Once inside, Ethan closed the door down.

Rachel clapped her hands. "Yay!" She kissed Kile's cheek. "Thank you, Big Guy."

"You are welcome." He slipped to the floor, coughing, still holding his chest with one hand.

The ramp closed, and the ship hummed.

"If no one objects," Ty said over the comm, "I'd like to get the hell out of Dodge."

Out of Dodge? What did that even mean?

"And if someone could please get the two unconscious people off the bridge, that would be helpful."

"Sorry!" Alanna said before the comm flicked off.

Cal stumbled from the sudden incline as Ty broke for the atmosphere. As long as they were bound for space, nothing else mattered.

Except, maybe, getting Dania and her friend to the med bay.

Cal caught his breath as Doc leaned over Kile.

"How bad does it hurt?" Doc asked.

"Significantly, you fool!"

"Hey!" Cal pointed at the commander. "Show some respect or I'll order him not to help you." He turned to Doc. "You got this?" Cal asked him.

Several small boxes that hadn't been secured slid past them. "Yeah, go. I'll get him to the med bay and then I'll need to look at Dania and Alexander."

Cal looked at the metal frame of the huge storage locker they'd herded the animals into. "Are they going to be okay in there?"

Ethan tapped the side of the container. "As good as they can get for now."

That was probably the best they could ask for.

Cal waved Ethan forward. "Come on. I'll need help."

He and Ethan sprinted up the ladder. Once they got to the top floor, they held onto the railing so they didn't fall backward.

The ship started to level as they stepped onto the bridge. In the main window, the clouds gave way to darkness and twinkling stars.

"I've got a lot of static around the planet, boss," Ty said.

That was never good.

Cal motioned to Dania. "Do you think you can slide her down the hall to the med bay?"

"Yeah, I got her." Ethan put her hands under Dania's arms and drew her out.

"We've got incoming!" Alanna announced.

Of course they did.

Cal grabbed Alexander's arms, pulling him through the door.

Doc met him outside. "Did I hear there's trouble?"

"There's always trouble."

Doc pointed down the hall. "Rachel is taking Big Bad to the med bay for me."

"And he's going of his own free will?"

"I think he's pretty screwed up. More than he wants to admit."

Cal wasn't sure if that was good, or really, really bad.

Doc slipped his hands under Alexander's arms. "I'll take him—you get back to the bridge." He grabbed Cal as he stood. "Hey, don't let Alanna jump. I don't like the way she was shaking before. I want to make sure her wounds haven't gotten worse."

Cal grimaced. It would be very like Alanna to have a secondary infection from those gunshot wounds and not tell anyone.

"Understood."

Doc pulled Alexander's lax form back toward the med bay. Cal tensed. He'd spent years trying to keep away from enforcers, and now there were three of them on board. All incapacitated.

And they had incoming.

And Alanna was probably hurt.

"Doctor Pete!" Rachel called down the hall.

"Coming," Doc yelled as Cal headed back into the bridge.

The ship rumbled beneath his feet. Moderate fire lit up the screen. Nothing the *Renegade* couldn't handle.

That was just the start, though, and he knew it.

Cal needed to figure out a way to get out of this mess in one piece without Alanna or enforcer intervention. This would be an old-school escape, just like when it was only him and Ty onboard.

There was a lot more at stake now than a couple of guys with no families back home to worry about.

They needed to be fearless.

He just hoped they remembered how.

IN THE WINDOW, three freighters twice their size bared down on them.

Figures. Cal slipped into his chair.

"Alanna, do you have a jump in you?" Ty asked.

"She does not," Cal said. "Doctor's orders." He flipped on the comm. "Ethan, are you ready to give that alien hardware a test drive?"

"I'd rather do it when no one was shooting at us."

"Then you have about fifteen seconds," Ty said.

"Not gonna happen."

"Just let me know when you can do some magic." Cal flipped off the comm.

The freighters turned on them, aiming gun turrets that were made to protect the ships from pirates, but they'd still do enough damage if they were hit.

"This is not going to be fun," Ty said.

"This is the *Star Renegade*. Just outfly them."

A smile burst across Ty's face. "Yes, sir, Captain, sir!"

They banked down, shooting past the first ship. A spray of sparks shot over their bow.

A large clang reverberated through the hull.

"What was that?" Cal asked.

"I'm not seeing any blast patterns."

"Sounded like something hit us," Ty said.

Cal flipped the comm. "Ethan, is the hull integrity okay?"

"Looks okay," Ethan shouted. "I didn't like that sound, though. I heard it all the way back here."

As long as they weren't going to spring a leak, they'd worry about it later.

Four more cruisers glided into view.

"What the frig?" Ty said, pressing buttons. "This is just a tiny little planet. Where are all these ships coming from?"

"It's a tiny planet with a governor who had a lot of security."

"Don't they know he's dead?"

"It looks like they don't care."

Or, more likely, there was a really pissed-off heir. Or one happy heir who knew the value of the incapacitated enforcers trying to break through their defenses.

A hum filtered through the exterior walls.

"What the blazes is that?" Cal asked.

Sizzling lines of light sparkled across Cal's panel.

Ty cursed beside him, jumping up and pulling off his flight coat. "I hate, hate, hate, getting hit with tech I've never seen before." He threw his coat over the sparks, and when he lifted the fabric, the small lightning bolts were gone.

"I can't believe that worked!" Alanna said, removing her own jacket and smothering her panel of miniature lightning bolts.

"Me, neither." Ty threw his jacket to Cal before flipping on the comm. "News flash! If you have a lightning storm in your instruments, you can smother them like flames. Don't know why, but it works."

Cal smothered the last of the bolts in the room as Ty swerved around another ship.

"I hope those electric charges didn't damage anything." Cal slipped back into his seat.

Ty sent a series of short-ranged shots over the bow of the largest ship. "I'm kinda busy at the moment, or I'd check."

"I was just thinking out loud." Cal's fingers flew over the instruments as he centered the forward weapons array on the main engines of the largest freighter and fired.

A smaller ship flew right into the flight path and exploded.

"Whoa!" Ty banked up from the debris, but something still slammed into them.

Ethan came over the comm. "This is your friendly engineer reminding you all that it is *really bad* to let things hit you!"

Cal grit his teeth. "Are we okay?"

"Yeah, but is there a reason we're having so much trouble with these guys?"

Ty grunted, like he was fighting with he controls. "I was thinking the same thing. These guys are way too well-funded, and there are still ships lifting off the ground."

Cal flipped the comm. "Ethan? We could really use that extra boost."

"Come on, boss, I'm trying!"

Cal switched off the comm. Ty spun the *Star Renegade* up and around a small ship, but three more took its place. Ty cursed, shaking his head.

"We're screwed, aren't we?" Cal asked.

"Pretty much." He glanced down at the instruments.

"Not quite yet," Alanna said.

A light purple haze formed around them. Alanna stood beside her nav station, blue gears already spinning.

Cal reached for her. "Alanna, no!"

"I'm fine!" She pressed the center of the floating blue ring.

The bridge stretched and fogged before springing back into shape. Outside, different stars twinkled back at them… and no ships.

"Three minutes!" Ty stood and turned to Alanna. "You are the queen, you know that?"

She held up her hands. "I know, I know."

Her eyelids seemed a little heavy, though.

Ty placed his hand on her shoulder. "Do you have another jump in you, in case of emergency?"

"Yeah, I'm tired, but I'm strong enough." She checked her readings. "I don't think I'm going to need it, though."

"We can't need it," Cal said. "Doc is going to give me hell for that one. We can't jump again."

Alanna waved her hand at him. "I'll take care of Doc."

Cal leaned toward her. "With an exam?"

She quirked a brow. "What?"

"He's afraid you're hurt, and that's why your gears were flipping on the planet."

She snorted. "My gears were flipping because I thought you were all dead. I was freaking out." She pointed to herself. "I'm fine."

"If you're fine, then let him check you over and give you the all-clear. It will make your life easier—and mine."

She turned back to her console, shaking her head. "Whatever."

"That's three minutes," Ty said. "We're clear." He looked

closer at his panel and snorted. "And on a perfect course to the Trillian Cluster."

Cal double-checked his panel. "The Trillian Cluster?" They were supposed to head toward Bane space. Not that Cal had intended on complying, but he'd planned on at least making it look that way. That was a little hard to do when you were headed in the complete opposite direction.

Cal turned his chair toward them. "That's going to piss off everyone's favorite commander."

Alanna reached up and pressed a button on an overhead panel. "Do we have any food for a Trellan jungle boar and whatever that other thing is in the cargo bay?"

Cal sat back. "No."

"Then, as the navigator, I made an executive decision and plotted a course to somewhere that did. If he's got a problem, he can take it up with me."

Ty snickered. "You planning on having Rachel stand behind you?"

"Of course," she said. "I'm no dummy."

The only problem was, this sent them closer to the pirate sector—the last place Cal wanted to be near with three disabled enforcers on board. However, it was also farther from Cartek space, which was the top priority. The longer Cal had to figure out that little problem, the better.

Ty tugged Cal's shoulder. "Can I talk to you for a sec?" He glanced at Alanna, then headed out of the bridge.

Interesting. Since when had he wanted to keep anything from Alanna?

Cal followed him into the hall and shut the door behind him. "What's up?"

Ty took a deep breath and let it out slowly. "Alanna keeps talking about that new enforcer like he's something special, but I don't have a warm and fuzzy feeling about all this."

Cal's muscles tensed worse than they had during the battle. "From the looks of him, it's going to be a while before he's conscious no matter what. But I agree. I want to talk to Dania about how we all keep breathing now that we have what Kile wanted."

Ty shook his head. "You know me, I'm usually the optimist. I have a really bad feeling about this."

"Let me get down there and see what's up." Cal pointed to the door. "I need you on the bridge. If we're going to drop off those animals, I want to do it fast." He started walking down the hall. "We need to get back to neutral space. I hate to say it, but the closer to the Banes we can get right now, the safer we'll be from whoever was funding all those ships we were just running from." And the less of a chance that the Carteks will pop up unexpectedly and expect their bounty.

"Roger that."

Cal headed down the hallway. Usually, after running and escaping with an illegal cargo, they'd celebrate. The people who they usually stole from had too much money to worry about small losses, and Cal hit different places every time to make sure no one ever started to care.

The place they'd messed with this time housed the type of people who held a grudge, and he'd stolen something personal. Some*one* personal. If the governor really did have an heir, they would be after the *Star Renegade*, and soon. Unless…

Cal hit a button on one of the comm panels, signaling the bridge. "Alanna?"

"Yeah."

"I have an idea. Scramble a signal and shoot it out on all

the royal channels. Tell the Banes that we tracked a stolen enforcer, male, pretty and blond, to Cerberus."

She snorted. "That will keep them busy for a while."

It would also make anyone already sent after the *Star Renegade* turn back to protect the planet. Even better, it may force the Carteks to lie low for a while, giving Cal more time to…to do what, he had no freaking clue. He needed to come up with a plan better than staying one step ahead of them and not dying.

"That's very mean, boss," Ty's voice said. "Brilliant, but mean."

Cal wasn't above being mean at the moment. "Make it happen. Then keep running scans. I don't want to be blindsided." There were far too many enemies out there right now, and not enough friends.

"On it," Ty said.

Cal placed his hand on the med bay door control.

Now, to do a little damage control.

THE DOOR SPLIT OPEN. On the far side of the room, Doc adjusted a bag running fluids...or something...into Alexander's arm. Closer to the door, on Cal's right, Dania lay on a gurney, her eyes closed, lips parted, the machine pumping Doc's artificial pathogens into her.

Cal's stomach fluttered. They'd come so far. He needed to believe Doc's brilliant mind would be enough to save her.

On the left, Rachel lay on a gurney on top of Kile, who seemed to be asleep.

Doc looked up, and Cal pointed to the stowaway.

Doc shrugged. "She's convinced we're going to try to hurt him."

"Well, you did knock him out right in front of her."

"True, and I did it again as soon as she got him on that gurney, so I guess the fear has merit. She refuses to leave."

"And the reason she's on top of him?"

"I guess she figures if I try to do anything to him, I'll wake her up." He turned back to Alexander. "I was a little too busy to argue."

Cal moved to the side of Dania's bed and smoothed a few

stray hairs back. She'd given Alexander the last bits of strength she had…the tiniest pieces of energy left over from her prince—not enough for her to do magic, but probably the last bits holding her body together. She knew it would probably kill her. Still, she'd done it on the slim hope of saving some guy from her past life.

Something tugged inside Cal's gut. He tried to push it aside, but it only got worse.

On the far side of the room, Doc adjusted the blanket around Dania's friend. The younger enforcer's platinum-blond hair flowed across his pillow, making him look elven, even in his sleep.

Did she love this guy? Was that why she was willing to give him everything—to maybe give her life to save him?

Cal closed his eyes, gritting his teeth. His cheeks heated. His fists shook with the need to hit something—maybe even Alexander, unconscious or not. Of course, unconscious was probably the only way Cal would live through it.

He needed to keep his cool because once Alexander and Kile were awake, he'd probably have to deal with two enforcers ready to pass judgement on this ship. And, more importantly, the crew.

Dania moaned in her sleep, and Cal took her hand.

She looked so helpless. He wanted to stay here and stand between the reality of the Banes' legacy sleeping in the other two beds and the woman who'd given up everything she'd known to get away from them.

He steeled himself. He was just one man. A normal man.

Enforcers were the power in the galaxy because of what they could do to *normal men*.

Still, he'd put himself between her and them, for all the good it would do.

Rachel's body rose and fell as she lay on Kile's chest. The commander didn't look half as horrifying on that gurney. Alexander looked like a sleeping angel, much like Dania. There was a reason that the slavers went for the weak ones, or the untrained, and they'd seen it today. The kind of power the enforcers wielded was unfathomable. The only chance to kill them was when they were asleep.

Cal looked back over to Alexander, then Kile.

Even knowing the threat they posed to the crew, he didn't have it in him to kill anyone in their sleep. There had to be a better way.

Of course, he also needed to worry about the Carteks. How long until they came, expecting payment for the technology they'd given Cal?

He released Dania's hand and stepped back. In simpler times, he'd hidden under his bedsheets to keep all the monsters away. Things hadn't been that easy in a long time, though—not since the day the enforcers had landed and taken his father away from him.

Cal had learned the hard way that problems—*real problems*—didn't work themselves out. He had to face them head on.

He just didn't know how.

Cal shook his head. He'd have to wake up Kile and Alexander eventually. No matter what, there would be trouble. The question was, how much trouble, and if battle lines were drawn, would Dania cling to her past or reach for the future she'd fought so hard to make a reality? Would she still want to stay, or would she go back to Keveron with her friends?

"Cal?" Doc waved him over. He stared down at Alexander.

"Everything okay?"

Doc rubbed his chin. "For now, yes. Do you notice anything strange about this one?"

The blanket was tucked around the enforcer's waist. His silvery hair floated a bit, and his chest rose and fell rhythmically over annoyingly broad shoulders. He looked like any other enforcer, with the exception of him not killing anyone at the moment.

The door slid open. "Everything looks good. We're on course." Alanna walked toward them and gazed down at Alexander. "Is he okay?"

"He's stable." Doc pointed to his patient. "Maybe you can help me out. What do you see?"

Her eyes widened, and her cheeks heated. "Umm...what am I looking for?"

"Look at the sharp edges in his face and cut of his nose." Doc gestured downward. "Look at his abs, and the way they cut into his hips."

Yeah, Cal got it, the guy was hot. Did it have to be a topic, though?

"Your point?" Cal glanced at Dania, and his hands clenched into fists again.

Doc looked up and sighed. "Maybe this will help you get my meaning." He lifted the blanket and pointed under.

Cal frowned. "I am *not* looking under the blanket."

Doc's face remained stoic. "Look under the blanket, Cal."

He was kidding, right? "No."

Doc shook his head. "Okay, Alanna, how about you?"

She leaned past Cal. Doc held the blanket up higher.

Alanna gasped, covering her mouth. Her eyes opened up like saucers.

Doc lowered the blanket. "I know, right?"

Alanna lowered her hands. "He's..."

"Huge."

Alanna stepped back. "I mean, that's not normal, right, I mean, he's…"

"Perfect, like the rest of him."

Cal glanced back to Dania, his blood boiling again. He gritted his teeth. "What's your point, Doc?"

Doc held his palm out toward the enforcer's bare chest. "None of this is normal. His angles are perfect. His arms and legs are in exact proportion. There are abs on top of his washboard abs."

This, Cal could see. "So?"

"Like I said, he's not normal. Humans are slightly off. And everyone has one feature that could theoretically be improved. But not him."

"What are you getting at?"

Alanna stepped closer. "He's like a doll."

"Exactly," Doc said. "He didn't grow this way normally. It's like he's been sculpted."

Her brow furrowed. "Like clay?"

Doc looked at Kile, then Dania. "They are all kind of pretty, aren't they?"

Cal considered what they already knew. "You told us that they pick kids at birth. Something about their blood. Maybe they purposely choose ones they know will be pretty when they grow up."

"Pretty is one thing. Genetic modification is another."

Genetic modification? Cal didn't like the sound of that. "Does this make him any more dangerous?" The last thing they needed was a genetically modified menace. A regular enforcer was bad enough.

"No." Alanna stepped closer to the bed, placing her hands on the rail. "This is the one who saved Peter." She looked at

Doc. "You remember, he could have kept walking, but he stopped and pulled that bullet right out of your chest."

Cal pursed his lips. "He's also the one who nearly strangled him to death."

Alanna's eyes widened. "What?"

They really needed to fill her in on everything that had happened on the surface so she would stop putting this death machine on a pedestal.

Doc pointed to the bruises on his neck. "It's true. Not to defend the guy, but that just confirms we're going to be dealing with a serious case of post-traumatic stress disorder."

Alanna blinked, looked down at the sleeping enforcer, then looked up at them and blinked again, like she was having trouble believing what was brutally obvious to those who'd been in that mansion.

She turned to Cal. "All I know is that he helped Doc out of the kindness of his heart." She pointed at Kile. "And that one yelled at him for it, like Alexander had wasted his time."

Cal held up his hands. "I'm just saying we need to be cautious." Alanna had always been the type to see only the best in people, and far too willing to overlook the worst. "When he woke him up the first time, he flashed out power that pushed us all back, even Kile. I don't want to be killed by accident."

"I'm all for not dying." Doc adjusted the drip in the enforcer's arm. "I have to admit, though, that we are on new ground, again, with this one. I'm not sure what they did to him to keep him in la-la land. For all I know, he could wake up angry at any moment."

Alanna folded her arms. "Or he could wake up smiling, happy that we saved him."

Too many variables, and far too many enforcers. "Let's

keep one of those containment fields around him, just in case."

Doc pointed across the room. "You want one around the commander, too?"

Rachel lifted her head from Kile's chest. "You will not put my Big Guy in a cage."

Cal shook his head and walked out. He wasn't past locking her up with him if they had to.

CHAPTER 44
CAL

DANIA'S EYELASHES FLUTTERED. Cal took a deep breath. That may have just been the most wonderful sight he'd seen in years.

Doc injected something into the bag of fluids running into her arm. "Okay, she should be awake in a few minutes."

And then they'd know if Doc's new mix of pathogens had worked or not.

Cal took another deep breath and released it slowly. He'd always known that her Kever pathogens would run out eventually, and that there was a chance the replicated cells Doc had created wouldn't work. He'd just never expected to be so worried about it when that day finally arrived and they'd get their answer.

Her lashes fluttered again. "Cal?" she whispered.

He grabbed her hand. "Yeah, I'm here."

His chest tightened. He'd made a point of being here when she'd had treatments before, and he would stay as long as he could this time. He was glad that she knew he was at her side.

She hummed, shifting across the sheets. "That's so good."

Cal narrowed his eyes. "What?"

"Cal?" Her head tilted to the side, and she moaned slightly. "More." She moaned again, licking her lips. "So good."

Doc snorted. "Umm, wow. Do you guys want to be alone?"

"What?"

Doc held out his hands as she moaned again.

Cal's cheeks flushed.

She'd said his name. Was she actually…?

"Oregano," she whispered.

Wait. What?

Doc laughed, covering his mouth. "Oregano? That's a new one."

Cal shook his head. He should have realized. "I've been teaching her how to cook."

He looked down at her. "Cook what?"

"Tomato sauce. What does it matter?"

Doc quirked a brow. "That must be some sauce."

Her lashes fluttered again.

She opened her eyes and frowned. "W-Why am I in the med bay?"

She tried to sit up, but Doc eased her back with a finger. "Take it easy there. I need to get a few readings. How do you feel?"

She blinked. "Tired."

Doc ran a flashing device over her. "Tired like you're just waking up, or tired like you could sleep for another week?"

"Another week…what?" She blinked hard again and tried to get up again.

Cal grabbed her shoulder and eased her back. "Hey, listen to the doc. You've had a rough couple of days."

Dania scratched her scalp. "Days? How long have I been here?"

"Almost three days now." Cal squeezed her hand.

"I kept you asleep on purpose." Doc adjusted the bag beside her. "I gave you almost a double shot of pathogens—everything I had ready for your next treatment, plus some of what I had brewing for next time, hoping it would give you the boost you needed."

Dania rubbed her eyes. "Did something happen to me?"

"You don't remember?" Cal asked.

"Everything is fuzzy." She closed her eyes. "I remember walking, and trees, and a big stone building." She shook her head. "Is that right?"

This wasn't good. Cal was hoping she'd recall Alexander waking up and nearly killing Doc. He needed her to understand what they could be facing.

The furrow in Dania's brow faded.

Her eyes widened. "Alexander!"

She sat up and turned toward the far side of the room, where her friend lay. Cal reached for her, wanting to wipe the tears from her eyes.

But she tossed off her sheet and sprang from the bed. "Alexander!"

"Dania!" Cal grabbed for her, but she slipped from his grip. The tubes leading from her arm tugged at the bag attached to her bedside.

"Sweetie!" Doc grabbed the bag and ran with her. "Honey, your fluids! You need to lay back down."

"Alexander!" She placed her palms on the enforcer's stomach, his chest, his shoulders. "Alexander!" She spun toward Doc as he hung her fluid bag on the metal hanger beside the other gurney. "What's wrong with him? Why is he asleep?"

Doc held up his hand. "He might be okay, but he also might not be."

"What does that mean?"

"It means that I don't know. I haven't woken him up yet."

She parted her lips. "Why not?"

"Because last time he woke up, he almost killed me."

Not to mention throwing them all back like they weighed no more than leaves on the wind. If that was what her friend was like wounded, what would he be like fully charged?

She glared at Doc before her gaze lowered to the bruises on his neck. "That's not who Alexander is. He was confused."

Confused and lethal. She had to see that. Certainly, she wasn't that blind to the weapon that this guy was.

Doc massaged his throat. "Honey, I know he's your friend, but he's been through a lot. He doesn't know me, and he doesn't know this ship. If I were him, I'd consider me a threat, too, and he's pretty strong—as I found out."

She frowned, looking at Alexander. "Wake him up."

"I will. I was just waiting until you were here."

Cal eased forward. He hadn't agreed to waking the guy up today.

"Wake him up now!" Dania shouted.

Doc held up his hands. "Like I said, he's been through a lot. With you, I had a game plan. With him, I'm figuring things out still. I need to do this in steps, both for his safety, and for the rest of us."

Cal waited for Doc's words to sink in. Dania seemed to

listen to Peter. Hopefully, she'd realize this was the right thing to do.

She glanced at Doc, then returned her attention to her friend. "He would never hurt me."

"That's what we're hoping." Cal stepped closer. "And that's why we all agreed not to even start thinking about waking him up until we knew you were here, just in case."

Dania stood. "Well, I'm here."

And, apparently, just as strong and forceful as ever. Cal knew that she cared about this guy. He was a little stunned by how much, though.

He reached for her. "Let's give Doc room to do what he needs to do, and I think you need to get back to bed."

She pushed him away. "I'm fine."

What was it with women telling him that they were fine? She wasn't fine. She had tubes attached to her arm.

"Dania, come on."

She glared at him, then smoothed her hands over the enforcer's annoyingly beautiful face.

"Alexander?" she whispered. "Alexander, I'm here." She kissed his temple, his cheek, and then…

Cal tensed. His hands clenched into fists as she leaned down and covered Alexander's lips with her own.

He took a step back, gritting his teeth as she knelt beside the bed and placed her head on his arm. The weapon Doc had given him when Dania had first boarded, the tiny gun calibrated to take down an enforcer, itched in the side of his boot.

One shot. That's all it would take.

Tears streamed from Dania's eyes. "I'm sorry," she whispered. "I should have been there for you."

Cal's stomach sank. What was he thinking? That guy was unconscious. Completely helpless.

He took another step back, looking down.

Dania was never his to begin with. They had tomato sauce. Nothing more.

Like Dania had said, this guy meant everything to her. Cal was her friend. Her captain. Her star-blasted cook.

Doc slapped him in the arm. "Stop it."

Cal rubbed his biceps. "Stop what?"

"Stop acting like an angry, abandoned puppy. Get off your testosterone-enhanced stupidity trip and look at what's happening here."

Dania hugged the guy's arm like it was a lifeline.

Cal grimaced. "Look at what?"

Dania leaned up and laid across Alexander's chest.

It was more than obvious what was going on here.

Doc slapped him again.

"Ow." Cal rubbed his arm.

"I said, stop it."

Tears welled in Dania's lashes as she closed her eyes, still lying on Mr. Perfect's chest. Cal had been an idiot to think that he ever could have had a chance against someone who looked like that.

Doc looked up at the ceiling. "Alanna and Rachel are right. You're a complete idiot."

"What?"

Doc pointed at him. "Don't move."

Cal folded his arms. "Fine."

Doc leaned on the edge of the bed and handed Dania a tissue. "So, this Alexander guy is pretty great, huh?"

She took the cloth and wiped her eyes. "He's everything to me."

Cal cringed. Nothing like pouring salt on a freshly opened wound. He didn't have to stand here and listen to this, though. He turned to leave and smashed his face against a hazy magnetic barrier.

A slight smirk appeared on Doc's lips, but he didn't take his eyes off his patients.

That devious moonsnake had trapped Cal in the same confinement circle he'd made for Dania!

"I guess I can't blame you," Doc said to Dania. "He's a really nice-looking guy."

Dania shrugged. "I guess."

"You guess?" Doc glanced at Cal. "Please, girl. He's got abs on top of his abs, and that long, gorgeous hair?"

Cal grimaced. Was Doc intent on torturing him? Things were bad enough!

"I guess I never really noticed." Dania sighed, her gaze on her Alexander's closed eyes. She trailed her fingers along the side of his face, and a little piece of Cal died inside. He turned away. He might have been stuck here, but he didn't have to watch.

"What did you mean, when you said he meant everything to you?" Doc asked her.

What did he think she meant? Wasn't it obvious?

The dumb thing was, Cal had gone to that planet to help save this guy. The way she'd reacted when she'd found out Alexander had been taken by slavers…he should have realized the way she felt about him. He could have saved himself some grief.

Dania sniffed. "Alexander and I grew up together. I just can't imagine a world without him."

"Interesting, so that would make him more like what…family?"

Family? Cal spun back to them.

"Yeah," Dania said. "He's the closest thing to a brother that I'll ever have."

The knife lodged in Cal's chest yanked itself out. He took a painful breath.

Had he heard that right?

Doc beamed. "A brother, huh?" He looked at Cal. "What do you know about that?"

Doc pressed a button on the wall, and the magnetic field around Cal disappeared.

Cal stood for a moment, shaking. He wasn't sure if he was still angry, or if he was shaking because he felt like a fool. He needed to get a hold of himself.

Cal walked over to the bed and put his hand over Dania's. "We're going to do everything in our power to help your friend."

She eased up, holding the edge of the gurney, and put her arms around his neck. "Thank you."

She trembled, and her weight suddenly fell on him.

"Whoa there." He lifted her into his arms.

She grabbed her forehead. "I'm sorry. Maybe I am still a little tired."

Doc ran over and adjusted the lines attached to her fluid bag. "One of these days, you people are going to listen to me when I tell you to stay in bed." He grabbed the bag and walked beside Cal as he helped her back onto her gurney.

Doc pointed at her. "Now, stay like a good girl." He turned to Cal. "You. Out."

Cal held up his hands. "All right, all right."

Dania fisted her blankets while he backed away.

A deep ache seeded in Cal's chest.

Did she think of Cal and the rest of the crew as family, the same way she felt for Alexander?

Was there something there, between them, or were they just really good friends?

"Cal," Doc shouted. "Out!"

"I'm going!" He flicked a glance at Alexander as he passed.

One problem solved. Now they just had to make sure Mr. Perfect didn't freak out when he woke up and accidently kill them all.

CHAPTER 45
DANIA

THE DOCTOR MANEUVERED around Dania's bed, shining a light in her eyes. She wasn't sure this light had any true medicinal purpose, but it didn't seem any harm to comply.

"Everything looks better than I expected," he said. "It seems like those pathogens are holding."

"That's good, right?"

"Definitely." He placed the light in his pocket. "I want to keep an eye on your readings, of course, but from what I can see, you're as good as new."

Well, maybe not quite as good as new.

Dania drew in a deep breath. Across the room, Rachel glanced at her, then rolled up Kile's blanket and threw the thick, white material into the recycler.

Kile hadn't moved since they'd woken Dania up. They couldn't keep him that way, though.

Alexander lay on another bed, with Alanna seated beside him, reading a paper book with a ripped cover out loud. Now that Alexander was reasonably safe, as soon as Kile was awake, he'd want to head back home, and there was no doubt that her commander still intended to take both her and Alexander with him.

A shiver ran down her spine. The crew would fight for her if they had to. She knew they would.

And if they did, Kile would slaughter them, and she wouldn't be able to stop him.

Humanity had so many bonuses, and one horrible flaw she wasn't sure she, or they, could live with. And that was their inability to stop an enforcer.

She looked back to the doctor. "Do you think I'll ever regain my powers?"

He gave an exaggerated grimace. "Like I said, I've only been targeting keeping your organs working. All those crazy powers are the part of the whole enforcer scenario that I've never understood. But maybe." He rubbed his chin. "How about you try something simple?"

"Simple," she whispered, staring at the top of the pen light sticking out of his pocket.

She held up her fingers and willed the small metal device into her hand.

Dania gritted her teeth, drawing on the atoms, the air, the components within. Her hand shook, but the device remained.

Peter looked down at his pocket. "I'm guessing that should have been easy."

"Child's play." Her eyes burned, and she wiped the dampness from them.

"Hey." The doctor sat beside her on the bed. "I've been thinking about this, imagining what it must be like for you."

"You can't even imagine."

"No, I can't, but I guess it would be like losing my hands." He held up his palms. "These are everything to me.

Not just to me, but to the crew. I can't be much of a doctor without hands."

Dania folded her arms. "Your point?"

He lowered his arms. "Well, the point is, that if I lost my hands, I would feel helpless for quite a while. But then my humanity would kick in."

She frowned at him. "What does that mean? You can't grow back hands."

"No, but I can adapt. I'd figure out how to live without my hands. For instance…" He shifted his weight, sitting on his palms. "Now, I need my pen light in my pocket." He reached down and tried to grab it with his mouth. He stretched but couldn't quite reach it. "Hmm." He looked up at her. "You know what? Can you grab that for me?"

"Of course." She plucked the light out of his pocket.

A smile burst across his face.

"What?" she asked.

He shifted again, freeing his hands, and pointed at the light. "You didn't even think about using your power to pick that up. You used your hands. You adapted."

She sighed. "That's a bad example. I can't use my fingers to defend myself." Or anyone in this crew once Kile woke up. This wasn't just about using her power. It was about defending the people she cared about.

Peter pointed at her. "But you can use those fingers to pick up a gun. So what if you can't throw fire or any of that other crazy stuff? Don't underestimate the power of a well-calibrated weapon."

She sighed. Maybe he was right.

She *hoped* he was right.

Kile took a deep breath in his sleep. The problem was her commander had been programed to be ruthless. She was certain of this because she had reviewed his conditioning protocols. He had his orders, and there would be little way to stop him from fulfilling those directives outside of killing him.

She had to find another way out of this. She just wasn't sure how.

Across the room, Alanna closed her book and placed her hand on Alexander's as she leaned over and whispered something into his ear.

"What are you reading to him every day?" Dania asked.

"Oh, this?" Alanna looked at the worn cover of the old-fashioned paper novel. "*A Tale of Two Cities*. It's Dickens."

Dania tilted her head. "Dickens?"

"Yeah, you know, '*It was the best of times, it was the worst of times*,' and all that." She held up the book. "I don't know, it's a classic. My mom used to read it to me when I was sick."

Alexander's eyes remained closed. His breaths were rhythmic, as they had been since Dania had woken up.

"Do you really think he can hear you?" Dania asked.

Alanna pulled the novel closer to her chest. "I don't know. My mom always believed in the power of positive thinking, and the power of family and friends."

Dania narrowed her eyes. What did this have to do with Alexander?

Alanna looked to the other side of the room, where Rachel tucked in Kile's sheets. "The commander has Rachel doting on him all the time. Heck, she even climbs into bed and sleeps with him every night." She turned to Dania. "All the guys and I come to see you every day, and I can see it in your face—it brightens you up."

Dania did enjoy visits from her friends. Even Ethan, who

everyone seemed to throw out like they thought he was annoying her.

Alanna held out her hands. "Alexander doesn't have anyone besides you, and it just seemed wrong to leave him alone lying in that bed like that all the time." She turned to him. "I guess I hope some part of him can hear my voice, and it will make him feel better knowing he's not alone."

"You are just the sweetest little thing." Doc hugged Alanna from behind. "Isn't she the sweetest?"

Actually, it *was* pretty sweet. Odd, how Alanna had no fear, while all the others looked at Alexander like he was a bomb that could explode at any minute.

The door slid open, and Cal entered.

His gaze met hers. "Hey, look at you, sitting up! You look great!"

Dania dragged her fingers through her tangled hair. She was sure she *didn't* look great. She'd love some time in one of their warm water showers, and to have her hair styled by Alanna's machine.

Rachel kissed Kile and skipped over to Dania, jumping to a stop like she'd seen children do getting in a line for sweets.

"So you're feeling better?" She placed her hands behind her back and looked at Peter. "Is Dani cleared for duty, Doctor Pete?"

"Yeah, she's probably healthier than I am at the moment."

"Great!" Rachel spun to Cal. "Then can we wake the Big Guy up? You promised."

Cal frowned. "I didn't promise."

"Yes, you did! You promised as soon as Dani was up and about, we could wake up my guy, too."

Had he actually said that? This was one more complication he didn't want to deal with. "We're only a few hours away from Trellis. How about we let the boar loose, like we all agreed to and…"

"How about we wake the Big Guy first? He'll want to see our new friends off, too."

Cal's cheeks reddened. "I have enough to worry about making sure those animals don't break loose and eat us."

"That's why you need the Big Guy. He'll keep us all safe."

Cal pointed at Kile. "The last thing on his mind is keeping us safe. He might not even allow us to land."

Rachel lifted her chin. "He will if I ask him to."

Cal shook his head. "Listen, I know you think he cares about you, but…"

The small woman's temperature spiked. "He does! You don't know him like I do."

"Rachel, he's an enforcer."

She pointed at Dania, nearly touching her nose. "So is she, but no one had any trouble waking her up."

"She's not promising to kill my crew."

This was true, and he certainly could not expect the same from Kile. Although her commander *had* made an uncharacteristic concession for Cal's ship.

"He did promise to give you a head start," Dania said.

Cal gaped at her. "Are you really saying we should wake him up?"

"We can't leave him like that." And maybe if Rachel was adamant about setting the boars free, she'd be enough of a distraction for them to wake Alexander. That way, Dania would have someone else on her side when Kile inevitably turned on her.

Alexander's chest rose and fell in a gentle cadence. At least, she hoped her friend would be on her side. Did their history mean as much to him as it did to her?

Would he listen to reason, or would he be just as blind as she had been?

As Kile *still was*.

Moreover, if Alexander wasn't on her side when he woke, what would she do?

What *could* she do? Use her hands…against fully charged primordial energy?

She gulped. The doctor was wrong. A well-calibrated weapon was no match for a fully trained enforcer.

CAL RUBBED HIS FACE. He'd never expected Dania to turn Team Kile. She had to know that he was a danger to everyone on board.

His ears started to ring. The last thing he needed now was another headache. "Are you sure you want to wake him up?"

She closed her eyes and looked down. "No, but we can't leave him asleep like that. Geron is already looking for me, and for Alexander. We don't want him looking for Kile too. Let alone finding us all here, under your care."

Care was an interesting way to put it. Peter had basically put the commander in a sleeping prison, but the doctor had said the same thing. It was dangerous to keep him under for much longer.

Cal puffed out a breath, dragging his fingers over his scalp as he watched the enforcer's hair glide about like he were charged with static. They all looked so harmless when they were sleeping.

"What can we expect when he wakes up?" Cal asked.

Dania took a step toward her commander's bed. "Well, from my recent experience waking up from a chemical stupor, the first thing he will do is go through his programming, his missions. His first thoughts will be what is most important to him."

Doc elbowed Cal's arm. "They think about what's most important to them first, huh?"

Cal narrowed his eyes at him.

"The first thing Dania said when she started to wake up was your name."

Cal shook his head. "She was dreaming about tomato sauce."

Doc poked his ribs. "She was dreaming about *your* tomato sauce, and don't you forget it."

Dania turned toward them. "His mission was to find Alexander. I would suggest giving him a clear line of sight so he can see him. It will keep him from lashing out and maybe hurting someone."

That was probably a really good idea. If the commander knew he'd been knocked out again, he might not be too happy with Doc.

Rachel looked up. "My guy won't hurt anyone. He actually has a soft spot for all of you." She grimaced. "Except Cally. He thinks you are—how did he put it?—*an annoyingly inefficient waste of breathable oxygen.*" She wrinkled her nose. "That didn't sound very good to me."

Cal sighed. *Great.*

Dania moved closer to Cal. "It might be a good idea if you aren't the first person he sees. There is still a price on your head, even if your capture is no longer Geron's top priority."

How could any of them possibly think this would go well? "Are you sure this is a good idea?"

Her brow furrowed as she looked at her commander. "Now is probably the best time. No matter what anyone thinks, Rachel is a valuable asset when it comes to dealing with Kile. She's here. She might not be later, at a time when we no longer have the option to wait."

"Hey, I resent the insinuation I'd leave my guy," Rachel said. "I ain't going anywhere."

Which right now was a good thing.

"All right," Cal said. "Let's get this over with."

Dania moved to the left, giving Kile a clear line of sight to Alexander on the far side of the room.

Doc injected something into the bag attached to Kile's arm. "Here goes nothing."

Cal scratched the back of his neck. "Will it take as long for him to wake up as it took Dania?"

"You got me. No other human has ever had a chance to study an enforcer let alone treat one. I'm basically making all this up as I go along."

"Your educated guess?"

Doc's lips thinned. "Big Bad is in a lot better shape than Dania, and his pathogens are real." He leaned closer to Cal. "My educated guess says we should have put him in an airlock when we had the chance."

"*Now* you tell me?"

"You wouldn't have done it anyway."

The enforcer groaned. His head moved from side to side.

Rachel stepped forward, while everyone else stepped back.

"Keep a clear line of sight to Alexander," Dania reminded the crew.

Rachel waved her off. "Yeah, yeah, whatever."

The enforcer's eyes sprang open and he took a deep breath, like he'd been stuck underwater.

"Quirky!" He sat straight up in the bed, gasping. "Quirky?"

She jumped to him, crawling onto his lap. "I'm here!" She grabbed his face, covering him with kisses. "I'm here. Everything is okay."

Dania seemed frozen, her lips parted.

Doc moved between Cal and Dania and whispered what they were all probably thinking. "The first thing he thought about was Rachel?"

"Somehow, she became his most important concern." Dania shook her head. "That shouldn't be possible."

Cal folded his arms. No, it shouldn't be possible. But neither should it have been possible to catch a general, shoot her up with fake pathogens, and free her from the control of a domineering prince.

That's twice in a row that Ty and Ethan's insane plans had worked. Maybe Cal needed to give them credit more often.

The enforcer grabbed Rachel's face, looking into her eyes. "You're okay? You are not harmed?"

"Why would I be harmed?"

"What are you talking about? They were shooting at us."

Rachel leaned back. "Wait, that was like, days ago. What is the last thing you remember?"

The enforcer looked down. "Something wrapped around my neck, and I remember you screaming."

She touched his face. "We got out of there. And we got back to the ship. Do you remember helping the guys get the boar and the other animal into the cargo container?"

He wiped his eyes. "Yes, of course. It's coming back."

Dania pulled Doc and Cal away. "That's not good. His memory should be sharp. All of our memories are enhanced.

Actual memories of our past should be like watching a news feed. Clear and exact."

"Alexander!" Kile pushed Rachel back but still held a firm grip on her shoulders. His eyes fixed across the room.

Doc inched forward. "Your friend is okay. I'm giving him fluids and proteins. I'm trying to flush out all the gobbledygook that was in his system."

The enforcer glared at him. "Gobbledygook?"

Doc shrugged. "To be honest, I can't even figure out the chemical makeup of that stuff he was floating in. I figured the safest thing to do would be to flush it all out."

The enforcer flung his legs over the side of the bed. "You can't figure it out because you are not a real doctor. He needs competent medical care."

"Hey," Cal said. "Peter is a damn good doctor. I don't give a fading star that he doesn't have an official seal next to his data records."

The commander's nose flared. "Well, I do. Tell your pilot to plot a course to Keveron."

Right to the executioner's doorstep?

"Not going to happen," Cal said.

"What?"

"We're actually heading in the opposite direction. We just entered the outer reaches of the Trillian Cluster."

"Why? I need to get..." He shook his head, like clearing a fog. "I need to get Alexander home."

Rachel touched his cheek. He closed his eyes and seemed to lean into her palm. *Interesting.*

"We need to go to Trellis," Rachel told him. "We have to drop off the boar, remember?"

The enforcer's expression lightened. His brow pinched, and he dragged his fingertips down the side of her face. Cal had seen so much death, so much destruction at the hands of enforcers, he never imagined one…especially this one…could touch someone with such affection.

Kile closed his eyes, looked down, and then turned to Dania. "You look like a shell of your former self. Can I take for granted you do not have the strength to feed me?"

Dania flinched. "I don't think I can." She glanced at Doc.

"I don't think that's a good idea to even try," Doc said.

There was that *feeding* thing again. Kile had said it was an exchange of energy. Did that mean the commander was wearing down? Would that be good for them or bad?

Part of the plan…the optimistic plan…was dumping Alexander and Kile as payment to the Carteks. He hadn't worked out how to bargain for Dania yet. This very flawed scheme only had to work long enough for the Carteks to remove the alien squeeze bomb from the comm juncture.

Cal would refuse Rgrythei's offer to turn the tech back into a shield. It was too risky. He just wanted the damn thing off his ship so they could get away free and clear.

This plan all hung on Kile's ability to fight off the Carteks, though. The commander was no friend to the *Renegade* crew, but Cal still couldn't send him and Alexander to slavery or death. It just wasn't who Cal was.

"I can't even sense your presence." Kile grimaced, like the very sight of his former commander hurt. "How can you stand it? How can you live with yourself, knowing you are so much less than you were?"

Dania reset her footing, but her eyes saddened. "This is who I am now. And I'm happy."

Damn right. But her forehead wrinkled. Was she having second thoughts?

"Happy?" The enforcer's lips twisted. "You shouldn't be.

It's disgusting." He turned to Cal. "Unlike my general, who has gone insane, I am not okay with withering away and dying. Once we drop off Miss Quirky's animals, we need to head back to Keveron."

Did he think Cal was stupid? "I'm not taking this ship anywhere near Keveron."

Dania pulled Cal away. "Kile is hurt."

"That doesn't mean that I'm sacrificing the crew."

"No, but you need to understand what's going through his head."

"That he wants me dead? That he doesn't care if anyone on this ship dies as long as he gets Alexander home?" A dull ache started behind Cal's right eye.

She shook her head. "It's not that. He was directed to save Alexander. He's already done that. His base orders have kicked in. The same ones that made me almost get you all killed."

Cal frowned. What was she talking about?

"When I was hurt, when I was getting weaker every day, all I could think about was getting home to Geron." She touched her chest. "It's programmed into us to go back to him if we can no longer function, or if we're seriously hurt and without a healer." She looked over her shoulder, to where Rachel was in the enforcer's lap again whispering something into his ear. "He's too brave to admit it, but he's severely disabled."

Doc held up a data pad and waved it. "This little doohickey tells me he still has enough of a pathogen payload to kick all our asses."

"So did I, if you remember," Dania said. "I was the weakest I'd ever been, but I still opened a black hole. He won't admit it, but he's scared, and he will get home, one way or another."

Maybe, but if that happened, it would be under Cal's terms.

He walked over to Kile. "You can't ask me to take this ship all the way to Keveron. The Banes know the *Star Renegade*. They're looking for us."

"This is not my problem."

"But it should be. We'll be overrun. We'll get boarded. They will kill everyone on board." Time to drive the point home with the only collateral he had. "Rachel is on board this ship. Do you think they'll have a second thought before cutting her down?"

The enforcer flinched, then looked to the side. "You have a point."

Rachel hugged his arm. "You don't have to go back."

He tugged away from her. "After we drop off the animals, we will head in the direction of Bane space. Then we will formulate an alternate plan that will not end in the ship being boarded."

Good. That was at least something. Hopefully, they could come up with a plan that left the ship...and the crew...in one piece.

CHAPTER 47
CAL

CAL STEPPED into his quarters and sighed as the door closed behind him. He rubbed his eyes as the dull throb behind his right eye started to gouge out the inside of his brain. He held his head and breathed in through his nose, out through his mouth, just as Doc had taught him.

The top of his throat started to burn, and he took another deep breath. He couldn't start vomiting again. His crew needed him.

He shielded his eyes from the harsh illumination. Doc had warned him light could make the migraines worse.

He tapped the panel on the wall. "Lights, lower by fifty percent," he whispered, and the room darkened.

His head still throbbed, but the stabbing sensation subsided. Any other day, he'd make his way back to the med bay, but Doc had enough to deal with, and the last thing he needed was Kile knowing about these star-blasted headaches he'd been getting.

A tone sounded on the comm panel beside him, and Cal trembled, closing his eyes. He definitely didn't want to talk to anyone right now. Maybe if he ignored them, they would leave him alone.

He walked toward the bathroom, and as he passed the bed, the center comm panel pinged. He flinched. There were no motion sensors in his room. Was it a coincidence?

Even the low light started to hurt, and he continued into the bathroom. As soon as he stepped inside, a tone sounded from the vanity mirror comm.

Cursing, he hit the button. "What?"

Static sizzled over the speaker. Cal blinked and squinted as bright white characters flashed across the screen. He winced, turning away. "What the hell?" he whispered.

The daggers stabbed into his eyes again. Who in the name of Jupiter's moons would be sending him texts? He lowered the lighting on the screen and started the message over.

Three enforcers: As agreed

Drop-off location Hitus Two
Rear exterior station

The Carteks! Sweat beaded on his brow.

Taking slow deep breaths, and searching with half-closed eyes, he checked the time stamps. The text had been transmitted three times. Once when he'd entered his quarters, sending straight into his door comm, the second time as he'd passed his bed, and then a third time here. The star-forsaken alien tech could track where he was standing!

His stomach churned. Cal leaned over and puked into the toilet.

They knew that Alexander was on board, and now Cal was expected to pay up.

He retched again, wiped his face, and looked back to the screen. Hitus was halfway across the galaxy and not far from Elbus, which meant that the Carteks probably hadn't penetrated any deeper into Earth's holdings. If Cal could just avoid that part of space...

He closed his eyes and took a deep breath. He couldn't hide forever. But he also wasn't giving up Dania without a fight.

CHAPTER 48
CAL

A FEW HOURS of sleep while Ty flew them to Trellis had wrestled Cal's headache to a dull roar. They'd entered the jungle planet's atmosphere about an hour ago, and now they needed to drop off their furry passengers before Cal figured out how to deal with the enforcers, and the pending Cartek problem.

His sight wavered slightly, and he closed his eyes. Doc had been working with Dania all morning, checking on her pathogen levels. Once they were done, he'd see if Doc could do a little magic and fix his brain again. He needed to be able to think straight.

Cal walked onto the lower deck as Ethan and Ty maneuvered the cargo container holding the animals to the edge of the landing platform.

Rachel and Alanna stuck their heads through the opening. Outside, a dusty, brown surface led to dense trees at the base of a mountain rising high above.

"They're coming closer," Alanna said, holding up an infrared scanner.

Rachel pointed. "There they are!"

The trees and bushes shifted before a dozen massive, tusked creatures moved into the clearing, followed by dozens more. They walked in groups of two and three. It almost looked organized, like a military show of force.

"They don't look all that extinct to me," Ethan said.

Alanna tapped Cal's arm. "Good call, landing on the opposite side of the planet from the colonists."

Cal agreed. "Too bad we can't relocate the rest of them out here as well." The sad fact was that humanity rarely stayed in one area of a planet. History showed that they spread like cosmic locusts, overtaking entire worlds in the name of progress—taking little heed of what damage they might do.

These boars were big and dangerous, but they were probably protecting their homes. To the settlers, though, they were just one more thing in the way to getting the beautiful worry-free home they'd traveled halfway across the universe for.

The boars waved their tusks and snarled as they approached the ship. Kile stood behind Rachel. The air about his right hand came in and out of focus, like he was holding power ready to throw. If all went well, he wouldn't need to use it.

As they anchored the container into position, Rachel placed her hand on the modified, barred-in window Ethan had installed. "You're home! We're going to let you out in a minute."

The boar snarled and lunged for her. So much for Rachel's animal diplomacy.

Kile pulled her away, but she pushed him off and walked back to the bars.

She pointed at the boar. "Hey, is that any way to treat someone helping you out? Sheesh!"

"She's pregnant," Alanna said. "And she's been stuck in that box for days. I kinda can't blame her."

"Do we put the ramp down?" Ethan asked Cal.

The other boars were circling below the entrance to the ship, snarling. They were lined up two by two. A chill ran down Cal's spine. No wonder the settlers were so afraid of them.

"They're not attacking," Rachel said.

Ethan snorted. "Probably because they know they can't reach the tasty humans from this height."

"That's a good point," Ty said. "What do you think they're going to do when they have a nice convenient gangway to run up?"

The largest boar kept stopping and looking directly at the opening. Ty and Ethan, for once, echoed his own thoughts.

The mama boar scratched at the door to her container. A light whining sound came from inside.

Rachel crossed her arms. "We can't ask a pregnant mother to jump thirty feet to the ground."

This was true. Cal pinched his brow as the ache deepened. There were way more boars down there than people up here. But maybe it didn't need to be so difficult. Cal turned to Kile. "Can you lift her down? Grab her with air and set her nice and easy on the grass?"

The enforcer folded his arms. "I could."

Rachel's eyes widened. "He could not!" She spun and pointed at the commander. "You said that was like turning the air into a giant hand. What happens if you drop her or squeeze her?"

"I have never dropped anyone." He glanced at Cal. "Unless it was on purpose."

Cal bit his tongue. He still had bruises from that fall.

Rachel shook her head. "She's pregnant. There is no way I am letting anyone touch her. It's bad enough she had to make this trip in her condition!"

Cal held up his hands. "Fine. Lower the damn ramp." He looked at Kile. "Can you stop them from running up the gangway?"

The enforcer quirked a brow at Rachel. "I don't know. Am I allowed?"

"Stop being snarky. You know that's okay." She pointed in his face. "But don't hurt any of them. They're extinct."

Ethan scratched his head. "Technically, they aren't extinct. There are a ton of them out there. I think we're going to have to reclassify them as endangered."

Rachel shoved him. "Stop being all smart-like. Endangered, extinct, it's all the same to me. We didn't give her a ride home just to hurt her or the other nice boars."

Cal leaned out the door. The tusks on the boars below were twice as long as the ones on the boar they'd freed, and they looked like they'd been razor-sharpened. *Nice boars* wasn't really the term he would have chosen to describe them.

Cal waved Ethan to lower the ramp. "Let's just get this over with, please."

The crew stepped to the side as Ty raised the door to the cargo container.

Kile grabbed Rachel's arm, holding her from the ramp.

She yanked away. "Quit it."

He pulled her back. "If one of them should hurt you, there would be no more concern about them being endangered because I would make them extinct today, in an instant. Do you understand?"

The large boar lumbered out the door, her mouth open, panting. She looked even larger, her heavy belly sagging. Maybe they'd just saved her in time.

"You are such a worrier," Rachel said, shifting so Kile couldn't grab her again.

Oddly enough, the commander didn't reach for her again.

Ty glanced at Cal with that all-too-familiar *I told you so* look.

Cal had to admit that he'd never thought their crazy plan would work. The enforcer could easily make the woman do whatever he wanted. Yet he hadn't.

The boar stopped on the ramp, raised her head, and roared. The dozens below bellowed with her. It was odd, like she called to them, and they all answered. Cal didn't know a lot about animals, but this didn't seem like normal behavior.

"Where's the little one?" Rachel leaned into the opening of the container. Her brow furrowed before she stepped inside. "It's gone!"

"What?" Cal moved closer. "If that thing has gotten loose on the ship…"

Rachel cried out, stumbling backward onto the gangway. A ball of fur the same color as the container rolled out, hitting Rachel's leg. She floundered, her arms swinging in the air, before she slammed onto the metal plating about ten feet down the ramp.

"Ow!" Rachel rubbed her rear, looking over her shoulder at the smaller animal as it ran around the larger boar.

"That wasn't very nice!" she told it.

Kile shook his head but didn't intervene. Cal supposed he'd figured out that he'd only get in trouble if he tried to help. Unless, of course, Quirky thought help was necessary, in which case, he'd better learn to read minds, because she probably wouldn't tell him before she started yelling that he didn't care enough about her.

Cal backed up and leaned against the wall as the mama boar lumbered to the middle of the ramp, another ten feet or so from Rachel. The little guy still scooted around the larger animal like a cheerleader. The boars below bellowed, some standing on hind legs and curling their front claw-hooves. It almost looked like they were all encouraging her down the slope.

It seemed the boar drop-off, at least, was going well. Cal closed his eyes, and the stinging abated slightly. Maybe that was all he needed...a normal day without having to worry about dying.

A tone sounded on the comm beside him. He did a head count on the deck. The only people missing were Doc and Dania, but the message didn't appear to be coming from the med bay.

Cal hit the comm. "Talk to me."

Static filled the line.

Cal frowned. "Doc, you there?"

The screen flickered, and bright white characters flashed on the black screen.

Drop-off location Hitus Two:
Rear exterior station

Not Trellis
Not Trellis
Not
Trellis

Cal stared at the screen. He knew full well that this wasn't Hitus. He wasn't an idiot. The last message hadn't given a time for the rendezvous. Did they expect…

The ship shook. Ethan and Ty cursed.

Cal grabbed a cargo hook on the wall. He hadn't seen any reports of seismic activity on this planet. "What was that?"

Lights flashed outside. Rachel stood, wide-eyed, and ran for the ship as a shimmering glow started closing over the hull.

"Quirky!" Kile raised a hand and Rachel's feet left the ground.

She flew through the doorway, flailing her arms and screaming, just as the glow slammed across the opening with a boom and a sizzle of sparks.

Rachel shrieked and fell to her knees, clutching her hand.

Alanna held on to her as blood dripped to the deck.

"My hand!" Rachel screamed. "My hand!"

"Quirky!" Kile raced toward them.

A small puddle of blood pooled at her side. *Dammit!*

Something creaked outside, followed by a metallic clang. The ramp—it was gone. Severed by the Cartek shield.

Rachel sobbed, while Kile held onto her hand. The girl was lucky to be alive.

The ship rumbled again. "What the hell?" Cal raced toward the glow.

"Stay back!" Ethan called. "That barrier sliced right through the ramp. You won't last a second."

Cal skidded to a stop, gaping at the shimmering glow outside the door. The gangway had fallen, then got hooked on the landing gear below. A sharp, scraping noise echoed throughout the chamber as the left side of the ramp slipped off the metal frame it had fallen on. The boar roared as she fell, clawing at the part of the gangway still leaning on the landing gear as her rear legs swung free, dangling toward the ground and shaking the frame she clung to.

Rachel pushed Kile away from her, clutching her bleeding hand. "Let me go! Save the boar! She's extinct!"

"I don't want to be extinct, either, if anyone cares." Ty fumbled with the door controls, but they didn't seem to work.

Ethan hit the comm. "Doc, it's now or never!"

"I'd rather it was never," Doc said over the speaker.

The hull creaked again. This was it… Cal hadn't complied, and the Carteks were going to crush them.

Cal blinked, his vision hazy. "We're going to die anyway, so if you two have an idea, I say run with it!"

"Here we go!" Ethan called.

Cal grabbed on to the side of the ship, but he really wasn't sure what good it would do.

The shaking stopped. The glow outside winked out.

Cal held his breath until Ethan punched his fist in the air and *whooped*.

Cal released his hold on the wall hook. "What did you do?"

Ethan's grin lit up the cargo bay. "We used the—"

"Who cares?" Rachel stood, clutching her hand. "Are we going to die?"

Ethan gaped at her. "Not today."

"Good." She pointed out the door with her chin. "Then can we please save the boar?"

The smaller animal skittered along the edge of the half-fallen ramp, while the pregnant mama still clung to the side of the ramp, her lower claws scraping against the metal hanging below her. The animals on the ground circled just underneath her, either hoping to cushion her fall or ready to eat her if she did.

"You told me not to use my power to lift her," Kile said.

Wind from outside whipped through Rachel's hair. "Well, I changed my mind!"

The commander muttered through clenched teeth. "I could have done this the first time." He raised his hand and the snarling animal rose into the air, floated from the ship, and eased to the sandy surface below. The wild boars closed in on her, rubbing their hides against hers in some sort of odd greeting.

"Where's the other one?" Rachel leaned out the opening.

Several of the smaller creatures clambered among the boars. They all looked the same to Cal, similar creatures in varying shades of color comparable to the hull of the ship. Their animal could be any one of them.

Rachel backed away from the opening. "I guess he fell. What if he got hurt?"

This girl definitely had a problem focusing on the right priorities.

Which, right now, was staying alive.

They'd gotten one solid directive: Don't touch the tech. The Cartek had sworn that they would know. Had Ethan and Doc done something to accidentally set it off?

Cal turned to Ethan. "What the blazes did you do?"

"Doc and I have been working on it since the last time that thing went off."

"You weren't supposed to touch it. Did you miss the part where it might explode?"

Ethan held up his hands. "Relax, boss. We're still here, aren't we?"

Yes, they were here, but was it luck, or ingenuity?

The engineer pointed at the screen. "We used their own tech against them."

"What do you mean?"

Ethan beamed. "We fired up the transient spatial inhibitor to create a shield of air between the new comm juncture and the ship. We used the same type of system the alien tech used, but instead of shrinking, we expanded the air pocket." He pointed at a representation on the screen. "Right now, it's detached, but only by microns." He turned back to Cal. "Don't you see the beauty in that? It thinks it is still attached, but it isn't! So if it goes off, it will crush itself, not the ship."

Cal rubbed his forehead. "That shouldn't have worked."

Ethan shrugged. "But it did. That's all that matters." He turned to Alanna. "We don't have a secondary comm juncture anymore. Sorry about that."

Alanna dragged her fingers through her pink-tipped hair. "I think I can forgive you."

The question was, though, was this fix permanent, or were they still in danger?

"It appears that your engineer has once again shown his worth." Kile frowned at Rachel's hand.

She burst into tears. "Don't look at me like that! I'm ugly!"

Kile's eyes widened. "I didn't say…"

She held up her hand. The tip of her left pinky was severed and burned just below the first joint.

Cal's jaw dropped. That was bad, but nowhere near as bad as it could have been.

Rachel wailed louder. "See? Even Cally thinks I'm ugly!"

Kile's eyes blazed. "Tell her she isn't ugly!"

"You're not ugly!" Cal shouted. "I mean, it's not even

noticeable."

Rachel held her hand close to her face. "I'm maimed! Disfigured forever!"

The edge of her pinky joint was dark. Was that from the alien tech, or had Kile tried to cauterize the wound? It didn't seem to be bleeding anymore.

"Rachel, I'm sorry you got hurt. I'm just glad the commander got you inside and your whole body wasn't cut in half when that shield slammed down."

Her eyes widened.

Cal got ready for another round of waterworks, but instead, Rachel threw her arms around the enforcer's neck.

"You saved me." She kissed him. "You're my hero!"

A slight smile touched the commander's lips. "That being said, I think the doctor should look at you, despite his incompetence. You *did* just experience an unexpected amputation."

She leaned away from him. "Yeah, okay."

Below them, the broken ramp still hung on the edge of the landing gear. That was going to cost a small fortune to fix.

He turned back to Kile. "Before you head to the med bay, can I trouble you to float the rest of the ramp back into the ship so we can get it repaired at the next way station?"

The enforcer sighed like it was an inconvenience, but the long, metal ramp floated back up and slipped into place.

Good. Now, at least, they'd be able to fly. That was one step in the right direction. Cal didn't know if Doc and Ethan's air pocket would work forever, but either way, they needed to be mobile and ready to run at any second.

The only certainty was that they wouldn't be able to hide from the Carteks forever.

CHAPTER 49

DANIA

DANIA RACED for the ladder to the lower decks, calling over her shoulder. "Are you sure the weapon has been disabled?"

Doc threw a bag over his shoulder. "We're alive, aren't we?"

Dania wished that were a good enough answer. Most likely, they'd gotten lucky, but the Cartek Empire was years ahead of other races in the pursuit of artificial intelligence, all of which they used in their weapons. If Peter and Ethan had thwarted the threat, chances were the AI was calculating a way around the problem.

She jumped onto the lower deck just as the frame of the landing ramp slid into place with a clang. Kile lowered his hand and stumbled until his back hit the wall.

Dania gasped and ran to him, but Rachel reached him first.

The woman grabbed his shoulder. "What happened?"

Dania placed her hand on his other arm. "Are you all right?"

He looked at the floor and took a deep breath. "I do not think so." After taking another slow breath, he looked at Dania. "I need to get home."

His face had paled. More pale than even an enforcer should have been. His eyes had also darkened somewhat, losing the enforcer's crystal blue hue. Had she looked so sickly when she'd first started to lose her strength?

Rachel's eyes glistened with tears. "He helped me with this." She held up a hand with a missing digit.

Dania gaped, but it looked sufficiently healed.

Rachel lowered her hand. "Then he used his magical mojo to help the boar off the ship, and then he floated the broken ramp back into place." She wiped her nose on her sleeve. "Is he gonna be okay?"

The answer was complicated, and it involved pathogen treatments or fulfilling his request to return home. For now, there wasn't much they could do.

Dania released him. "He'll need rest." It wasn't a lie. It wouldn't save him, but he'd regain some strength.

Cal tapped Ty's shoulder. "You heard Big Bad. Let's get moving."

Rachel helped Kile up, and he leaned on her as they walked toward the ramp to the crew quarters.

Peter stepped onto the deck. "You guys all right?"

Kile shook his head. "Quirky needs medical attention."

"I'll be up to see you in a bit," Rachel said. "I want to get the Big Guy in bed first."

The doctor let them pass and moved beside Dania. "Big Bad doesn't look so good."

Cal closed the cargo bay hatch, watching them leave. "He used his power and got weak, just like Dania used to."

Kile leaned on Rachel as they reached the accessway. He

glanced back, and when his eyes met Dania's, he straightened but still held on to the woman as they ascended.

Dania folded her arms. "He's very proud. He won't admit it, but he's tired, and he's probably scared. I know I was when my power started to drain."

Doc bit his lip as Kile and Rachel reached the top of the accessway. "If he's tired, he might lash out and do something *unfortunate.*"

Cal smirked. "Like call up a black hole and get us stranded in the middle of nowhere?"

Dania's lips parted. Her cheeks heated. She hadn't meant to strand them in the uncharted regions. That had been the furthest thought from her mind!

Cal laughed. "Hey, hey, I'm sorry. It was just a joke."

Dania hugged herself. "It wasn't funny."

Cal moved closer, touching her cheek. "Hey, I'm sorry."

The words still hurt, but the touch warmed her skin. A deep ache formed in her belly, a need not unlike the pull of her sponsor.

Why did that happen every time he touched her? The captain had no powers, no primordial energy. Humans were just...*human.*

Ethan walked toward the ladder, tossing a piece of metal from one hand to the other. "If you're going to live on this ship, you need to learn to take it as well as dish it out, General. Them's the rules."

More odd phrases. She cocked her head.

The engineer pointed at her with the metal. "It means you need to take a joke for what it is, and not get offended."

Dania supposed Ethan would know that better than any of them.

Ty inched closer to Cal. "Do you really want me to head us toward Bane space?"

Cal looked at Dania. He seemed to search her eyes, but what was he looking for? If it was an answer, she didn't have one. Even in his current state, Kile was a threat. They all knew that.

Cal turned back to his first mate. "Yeah. We made a deal, and we won't welch on it." He looked down. "Not this deal, at least," he whispered, barely audible.

If her hearing weren't enhanced, she probably wouldn't have even noticed.

Dania tilted her head. What did he mean by that?

Above, Rachel and Kile slipped through the door to the floor above.

"We need a solid plan," Cal said.

"Like drop and run?" Ty tugged at his hair. "If he's that messed up, he might even let us go without a fight."

"There is one other little detail," Peter said. "One that really isn't all that little."

They all turned to him.

"Even if we intend to drop and run, we need to wake up the other enforcer. Kile's too weak to take care of Dania's bestie unless they walk off the ship together."

Dania shivered. He was right. They needed to wake up Alexander, and once they did, Kile would probably do everything in his power to turn her friend against her and the crew. The only questions was: How easily could he do that?

When Dania had last seen Alexander through the glass of his ship, he'd begged her to come home. Would Alexander still want that, or would he listen to her…maybe even stay?

Her heart fluttered, and she held her hand over her chest.

She hated not having her powers, but the freedom of choice...discovering who she really was...this was like nothing she could have imagined.

Every day was a new experience, with an excitement so much more powerful than any rush of primordial energy. Alexander deserved this kind of freedom as well.

Peter looked at each of them. "I just want to make sure everyone understands that when we wake Mr. Perfect up, we're going to have two of them to deal with." His brow creased. "Do we really want to do this?"

"Yes," Dania said.

There was no question. She needed to know if Alexander's loyalty still lay with her. If it did, she might be able to save him as well.

Cal drew in a deep breath before expelling it slowly. "She's right. We didn't save him just to leave him helpless so he'd get caught again...or worse."

He grimaced. His thoughts seemed lightyears away. Cal pinched his brow like he did when he had a headache, but he also seemed to be working through something. Was he really that worried about Alexander?

He turned to Dania. "We'll wake him up."

She straightened. It was the right thing to do, and she'd finally get to speak to her friend again. She couldn't wait to show Alexander all she'd learned, to introduce him to her new friends, and to Cal.

Dania blinked. Why had she singled Cal out from the others?

A chill ran across her skin. Part of her, the human part, kept casting aside the reality of Cal's death sentence. His innocence did nothing to erase that, not until she convinced

Geron to acquit him, which she wasn't sure would ever happen.

"Okay." Peter started walking toward the ladder. "I hope you all know what you're doing."

Dania shivered. She hoped so, too.

NO MATTER how much Cal rubbed his palms together, they continued to sweat. It seemed like every time they got out of one bad situation, they got ready to step right into another one.

On the other side of the med bay, Dania leaned over Alexander's bed, holding his hand and talking to him like he was awake. Her expression seemed so sweet and full of hope.

This guy really meant a lot to her.

Cal grimaced, turning away. What would happen to her if this went bad?

Would she snap?

Decide humanity was too hard?

Would she take off with her commander and return to that star-blasted prince?

And if she did, would Cal one day have to face her as an automaton again? Would she execute him without a second thought, despite all they'd been through?

Doc nudged him. "Whatever you're thinking, it's not leading to any good."

As usual, his friend was right.

Doc tapped on his data pad, frowned, and then glanced at his patient. "Do you still have that gun?"

Cal cringed. In many ways, he'd wished he'd destroyed the weapon. His stomach sank, knowing he'd kept it so close over the past few weeks because Kile, even though he'd softened due to Rachel's odd charms, was still a threat. "It's in my boot."

"Good. You need to know something."

"I don't like the sound of that."

"Neither do I." Doc looked over his shoulder. "I ran a check on our new friend's pathogen levels, and they're through the roof."

Wait. What? "How can that be?"

Doc shifted his weight. "Well, I may have injected him with some of the pathogens I had brewing for Dania."

"You did *what?*"

"Well, the half-baked ones worked so well for her, I figured they'd help him, too."

"And now he's overloaded?"

"I don't know. Maybe it has nothing to do with that. Maybe whatever Dania gave him regenerated what he already had, but he's stronger now than Kile was when I first scanned him." He stared at Alexander again. "That boy is not going to wake up weak and feeble."

And he has no idea where he is, or why he's here.

Alexander was a ticking time bomb, just like Dania had been…or maybe worse.

Across the room, Dania leaned over and kissed her friend's cheek.

"We can't just shoot this guy, no matter what happens. It would kill her."

Doc took a deep breath. "The gun is just a precaution.

You need to understand that post-traumatic stress is a real thing." He lowered his eyes. "You didn't see the data streams on Cerberus, but believe me, they basically tortured this guy." Doc looked up. "From all the research I've done, there is a really high chance that Alexander won't be the same person she knew."

The truth was, the person she knew was an enforcer. Even though he'd saved Doc back on Midway Station, any change would be a change for the better. It was a long shot, as far as hopes go, but it was something. Cal would cling to that, for Dania's sake.

The door slid open, and Kile entered. He grimaced at Dania before joining them.

"Where's Rachel?" Doc asked.

"Miss Quirky is sleeping." Kile's brow furrowed. "I thought it better that way."

Doc narrowed his eyes. "She's a decent assistant. I could have used her help."

"Quirky is an exemplary medical technician, and I do understand that you are a less-than-capable doctor, however..." He pursed his lips. "Her *enthusiasm* tends to be a liability." He looked toward Alexander. "I do have concerns about Alexander's state of mind when he wakes up, though. I wanted to make sure I was here."

Cal cringed. Kile had seen the data streams as well, and he'd blown a fuse, breaking Alexander out of his glass prison with one angry whip of his power. If it were really as bad as these two thought, was there any chance that Dania's friend would be okay?

Sweat beaded Cal's brow. They had another live wire on their hands, and they had no idea if it was going to spark or not.

He shifted his footing, and his gun pressed against the inside of his boot. He really hoped he wouldn't have to use it.

Doc held up a syringe. "Ready to do this?"

No, but Cal nodded anyway. There was no use in postponing the inevitable.

Dania looked up when they approached.

"We need to be prepared in case he lashes out," Kile told her. "The last things he will remember will be…" He grimaced. "Unpleasant."

A slight red tint shone in her eyes before she wiped them. "I'll sit here with him. I'm his general, and I'm his friend. He won't hurt me."

A flush of heat spread through Cal. If that guy woke up, guns blazing, he didn't want Dania to be the only thing in the line of fire.

"She's right," Kile said. "She is probably the safest face for him to see first."

Doc glanced at Cal.

He wanted to tell them *no*—to wake the guy up alone inside the strongest confinement barrier possible. That was the safest thing to do…keep him in a cage. But that might make them no better than the last people who'd floated him in that giant fish tank, and he might never trust them again.

"Cal?" Dania's eyes pleaded.

She needed to save this guy maybe even more than Cal needed to save her.

When had all of this become so damn hard?

Cal turned to Kile. "Are you ready in case we need a little enforcer intervention?"

The commander hesitated before he answered. "I've slept, but I'm weak." He looked at Alexander. "But I would assume that after so long, he will be even weaker."

Oh, boy, did he have that wrong.

Doc looked at Cal before his gaze traveled down to Cal's boot.

Cal closed his eyes. This had to go better than they all feared. If Cal ended up being the one to pull the trigger, killing Dania's best friend, he'd lose her forever.

He flinched, like he'd been sliced with a knife.

Was that it? Was he more worried about losing Dania than this guy's life?

"Cal?" Doc asked.

"Yeah," Cal said. "Let's do it."

Doc placed the injection, then stepped back.

"How long will it take?" Dania asked.

"I wish I knew." Doc tossed the syringe into the recycler.

Kile folded his arms. "You all keep forgetting that this man is not really a doctor."

Heat flushed over Cal again. "That's none of your business, Commander. I'd gladly place my life in Doc's hands."

Screw what anyone thought—Cal would back his crew. They were on board the *Star Renegade* because he trusted them, and that was good enough for Cal.

Doc smiled at him, but his brow still furrowed as he stared at his patient. What they all needed to understand was that human medicine—*any* human medicine—had no idea what they were dealing with when it had to do with enforcers. This had nothing to do with Peter's skills.

Alexander twitched. His head tilted back, his brow pinched, and he groaned. "Dania."

Cal's hands formed fists. Dania had thought of Cal first.

Kile had thought of Rachel first.

And this guy thought of *Dania?*

Cal rubbed his face. He couldn't read into that. Dania had

already told them he was like a brother to her. Still, it was hard not to hate him when she was right there, holding the guy's damn hand.

"I'm here," Dania whispered. "Everything's okay."

Cal really hoped that was true.

The guy's lips twisted, and his cheeks lit up a bright pink. He grunted, like trying to ward off a pain deep inside him. His back arched and he opened his mouth in a soundless scream.

"Alexander!" Dania cried.

"What the hell?" Cal asked.

Doc ran a scanner over him. "I don't know. His heart rate is through the roof, but everything else is fine."

Kile shook the bed. "Alexander. You're safe. We got you out!"

"Dania!" the younger enforcer screamed, his eyes still closed.

"I'm here!" Dania called, gripping his hand. "Alexander, please, wake up!"

The doorway opened, and Alanna slipped beside Cal. "Yikes. This doesn't look like it's going well."

"Yeah, you're not kidding," Cal said. "You should get out of here." The last thing Cal wanted was someone else in the line of fire.

Alexander sat up. His eyes opened wide and glassy.

"Alexander?" Dania released his hand, reaching for his face.

He sucked in a deep breath and his hand shot out, wrapping around Dania's neck, just like he'd done to Doc in the mansion.

"Dania!" Cal leapt toward the bed and slammed into a shimmering wall of light. He cursed. "Doc, take that damn barrier down."

"It's not me!"

On the other side of the bed, Kile punched against the shimmering light while Dania clawed at the hand around her neck, gasping for air.

The barrier sizzled as Cal slammed it with his own fist. His knuckles burned with each blow, but he didn't stop. This was not happening again!

"Alexander, that's Dania!" Kile continued to pound against the barrier on the opposite side of the gurney. "That's your general!"

Dania's gaze flicked to Cal as her face turned a light blue.

Cal's heart hammered against his ribcage. "Shit! Doc!"

"I see it! I just can't get to her!"

Alanna moved beside Cal and placed her hand on the shimmering shield of light. "Alexander, stop! This isn't you!"

Dania twisted, kicking against her friend's grip. Alexander's hair flew about as if he were underwater.

Alanna pressed against the barrier. Sparks gathered around her fingers. "Alexander, I saw you heal Doc. I heard you give Kile good old-fashioned sass." She wiped her brow. "Whatever it is that happened to you, you need to remember who you were before. You need to remember Dania."

Alexander's wide, lifeless eyes turned toward the navigator. His expression was blank, soulless, before his right hand punched through the barrier and wrapped around Alanna's neck, too, pulling her inside.

"No!" Cal leapt for her, grabbing her waist, but Alexander drew her right beside the bed—and Cal with her.

Cal clawed at the hand around Alanna's neck, but the enforcer's fingers didn't move. Dania hung from Alexander's other hand. Tears streamed from her eyes and her head started to loll. Cal tried to reach for her, but she was too far away unless he let go of Alanna.

Dammit! He couldn't try to save them both!

"Cal!" Doc called through the barrier. "Your boot!"

The gun.

Cal released Alanna and reached for the weapon. He pointed the barrel at Alexander's head. One shot. At this distance, that's all it would take.

"Cal, wait!" Alanna held out her hand. "He's not hurting me!"

Cal eased off the trigger. "What?"

"He's holding me, but he's not hurting me!"

Dania fell to the bed in a heap. The enforcer turned his wide crystalline eyes toward Alanna again.

"It's me," Alanna said. "Remember?" She choked out a breath. "'It was the best of times. It was the worst of times.' And, umm..." Her eyes flicked to Dania, still crumpled on the bed beside her. "Then there's something in the next paragraph about wisdom, and something else about foolishness, I think." She sniffed. "This would fall under foolishness, Alexander. We're your friends."

Cal tucked the gun in his waistline and moved to the other side of the bed, closer to Dania.

The enforcer tilted his head, still looking at Alanna as she continued to quote from the book she'd been reading to him.

Cal placed his hand on Dania. She was so still. So lax. "I don't think she's breathing."

Doc ran a scanner over her from outside the barrier. "She's not. There's hardly any oxygen getting to her lungs." Doc lowered the scanner. "He crushed her larynx." His gaze met Cal's. "He-He killed her."

A deep pain ripped through Cal's chest. He gulped, running his fingers through her hair. *No... It couldn't be...*

The enforcer looked down.

"I don't believe it." Alanna clawed at the hand around her throat. "Come on, Alexander. Remember. Remember who you are. Remember Dania!"

"Dania," Alexander whispered, releasing Alanna.

Alanna leaned on the gurney, holding her neck, panting.

Dania lay still. Gone. How was this possible?

Doc slammed his fist against the barrier, clutching his data pad in his other hand. "We need to put a tube in her neck!"

Cal lifted his head. "A what?"

Doc's lips quivered. "We can still save her!"

Alanna leaned closer. "Like what kind of tube?"

Doc pulled a pen light out of his pocket. "Something like this."

But he was on the other side, and they were stuck inside this barrier with a guy who might snap again at any moment.

Alexander looked up and blinked again. "Dania?" He squinted like he could barely see. "Dania!"

Dania's limp form rose into the air.

"No!" Cal grabbed for her, but a shock zapped him, forcing him back. "Dania!"

Alanna held up her palm. "Cal, wait!"

The enforcer lifted his hands and a soft glow illuminated his fingertips.

His eyes clouded with tears. "Dania, I'm sorry. I'm so sorry."

Alanna reached for Alexander.

"Stop!" Cal said. "Keep back!"

Alanna shook her head. "No." She touched the enforcer's shoulder, then the side of his face. He turned to her.

"You have so much power," Alanna whispered. "Remember what you did for Peter? You floated that bullet right out of him."

"This isn't a bullet," Doc shouted through the barrier. "Her windpipe is crushed."

"But she's not dead yet, right?" Alanna asked.

Doc looked at his medical device. "Well, no, but she can't breathe. We need to find a way to get her air—and fast!"

Alanna brought her other hand to the enforcer's face. "You can save her. I know you can."

Alexander's hair whipped up. His eyes widened again.

"Alanna, get back!" Cal bolted to the other side of the table and pulled her away.

They swung to the edge of the barrier as the shimmering shield winked out and they stumbled right through. Doc Grabbed Alanna and Kile moved closer to Alexander as a glow surrounded Dania.

Alexander drew her tight to his chest. "I'm sorry," he whispered. "I'm so sorry."

The haze around them pulsed with white light before fading.

Doc slammed his light on the edge of a counter, emptying out the contents. "I can still save her." He reached for Dania, but as soon as he touched her, a flare of white light flashed out, pushing him back.

Kile moved closer, only to be pushed back by the same white light. "Alexander, let the incompetent human help!"

Dania still lay limp on her friend's shoulder. Doc stood a few inches away, shaking, holding the empty cylinder in his hand, ready to do what needed to be done but unable to get to her.

Cal gulped. Dania had been so alive before, so full of hope —only to be strangled by the very person she'd come to save. And Cal had helped bring him on board.

If he'd only said *no*, told her it wasn't worth the risk…

She would have hated him, but she'd still be alive.

Alexander started to sob, holding Dania to him.

"Dammit!" Cal approached the light. "Let us help her!" A bolt of heat slammed him in the chest, driving him back.

This was worse than any of them had anticipated. This guy was stronger than Kile and absolutely insane. Cal fingered the gun in his waistline.

Doc's eyes widened. He shook his head at Cal, then pointed his chin at the sobbing man clinging to Dania.

Who cared if the enforcer was showing remorse? That didn't change what he'd done, and who'd he'd done it too. They had one chance to save her, and if Cal had to go through Alexander to do it, he would.

Cal tightened his grip on the gun.

Alexander leaned back. "Dania?"

Her body jolted. She drew in a breath with a deep wheeze as her eyes opened.

Cal gaped. "Dania?" Could it be?

Alexander grabbed the sides of her face. "Again. It will hurt, but you need to breathe!"

She drew in another breath, then another.

Cal pushed the gun back into his pants and ran to her. "Dania?"

She coughed, grabbing her neck. Alexander shoved Cal back.

"Stop!" Alanna jumped between them. "Cal's a friend."

Alexander's brow knotted. "Who are you?" He shook his head. "Your voice. I know your voice."

Screw that. What did it matter? "Dania?" Cal reached for her.

She held her throat and nodded, but her eyes were not on Cal. They were on the man with the flowing, blond hair. The man who'd nearly killed her.

Alexander pulled Dania back into his arms. "I'm so sorry." He held his head like it throbbed. "Everything…it hurts. It's a fog."

Kile touched his shoulder. "You've been through a lot. You need to rest."

Cal gritted his teeth. *Through a lot? He nearly killed Dania!*

Doc grabbed his arm. "Calm down, boss. Either one of them could still pull your spine out with their fingertips."

Alexander reached out and touched Dania's throat again. "You could have died."

"But I didn't." Dania's sweet, melodic voice sounded old and torn. She coughed again. "You saved me, as you always do."

Alexander's hands trembled as he covered his face. "It-It was dark. There was water, but I could breathe."

"They had you floating in some sort of psychotropic liquid," Doc said. "I would have liked to have analyzed it, but we had to break the glass to get you out."

The enforcer held both sides of his head. His hands trembled. "Dania?"

"I'm here."

He lowered his hands. His eyes were red and those perfect features were twisted into something drawn and ugly. Alexander choked out another sob.

Dania climbed up higher on the bed and put her arms

around him. "I'm sorry I didn't get there sooner. I tried. I came as soon as I could."

Alanna pulled Cal back as the enforcer sobbed on her shoulder. "Maybe we should give them some room."

"*Room?*" Cal turned to her. "He nearly killed her."

"But not now."

Cal closed his eyes. He wished he had her optimism. But someone on the crew needed to be a realist.

Doc tapped a screen on the wall.

"What are you thinking?" Cal asked, as Dania patted down her friend's floating hair. "Am I overreacting?"

Doc shook his head. "I think he's just as messed up as I'd feared." He pointed at them. "But that's encouraging."

"Crying is encouraging?"

"Crying is a huge stress reliever. As guys, we're told it's not manly to cry, so we hold it in, and that's why we snap at times. If we all learned to let it out like that, we'd probably be happier in the long run."

"You want us to cry to make us happy?"

"It does sound ridiculous when you say it like that."

Kile appeared behind them. "Are you going to do something about this?"

Doc looked past him. Dania still clung to Alexander's shaking shoulders. "What do you want me to do?"

"Stop this. He is not weak. He is an enforcer. Do something."

"Like what? The guy has been through a nightmare. What he needs is time. Time, and knowing that his friends are still there for him."

Alexander sobbed again, clinging to Dania.

She was there for him, after he'd nearly killed her. If he

wasn't already permanently damaged, he probably was now, even if he had saved her in the end.

"You're right." Alanna started walking back to them.

"Where are you going?" Cal asked.

"He remembered the sound of my voice. Maybe I can help."

Oh, hell no. He'd just had his hand around both Alanna's and Dania's throats. Cal wasn't leaving him alone with either of them ever again.

He took a step and Alanna spun, pointing at him. "Stop. Just stop."

Cal hated when she used that voice. It reminded him of his mother.

Alanna rubbed the guy's back, talking in his ear. After a few moments, the sobbing subsided. She looked up to Cal and smiled.

Damn. When she was right, she was right.

Which was most of the time, now that he thought about it.

"Cal." Dania held her hand out to him. "I'd like you to meet Alexander." She smoothed back her friend's hair. "Cal is our captain. You're on the *Star Renegade*."

Alexander blinked a few times. "*Star Renegade?*" He turned to Cal. His eyes narrowed. "Calvin *Espinoza?*"

Kile snorted what may have been a laugh before covering himself. "Yes, Alexander, that is Calvin Espinoza."

Cal readied himself to grab the gun again. Kile might as well have punctuated that with, 'The man wanted for Filluck Palogivan's murder.'

Alexander's hair took flight again.

Alanna stepped between Cal and the enforcer.

Was she out of her mind? "What are you doing?"

"He won't hurt me." She shifted her weight. "At least, I hope not."

Dania grabbed her friend's arm. "Don't," she rasped. She started coughing again, shaking her head and pointing at Cal.

Cal looked to the door. The safest thing to do might be to get out of the room before the fight started. If he had to face this, he needed to face it alone, where the rest of the crew wouldn't get hurt.

Alexander frowned at the marks forming on Dania's throat.

She coughed once more, before she looked up and said, "Cal didn't kill Filluck Palogivan."

Alexander cocked his head. "Of course he did. This has already been decided."

Dania massaged her throat. "They decided wrong."

Great. They were at square one for the third time.

Alexander glanced at Cal. "Geron wants his head."

"I know," Dania whispered, wincing like each word hurt.

Cal was more than ready to punch someone. "Is it a surprise to anyone that your wonderful sponsor didn't share with his people that I'm innocent?"

Kile sneered at him.

"What?" Cal said. "You can't possibly think he's still the best thing since the invention of the galactic modulation engine."

"He is that and more," Kile seethed.

"Gentlemen." Dania held up a hand, then turned to Alexander. "I will show you the evidence," she rasped. "You can kill Cal later if you don't agree we should discuss the execution with Geron."

"He's still guilty of smuggling," Kile said.

"But so am I," Dania said.

Alexander blinked rapidly like he could hardly see. "What? Smuggling?"

Dania tucked back his swirling hair. "It's a long story." She coughed again. "We have a lot to talk about."

Alexander held his head.

Doc inched forward, holding up a scanner. The enforcer jumped, grabbing the sides of the mattress.

"This is Peter," Dania said. "He is a talented doctor."

"He's not a doctor," Kile pointed out.

Dania sighed. "Okay, he's a medical practitioner."

"Without a license." Kile folded his arms.

Doc mimicked his stance. "You weren't all that worried about that when your girlfriend lost half a finger." He pointed at him. "Or when you were lying on the deck after you'd been shot multiple times. You are not a very gracious patient, by the way." Doc turned back to Alexander. "May I treat you? It's up to you. I don't want you to melt my face off."

Alexander rubbed his eyes. "You seem familiar."

Doc tapped his chest. "You pulled a bullet out of me on Midway Station."

Alexander kept blinking, looking down.

"Are you having trouble seeing?"

The enforcer nodded. "Everything is blurry."

"Why don't you lie back down? I'll try to see if I can figure out what's wrong."

Dania coughed again, holding her throat.

Doc frowned before turning to Kile. "Do you think you can wake up Rachel now? I really could use some help."

The commander's brow furrowed as he looked at Dania. If Cal didn't know any better, he might have thought the guy actually cared about his general.

"I will wake her." Kile glared at Cal before heading out the door.

"That man does not like you," Doc said.

"He never has."

"Because you're a murderer," Alexander said, easing back on his pillow.

Dania tapped his hands. "We'll discuss the murder charge later. Would you please just let Doc help you?"

Alexander nodded.

Dania started walking toward Cal, but the enforcer grabbed her wrist.

"Where are you going?" he asked. "Don't leave."

Dania inched back to him. "Let me get a chair and I'll sit beside you, okay?"

He nodded again.

Dania squeezed his hand before she walked with Cal. "He's going to need time," she said.

"So I see."

She grimaced. "He really is a good man."

Cal glanced down at the finger-shaped bruises forming on her neck. "I'm sure he's a great enforcer."

"He's also a great person."

Cal hoped it was true. Even more so, he hoped that Dania didn't love this guy more than she loved her freedom.

DANIA STEPPED INTO THE LOUNGE. Alexander strode in at her side, wearing the brown-toned clothing they'd purchased for Kile on Cerberus. He stood tall, his hair flowing freely, alive with primordial energy. Yet beside the outward show of strength, he walked slower than he had in the past. Dania may have been the only one able to notice such a slight change, but it worried her.

On the far side of the room, Kile stood facing away from them in his opalescent uniform. The commander clasped his hands behind his back as he stared out the window. Neptune loomed in the distance, a lone purple-blue orb hanging in space.

"The Earthan Cradle system was not exactly the destination I had in mind," Kile said, not turning.

"I think it's the perfect destination," Alexander said. "It's far enough from Cerberus to avoid any previous entanglements, and Neptune Nine is a capable port. We'll be en route for home before you get a chance to become any more uneasy."

Kile spun. "I am *not* uneasy."

Alexander gave a slight bow of his head. "My apologies, Commander. It was a poor choice of words. However, Neptune Nine does have an excellent communications array. Keveron will send transport expediently." Alexander wove his fingers around Dania's. "Geron is going to be so happy to see you. He's been like a lunatic, knowing you were out here alone, dying."

Dania cringed. She'd never meant to cause her sponsor pain. But she was only one of many under his charge. Certainly, her loss hadn't affected him that much.

She lowered her eyes. "He's lost enforcers before."

"He hasn't lost *you.*" Alexander lifted her chin with his other hand and searched her eyes before his gaze carried over the bruises on her neck.

Dania wanted to turn from him and hide the marks. She knew what he was thinking—that the bruises should have been gone by now. They would have been gone if she were still whole—if she were still an enforcer.

"I'm not even sure how you've survived in this condition. But no matter." He lowered his hand. "As soon as Geron returns your strength, I'll be able to heal you properly. You will be your old self within a matter of days."

"She does not want to be her old self." Kile folded his arms. "She likes being feeble and weak."

Dania cringed. Nothing could be further than the truth, but Kile was incapable of understanding that she no longer wanted to be controlled.

Alexander frowned. "Ridiculous. She looks like she's near death." His eyes carried over her again. "How have you survived so long like this?"

Kile stepped closer. "Their repugnant excuse for a doctor did something to her. Some sort of experimental medicine that will no doubt kill her in time. He should be executed for even touching her."

Dania sighed and looked down. Everything he said was the truth, but it was also incredibly narrow-minded. Incredibly *enforcer-minded*. There was no use in trying to convince him of what he knew in his soul was true, even if that truth was incorrect. She shivered, realizing that she'd been no different less than a year ago.

"It's all right," Alexander said. "Whatever it is, I'll fix it." He squeezed her hand. "It will be good to be home again."

A flush of warmth spread through her. It *would* be good to be home. Geron would return her strength, and she'd be with Alexander again. Happy. But at the same time, that would be horrible. She'd lose everything.

Her stomach tightened as her past fought with her present, both struggling for control.

The overhead comm went off. There was scratching, and someone's muffled voice. Then, Ethan said, "Oops. Sorry I hit the button by accident."

Dania laughed.

"Incompetent," Kile said. "All of them."

Maybe they were a little incompetent, but their faults made them wonderful and unique. Each member of the crew was different, with their own strong and weak points. Yet together, whether or not Kile wanted to admit it, they were formidable. If they hadn't been, the enforcers would have caught them years ago.

Alexander pulled her closer. His brow knitted.

He'd always been far too good a judge of her moods.

"When we get home, we need to spend time in the queen's gardens."

The gardens had always been their playground, but... "I

think we're technically still banned after we knocked those nests out of the trees when we were children."

"So many memories." Alexander squeezed her hand again. "So many *good* memories." He leaned closer, his eyes searching hers. "You *are* coming home with me, aren't you?"

The door opened, and Cal walked in. He stopped short, his gaze falling on their clasped hands. His temperature spiked as his gaze latched on to Alexander's.

There was a challenge in their eyes—a startling protectiveness from each of them.

Dania's future was wedged somewhere between them, both sides tugging, and both sides feeling right.

The only question was: Which side was really home?

CAL GRITTED HIS TEETH, dragging his gaze from their clasped hands to Mr. Perfect's smug grin. Dania may have only thought of this guy as a friend, but Cal knew better. This guy was being territorial, and every ounce of Cal's soul was ready to push back. He wasn't giving up anyone in his crew. Especially Dania.

Alexander's hair whipped around like a gale had blown through the lounge, a grim reminder to Cal, without Doc nudging him, that the enforcer had enough power coursing through his body to take out Cal and everyone on this ship without breaking a sweat.

Cal wouldn't give Dania up so easily, though. He just needed to figure out a way to keep her and not end up dead.

Rachel bounded through the door behind him. "There you are!" She ran to Kile and gave him a hug before looking out the window. "Ew, is that Neptune?"

Kile nodded.

"It's ugly. Do you really want to go there?"

"No. I'd rather go to Keveron, but apparently, this is as far as our cowardly captain is willing to bring us."

Cal steadied his breathing. Things were bad enough. He wasn't going to let this guy bait him. "It's a good landing site. Plenty of traffic. If your prince doesn't come for you, it will be easy enough to buy passage on a freighter."

"What's it like on Keveron?" Rachel asked. "Will I like it?"

The commander's brow furrowed.

Dania's eyes widened.

Cal shifted his weight. Had Kile not told her yet?

The enforcer took a deep breath before looking away from her. "You are not coming."

She leaned back, still holding his shoulders. "What?"

"It's not feasible for you to come to Keveron. It would not be safe."

Rachel narrowed her eyes. "Not safe? Why?"

Dania released Alexander's hand and stepped toward her. "Geron would see you as a liability, Rachel. He needs his enforcers focused."

She scowled. "My guy is focused."

Cal bit back a laugh. The high and mighty enforcer had caved to her whims more times than he could count.

Kile removed her hands from his shoulders. "I won't risk you, Quirky. My sponsor would not understand."

"But I thought he was a nice guy. I thought he would want you happy."

He shook his head. "He would not want me *that* happy."

Rachel stared at him for a minute, then reset her footing. "Fine. Then stay here."

Kile cocked his head, gaping.

She lifted her chin. Cal had seen that stance before. Rachel Quirky was used to getting what she wanted—probably because Big Bad had caved so many times before.

"It's the only solution," she said. "I'm here. I can't go to Keveron, so you stay here. End of conversation."

Kile's gape widened. "It is far from the end of the conversation."

True, but it was a darn good start.

For the first time in maybe ever, Cal was glad Rachel was being...well, *herself*. This opened the door to complete Ty and Ethan's crazy plan to make Kile stay, which could quite possibly end up working.

"She's right," Cal said. "You could stay if you wanted. You're good in a fight. And hey, even not in a fight, you just *being you* looks imposing enough to scare people off. We could use you."

"To smuggle?" he asked.

"Don't knock it until you try it. You might be surprised how fulfilling it can be."

Kile pursed his lips. "I highly doubt it."

Rachel cupped his cheek. "But that would mean you could stay. Don't you want to be with me?"

"Wanting to be with you is not the issue."

Dania's eyes widened, and Cal got it. That was a huge admission for an enforcer. Especially *this* enforcer.

Kile touched Rachel's cheek far more gently than seemed possible for such a large man. "I do want to be with you. I just..."

Rachel's bottom lip quivered. "You just want to be with your prince more?"

He sighed. "Yes."

Rachel reared back and slapped him so hard, the sound echoed through the lounge.

Kile gawked, rubbing his cheek. "Did you just hit me?"

"Yes, I hit you. How can you say that? After all we've been through!"

"You need to understand that this has nothing to do with you. This would mean turning my back on my prince." He glanced at Dania, fire in his eyes. "No enforcer worth the air that they breathe would ever forsake their sponsor."

Dania cringed. Her cheeks flushed, and she looked down.

Cal's chest clenched. Did that mean she wasn't going with them?

"He's right," Alexander said. "For your own safety, Miss Quirky, you need to stay behind. The three of us will go, and give the *Star Renegade* the head start that the commander promised before we relay your location to our people."

Dania stepped forward. "We are not relaying any location to anyone."

Cal stiffened. Did that mean she *was* going with them? This was driving him crazy.

He resisted the urge to yank her out of the room and find out what was going on in that beautiful head of hers.

Alexander turned his ghostly crystal eyes to her. "They are criminals."

Dania swallowed. Her hands shook as she lifted her chin. "And so am I. I'm not going back with you, Alexander."

The weight of a million worlds lifted from Cal's shoulders. He took a moment to gloat over Mr. Perfect's wide eyes and surprised stare.

Behind him, Rachel whimpered to Kile, "If she can stay, why can't you?"

Alexander stayed focused on Dania. "You have to come back. Look at you. You're dying."

"I'm not dying, and you know it," Dania said. "You're too good of a medic to not recognize that they've healed me."

"You didn't need to be healed," Kile spat, disregarding Rachel's tears.

Dania stayed calm. Collected. Very much the general that she always had been. "On that, we disagree."

Cal bit back another grin. *Take that, Big Bad.*

The shift of Alexander's hair slowed as he approached Dania. "You can't stay here."

She placed her hand on the enforcer's chest. Cal cringed but settled himself.

Dania had said she was staying. That meant she'd made her choice, and the choice was not Alexander.

"I *can* stay, and I will," Dania said. "I don't belong on Keveron anymore."

He slid his hand over hers. "But we need you. You're our general."

"Not anymore."

The room seemed to still as they stared at each other. Cal took a shaky breath as they stood there, holding hands. *Dammit!* He wished one of them would say something!

Alexander blinked, then turned to Kile. "She is unwell and incapable of caring for herself. I'll stay behind and keep her safe."

That—*wasn't quite* what Cal had in mind.

Kile's hair wafted through the air. "What?"

"I am her healer and her protector. I am coded to be at her side."

"This is not what Geron wanted."

Alexander's expression remained level. "Yet this is what it is. Our sponsor gave me this charge. He would expect me to fulfill my duty." He glanced at Cal. "No matter how unsavory."

Cal's nose flared. This was not the way this was supposed

to go. He didn't want this guy on his ship, let alone anywhere near Dania.

Kile's face reddened. "This is ludicrous. I cannot allow this. Geron tasked me with bringing both of you home."

"No, he didn't," Dania said. "You told me that saving Alexander was his top priority. You told me all of Geron's assets had been redirected to saving his healer. You've done that. You didn't say that you were directed to bring him home."

Kile looked to the side before leveling his gaze back on her. "A technicality—one that does not overcome the directive to bring you home as well."

"Did he tell you to bring *me* home, or his general?"

"You are one in the same."

Dania held up her hands. "Look at me. As you have so adamantly pointed out, I am weak and useless. The general I once was is gone. Dead."

"You are not dead."

"But she also no longer holds the power of a general," Alexander noted. "She has no primordial energy running through her. She's no better than a human."

"Then you should not be following her anymore, either," Kile said.

Alexander shook his head. "Geron directed me to protect Dania at all costs. Not my general."

"You are twisting words."

"No," Alexander said. "I am using the leeway my sponsor gave me to keep Dania protected until she comes to her senses." He pointed at her. "Do you really want to leave her alone like this?"

"No. I want to drag her home and throw her at the mercy of our sponsor."

"This is out of your hands, now, Kile," Dania said.

The commander shook his head. "I cannot allow you to ruin Alexander like you've ruined yourself."

"I believe we have a different definition of *ruin*." She looked at Mr. Perfect and then back to Kile. "If Alexander wants to return home at any time, he'll be free to go. But it's the right thing to do to give him a taste of freedom, just like I had, and let him make the choice on his own." She glanced at Rachel. "Just like you're doing now."

Rachel wiped her nose on her sleeve. She returned to Kile and buried her face in his chest. "Please don't go. I know you never said it, but I thought you cared about me."

Alexander watched them for a moment before he looked at Dania. "I am not staying here for freedom. I meant what I said. I'm here to protect you and, ultimately, bring you home."

"I realize that," Dania said. "But I'm looking forward to you seeing the galaxy from a different set of eyes."

"My eyes are fine."

She smiled. "I know."

Cal gritted his teeth. He didn't hate many people, but Alexander had quickly jumped to the top of his list.

Rachel sniffed, clinging to Kile. "Please stay."

The commander wrapped his arms around her and breathed in a deep whiff of her hair. "I do care about you. More than I ever expected to."

She pulled back, her eyes wide and hopeful. "So you'll stay?"

He shook his head. "I'm sorry, but the draw to my prince is far stronger than any urges my body has."

"Urges your body has?" Rachel's arms fell to her sides. "You know what? Screw you, Commander." She slapped him again. "Go back to your stinking prince. I hope he does it for you."

She ran from the room. Her sob broke free before she got through the door.

"Quirky!" Kile took two steps for the door and stopped. His eyes fell on Dania and Alexander before he straightened, as if bringing himself to military attention.

He grimaced at Alexander. "Do you really want to stay here and get slapped?"

Alexander looked at the door Rachel had run through, and then back to Kile. "I'm actually quite interested in experiencing whatever it is that got you slapped."

Kile's nose flared. "Do. Not. Touch. Rachel. Quirky."

Alexander bowed. "Orders understood, Commander."

"Unless she needs medical attention," Dania said.

Kile's nose flared again.

Dania held up her hands. "I'm just making that clear."

The commander growled before he turned toward the window, where Neptune's blue-green glow filled the space behind its Ninth moon.

Ty's voice came over the comm. "We're cleared for landing, boss. Should I take her in?"

Only the light hum of the ship's engines permeated the room.

"What's your final decision, Commander?" Cal asked.

Kile didn't turn. "I am an enforcer. My place is beside my prince."

Rachel's sob echoed down the hall.

"Are you sure?" Cal asked.

The hum of the engines swirled three times.

Kile took a deep breath. "I am quite sure."

So much for Rachel's feminine charms.

Cal hit the comm. "We're a go for landing."

The commander continued to stare out the window. Still and unyielding.

"Really?" Ty said.

"Yeah, really."

Ty cursed before switching off the comm.

The weight of reality set in. Cal needed Kile. If the Carteks came and Kile wasn't onboard…

Cal shook his head. The squids couldn't expect a human being to control an enforcer. If the commander wanted to leave, there was nothing Cal or anyone on this crew could do to stop him.

If the Carteks caught up with them, that would leave him with only Alexander to trade if Cal was lucky enough to convince them that Dania wasn't really an enforcer.

Dania smiled at her friend again.

She'd never forgive Cal for betraying Alexander. If the Carteks showed up right now, or months from now, he was screwed. He'd made an unbreakable deal with no happy endings.

Kile turned and headed for the door. Cal followed, with Dania and Alexander behind him.

The commander stomped his boots on the floor tiles, the sound reverberating through the hall, as if each step held more meaning than the last. A slight heat emanated off his uniform and his hair took flight again.

Maybe Rachel *had* gotten under his skin. Could he be having second thoughts?

The commander stopped at the exit and stared at the closed doorway.

"The ramp's still broken," Cal said.

Kile seemed to make a point of not making eye contact. "I do not care."

Cal glanced at Dania. Could she command him to stay? If she did, would he even listen?

She lowered her eyes. "Open the door."

Cal sighed. He'd wanted Kile off the ship from the moment the enforcer had stepped onboard, but now that they'd reached the crossroads, Cal wished that Ty and Ethan's plan had worked. Yes, Kile was weakening, but he'd rather face the Carteks with two enforcers than only Alexander and the *Star Renegade*'s dumb luck.

He could confess, tell them all everything, but that would just drive Dania into Mr. Perfect's arms. She'd probably jump off the ship with her friends and never look back, and Cal wouldn't blame her.

He needed to find a way out of this. He just didn't know how.

Cal hit the control, and the accessway opened to the landing platform thirty feet below.

The commander turned to his former general. "Are you sure you want to stay with these imbeciles?"

Dania slipped her hands around Cal's arm. "I like these imbeciles."

Kile's lips twisted. "Revolting."

He turned and jumped from the ledge, landing softly on the ground.

Cal placed his hand over Dania's. She was warm, smiling, and—most importantly—she was still here, aboard the *Star Renegade*. He took a slow, deep breath, letting his stomach settle.

The other enforcer stepped to the opening and watched Kile leave.

Cal would still have to deal with this guy. But unlike Kile, this one's loyalties didn't seem quite so cut and dry. If Dania could convince him that freedom was obtainable, maybe Cal could come clean, and they'd be able to figure this out together.

They just needed to keep one step ahead of the bad guys until that happened.

Kile stormed from the ship without looking back. Normally, Cal would have called the station maintenance crew for repairs to their cargo ramp, but instead, he closed the door.

The commander had only promised them ten minutes, and he seemed pretty pissed. Chances were, he wouldn't give them a second more.

He hit the comm. "Ty, get us out of here. Alanna, prepare to do your magic."

"Magic?" Alexander asked.

"Just a human exaggeration for moving at high speed," Dania said.

She glanced at Cal, and he nodded. They'd managed to keep Alanna's jumping from Kile. It was probably safer to keep her ability a secret from Mr. Perfect, too.

Alexander clasped Dania's hand again, and it took everything Cal had not to give the guy his first slap of humanity.

"We're going to be okay," Dania said. "I think you'll like it here."

The enforcer didn't look so sure, but he wasn't threatening to kill them all. That, at least, was a step in the right direction.

Kile was already far out of view before the door sealed shut. The floor hummed as they left the ground.

Cal expected to feel at ease, but the commander's absence

created a boatload of new problems. Not that it mattered. Cal had a bad feeling they hadn't seen the last of the commander. Hopefully, whatever Kile had learned about humanity while he was here would be a boon in the *Star Renegade*'s favor. If not, the power of the royal family might come crashing down on them.

Again.

Cal grimaced. Who was he kidding? There was no question about it. Kile was probably already tapped into the network, giving that blasted prince the *Star Renegade's* location.

Cal hit the comm. "Ty, we've got ten minutes before the enforcers will be on our tails."

"I guess it was fun while it lasted. We're clearing the atmosphere now."

"Good. Alanna?"

"Making calculations. Do you care where we go?"

Cal shook his head. "Anywhere but here."

Ty cursed over the comm.

"What?" Cal asked.

"We got incoming!"

"That was not ten minutes!" Cal ran toward the bridge, shouting over his shoulder at Dania and Alexander. "Your commander lied."

Or maybe he'd never actually promised a full ten minutes. He'd said he *may be inclined* to give them a head start.

Damn enforcers and their literal technicalities!

Cal squeezed through the door to the bridge and raced to his chair. Three cruisers bore down on them. Nothing new, just another day on the *Star Renegade*.

For now, they'd just have to do what they did best.

Run like hell.

Ready to blast off with book 3?
Order Star Bandits Uprising: Renegade Storm now!

Want to hear updates on future books and a few odd meanderings here and there? Sign up for my newsletter here.

https://www.subscribepage.com/s2b4f1_copy4

If you loved Renegade Thief, it would be awesome if you'd leave a review! Even a few kind words may help others discover *Star Bandits: Uprising*, and more readers mean more books for everyone to enjoy!

Thank you!

--Jennifer

ACKNOWLEDGMENTS

Writing and editing during a global pandemic proved harder than I'd expected. This was a year of working from home, layoffs, unemployment, home schooling...you all know the drill. I'd like to thank my family for not tearing each other apart while being cooped up in the house, and for working together to keep everyone safe.

Thanks to Ashley, Jenny, Julie, Tobie, Mel, Shaila, Gwen, and Erin for helping me keep it together. Thank goodness for the internet, because we were able to stay in touch despite social distancing. Seriously...I may have gone nuts without you guys.

I never trust myself to notice when something is "missing" in my own work. Sharon Hughson and Shaila Patel, thank you again for looking over the first draft of the manuscript and showing me where it could be stronger. I really appreciate your help!

Thank you to my editors Amy McNulty and Tandy Boese. I still shake my head when I see all the errors you catch. One day I will write a manuscript with less than a hundred typos. (Hey, a girl can dream.)

And, as always, a special thank you to YOU for reading.

I hope you continue to love the worlds and cultures I've built. Star Bandits is a labor of love, and there is more to come!

Catch you soon, one galaxy to the right, and straight on until morning.

--Jennifer

ABOUT THE AUTHOR

Jennifer M. Eaton hails from the eastern shore of the North American Continent on planet Earth. Yes, regrettably, she is human, but please don't hold that against her.

While not traipsing through the galaxy looking for specimens for her space moth collection, she lives with her wonderfully supportive husband, three energetic offspring, and a duo of poodles who run the spaceport when she's not around.

During infrequent excursions to her home planet of Earth, Jennifer enjoys long hikes in the woods, bicycling, swimming, snorkeling, and snuggling up by the fire with a great book; but great adventures are always a short shuttle ride away.

Read more from Jennifer M. Eaton

www.jennifereaton.com